THE BOG LADY

THE BOG LADY

By
Terry Oliver Mejdrich

To Gunner Patten,
Best Wishes
Terry Mejdrich

iUniverse, Inc.
New York Lincoln Shanghai

THE BOG LADY

All Rights Reserved © 2004 by Terry Oliver Mejdrich

No part of this book may be reproduced or transmitted in any form or by any means, graphic, electronic, or mechanical, including photocopying, recording, taping, or by any information storage retrieval system, without the written permission of the publisher.

iUniverse, Inc.

For information address:
iUniverse, Inc.
2021 Pine Lake Road, Suite 100
Lincoln, NE 68512
www.iuniverse.com

This is a work of fiction. Names, characters, places, and incidents are either the product of the author's imagination or are used fictitiously, and any resemblance to actual places, events, or persons, living or dead, is entirely coincidental.

ISBN: 0-595-30806-6 (pbk)
ISBN: 0-595-66203-X (cloth)

Printed in the United States of America

For Grandfather, Charlie, Forrest, Lora, Bill, Lynn, Jerry, Maclin, Jonathan, Sharon, Mr. Bell, Alfred, and the supporting cast for helping me tell their story.

ACKNOWLEDGEMENTS

A heartfelt thanks to editors Donna Nelson, Darlene Mejdrich, Therese Olejniczak, and Lisa Jordon for their help, encouragement, and suggestions, and to Larry Hanken for sharing his knowledge of law enforcement and firearms. Thanks also to Sandra Hanken for providing the cover graphic. A special thanks to my wife, Darlene, for putting up with the clatter of the keyboard at one o'clock in the morning.

THE BOG LADY is a stand-alone story. However, the characters and setting are carried over from the first book in this series, **A MAMMOTH RESURRECTION**. Although this story is self-contained, those who have read **A MAMMOTH RESURRECTION** will have the benefit of the background of what has led up to the events depicted in **The Bog Lady**.

PROLOG

Twenty-seven years before the present

The three men and three women, all smartly dressed in tweed suits and conservative pantsuits, and smelling of aftershave and perfume, followed the middle-aged Native American man into darkened confines of his home. A knotted leather strap kept his long, gray streaked hair centered down the middle of his back. Unlike his guests, the man was dressed simply in a well-worn shirt, pants, and moccasins made of soft brown leather, and the strong aroma coming from his body was a blend of sweat, pine needles, and soil. The knees of his pants were dirt-stained and moist, as were his hands.

    The guests nodded politely to the woman of the house as they passed by her kitchen. Her hair and skin color were the same as the man's, and she wore a plain forest green housedress. Her lips were pressed together in a neutral expression, but she couldn't restrain a slight negative shake of her head. She held up a long slender fish with massive jaws displaying a long entailing gash down the length of it's white belly as they filed past to the living room.

    Their host gestured with his soiled hand toward the faded blue sofa and the women sat down primly on the cushions, while the men remained standing behind them. Looking at the group from across the room, the Indian was reminded of one of those old-time pictures, where the women were in their place and the men stood protectively behind. The woman of the house watched until they were out of view and then went back to gutting the Northern Pike, shook her head slightly, and rolled her eyes. "Here we go again," she muttered under her breath.

In the living room, a white woman smiled widely, a forced smile for politeness, but didn't look directly at her host. Instead her eyes swept the cluttered room that was filled with piles of books and magazines. The combined odors of the stale stacks of magazines and a sustained human presence made her stifle a sneeze. A television set sat on top a three-foot stack of *Geographic* magazines, and animated cartoon characters flitted about the television screen but made no sound, the volume muted. The glass-topped table that separated her small group from the Indian had several open books and magazines in various stages of completion.

"We won't keep you from your garden long," the woman began. "Did you have a chance to read the literature I left with your wife last month?"

"Yes," the man replied, as he sat down on a worn overstuffed chair across from them. The chair was frayed and currently light brown, but what the color had been originally was impossible to tell. The Indian silently studied his guests. One couple was African American, one was white, and the other was of his own race. A well-balanced group, he thought. This was different than the usual all white visitors that occasionally stopped at his doorstep. They all wanted to talk about their religion, getting saved, and how sorry they were for the wrongs that the white man had committed against the Indian people. Normally, he made himself very busy when these people arrived, but this mixed race entourage gave him cause to be curious.

"And?" the woman pressed.

"It is not the first time I have read the white man's creation story. And the pages of words you gave me were just the same."

"Well, of course," the woman laughed nervously. She looked at her companions for some assistance, but they were content to let her do the talking. "That's the point, isn't it? It's God's word, and it never changes."

"My people, too, had a creation story. It is pretty good. There were miracles, and some sex with animals. Would you like to hear it?"

Suddenly red-faced, the woman groped for words. "Oh? Goodness, no. I mean...you must know that...well...you know that was just a fable passed down from one generation to the next. It didn't really happen. My miracles are real."

"Why should your miracles be any more real than mine?"

The woman smiled the thin smile of frustration and anger. She didn't like being led into a corner, which was clearly what this man had intended from the beginning. She was not about to play his game, and remained silent.

"We want you to know, brother, that we are saddened by the white man's treatment of the Indians." It was the black man who spoke. "They stole the land from you."

"Nobody has taken anything of importance from me."

"I just meant your people."

"Who are my people?"

"Well, the Indians."

"Maybe I am Jewish."

"You don't look Jewish."

"And what does a Jewish person look like?"

"Not like you."

"And maybe you are an Indian."

"No. My parents descended from Mississippi slaves."

"Maybe being something does not have much to with what you look like on the outside."

"That's...interesting," the white woman said, clearly not following the man's reasoning. There was a prolonged silence, and finally the man of the house began to speak.

"This thing about stealing land. The Jewish people believed their god gave them their land. But pretty quick the Arabs caught on and said that the land was given to them, too. That is where the Indians went wrong. They should have told the Pilgrims, sorry, but your god already gave this land to us. This was something the Pilgrims would have understood."

"As I stated," the woman interrupted, "taking the Indian land was wrong."

"But not so wrong that you are now willing to give it all back."

"Well, I just meant..."

"I will tell you now what I think. I do not think Mother Earth was given to any one race. The Europeans took most of the north and western lands of the Great Lake, *Otchipwe kitchi gami*, from my ancestors, the Ojibwe. But before that the Ojibwe took the land on which you stand from my wife's ancestors, the Lakota. Before that the Lakota drove out the Woods People. If all people gave back all the stolen land, it would have to go back to the animals of the forests and plains. In the final days, we will follow the ancient beasts into the *wanendagwad*, the forgotten, unless the race of good men, *anishinabe*, draws a line in the flow of time and say the past is no more. The future starts here. That is what I think."

"God has a plan..." the woman began, but let the thought trail off to silence.

"In the Great Mystery there are many plans for the many different people."

The Native American man in the group of guests spoke for the first time, and his voice was thick with scorn. "Your words are old and useless, your ways extinct. The very first contact with European settlers ended the Old Ways. There are no old Indians anymore. Now there are only new Indians with cars, homes, and jobs like everyone else. The Old Ways are dead."

"Sometimes the Old Ways are the New Ways," the man reflected. "And you are wrong. It is you who are dead."

The gray dusty clay of dirt roads clung to the sides of the pickup, obscuring most of its light blue color. The morning sun reflected off the side mirrors as it turned off the asphalt highway onto the dirt. The brakes squealed, metal on metal, when it came to a halt in front of the weathered white house that was badly in need of a coat of paint. A ten-year-old boy bolted from the pickup and sprinted up the evergreen shaded path, flung open the front door, and ran in without knocking. His parents, a well-muscled man with fair skin and blond hair and a woman with copper skin and black hair, followed more slowly, stretching stiff joints after the two hour ride. They both wore blue jeans, light blue cotton shirts, and work boots. A tall Native American woman dressed in a simple forest green housedress came outside to greet them.

"Hope you don't mind the unexpected company," the man said. "We're on our way to Valley City, and, of course, Charlie wanted to stay with his grandfather."

The boy came back out of the house. A look of disappointment clouded his face.

"Where's Grandfather, Grandmother?"

"Out somewhere, Charlie," Grandmother answered. She turned her attention to the boy's parents. "We had a carload of holy-rollers here earlier. Three men and three women. I felt sorry for them. Gerald invited them all in, proceeded to get them damn good and mad, and then said he had to go take a leak and left. It took them a half hour to realize that was his way of saying good-by. That was over an hour ago, and I haven't seen him since."

"That's my father," the woman said, throwing up her arms. "Everything all right?"

"You know your father. No matter which way you argue, he'll take the other side…out of pure orneriness. He's somewhere on one of his 'thinking' expeditions." She smiled and rolled her eyes upward, as if to share some mutual joke. "He'll show up as soon as he realizes Charlie is here. What's in Valley City?"

"Squeeze chute with a self-catching head gate," the man explained. "The bandits around here want twelve hundred for a beat up used one. I found one out in Dakota for six hundred."

Grandmother remained quiet, and only her daughter would realize she was puzzled. "A squeeze chute is a narrow pen that holds cattle when you have to work on them," she explained to her mother. "It keeps them restrained and quiet for dehorning, castration, and shots."

"I wonder if it would work on Gerald?" the older woman mused, and a mischievous smile turned her lips.

"I'm getting too old, well maybe smart, to be bulldogging eight hundred pound steers," the blond man explained. He turned to his wife. "We better get going if we're going to be back to the farm before dark. Hope everything works out between you and Gerald," he added to his mother-in-law.

His wife grabbed him by the arm and pulled him toward the pickup. "Good-by Mother," she said over her shoulder. Once back in the pickup she began to laugh. "You almost gave it away."

"Gave what away?"

"Didn't you see Father?"

"No, but I assume he was in hiding."

"One of these days he's going to have to change his hiding place."

"Where was he?"

"Right above us on the roof. He motioned me to silence as soon as I spotted him."

"And your mother doesn't know?"

"Of course she knows. It's just her way of keeping track of him. What trouble can he get into on the roof?"

The boy with short black hair had searched the house twice, followed the path through the back yard, across the stream, and then back to pine ridge that overlooked the blue waters of the lake. The object of his search was not there. He returned, found Grandmother in the house, but she insisted she had no idea where Grandfather was. Discouraged, he sat down on the rough planking of the front steps, his chin in his hands. Somewhere, someone chucked.

"Grandfather?"

"Hello, *Amikons*."

The boy ran around the house once more and returned to the front.

"Where are you?"

"Look up, *Amikons*."

"What are you doing on the roof?"

"I have been watching you."

"Can I come up there?"

"There are some places you cannot go."

The man was of medium height, and stockily built. Even bands of gray ran through his straight black hair, which now rained down his back. His brown face showed very little emotion, and seemed set in an expression just on the warm side of neutral. His simple clothing and moccasins were made of soft buckskin leather.

The ten-year-old boy wore a tight fitting white T-shirt, blue jeans, and black tennis shoes. His black hair was cut short. His skin was a shade lighter than the man's, but their rounded faces, except for age, were virtually the same. The two sat at the base of an old growth white pine that sheltered them from the heat of the midday June sun. The pine and several others grew along a ridge that dropped steeply to the sandy shores of a northern Minnesota lake. A loon laughed in the distance, and the surrounding forest was alive with animal and insect voices, and filled with the pungent odor of pine needles.

"Your mother told me on the phone you lost the contest."

"A girl beat me."

"Yes. That is what your mother said."

"Sorry, Grandfather."

"Sorry? Tell me about it."

"The questions were pretty easy. Just math stuff. Pretty soon it was just Jean and me." The boy hesitated, and the man waited patiently for him to continue. "Then the questions were about Geometry."

"That should have been easy for you."

"It was. I was the only one in the class who the teacher let study the Geometry book."

"Yes. I know."

"Jean was stumped on one about triangles." The boy looked down, and hesitated. "Can we talk about something else?"

"I am suddenly very interested in triangles. What was the question?"

The boy looked away, and read the words off an invisible page. "If one of the smaller angles of a right triangle is twice the other, what is the measure of each?"

"That sounds complicated."

"Oh, no. It's easy. They have to be sixty and thirty, because the other one has to be ninety. It's kind of trick question."

"This is interesting."

"It's just math."

"No. I mean this contest is interesting. Jean did not know the answer. Charlie did know the answer, yet Jean won."

"She was crying, Grandfather. Her mom and dad were watching her."

Again the man left a silent space for the boy to fill.

"I told her the answer," the boy said finally. "No one heard. I guess I cheated."

"You let her win. Does it bother you that you did not win?"

"Not really. But then afterward, Jean…she laughed at me. She said I was a fool for letting her win. And then she did some other stuff."

"You were not a *gawanadisid*. In the Old Days the strongest, fastest man of the tribe would often hold back so as not to embarrass those that were less capable. It was a good thing you did, if not for Jean, then for yourself."

"Then you're not disappointed in me?"

"You are my grandson, the greatest gift a man can receive. I will never be disappointed in you."

"But the contest…"

"It is not important."

"But…"

"These contests, they are a sickness of the modern world."

"A sickness?"

"It is a sickness when only the winner is appreciated, and others are regarded as failures. In the forest of ideas, all are worth consideration, and their worth is not made lesser or greater by a contest."

"But you've told me of the games the Old Ones played."

"Games, yes, but they were never meant to show who was the best at anything."

"What were they for then?"

"To have fun, and to impress the young women."

"Did you do that?"

"Me? No. These Old Ways are even older than I am. And, it seems, the women today are more interested in who wins contests. Except for your grandmother."

"Grandmother?"

"She was a young woman once, you know. We were two different people but our hearts were the same. We didn't need a contest to tell us that."

"And what about me, Grandfather?"

"Do not get involved in these contests. They seek to measure you by the standards set by others. Set your own standards. It is the only contest that matters."

A long silence followed, but it was not the awkward silence of two people trying to think of something to say, rather the peaceful silence of two people who appreciate each other's company.

"Who is the most important person?" the man asked quietly.

"The President, I suppose. Or maybe some rich guy…I don't know."

"It's you."

"Me?"

"Without you, if you didn't exist, there would be nothing."

"I don't understand."

"Every time you look at something, think of something, it comes into *aiawin*, existence. Before that it was only possible. You made it a certainty."

"Grandfather. Are you fooling me?"

"Each person creates his own Universe," the man said and he swept his right arm in a broad arc to emphasize his statement, "and it is limited only by what he chooses not to see. The Great Mystery sings to us, but most cannot hear above the sound of their own heartbeat."

"Did a great spirit tell you that, Grandfather?"

"I think some white guy wrote it in a poem. Nevertheless, a man's Universe is limited only by the strength of his fears. Always question and seek to know, and you will get closer to, not farther away from, the Great Mystery."

"That sounds easy enough."

"I only wish it were." The man smiled slightly and looked at his grandson out of the corner of his eye. "So what was the 'other stuff' that Jean did?"

"Something really gross, Grandfather. She kissed me on the lips."

"And how did that feel?"

"Pretty yucky."

"It is disgusting. But after a while, you will get used to it."

Sixteen years before the present:

The forty-something woman wore a black hand-woven veil over her face, not to hide her tears, but to hide the fact that there weren't any. Her black dress matched the suits of the two young men that stood on either side of her. The only drops of moisture present were those that came down as a light drizzle from the thick layers of stratus clouds above. A man's low voice was droning on and although he was directly across from her, the sound seemed far away. The woman's hair was naturally red, but she had always preferred to dye it black. Old Man Franklin Wrightham had insisted she leave it red, however, but now there was no one to stop her from doing as she liked. She was head-turning attractive, but her well-hidden insecurities kept her in front of a mirror for hours, applying makeup, then removing it, then reapplying it to get it just right. It was usually too much. Her walk was one of an aristocrat, back straight and stride purposeful, even though she came from humble beginnings. She stared at the dark hole in the cold ground, and the knotty pine casket that lay at the bottom. "My god," she thought to herself, "I never expected the old fool to live this long."

There had been times when she had been tempted to return to Luke James, the other man in her life. Even beg him to take her back. He was still raking in the cash with his evangelist routine. He even had a regular show on cable. He had found his niche, vigorously attacking the evils of science and humanism. She had called him once, left a message, but he never returned the call. In his present position as a tele-minister, she finally realized, he would not want to acknowledge his ten year affair with her, much less the fact that they had a son together while she was married to someone else. He was certainly a coward, but, if nothing else, he had been a competent lover, and her return to Franklin Wrightham, her lawful husband, had ended her social life. Since that time she had been a virtual prisoner. Wrightham had said the men he assigned to her were bodyguards. In reality, they watched her every move, never allowing her the opportunity to indulge in any personal gratification, social, sexual or otherwise. She had made a blatant attempt to seduce one of her guards even though she found him brutally ugly, but he hadn't taken the bait. In fact, he had simply laughed at her. "With what I'm getting paid," he'd said," I can buy any woman I want. Why should I screw myself by screwing you?"

A faded green blanket that was supposed to look like grass covered the mound of dirt that would soon cover Wrightham forever. The others were leaving now with faces properly yet artificially solemn, filing away to the buffet, having done their duty to the family. She smiled to herself. They didn't want to be there any more than she did. Franklin Wrightham had not been a particularly well-loved man. He had simply been rich. He had also been a bastard, and not in the familial sense. Now, after twenty years, her marriage to the cranky old tyrant was about to pay off. After a few brief formalities, his wealth would be hers. All nine hundred million. She reached down and with fingers tipped with long bright red artificial fingernails, grasped a handful of dirt, and flung it on the casket. "Good riddance," she muttered.

The two young men repeated her action, which they mistakenly took to be a sign of respect. They were obviously sons of the woman as all three had the same red hair and fine features. Both were shorter than average height, and for young men, looked fragile.

The older of the two had repeatedly exchanged glances with an attractive and petite woman that waited patiently at the fringes of the crowd. Her dark brown hair framed a knowing and devilish expression, and her resemblance to his mother was striking. In less than an hour they were heading to Europe for some R&R. Dressed provocatively in a black dress with ample cleavage, her body covering was inappropriate for the serious occasion, yet everything about her said she didn't care. While others were properly solemn, the corners of her delicate mouth betrayed the amusement she felt for the ongoing performance.

The younger of the two, however, was apparently moved by the ceremony. His eyes were red, and he wiped his nose quickly with a white handkerchief. The mother noticed his show of emotion.

"Maclin. Stop that damn sniveling. He wasn't even your father."

The young man straightened, and made a noticeable attempt to suck it up.

"That's better. And you, Jonathan. Your plans to go whoring in Europe are hereby cancelled. I had Alfred check into your latest little honey. She's a groupie and a gold digger, and almost twice your age.

Besides, we have a three o'clock meeting with Alfred and the executors for the reading of the will. I expect you to be there."

"Of course Mother. Whatever you wish."

"You have two hours to kill. Do what you want. But be in the den at three precisely." The woman abruptly turned and walked away. "I need a stiff drink," she added to no one in particular.

"What's your problem?" Jonathan said to his half brother when their mother was some distance away.

"He said he was going to give me the yacht," Maclin whined, and seemed on the verge of tears again.

"What?"

"The old bastard died before he gave me the yacht!"

The air smelled of stale cigar smoke and nearly everything in the room appeared to be old, handcrafted and dark brown, from the oak paneling to the circular table and chairs. A light green sofa, which seemed totally out of place in the otherwise masculine décor, occupied a place adjacent to the table. Outside, a long narrow breach in the clouds allowed brief rays of sunlight to enter the huge bay window of the room. The woman began to speak before the last chime from the handcrafted grandfather clock had died away.

"We're all here. You may begin Alfred."

Alfred was a slight, thin man but with a face that seemed almost fat, and that would have fit better on an over-weight body. "This is all written down, of course, but Mr. Wrightham asked that you hear his wishes with his own voice." He took a tape recorder from a briefcase and placed it on the polished tabletop. Mrs. Wrightham and her sons sat on the sofa on one side, Alfred on a straight-backed chair on the other. Several men in suits stood around them. Some were security personnel, some were lawyers, some were bankers. All were middle-aged or past.

"Well get on with it," Mrs. Wrightham said nervously. She had been completely in control at the funeral, but now, with all the old man's wealth about to fall into her lap, her heart raced inside her chest.

"In a moment, ma'am. Mr. Wrightham asked me to say a few words first."

"What words?" She shifted nervously on the sofa, crossing her legs one-way and then the other.

"He asked me to tell you that he always loved you. Even when you left him to go live with Mr. James. He said also that he wanted Maclin—your son with James—to know that he would have an equal chance at his considerable fortune, even though he wasn't his biological son."

"An equal chance? At my inheritance? What are you talking about?" The part about Wrightham loving her swept past without registering.

"I believe it's all on the tape."

"Well stop mumbling and play the damn thing!"

"As you wish, ma'am." No one uttered a sound as Alfred pushed the 'play' button. For several seconds there was only static, and then a too loud voice erupted from the speaker. Alfred quickly adjusted the volume, reset the tape at the beginning, and the surprisingly strong tones of a ninety-year-old man filled the room. His words were clear and thoughts lucid, and it was obvious this man was in complete control of his faculties.

"First of all, you can bet your ass I'm as mentally capable as anyone in the room, so I'm not going to go into all that being of sound mind crap. Second, with the possible exception of Alfred, I'm certain that no one is shedding any tears over my demise. That's neither here nor there. I didn't get rich by being a nice guy. My only concern at this point is that the family fortune is not only maintained, but also grows at a rate proportionate to its present rate of increase. When, dear wife, you get over celebrating my death, I want you to personally conduct an inventory of all family assets. Jonathan, you have the temperament to carry this family forward, but lack

experience. I have a plan that will help. Then there's Maclin. What can I say? I'm going to give you the same chance as your mother..."

Mrs. Wrightham reached over suddenly and turned the recorder off. "What the devil is going on here? This isn't a will. The old fool is still giving orders from the grave."

A gray haired man in a business suit stepped forward. "As your legal representative, Mrs. Wrightham, I must tell you it is in your best interests to hear what the 'old fool' has to say." The woman shrugged and Alfred restarted the tape. Wrightham's voice continued.

"...and Jonathan. I am, therefore, providing each of you with one million dollars. It's not a gift. You have one month to at least double that amount. How you do that, I don't care. You may work together and share the reward, my entire fortune, or you may work separately The one or ones who are unable to double their stipend will lose everything. Alfred has all the legal crap on hard copy. If there is no clear winner, or if at any time some tragedy would strike and there are no heirs, half of everything goes to the University of Southern California for their cancer research effort and the other half to the Ginnus foundation. No matter what happens, however, Alfred will receive a yearly payment of two hundred thousand dollars for the rest of his life. That's just about it. Get to it."

"I can't believe this," Mrs. Wrightham said after a stunned silence.

"We can work together or separately," Jonathan said thoughtfully.

"What about the damn yacht!" Maclin exploded.

What few maternal instincts Mrs. Morgan Wrightham might have had were quickly smothered by the realization that she could easily end up a pauper if she didn't come up with another million dollars in a month's time, truly an impossible task. Even though she was married to a millionaire, her own personal bank account registered only a fraction over fifty thousand dollars. Her sons were young and could seek their own fortune, she quickly concluded. She had one foot solidly in midlife, and had no intention of starting again. The others had left, leaving her and her two sons alone in the room.

"I have an idea," Jonathan said interrupting Morgan's sour mood. "I think I can make this work for all of us. But I'm going to need a half-million dollars from each of you."

"Just how stupid do you think we are," Maclin said sarcastically. "You get our money, turn it over to Alfred, and you're home free."

"You'd have to trust me. We can all win here. I think that's what Father was getting at. We have to work together."

"I don't trust you in the slightest. You can count me out," Maclin said. "I have an idea of my own." He exited the room without another word.

"And you Mother?" Jonathan said turning to the woman.

"I know where you're headed. The question is which one of us will have to do the trusting?"

"I leave it to up to you."

One month later Jonathan Wrightham and his mother, Morgan, entered the rustic den of the Wrightham estate. Maclin was already present as were Alfred and several estate lawyers. Both Morgan and Jonathan ignored them as if they were part of the woodwork. Carefully ordered papers and documents sat on the polished tabletop. Maclin noted his mother and Jonathan walked arm in arm, laughing at some shared joke, and took seats across from him. They did not look in his direction, and seemed oblivious to his presence.

Maclin Ethek didn't want to be there, he had no bargaining chip, but hoped he would come away with ten or twenty million. It wasn't that much to ask. His plan for turning another million on his own had failed. Not only had he not secured the extra million, but also most of the original million had evaporated.

Alfred cleared his throat to get everyone's attention.

"As you are quite well aware, at this time I need to have a financial disclosure from each of you. If you have no objection, may we start with you Mrs. Wrightham?"

"Certainly. My account reads two million dollars, and a few thousand dollars change." She handed him a notarized statement from the bank.

"And you Jonathan?" Alfred continued.

"My account reads…reads zero."

Maclin suddenly felt better. A lot better. He would not be the only one with his begging shoes on.

"And you Maclin."

"At least I beat Jonathan. My account reads two hundred fifty thousand dollars," he said with some reluctance. "I know. I didn't make it. It wasn't my fault. It was the damn accountants."

Alfred picked up a piece a paper and read: "By the authority invested in me by the stated and duly notarized wishes of Mr. Wrightham, I declare Morgan Wrightham the legal head of the Wrightham estate, and recipient of all the powers, assets, and privileges that that ownership entails, as long as she shall live."

Morgan Wrightham wasn't surprised, and, in fact, felt a great calm engulf her. The family fortune was secure in her hands, and she would have little to do the rest of her life but indulge herself in whatever or whomever she desired. Someone else would make all the boring investment decisions. Things couldn't have worked out better.

For the first time since she entered the room, she looked directly at Maclin and then Jonathan. "I have two orders of business to take care of immediately," she began. "To my son, Jonathan, I grant forty-nine percent of all Wrightham assets—except for one small thing—and with the bulk of the family fortune to fall to Jonathan upon my death. And to Maclin, I grant one well-used yacht."

From the depth of his being, Maclin Ethek began to scream, cursing his mother, cursing his half-brother, cursing all that were present, and then the world in general, promising vengeance if it took him the rest of his life. He was still screaming when a towering security man forcibly moved him outside the main gate of the Wrightham mansion.

After the tirade, Jonathan turned to his mother with a warm smile.

"It seems my faith in you was justified, Mother."

"I don't care about running this ship. You can handle the business end, and have nearly all the money. I plan to quietly slip away into shadows, and live sinfully and comfortably for the rest of my life. All you have to do is leave me a blank checkbook, which I promise not to abuse too badly. Mainly, I'm going to hire a young, handsome man, several actually, with lots of endurance."

"Maclin could be a problem," Jonathan surmised. "He is a...a..."

"Fool?"

"Most assuredly, but it is not wise to have him for an enemy. There was blood in his eyes when he left."

"What are you suggesting?"

"A nice quiet family outing to recover from Father's death, and to spend some quality time together. I'm thinking a few weeks at our lodge at the lake in Minnesota would do us all some good. Maybe we could even make this a yearly thing. The helicopter has been completely tuned after our Alaskan trip. It's still equipped with floats and can land on land or water. Alfred is a very capable pilot and can handle the details. We could leave tomorrow."

"Even Maclin?"

"Even Maclin. I think I can persuade him to come, if I throw in a few thousand."

Morgan Wrightham considered for several seconds. "Why don't you bring along your little honey? She may be an interesting distraction."

"Don't worry mother. She's nothing to me other than a temporary diversion. Expendable and replaceable. I plan to get a new model every year."

"I've trained you well. I am wondering about Maclin, however. What if he refuses to join our family outing?"

"Then it would be just you and me, Mother."

Chapter 1

Somewhere in the foggy distance, a girl-child's voice called to him softly. But he was too tired to get up.

"Let me sleep," he called back.

"Daddy. Come quick. There's someone here," the voice now demanding.

"Don't talk to strangers," he insisted, and rolled over in the leaves.

The excited voice turned suddenly frantic. "Daddy, there's someone here! Help me!"

"I'm coming!" he called, now fully aware and on his feet. The odor of decaying flesh smothered him as he began to move toward the voice.

Something was terribly wrong. His feet grew heavy, and looking down, he noticed that each foot was set in a human skull, and the more he tried to run the heavier his feet became.

The girl was panic stricken now, "Daddy! Daddy!"

Suddenly, an invisible force propelled him down a long path lined with massive tree trunks into a clearing in the wood, where a little girl in a flowing white dress pointed into a massive hollow tree. He recognized his daughter, but as she had looked many years before.

"Come quick, Daddy. Something's in there. In the dark. Look and see."

Every fiber of his being told him he didn't want to see what the little girl was pointing at, but he couldn't stop his forward movement, couldn't close his eyes, couldn't force his head to turn another way, and as he looked into the dark place, couldn't help but see a rotting corpse gazing out at him with two sunken holes for eyes, or see its bone fingers grab the little girl by the arm. She screamed, a piercing, panic-stricken blast that froze his soul, and he could only watch in horror as the thing that was no longer alive began to drag his daughter into the hollow tree.

Frantically, he tried to dislodge the fleshless bones from her arm, but the grip was like iron. In desperation, he pulled one of the skulls from his feet, and began pounding his attacker. It seemed to help, as there was a pause, and then the thing that was not alive began to plead, "Stop. Stop." Beams of light began to penetrate the gloom, and in the growing light a woman's face began to appear.

"Jesus, Steve. Are you trying to kill me!"

"What…what?"

"Another nightmare?"

"Another nightmare," Steve admitted. "What happened?"

"You were thrashing around, and when I grabbed your arm to try to wake you, you started whacking me with the pillow. How many does this make now?"

"Bad dreams? About one a week."

"More like two or three a week and for nearly a year. Your daughter overcame hers, but you can't seem to get it out of your head. I can't take this any longer. For your sake and the sake of our marriage, you have to get help."

Steve McGraig looked at his wife who had fled the pillow assault and was now sitting on the edge of the pink stuffed chair by their bed. She wore a rose-on-white nightshirt, strands of disheveled dark brown hair hung down over her face, and deep lines of concern dented the space between her eyes. "You're right," he said finally. "I know what I have to do."

"And that is?"
"Get back on the horse."

Steve McGraig always believed that when you fall off a horse, metaphorically speaking as he did not actually ride horses, you pick yourself up again and get back on. To give up even once would set a precedent for the next of life's challenges, and initiate a pattern of living that was not, in his view, the manly thing to do. However, even he had to admit heading up north this time caused some distress. It was ridiculous, he rationalized, to think that anything like what had happened in the deep woods of Northern Minnesota the previous year would ever happen again.

While on a father-daughter grouse hunting trip, Jennifer had been the one to stumble onto the gruesome remains of two men who had met a violent end. He, however, was the one having the most difficult time dealing with it. Even when fully awake and after the passage of several months, he could vividly see the grotesque and partially decomposed faces of the two men.

Because of the decidedly unsettling dreams, he began to fear the darkness, and the lack of sleep was having a serious effect on his general health. He was lucid enough to recognize the symptoms. Lack of appetite, frequent and deep depression, lack of ambition, morbid thoughts, and a disinterest in sex. It was like slipping down the sides of a deep well, and no matter how hard he tried to claw his way back up, he kept sliding inexorably downward. On the surface, it all seemed so cowardly; after all, the dead cannot hurt you, but try as he might he couldn't wipe the images from his mind or clear the awful stench from his nostrils.

Despite his wife's prodding, he was not, however, going to see a shrink under any circumstances. Real men didn't go to shrinks. They sucked it up and dealt with it. In his mind a trip back to the scene of the incident in the northern forest was the equivalent of the 'getting back on the horse' mentality.

As he, his wife, and Jennifer, who was now fifteen years old, drove from their suburban home near St. Paul in the light blue and white Explorer, the anxiety that steadily grew inside forced him to stop at a campground fifty miles short of his intended destination. The campground on Washburn Lake was near a ranger station, and that added a degree of comfort. They selected a campsite under a cluster of white pine trees, and began setting up their camp. The activity began to make him feel better. Certainly, after a few days, he'd be able to continue on to where he and Jennifer had discovered the dead men. He told himself that once he confronted his fears in the clearing in the woods, he could begin repairing his life.

For a typical summer day, the area was practically deserted, as only a dozen or so campers occupied the Minnesota DNR campground on Washburn Lake, and each had picked a site as far removed from the others as possible, providing each with a considerable degree of privacy. Mature white and red pine covered most of the four-acre camping area, and their pruned solid trunks reached twenty or thirty feet above the brown and needle covered ground. The land sloped away to the north for fifty yards and ended at the public boat landing and swimming beach. Primitive bathroom facilities, labeled Bucks and Does, occupied a place well away from the campsites in a grove of balsam trees. A single hand-pumped well provided pure cold water for drinking, washing, and cooking.

Once a day at five o'clock a young man with blond hair, facial fuzz, and denim bib overalls drove around the campground in a decaying yellow Chevy pickup truck selling bundles of firewood. On the third day of their stay, Steve McGraig noticed the driver and truck had changed. The new driver had dark hair, and looked as though he might have Native American ancestry. New clothes, a tan shirt and dress slacks, were about a half size too small, and his stomach bulged outward slightly stretching the buttonholes. From earlier conversations with the first man, McGraig had learned he was a local sawmill worker.

As he paid the new driver for three bundles of firewood, he decided to initiate a conversation. Somehow, this man didn't look the part.

"So Larry sick today?"

A blank look spread across the man's face followed by the dawn of recognition. "Oh, Larry. He took a couple days off. I'm just filling in. You folks must be the McGraig family."

"How'd you know? Have we met?"

"Not directly, but we have something in common. We're both connected to the two men who were found dead up on the Ottertail point road last year."

"My daughter and I found them."

"I know. I'm something of an expert on that case. My name is…is Charlie Johnson."

"Charlie Johnson. I know that name. You were connected to the investigation of those two men somehow."

"I don't mean to brag but I occasionally have to help out the local authorities."

"Now I remember. You're the woodsman, the tracker guy. They say you have some kind of honor code you follow."

"Honesty is the best policy. Right? And I come from a Native American family, and learned all about the woods stuff from my grandfather."

"We've been seeing this really big woodpecker. Almost the size of a crow. Any idea what it is?"

Johnson seemed momentarily puzzled, but then answered, "Pine…it's a Pine Woodpecker. Very rare. Consider yourself fortunate to have seen one." A few silent moments passed as Johnson looked around the campsite. "So where's your daughter now?"

"She and her mother went down to Brainerd shopping for the day. They should be back soon."

"You plan to stay at the campground long?"

"A few more days."

"Well, stay as long as you like. This really is God's country. Quiet, peaceful, safe. Have you tried any of the hiking trails?"

"Not me, but Jennifer does the jogging thing every morning."

"Oh does she now. A star athlete, I suppose. Dedicated. Up every morning at six?"

"Make that day break, whatever time that is. I just tell her not to wake her mother and me. I'm not that dedicated."

"Hey, I hear you. The bones just aren't what they used to be. Well, better get going. Have a nice stay."

Steve McGraig watched the pickup as it disappeared down the dusty trail and back to the highway. In sharp contrast to Larry's pickup, this was a brand new silver Silverado. McGraig wondered if there might be more money in selling firewood than he thought. His wife and daughter appeared moments later in the Explorer, and they began to settle in for a relaxing evening. If he could get through this night, it would make four in a row without a nightmare. It was a hopeful beginning, and yet he couldn't shake the feeling that something was not quite right.

In any serious altercation, Sheriff Forest Bodeman was someone you'd pray was on your side. Huge by any standards, in width if not his six-foot height, his most noticeable features were his massive shoulders and upper body strength. Like a professional football linebacker, which he had been in his youth, he was built like a wedge, and, even though Bodeman was well into middle age, there were few sane men anywhere that would consider a frontal assault without first getting their personal affairs in order. His deeply tanned and fissured face was that of an oil-rig roughneck, and crowned with thick white crew-cut hair about an inch long that stuck out like the bristles of a wire brush. His slightly large but perfectly symmetrical ears lay windswept against his skull, nestled in the white hair.

Blunt, frank, and honest to a fault, he said exactly what was on his mind, and had only marginal tolerance for stupidity and none for ignorance. His deep gravelly voice seemed to erupt out of his massive chest, startling those that did not know him, and that, together with his great bulk, had been rumored to have literally scared the piss out of more than one unprepared suspect. His election to county sheriff had been a landslide, even though he spent not one nickel on a campaign. He simply said he'd accept the job if the people wanted him. He'd spent several years working as a deputy, and his reputation, alone, was enough to stuff the ballot boxes in his favor.

His young wife had left him years before for greener pastures, leaving him to raise their daughter, Nicole, alone. Nicole, whose former marriage had ended abruptly upon the death of her husband, had produced a daughter of her own, and now father, daughter, and five year old granddaughter, Mary, shared the same home on a quiet southern bay of a great starfish shaped lake in the woods of Northern Minnesota.

Bodeman's job took him to the nearby county seat each day where, even in one of the most rural areas in the country with only a wide scattering of homes, there were still plenty of people who found creative ways to mess up their lives.

Sheriff Forrest Bodeman shuffled through chaos on his desk in his office at the Emergency Services and Law Enforcement building. Normally his desk was the only organized place in the cluttered room. It now contained the contents of one file drawer, and he rummaged through the pile of papers like a man possessed. The office secretary, Pam Calway, a white haired middle aged woman of Native American decent, poked her head in the door, took one look at the mess, and turned to leave.

"Hold it," Bodeman called after her. "I need to talk to you. Have you seen my speech? I know it's in this room somewhere."

For her own safety, Calway stood just outside the door and surveyed the room. "I can't imagine why you can't find it. Ever heard of organization? Try the top left drawer of your desk under your gun."

Bodeman pulled open the drawer, extracted his 9mm service pistol, and removed a brown manila envelope. He nodded a thank you, and was going to let it go at that, but reconsidered.

"I have an idea. Why don't you go deliver my speech to the civic club? I'm not worth a damn at these things."

"Sorry. Your uniform wouldn't fit. Just don't start cussing and you'll do fine."

"I'll bet you fifty bucks this whole thing is a set up."

"A set up?"

"The etiquette police and crook huggers will be there in force hoping I'll say shit, or some slanderous comment. Something they can use against me in the next election. I hate this political crap. I'd rather face a loaded forty-five any day. At least I know what I'm up against."

"I'll cover that bet, and not everyone that will be there thinks you're an insensitive ass," Calway grinned. "Only those who know you."

"And that coming from my only friend."

"Don't flatter yourself."

"Ouch!"

"Just go and be Forrest Bodeman. If you try to be nice now, they'd just think you'd lost your mind."

"I must have. I agreed to this. I *hate* this political crap."

"You're the sheriff. The main man for the county. People look up to you. Who else would be more appropriate to spearhead a be a good citizen campaign?"

"God, that sounds lame. Who ever thinks this stuff up?"

"It came from the state."

"Probably from some PhD who couldn't find a real job."

"Still, it's not a bad idea."

"Just naïve, stupid, and a waste of time. The good are already good, and the bad will just get a good laugh out of it."

"Don't worry. We'll suffer along without you this morning. If something important comes up, there's always your cell phone. A word of advice, however."

"Fire away."

"Man who step in shit not watching where he's going."

"Man who step…where'd that come from?"

Calway swept her eyes around the room, grinned, and closed the door.

It was only four blocks to the Wagon Wheel where the civic club was meeting, but Bodeman decided to drive. His personal police vehicle, a dark green, '95 Eagle sports cruiser, was fully capable of a hundred forty miles per hour, and rarely did he use a standard patrol car. He was, however, in no hurry now, and even as he drove into the parking lot of the steak house, his mind searched for some way to get out of it. Maybe Calway was right, however. Some good might come of it, and he was the logical man for the job. Yet, it would mean speaking to civic groups and school boards, church congregations and students. There would be articles to write and radio announcements to make. Maybe even TV appearances. The focus was supposed to be on drug awareness and young people. He easily visualized a group of first graders scattering in a panic the first time he opened his mouth. Yet, this is what the new generation of cops was supposed to be. A kinder, gentler breed. Use psychology. Don't shoot, talk nice to the criminals.

"Can't do it," he admitted to himself. "This dog really bites."

Audrey Bechworth, the president of the civic club, walked up to Bodeman's car, and opened the door for him. Bodeman noticed she had spent a great deal of time in front of the mirror filling in here, adding color there, in hopes of removing about ten years from her appearance. Her light brown hair, which was curled and puffed up on top of her head, showed just a hint of gray at the roots, but, together with a gray suit much like a man's, created the image of a typical businesswoman.

"Hello, Sheriff," she said as Bodeman raised his considerable bulk out of the small sports car. The greeting carried the neutral tone of a banker. Her above average height put the two at eye level. "So glad you could come today. Truthfully, I didn't think you would go through with this."

"That makes two of us. I'm not convinced I'm the man for this job."

"I'll be perfectly candid with you, Sheriff. Neither am I. To be frank, I don't think you have the necessary social skills."

"Then why in the hell did you ask me?"

"Because sooner or later you'll fail, and then maybe the people of this fine county will see fit to elect a sheriff who does have the necessary social skills." Audrey Bechworth pushed the on-switch on a miniature tape recorder in the pocket of her suit coat, and braced herself for the verbal assault that she hoped was coming. Instead, Bodeman simply smiled.

"I have to thank you twice."

"For what?"

"For proving me right and for making me fifty dollars richer," Bodeman stated, even though he had no intention of collecting on the bet.

The two stared at each other without speaking, Bodeman smiling and Bechworth confused. The sound of a cell phone interrupted their mutual contempt. Bodeman turned away to take the call. "I'm on my way," he said into the unit after nearly three minutes of silence, and then turned to Bechworth, who had become increasingly uneasy during the wait. "We'll have to do this another time. Duty calls. I want you to know that I do appreciate your candidness, if not your methods, and you may well be right. Times change, and different times require different tactics. Good-day, Ms. Bechworth, and one more thing."

"Yes?"

"Get a new tape recorder. Yours makes a peculiar humming sound."

There hadn't been a sense of urgency in the call. It had come from Joe Robinson, a forester who worked out of the DNR office near Outing. A camper at the nearby campground had come in at eight to report his daughter hadn't returned from her morning jog, and wondered if she had stopped in. Since Joe had only just arrived at the office himself, he had to say no. Robinson had accompanied the man back, and together they walked the three miles of hiking trails, where the teenager usually jogged, encountering no one. Now they were assembling a search party composed of volunteer fire fighters and emergency workers to comb the woods, and should be ready to begin the sweep in an hour and a half. Most likely the girl had left the trail, and gotten lost. The forester seemed confident that they would find the girl in time for the noon meal, but standard procedure was to notify the sheriff's office just in case. One red flag had gone up. Persistent calls into the forest had produced no response.

Robinson had explained the hiking trail wound through a section of wooded land roughly two miles square. Blacktop highways bordered it on two sides, a county road on the third, and a long series of private homes and cabins along a lake on the fourth. All the girl would have to do was keep walking and eventually she'd come to something man made. Robinson had reassured the McGraigs this wasn't the first time someone had gotten lost. Other than mosquito bites and a possible case of poison ivy, she shouldn't be any worse for the wear. For Bodeman, the call couldn't have come at a better time. He'd been one inch away from expelling a sting of expletives that would have certainly burned up the tape in Bechworth's recorder. When he thought about it, he wondered if he was starting to get soft, or even worse, diplomatic.

Bodeman mentally put time and distance together. He'd head east on Hwy 200, then south on Hwy 6. He briefly considered using the siren and lights, but even at a modest eighty miles an hour or so he'd still arrive well before the search party was ready to begin its work. Without a life-threatening emergency, it didn't make sense to tempt fate by weaving around the campers and boat trailers that clogged the highways during the summer months. He didn't resent them. It was the yearly pilgrimages of tourists to God's country that provided substantially to the local economy. Given the ten or fifteen minute cushion of time, he decided to make a pit stop along the way at someone's home who might just find the events at the campground interesting, if not at all challenging. Local legend had it this man could follow a flea's trail through the hair on a dog's back. If by some chance the search party failed, Charlie Johnson would make as good a backup as anyone could hope for.

Fifteen minutes later, Bodeman hammered a great fist on the weather-beaten door of a faded white cottage. There was no immediate response, and he absently glanced at his watch. At nine-fifteen AM, surely Johnson would be up and about. He cupped his hands around his eyes to shield the sunlight and peered into the dim interior through the front door window. Things, he couldn't be sure just what, seemed to be hanging from the ceiling suspended on dozens of white strings. It was, he realized, an assortment of edible wild food suspended and drying. Then he remembered. Johnson and one of the county deputies had gone off on a canoe trip somewhere, and probably hadn't returned. Yet, Johnson's old brown Ford pickup sat parked next to the house. He tried the doorknob, and found it unlocked. That told him nothing, since Johnson never locked his door. He was about to give it up when a female voice called from within.

"Just a minute! Keep your pants on. I'll be right there."

Moments later the door opened. A young woman appeared, slightly less than average height, blurry eyed, and dressed in only a man's long red flannel shirt. Long light brown hair fell haphazardly upon her shoulders and framed child-like features. She appeared solidly built, but not overweight, like someone who took physical training seriously. A look of panic swept across her youthful face when she recognized Sheriff Bodeman, her face flushed red, and immediately she fled back into the interior of the house. Less than two minutes later she reappeared, tucking her hair under a hat, and dressed in the official uniform of county deputy.

"Good morning, Sheriff," she said with formality, and then glanced nervously at her watch. "Am I late?"

"Relax Whitney. Must have been a late night. You're still on vacation, remember? Charlie around?"

"Out back on the pine ridge." Whitney braced herself for some comment, but Bodeman's expression never changed.

"Thanks," he said and started to leave.

"Sheriff, I…" Whitney began somewhat apologetically.

"What you do on your own time is none of my business," he stated, but then couldn't help but add with a crooked grin. "I like red in any color." He hesitated before continuing. "I'm heading down to the campground on Washburn Lake to check on a lost jogger."

"You need Charlie to help find him?"

"It's a her, and maybe. Want to ride along?"

"If I can help."

Bodeman nodded, then circled around to the rear of the house, and followed a gentle slope downward to where a stream formed the border between the tiny back yard and a forest of oak. He found the well-worn path and wound his way first through the oak, and then up onto a pine ridge. The ridge dropped away sharply to the shores of a quiet lake. A man sat under the limbs of a massive white pine and stared out over the blue waters. He sat very still, and long dark hair fell past his shoulders on his brown back.

"Good morning, Forrest," he said without turning.

"'Morning. Am I interrupting something? I can come back."

"You're welcome to stay." A long pause followed and then, "Grandfather sat under this tree every morning."

"I know."

"He said it was a good place to talk to yourself. I guess you could call that praying. But I come here to keep Grandfather's face in my mind, and to listen to the voices in the woods."

"It's hard to let go. That's why we have funerals, I suppose. A final parting. I just wish…"

"Grandfather died like the Old Ones he honored so much."

"But we never found his body."

"In the Old Days, the old ones would often simply vanish into the forest when they knew their days were done, or considered themselves a liability to the tribe. It was as if they didn't want to be found."

"Your grandfather was hardly a liability."

Lora Whitney appeared, having changed her clothes once more. The faded red plaid shirt was now tucked into a pair of well-worn blue jeans, and her long brown hair remained trapped under a hat. Johnson acknowledged her presence with a nod and slight smile. Whitney had heard the account of Grandfather's death many times from Charlie, and knew each telling was like medicine along the path to healing.

"It was near zero that morning in early November, going on three years ago now. Most of the small lakes were already frozen over, but this one was still open. He said he wanted to go out one more time in the canoe before the ice came in. He said good-by to Grandmother and never returned. When he didn't come in for supper, Grandmother went looking for him. She found the overturned canoe along the shore. In the frigid water, he couldn't have lasted more than a few minutes."

Bodeman and Whitney remained silent, letting the story unfold.

"We met right on this spot the day before. I can still remember him sitting with his back against the bark of this old pine tree that he loved so much. He told me then he was going somewhere, that he had to save a friend. It never occurred to me to question him. To me, he died right there."

"You couldn't know," Whitney said. "Let him go."

Johnson continued as though he hadn't heard. "Grandmother went to live with my parents near Duluth. I spent a week searching the shore and surrounding area for tracks, hoping I guess, but found nothing. Yet, I can't help but think that no one saw him get into the canoe, no one saw it capsize."

"We dragged the lake for three days," Bodeman added. "Some lakes never give up their dead."

"Now every time I come to this place I can't get past the feeling I'm missing something. All the things that Grandfather taught tell me there's a trail here, but I just can't find it."

"Let him go, Charlie," Lora repeated. "It's like you were saying when I arrived. He doesn't want to be found."

The three remained silent for nearly a minute, Bodeman shaking his head slightly and studying his feet, Whitney with her eyes focused on Johnson, and Charlie lost in his own private sorrow. Finally, he put that part of himself back into the box, and turned to the sheriff.

"So what can I do for you this morning, Forrest?"

"Jesus! I completely forgot," Bodeman exclaimed, and glanced hurriedly at his wristwatch. "We need to get down to the campground on Washburn. A lost jogger."

At least twenty vehicles, mostly pickups and SUV's, formed a long line along the access road to Washburn Lake Campground, and Bodeman had to pull out into the shallow ditch to get around them in the Eagle. The car was not designed for rough terrain, and he cringed at the sound of the underside scraping on gravel and rock. Johnson and Whitney followed in the Ford pickup, trailing Bodeman to where the line of vehicles ended. A group of thirty men and women that formed the search party were clustered around one campsite. As Bodeman exited his vehicle, Joe Robinson made his way through the crowd with a middle-aged man and woman in tow. Whitney arrived just as Robinson was making the introductions, but Johnson disappeared into the crowd.

"Sheriff, this is Steve and Margret McGraig. It's their daughter who's lost." Bodeman looked at each, recognizing concern, fear, and confusion in their faces. He nodded a hello and turned immediately to Robinson. "Fill me in," he boomed, startling the McGraigs to attention. Robinson deferred to the McGraigs.

"My daughter went jogging this morning and never returned," Steve began.

"Everything ok in your family?"

"What do you mean?"

"Any reason she'd want to run?"

"As in run away? Of course not."

"We're a close family, Sheriff," Mrs. McGraig interjected.

"Describe exactly what happened this morning."

"My daughter went…"

"I know your daughter went jogging. I want details, Mr. McGraig. What time was it? What did you hear? When did you contact Mr. Robinson?"

"You make it sound like we had something to do with this," Margret again interrupted, her voice straining with emotion.

"Your daughter may walk out of the woods right now, and I hope she does, but on the off chance that there's more going on here than meets the eye, I'm the one who gets paid to find out. I'm not accusing anyone of anything…yet. But if you want to find your daughter…"

Lora Whitney lightly touched Bodeman's arm and he abruptly stopped speaking and turned to face her.

"What is it?" he boomed.

"Can we talk, privately?"

Bodeman shrugged and moved several paces away with Whitney close behind.

"Permission to speak freely, Sheriff?"

"Of course."

"Bad morning?"

"What are you talking about?"

"You're scaring the hell out of these people."

"What?"

"Let me continue the questioning. Good cop, bad cop?"

"It hasn't been my best day," Bodeman admitted. "Go ahead. Take your time."

"Take my time?"

"Charlie asked me to buy him fifteen minutes."

"I'm not following."

"He wanted a few minutes to look around before everyone started trampling over all the tracks." Whitney nodded in understanding, as they moved back over to Robinson and the McGraigs.

"Mrs. McGraig," Whitney began with a broad comforting smile. "I'm presently out of uniform, but I assure you I am an official county deputy. Any detail you could give us will help bring your daughter home safely. We're basing this entire operation on the assumption your daughter used the hiking trial this morning. If she chose the highway instead, or went for a boat ride, or hitchhiked into town, we could be wasting a lot of people's time. See what I mean?"

Bodeman remained silent, watching Whitney work. She was a good cop, and he had to admit, in this case at least, tact was the more affective strategy.

Margret McGraig visibly relaxed. "It was just like the last three mornings. Jennifer rose early, probably around six thirty, and went jogging. At least she put on her green sweats before she left. Usually, she's gone for maybe an hour, and gets back just as Steve and I are getting up. When she didn't show up for breakfast, we waited until eight and then Steve drove over to the forestry station, and came back with Mr. Robinson. We walked the trails calling out her name, but didn't get an answer."

"Anything unusual happen this morning. Any unusual sound? Car door slam, splash out in the lake, that kind of thing."

"Nothing like that, at least that I heard."

"Did you see anyone suspicious? Maybe some stranger in the camp."

"No new campers have come in since we've been here."

"No change in the daily routine?"

"Not that I know of."

"There was one thing," Steve interrupted. "Probably nothing."

"What was it? It might be important."

"That guy, Larry, the one who comes around with the firewood, was sick, and some new guy took his place."

"That would be Larry Alberts from the sawmill out on '84," Robinson added.

"And?" Whitney continued, turning her attention back to Mr. McGraig.

"And I thought it was kind of funny, because Larry had this beat up old pickup, and the new guy was driving a brand new Silverado. Larry had on old work cloths, but the new guy looked like he was heading for a dinner date. I remember thinking the firewood business must be pretty good."

"That's it?"

"Ya, probably nothing, but you asked if there was anything different. And considering his connection to you folks..."

"What do you mean?"

"Well, you must know this guy. He works with you people all the time."

"Who?" Bodeman growled.

"It's that tracker guy. Charlie Johnson."

With a loudspeaker, Joe Robinson directed the search party and they moved off together in mass towards the blacktop highway. He intended to form a human line a half-mile long and march southward until someone located the girl, or they reached the homes on the southern end of the search area. If they didn't find the girl, they'd move the line farther east, and sweep back north. The process would continue until they located the girl or reached the second blacktop highway on the eastern side. The search would have to be started over again or reconsidered altogether if not successful. Steve McGraig insisted on taking part in the search, and left his wife alone with Bodeman and Whitney. She retrieved a cell phone from the Explorer and waited for some word from her husband. Bodeman and Whitney, with Mrs. McGraig trailing, moved over to the well pump for a drink of cold water. The temperature had already reached eighty degrees, too warm for most folks accustomed to the northern climate. Whitney sipped at the cold water, digesting what McGraig had said.

"It couldn't have been Charlie," Whitney stated. "Except for a couple hours, we were together all evening, all last week."

"Describe this man," Bodeman directed Mrs. McGraig.

"I didn't get a good look at him. Jennifer and I had been in Brainerd shopping, and saw him only briefly when we passed on the access road. He had long black hair, looked like he might be part Native American. Steve said he was very friendly. Seemed to know a lot about the woods."

"Could be Charlie, all right," Bodeman said. "Anything else?"

"You should talk to my husband when he gets back, but we've been seeing this huge woodpecker, and Steve said this man knew right away what it was. A pine woodpecker."

"Never heard of such an bird," Bodeman growled.

"Neither have I," someone stated, and the trio turned to see a man with long black hair and dressed in light brown buckskin clothing emerge from the forest. "Now pileateds are fairly common."

"Does this look like the man you saw yesterday?"

Margret McGraig looked closely at the newcomer. "Well, yes. Maybe. Except for the eyes. My husband should be here."

"The eyes?"

"The man in the car looked away as we passed. This man's eyes are…intense."

"Forrest," the man said calmly. "You want to tell me what is going on?"

"The McGraigs seem to think you might have been here last evening."

"This is Mr. Johnson?" Margret asked.

"The one and only."

"I've never been here before today," Johnson stated.

"Well, there are undoubtedly many Charlie Johnson's in the world. Could be a coincidence," Whitney reasoned. "Easy enough to check.

One call to the sawmill should be able to confirm the other man's identity."

"Why don't you do that," Johnson advised, "And see if Mrs. McGraig has anything further to add." He nodded toward their campsite. "Over there." Whitney understood, and moved away with the woman.

"OK. What did you find?" Bodeman asked, when the women were out of earshot.

"The search party is looking in the wrong area, which is fine, since they won't corrupt the real crime scene."

"Crime scene?"

"It's not pretty." Johnson glanced over toward the woman making sure they couldn't hear. Mrs. McGraig sat at the picnic table, head down on folded arms, with Whitney standing nearby talking on the cell phone. "What's the first thing you do in the morning, Forrest?"

"What? Well, I usually take a shower, shave, and make myself beautiful. What does that have to do with anything?"

"No, I mean the first thing."

"I take a long leak like everyone else."

"Precisely. Nature calls. That's what Jennifer McGraig did, also, and then went jogging. Only this morning she never made it to the hiking trials."

"For the love of Pete, quit jacking me around and spit it out. Where is she?"

"She's alive, or at least she was when she was led away. You'll want to get the BCA people in here. And keep everyone away from a hundred foot radius around the latrines."

"A kidnapping?"

"Looks like she went in to take care of business, and from the scuff marks on the ground, was accosted when she came back out. From there her attacker dragged her behind the buildings deeper into the balsam grove. There was a lot of commotion there, obviously a struggle, I can't tell what happened for sure, but…"

"But?"

"But there's an article of clothing. Looks like a green sweatshirt. I didn't want Mrs. McGraig to hear any of the details."

"Mrs. McGraig said her daughter wears green sweats."

"The two then headed north away from the highway deeper into the woods."

"So no vehicle."

"At least not close by. The man was in front with the girl in tow."

"Wonder why she didn't try to run?"

"The way she was weaving around, I'd say her hands were tied, and was most likely being led with a rope."

"Jesus," Bodeman exclaimed. It was not blasphemy, but as close as he could get to a prayer.

Mrs. McGraig had noticed the intensity of the conversation, and now returned with Whitney, who was clipping the cell phone to her belt.

"No man by the name of Charlie Johnson works for the sawmill," she stated flatly. "Larry Alberts does; however, he's in intensive care in the hospital in Brainerd. It seems someone beat him within an inch of his life with a blunt object." She turned to Johnson. "What'd you find?"

Johnson remained silent, deferring to Bodeman who opened his mouth to speak, but closed it without uttering a sound. This was going to get complicated in a hurry. The easy part would be to recall the search party, seal off the area, and notify the proper investigative authorities, who would then begin the analytical and objective investigation. It wasn't that he didn't have faith in the county's own people, but something this serious had to be handled by the best and the brightest—the Minnesota Bureau of Criminal Apprehension, the BCA, the state's equivalent of the FBI. The hard part was before him, telling this woman, and later her husband, that their daughter had been forcefully abducted. He wished some one else was available to take that responsibility. Audrey Bechworth was probably right. He didn't have the necessary social skills to handle this sort of thing. So he simply laid out the facts as Johnson had relayed them. Margret McGraig broke down as soon as the realization hit.

"The good news," Bodeman concluded, "is that your daughter is probably still alive."

"Why would anyone do this?" Margret cried. "We're not rich."

"There could be other motives, but stay close to a phone just in case."

"Other motives? Like what?"

"We have to consider people like a survivalist cult, or sexual predators."

"Oh my God!"

"Right now we need facts. About the only lead we have is the other Charlie Johnson, or whatever his name is, that was at the campground last night. We'll want you and your husband to come in and help put together a description and picture."

"Do you think he took our daughter?"

"Right now we'd just want to talk to him, but there is that possibility." He nodded to Whitney, and she led the distraught woman back to the picnic table.

"I can take about anything, but I can never get used to this part," Bodeman said looking at the women.

"I want to be a cop for a while, Forrest," Johnson said. "You know, temporary, like last year. I have a feeling, a connection to this I can't explain."

"What are you thinking?"

"A one eyed mule could follow the trail that this man is leaving."

"So, he's not very smart."

"Either that or he wants to be followed."

One hour later, the campground was empty, except for Bodeman, Whitney, and Johnson, several additional deputies who were called in to help secure the area, and one highway patrolman who'd picked up on what was happening on his radio, and followed his curiosity. Robinson had thanked the volunteers, several of whom he didn't even know, and sent them home. Bodeman and Whitney had made the rounds to the few other campers, searching for someone who might have additional information, but none had anything to add. They checked all ID's and compiled a complete list of who were present in the campground that morning. They found nothing glaringly suspicious, and when they were convinced none had anything to offer, had Joe Robinson tell them all politely to leave. Steve and Margret McGraig left for the Law Enforcement building in Walker in their Explorer, leaving the rest of their camp intact. Crime scene tape stretched across the access road where it made the final turn into the campground, and also along the shore by the boat landing. Usually only campground residents used the boat landing, but it was a public access, and Bodeman didn't want to risk having curious fishermen inadvertently contaminate the scene. Leaning up against the side of the patrol car, he conversed, now, with the highway patrolman and waited for the arrival of the investigative team from St. Paul. Whitney and Johnson remained by the well.

"If you're correct, this is not a good idea," Whitney was saying. "Someone capable of this is probably…"

"Capable of a lot worse?"

"A lot worse."

"I care about you, too," Johnson grinned. He was making last minute adjustments to a leather bag that hung from a long strap over his left shoulder.

"Think about it. Whoever did this is not…"

"Stupid?"

"He knew just when to strike, how to keep the girl quiet. It had to have been well planned. You're not following some…"

"Moron?"

"Yes, moron, and quit interrupting me!"

Johnson smiled, but Whitney was not amused. "You're the one who's supposed to be so damn logical."

"Did anyone ever tell you you're especially radiant when you're angry?"

"I'm not angry, I'm..."

"Upset? Oops, sorry."

"I'd slap you silly, if I thought it'd help. Put the pieces together. A man comes into camp who says he's you, a person known to be a tracker, and a man of honor. Then he abducts an innocent teenager, and heads off into the woods instead of doing the obvious thing and drive away. Doesn't that smell a little like a trap to you? He knows you'll want to defend your name, and he leaves an obvious path for you to follow. Abducting the girl just adds the perfect bait. There are a thousand places he could lay in ambush waiting for you to come bouncing down the trail like some stupid rabbit!" Whitney stopped and took a breath, her voice having risen to near shouting level, but Johnson remained silent. "Well, say something," she gasped.

"I think you've summed it up pretty well. You've overlooked one important point, however."

"What, your stubborn, bullheaded nature?"

"No. Why?"

"Why?"

"Why me? If what you say is true, then this man has singled me out for some reason. He used my name, and picked a victim with a connection to me. He's set out a trail of corn he's certain I'll follow."

"Well, prove him wrong. Stay here."

"I can't"

"Why not?"

"You said it yourself."

"Don't give me that honor crap. What good is honor if you're..."

"Dead? Have a little faith. I have no intention of dying."

"Well, at least take a gun."

"No can do."

"Why not?"

"I don't have a permit to carry."

"That's only for a concealed weapon and you know it."

"The extra weight would throw me off balance. Slow me down."

"If you won't listen to reason, then I'm coming with you."

"Sorry, this is a one man show. I couldn't put you at risk. Besides, I only received clearance for one."

"Clearance?"

Bodeman left the side of the patrol car and rejoined Whitney and Johnson. "About ready?"

"Yes."

"Do you have the cell phone?"

Johnson patted the side of his satchel. "Right here." He turned to Lora. "You going to be all right?"

"Me? What about you?"

"I'll be fine. Just keep the home fires burning."

"Here's the plan," Bodeman began. "Whitney, Robinson, and I are going to set up at the ranger station so we can use the wall sized Topo map they have of the county, and also the computer. Charlie is going to be calling in every half hour with his exact coordinates, thanks to the GPS unit Robinson provided. We can then determine how far he's traveled and were he is with the aid of the computer software."

"What about the crime scene?" Whitney asked.

"I'm leaving Deputy Martin in charge until the folks from St. Paul get here."

"I think that about covers it," Johnson said, and without another word or backward glance disappeared into the forest.

Whitney stared at the place where Johnson had vanished for some time. A bit of moisture appeared on her cheek, and slightly confused she wiped it away. Bodeman looked on in amazement. To his knowledge it was the first time this tough, seemingly unbreakable little woman had shed a tear. Whitney looked at the drop of moisture on her fingertip in wonder.

"Sorry, Sheriff."

"For what?"

"I don't usually get weepy. It won't happen again."

"Relax Whitney. It's not a capital offense."

Chapter 2

Finally, the brat had quit struggling against him. It wasn't going to help her anyway, and it was damn annoying. She was athletic enough to run circles around him, but lacked any real strength. Yet, she'd resisted more than anticipated, and he had to tie a rope around her wrists and to his waist to keep her moving along. Absently, he ran his left hand over the right side of his face where four fingernails had raked open the flesh. Good thing he'd gotten the duct tape over her mouth before she screamed her head off. If it was up to him, he'd end it right here, but there was the matter of getting paid a great deal of money, which wouldn't happen if the kid died prematurely.

Contact with the targets was supposed to have occurred four miles farther north, at a carefully orchestrated traffic accident, but the family had elected to stop at the campground. This had forced a total and hasty reworking of the plan, which had turned out much better than he could have hoped, except now he had to walk four additional miles through this god-awful forest filled with brush, ferns, and swamps to get to the hunting cabin. The terrain he had carefully studied and mapped farther north would be no problem, and there was an ATV trail to follow, but at present the woods and the kid were fighting him every inch of the way.

There had been no time to get the elevation maps that would have told him where the swamps were, and the aerial photos taken off the DNR website were the best they could do. Probably an expert could tell what was forest and what was swamp, but to him it was just various shades of gray. The photos did, however, clearly show the rivers, roads, and lakes, and provide enough information to tell him where he had to go, and what direction to get there. Thankfully, he was nearing the end of this part of it. He'd been through worse, but never in his life had he seen so many mosquitoes, or tiny flies that were enough to drive a man crazy. The bug spray kept the mosquitoes away, but the flies were unaffected. They buzzed around his head in clouds, burrowed into his hair, crawled under his clothing, and seemed to bite at will. Then there were tiny mites that he couldn't see at all that bit and bit but were impossible to kill. He'd heard of what the locals called 'no see ums' but he'd thought it was just a myth. What really irritated him was the kid seemed hardly affected. "And they call this God's country," he muttered under his breath.

The good news was a good part of the plan was running ahead of schedule. It had been total chaos at the campground, and his partner had been able to walk around at will, posing as just another volunteer, keeping him informed via the cell phone on what was going on. Once the campground had been evacuated, his partner had moved on ahead with the Silverado, hidden it away in the woods, and hiked into their final destination.

It turned out they'd been able to suck Johnson in right away. Using his name had been a stroke of genius, and he had enjoyed playing the part. He was dark complexioned enough to pass himself off as part Indian, but was of purely Italian descent. He got a good laugh out of that, remembering most of the 'Indians' in the early Hollywood westerns were actually Italian actors.

The personality profiles on Johnson had been correct and he was already on their trail, having fallen for the oldest trick in the book.

While his partner would be waiting at the hunting cabin, it would be Bullet's job to slow Johnson down if he came too close. He'd seen some whacked out dope heads in his life, but that character, the third member of the team, was just plain weird. Some kind of freak. Mostly it was his eyes. They didn't look like eyes at all, more like two red coals. Rumor had it he'd killed hundreds of people, even bit one man to death. If this operation went according to plan, he'd never have to look upon that hideous face again.

He checked his compass and map again. Right on course. The girl jerked back on the rope, a feeble if defiant effort, and he jerked back hard pulling her face down in the leaf mold. Too bad they had strict orders not to do any real damage until they reached the hunting shack. There the real party would begin.

Charlie Johnson moved through the forest like a dolphin through water. Soundlessly, the leaves and ferns slipped over the supple leather clothing, and his feet padded softly on the leaf-covered humus of the forest floor. Several things became immediately obvious. The man ahead was walking purposefully in a northerly direction almost dragging his prey behind, but he did not know the area. He did not avoid the swamps, and difficult terrain and undergrowth, but rather headed right through them, evidence that he was using a compass or guiding map and not his head. Also he was making no effort to conceal this path. The ferns lay trampled and small limbs were bent and broken. He estimated the man's progress at hardly more than a mile an hour, which was good news since it meant the girl was still alive and slowing him down. Because it is often easier to follow a trail than make one, his own pace was close to four miles an hour.

Johnson ran for several seconds, then stopped abruptly; watching, waiting, listening, and when he was reasonably confident of his own safety, ran again, repeating the pattern over and over. In the humid eighty-five degree heat of early afternoon, his body dripped with rivulets of sweat, and with the added annoyance of the insects, he found himself wishing it were twenty below zero. At forty minutes into the task, he checked the watch Bodeman had given him, and realized he was already ten minutes late for the first call-in. He veered off the trail to seek cover under a spruce tree that had lower branches sagging to the ground. He sat up against the trunk, invisible from the outside, removed the GPS unit, and dialed Bodeman's cell phone number.

"You're making good time," Bodeman said, after Johnson had relayed his coordinates, and Robinson verified his distance and position. "Approaching three miles so far. You're about a half-mile west of Hwy. 6. You're not that far from a gravel road, and a couple homes. Anything to report?"

"Just that this is way too easy. If I've done my figuring right, I can't be much more than a mile behind him. The girl is really slowing him down."

"The closer you get..."

"I know. Desperate people do desperate things. By the way, we never did decide what I'm supposed to do if I catch up to this creep."

"Just sit tight after you let us know where you are. Don't try to be a hero. Keep him under surveillance until backup arrives. I have some special folks ready to go on a moment's notice."

Johnson could hear another voice in the background, and then Bodeman added, "Whitney wants to know if you can tell time. You're ten minutes late."

"Just became too caught up in my work, I guess."

"She's says don't let it happen again, and Charlie..."

"Yes?"

"Since I am now your commanding officer, I'm making that an order."

"I knew there was some reason I never..."

The sound of a limb breaking caused Johnson to abruptly terminate the connection, and then shut down the unit completely, in case Bodeman decided to call back. He sat motionless under the protective limbs, and strained to hear a sound that might not be a part of the natural plethora of voices of the summer forest. It came again, the unnatural sound of a dead limb cracking under the weight of a flatfooted animal, certainly not a deer, more likely the human animal. It was coming slowly along the same trail, trodden now by three people, and from behind him. It was clear that while he was stalking the man and girl, someone or thing was stalking him. Even though he was barely twenty feet from the trail, the leaves and other vegetation made it impossible to see who or what was following him. Several minutes passed, as the intruder drew ever closer. Then an odor like a musty wet dog reached him and he sighed in relief. Only a bear, he realized, and began whistling softly. He stood, and quietly stepped from the protective cover of the spruce tree. A few feet away, a great black head reared up above the low brush. Its tiny eyes darted about, settled on Johnson, and then its jaws snapped loudly, a sign of agitation and warning. For a brief moment the two stood face to face, and the consciousness of a man and the instincts of an animal collided as their eyes met and locked.

"Why are you following me, Brother Bear?" Johnson asked as if he truly expected an answer. The bear responded with a deep-throated 'woof,' returned to all fours and crashed away through the bushes.

While generally less volatile then grizzlies, Johnson knew black bears could be killers, especially rogue males or females with cubs. When unarmed and in their suspected company, it was always a good idea to make some continuous noise like singing, whistling, or ringing a hiker's bell to alert them to the human presence. He remembered the joke about how to tell wolf droppings from bear droppings. The wolf droppings have the indigestible deer hair, and the bear droppings have all those little bells. In fact, black bear attacks were rare, and usually ran from man, but four hundred pounds of raging bear with four-inch claws and powerful sharp teeth was an animal to be avoided. This one had been merely curious, and wisely fled at the sight of a human. It was a good habit to get into as it might just save him come hunting season.

Johnson set off again and within a few minutes the trail led out of the generally low land, and up into a hardwood forest. There was very little understory, almost like a well-maintained park, and he could see far ahead around the tree trunks. He couldn't help but think the object of his search could also see him coming from the same considerable distance. Then he came to the trail.

Two ruts worn through the leaves and into the dirt indicated past use by single person ATV's, 4-wheelers. However, the impressions were not recent, probably created by last fall's hunters, who drove road vehicles as far into the woods as possible and then mounted their ATV's. The days of such practices were numbered in the state since what had started out as a few weekenders had turned into a multitude, causing considerable environmental damage. Each year the regulations were getting stricter, and there was talk of banning recreational vehicles from public property entirely. The man and girl had diverted onto the ATV trail, and Johnson suspected it was what the man had been aiming for all along. Minutes later, just as he was considering calling Bodeman again, an unnatural flash of light ahead brought him to a halt. The sound of a bullet whining past his head and smashing into a nearby tree came a split second before the sound of the rifle blast, and instinctively he dove for cover.

Charlie Johnson had not been particularly concerned about getting shot at, which is why he hadn't taken Whitney's concerns seriously. While certainly vulnerable to an ambush, he had assumed it would be a physical fight, if it came. He had been reasonably sure the man he pursued was unarmed, certainly he wasn't carrying a high powered hunting rifle, but the sound of the bullet whizzing past his head forced him to reconsider his thinking.

From behind the solid protection of a two-foot sugar maple, he quickly discerned the error in his reasoning. The girl was alone with only one man, but it was now obvious there was more than one man involved. Quite probably he had come in on the ATV trail. In fact, if there were two, why not three or four. Yet, when he thought about it, this place was a poor choice for an ambush. The shot was made from a considerable distance. Why hadn't his attacker lain in wait in the dense vegetation he had just been through, and shot him in the back if his intent was to inflict bodily harm? The thought occurred to him that the shooter's goal might not be to kill him after all, but merely warn him off. Yet, why then were they leaving a trail that a child could follow? There didn't seem to be any logical explanation, and yet one thing rang perfectly clear. These people had access to deadly force and wouldn't hesitate to use it. The bullet had hit a few feet from his head and dead center six feet up on the smooth white bark of a six-inch aspen tree. The entrance hole was a tiny circle under a half-inch in diameter, but the exit hole was a gaping and fractured mass of shredded bark and splintered wood. He could only imagine the impact on a human head. Yet, the hit was so exact it was almost as if the tree had been the intended target.

It seemed likely the attack had been a warning shot to suggest, in the strongest terms, that he abandon his pursuit. The next one might not be so suggestive. It was a safe bet the shooter was still watching, waiting to see what he would do. When he thought about it, he decided that would work in his favor.

From the satchel, Johnson removed a wrinkled mass wrapped in a one foot square piece of brown buckskin. He removed a bit of beef jerky, and set the rest aside. Next he took out the GPS unit and cell phone, and called Bodeman. Again he relayed his coordinates.

"Robinson ran the distance formula through the computer," Bodeman explained. "Only a mile this time. Run into trouble?"

"Just Brother Bear." He hesitated, considering whether or not to tell them about the bullet that just missed his head, and that the shooter most likely still had his scope trained on his location. He knew Whitney would be ear to ear with Bodeman, listening in on the conversation. If Bodeman knew all the details of his present situation, he would instantly order him to do an about face, he would say no, and then

Whitney would tell him he was crazy, which might not be far off. It seemed so much easier to keep his present predicament to himself. If the situation deteriorated, there was no way help would arrive in time anyway. He was alone with a lunatic, but then it wasn't the first time.

"A bear?" Bodeman demanded.

"Seems I attract wildlife."

"What's your situation now?"

"Eating lunch. Venison jerky and dried blueberries."

"Forget the nuts and twigs and remember what you're doing there," Whitney called from the background, and then her voice grew louder as she took sole possession of the phone. "Are you sure everything's alright?"

"The bear's gone. I guess he didn't like the way I smell."

"Something smells."

"What do you mean?"

"You've slowed up considerably."

"Just taking my time enjoying the scenery."

"Scenery, my you-know-what. You know I've had a bad feeling about this from the start. Watch your back."

"Roger that," Johnson confirmed. "Over and out."

Whitney set the cell phone on the corner table in the DNR office. She stood silently next to Robinson, eyes focused on Bodeman, and then looked away.

"What are you thinking?" he asked.

"He's lying through his teeth."

"You and I know Johnson doesn't lie."

"Then he has a severe case of selective forgetting."

For a hundred yards between the shooter and the maple tree, the ground rose and fell with a series of tree-covered ridges. Johnson lowered his head to the level of the ground and peered around the trunk. From that level, one ridge, perhaps fifty yards away, was high enough to block his line of sight. If he couldn't see past the ridge, then neither could the shooter.

It was going to be a matter of who would give in first, and the tracker who sat behind the maple tree a hundred yards away didn't seem to be in any hurry to go anywhere, and that was beginning to worry him. He'd placed the shot within inches of his head merely to slow him down, it wasn't supposed to deter him entirely and shouldn't have according to the personality profile, and yet careful observation through the variable power scope clearly showed a bit of the brown of the man's clothing behind the tree. Perhaps the shot had been too effective, perhaps he should have placed the shot farther away, but now he couldn't just saunter on over and tell the guy to get going, that he had a date with destiny in a run down hunters shack yet two miles distant.

The man with red eyes had been one of the youngest in the end days of Vietnam, and he'd earned a great deal of respect as a marksman. After Vietnam, he came home to nothing. Someone else had his job, and a bunch of kids broke into his house to have a keg party and managed to burn it down. No one gave a shit that he had nearly been killed a dozen times, there was no hero's welcome; in fact, his welcome had been a wad of spit from someone carrying a 'make love, not war' sign.

His wife and the child he never knew had been killed in a senseless car accident, struck broadside at an intersection by a shoe salesman who had left the corner bar two minutes earlier insisting he 'didn't need no help from nobody.' She had been a lover of flowers, and the one thing he did that really mattered was maintaining a bed of red roses on the place where mother and daughter were buried side by side. Yet, the tombstone had three names chiseled in the granite. After all the years, he still saw her face, heard her laugh, felt her touch. He would have given anything to have physically died with her because, in every way that mattered, he had. If there were such places, he was sure his wife and daughter had gone directly to the love of heaven, but knew he'd spend eternity in the fires of hell.

Always a loner, he'd tried working in the construction trade for a while, and although he enjoyed working around wood, found he had a difficult time taking orders from foremen who knew much less than he did. Eventually, he became a surveillance expert which meant he often hid for hours with a camera-scope, directional microphone, and headset listening in on rich old men screwing the maid, or unsatisfied wives out for a little extra when the husband was away on business. All was patiently and accurately recorded and handed over to the lawyers who proceeded to rip families and fortunes apart. He learned early on that so-called humanity was not equal to the animals; it was considerably lower. He had come to look at life as just another war, with strike and counterstrike, unavoidable casualties and collateral damage, where the most one could hope for was to win a battle or two because the war was without mercy and unending. He was about to end his own suffering, when he met someone, a sort of father figure, who brought him back from the brink, and introduced him to his family.

Yet, he hadn't intended to turn to the alternative occupation he ended up in, but one must find a path through life somehow, and his sniper skills were of little use in the mainstream civilian world. His first shot had been a famous CEO who had milked over two hundred million dollars from the pension fund, there had been several attempted and successful suicides, and when certain families couldn't get satisfaction in court, they'd hired him to take care of it the Old Testament way. He carefully studied each assignment, looking for what he considered a 'gross miscarriage of justice,' and he justified each execution by convincing himself that since these people had caused extreme hardship and the death of others and gotten away with it, he was merely doing what a fair and just society should have done.

He'd adopted several different names, perfected several alternative identities and disguises, and became so adept at character transformation that he wondered at times if he should have been an actor. There was the old hag complete with a lazy eye and bad teeth. His favorite persona, however, was the crazed psychopath, complete with red contacts, an eyebrow that twitched on command, and a silver tooth. If need be, he could produce a sneer that had taken several hours of practice in front of a mirror to master. Topped off with a shaggy dark brown wig and beard, there had never been anyone anywhere whom he hadn't fooled. Besides his very real activities, he'd seeded the underground with fabricated and horrific exploits to the extent that the worst of the worst would not cross the man known as Bullet.

Yet once down the trail he chose, there was no turning back, and from the first time years before to the present, his life's work had been a series of well-paid contracts. There really hadn't been that many, but then there didn't need to be. At two hundred thousand a crack and tax-free, one didn't need to be greedy. The money was to cover living expenses, since once in old man's family there was little need for anything else. In fact, most of the money he gave away. In the past twenty-five years, only eight bullets had left the barrel of the aught-six, and there had been only one miss. That had been deliberate, and that had been today.

The present situation was different from all previous. He was not acting under orders from anyone, but was free-lancing on his own. This man, Charlie Johnson, did not deserve to die, and he made sure his part did not call for it. The Indian seemed almost like a kindred spirit, and it had been curiosity as much as anything that made him decide to accept the contract. His directive called for a 'near miss,' or whatever it would take to cause a thirty-minute delay in Johnson's pursuit, and only if needed. It had been needed, but now as he glanced at his watch, he realized the time passed was over an hour, and still he saw a brown patch of the tracker's back sitting against the maple tree a hundred yards distant. Very slowly a wisp of suspicion began to crystallize into the stone of certainty. He was not the only one to have mastered deception.

It took Charlie Johnson five minutes crawling on his belly to reach the base of the ridge. From there he followed it eastward as it wound along the ground like a huge snake. Eventually, it disappeared into a cedar swamp, which provided him with dense cover. Everything hinged now on how long the piece of buckskin that had held his dinner would hold the shooter's attention, and just what he'd do once he realized the deception. He hoped it would give him enough time to circle around and pick up the trail once more. That would mean, however, that there was now a potential threat both in front of and behind him. Surprise and the forest would be his only weapons, and yet his greatest concern was how to keep Whitney out of the upcoming events. He was not good at fabrication, and although he hadn't actually lied, he'd left a gaping hole in the facts, which he knew hadn't fooled Whitney. Well, there was one little white lie. The coordinates he had relayed to them were not exactly where he happened to be.

The man known as Cook suspected that if one counted them all up, there were probably more hunter's shacks in Northern Minnesota than buildings over five stories tall. They existed in the real world, isolated from mainstream society, and yet were the creations of fantasy.

To a greater or lesser degree, all human beings, including and especially himself, possessed a residue of the hunter spirit, the desire for the thrill of the chase, and a yearning for a simpler existence. Yet in the complexities of modern society, the hunting instinct is systematically buried and smothered, or reshaped and reborn into the mental tools of capitalism. One may no longer hunt animals on a regular basis, but there is certainly still plenty of prey, and even competitors are fair game.

A man sits at a desk staring out the fortieth floor window at rooftops and wires, cement and steel, which some actually call beautiful, and begins to wonder. Is this all there is? Is there nothing more? Is there no escape from this dullness that some people call success? He rises before the dawn, gets ready for work, fights the traffic to work, plays the rumor game at work, fights the traffic back to the apartment, ingests the latest human cruelty from the box with the moving pictures, then watches some inane comedy to exercise the other facial muscles, takes a sleep aid to forget it all, so the following morning he can begin again. Success becomes a lie reinforced by the accumulation of things, happiness an illusion, life becomes meaningless. There is no purpose, except to fill a temporary slot in society, where there are millions of essentially identical slots. One morning he wakes up and realizes the last five, ten, or twenty years have simply vaporized. Where did they go? And more importantly, where has the spirit gone?

So is born the impetus for the rustic shack in the wood, an escape from the reality of a monotonous existence, where men search for fleeting shadows of what men once were. The crudeness is a deliberate construct of the subconscious mind. To build anything better would remind them of that which they're trying to flee. Yet, the cabin is irrelevant. The hunting rifles are irrelevant. It is the anticipation and the gathering for the hunt that is important, and provides a kind of therapy, a brief genetic remembrance of a time long past. For some it is a virtual lifesaver; for others it merely postpones the inevitable.

In the 'business,' one did not use given names, not even if your partner was your brother, especially if your partner was your brother. So in due time, the dark complexioned brother whose features came from his Italian heritage adopted the name Saulo, and the one with the lanky frame and pockmarked nose—who resembled the pizza delivery boy—adopted Cook. ID's were forged, portfolios fabricated, reputations built. Deliberate avoidance of real names was not so much a commandment, rather more like proper etiquette, and a violation would be on par with a raunchy fart in church.

Those successful at the business developed the attitude that there were always ears listening, because, for those who had the most to lose, a slip of the tongue could result in a flip of a switch. Yet for the most dedicated, the penalties for crimes against society never entered into the equation except that it added a keener edge to their skills, and the fact that a particular state did or did not use 'old sparkly,' lethal injection, or cyanide gas, or other means of capital punishment was irrelevant.

When Cook thought about it, the business seemed no different than the construction trade. The buyers created the demand, which was filled by contractors and sub-contractors, and the contractor's business depended on the quality of the product he delivered. The customer wrote the paycheck; therefore, what the customer wanted, the customer received. The Brothers, as Cook liked to call their contracting business, had done just about everything there was to do for hire, from stealing a million dollar thoroughbred Tennessee walker to a marketing scam, to kidnapping a new born child from a hospital nursery to expediting the demise of a wealthy tycoon. Never did Cook seek a portion of the take. It was like building a house. Once it was finished and you got paid, you moved on to the next house.

His present location was a house only by the crudest standards. It was a twelve by twenty box with a peaked roof, two recycled windows, one solid door, and covered with black tar paper. Built by one Jackson Grayling from Minnetonka on a forty-acre parcel he also owned, it was the pitiful outcome of a city dweller's dream to escape to the north woods, and live like a real man. The interior, however, showed the rewards of the dream before it went sour. Knotty pine paneling covered the walls, and the pungent aroma of the wood still overpowered the musty odor of disuse. There was a handcrafted wooden table and four chairs, a black freestanding fireplace, and bunk beds against the far wall. There was no indoor plumbing, yet one corner was the designated kitchen with a gas cooking range on the counter, a sink properly under the east window, and varnished wood cabinets below and to the right and left above. While the outside looked like a squatters shack, everything inside was new, or at least barely used. Cook was not concerned about Jackson Grayling making an unexpected visit. On the twelfth of May, he stepped off the top of the Maryland Hotel in Minneapolis, and found the peace he was looking for.

While Cook considered his brother an equal partner, he, by virtue of his superior mental skills, assumed the leadership role. He was insightful, even philosophical, and knew full well that to most people, his gangly frame and pockmarked face marked him ugly, but in the business where impressions were everything, this was a bonus. While he was analytical and calculating, Saulo was headstrong and impulsive and, admittedly, straining at the limits of sanity. He'd thought long and hard about assigning him the task of retrieving the kid. Both carried .38 caliber weapons, and he'd wondered about the wisdom of letting him take it with him. The contract called for her to arrive alive and in one piece, and given his brother's maniacal nature, that was an uncertainty at best. The deciding factor had been Saulo's resemblance to the main target, Charlie Johnson. The skin tone was similar, as was the long, black hair.

They'd accepted some strange assignments, but this one took the prize for weirdness, which matched the customer perfectly. He'd met the boyishly handsome man face to face only once, realizing immediately that he was by far the most dangerous man he'd ever met. Charming and charismatic on the outside, yet cunning, cruel, and corrupt on the inside, he had the financial resources and the power wealth buys to go wherever he wanted, take whatever he wanted, control whomever he wanted. What he had against this man, Johnson, was irrelevant to the mission, but by the look of the intended retribution, must be on par with murder.

Cook stood in the shadows of the solid branches of an oak near the cabin, tall and still like a skinny tree trunk himself, waiting for Saulo and the kid to arrive. The clearing had once been a homestead, the land long ago abandoned back to the public domain, before Grayling acquired it. If one looked hard enough, one could still find the outline of where the log cabin and barn had been. The once cleared forty-acre parcel had grown back in with mostly aspen, oak, and maple, with occasional mounds of dirt up to three feet high scattered throughout. The mounds were colonies of red and black ants, stable and thriving for over fifty years, that had moved in after the sodbuster's retreat. Thousands, perhaps millions, of diligent workers slowly yet steadily added to the accumulation of debris in each colony adding a few centimeters of height each year. A few colonies had been ripped apart by marauding black bears looking for a meal, but several still dotted open areas of the forest. Cook absently kicked at a mound with his toe and hundreds of soldiers poured into the depression, pinchers at ready, instinctively willing to sacrifice themselves to protect their queen.

The head of a man and girl appeared on the trail, growing into full bodies as they came up over a ridge. If Bullet had done his job, this brother and he would now have one hour to prepare, take care of the business, and move on to the next house.

It had only been for her father's sake that Jennifer McGraig accompanied her parents into the north woods. At fifteen years old, she was fast discovering her own world that, though shallow and self-centered, would be the transition from childhood to adulthood. The tug of her friends and social life was only barely overcome by needs of her family. She was having difficulty accepting the body fate had given her, and it somehow seemed logical that her parents didn't have a clue what she was going through. Her hair was too blonde—almost white, her lips were too big, nose too small, mouth too full, chest too flat.

Though completely horrified at last year's discovery of the rotting bodies, she had suffered little mental injury. Maybe it was youth, or a different character, but her nightly visits by the demons of the dark were few. However, she clearly saw the cumulating effects on her father. Someone who had always been easy to talk to, joke with, and milk an early advance on her allowance from, rapidly mutated into a quick tempered, solemn, and reclusive mental case. The family outing seemed like a good idea. The campground seemed like a good idea.

Running every morning so she could make the cross-country team seemed like a good idea. It seemed like forever, but it had been only a half day ago that it all went bad. One moment she was half asleep and the next she was fighting for her life with duct tape over her mouth.

The man who dragged her along had long, black greasy hair, swore constantly, and even though he had been nicely dressed, smelled like the latrines at the campground. Intellectually, she knew she wasn't supposed to resist, that statistically it was safer for her to remain passive and let him do whatever he wanted, but her instincts told her to fight. He had ripped off her sweatshirt, leaving her with just the halter top and sweat pants. She managed to deliverer a strong kick to the man's groin, slash his face with her fingernails, and finally resist every inch of the way through the forest. His clothes and her's were now dirt stained, and soaked with sweat. She gave her resistance all she had and then some, but it hadn't been enough.

She noticed he kept looking behind, and her hopes grew that someone was following, attempting to rescue her. Eventually, as the rope gradually wore into her flesh, the bruised and bleeding wrists simply ached too much, and she lapsed into the numbness of both mental and physical shock. Then came the rifle blast, and the greasy haired man started to laugh, a sick croaking sound that echoed through the woods. Defiance melted away in the face of gut twisting terror. It suddenly hit home. This man was not going to let her live.

The call was ten minutes overdue. Bodeman sat by the corner table drumming his fingers on the dark red wood. Whitney paced back and forth in the small space in front of the service counter like a tiger in a cage. Joe Robinson remained by the computer checking color aerial photos of the area north of the campground. He was in the process of overlaying a digital grid over the general area of Johnson's last contact.

"We can't just stand around doing nothing," Whitney suddenly exploded. "We have the manpower right outside the door. With all due respect, Sheriff, it's time to move."

"Charlie was ten minutes late last time. Let's give him a few minutes more."

"You gave him a direct order to call."

"It was a nice gesture, but you and I know the only orders he takes are from his own conscience."

"Not you too. I'm sick and tired of this honor…"

"Shit!" Robinson interrupted from his station.

"I wouldn't go that far," Whitney stated.

"No, I mean this," he said, pointing to the monitor.

"Assume I know nothing about what the hell you're talking about," Bodeman drawled. "What are you talking about?"

"When Johnson called in last time I just punched the numbers into the computer and it gave me the distance traveled."

"One mile. We know. So what?" Whitney said.

"So I just did the overlay…matched the coordinates with a physical place on the map."

"Isn't that good news? At least we know where he was when he called in last time."

"I ran the numbers again and there is no mistake."

"I hate it when people beat around the bush. Spit it out," Bodeman boomed.

"Well, according to this, Charlie was sitting in the middle of Rat Lake."

Seconds passed as the revelation sank into Bodeman and Whitney.

"Well either he misread the GPS unit…" Bodeman began.

"On purpose," Whitney finished.

"I think I can narrow down his whereabouts," Robinson said. He turned back to the computer, and started entering numbers and commands. A minute later, he turned back to Bodeman, shaking his head.

"Well?" Bodeman demanded.

"Just too many variables. The best I can do is put him somewhere inside a circle."

"How big a circle?"

"About a five mile circle."

For the first time since she arrived at the forestry station, Whitney collapsed into a chair. "Might as well be the moon," she sighed. "We never should have let him go alone."

He pushed the girl down backwards onto the chair, and while he held her there, his partner taped her firmly in place. Next he grabbed her roughly by the throat with his grimy left hand. Tears flooded her eyes as she tried to suck in air through her nose. With his free hand and one swift motion, Saulo grasped a loose corner of the duct tape and ripped it from her face, and was greeted immediately with an ear splitting scream. Cook nodded his approval. The brothers stepped outside the shack, but left the door open.

"Good set of lungs. Should do the trick."

"How long you going to let her scream her fool head off?"

"As long as it takes. We're a long way from the nearest home or regularly traveled road. Only one person is going to hear, and come riding in on a white horse. When he comes charging into the house, we use the tranquilizer pistol. Then we turn on the cameras, and up-link. Our benefactor wants to watch the final show."

"He has to be one twisted bastard."

"And we aren't?"

"You know what I mean. This is business. But to get a stiff one out of watching is just plain sick."

"He pays. We don't ask questions."

The sound of the human scream penetrated the woods, and Johnson fumbled with the cell phone dialing the memorized number at a full sprint. The scream came again filled with the raw emotion that is inexpressible in verbal terms. He heard Bodeman's voice, but didn't wait for the words to register.

"I have something," he gasped into the unit. "Stand by. I'll get back to you."

Driven by rage, Johnson raced up and over the oak and maple ridges with a surge of adrenaline that made him feel as though he could almost fly. The scream came again, much closer now, and the outline of a black dwelling appeared in a tiny clearing no more than fifty yards distant. Again the high-pitched wail taunted him and he was about to race blindly in…into what? Two men stood outside and appeared to be guarding the entrance. A memory fired of something Grandfather had shown him, and he abruptly stopped, sliding quietly behind a cluster of basswood trees.

He had been ten years old on a January day so cold that spit froze solid before it hit the ground, yet Grandfather insisted they go to the big pine on the ridge by the frozen lake. He said he was going to make a wolf venture out of his warm den. They sat together under the tree in the cold snow with a white blanket pulled up to their chins, and then Grandfather took a flat blade of dead grass from his pocket, placed it firmly between his thumbs, and blew threw the tiny place. The sound produced was a cross between a whistle and a scream.

Every few minutes, Grandfather repeated it. Soon he said, "Be very still. Brother wolf is coming across the lake." For twenty minutes they watched the lone wolf circle around, catching the scents in the air, as if it were searching for something. Twice it came up the pine ridge a stone's throw away. When it had gone back to its den, Grandfather explained every animal has a weakness that could be used against it. The grass whistle made the sound of a rabbit in death's grip, and the wolf was looking for an easy meal. "So you see the squeal of the rabbit can be used to catch a wolf. He does not realize that you and I are waiting for him."

Johnson removed the GPS unit, and the cell phone, and again dialed Bodeman's number. Before he had a chance to identify himself, Bodeman began.

"What do you have?"

"I'm within sight of the shack where they have the girl," he said quietly.

"Anyone see you?"

"Not from the cabin. I'm in a hardwood forest, with scattered openings. Lots of cover."

"What are you up against?"

"One man brought the girl. Another came in alone on foot. They're standing in front of the cabin at the moment. Too far away to see clearly. Also there's one somewhere behind me who knows I'm in the area."

"Doesn't sound like the best odds. Better sit tight until we can get there. What are your coordinates, and Whitney says no bullshit this time."

Johnson paused as one man reentered the shack, while the other made his way towards a four-foot square shed. The door was facing away from the cabin, and the man entered, already unlatching his belt.

"Sorry, have to run. Looks like something is about to happen."

"What are you going to do?"

"See if I can make a sound like a rabbit."

"Don't do anything stupid," Whitney shouted into the phone, but Bodeman shook his head.

"Connection's dead," He turned to Robinson. "You have to get me and the SWAT team in there as close as you can. Find the closest likely road. Probably one of the gravel roads we identified earlier. The coordinates he gave us for Rat Lake can't be that far off. We can only hope he has a chance to call back, before…"

"…he gets himself killed." Whitney finished.

Despite years in the trade and his calculating nature, Cook always became nervous just before the deal was about to come down. He didn't consider it a bad thing, a little nervousness caused one to be extra cautious, but a side affect of the condition had always been a need to clear the lower intestinal track and bladder. By his reckoning, the target was still a good way off, and this was as good a time as any to take care of business, and probe his mind for any overlooked detail.

This sortie, however, was pretty straightforward. Johnson had left the campground unarmed, and so, with the tranquillizer, it would be easy to capture him alive. His personality profile had predicted his movements precisely up to this point and there was not the slightest doubt that he would soon be racing in for the rescue. All they had to do was wait in the cabin, allowing the kid to make all the noise she wanted. Originally, it was supposed to be clean, quick, and easy. Then orders came to set up the cameras. The camera link was to be established with the buyer, they'd toy with their captives a bit, and then send them on their way to the Promised Land. Cook glanced at his watch, stood, and pulled up his pants. He felt…relieved…and opened the door. A brown blurry object raced towards his forehead, there was the instantaneous thought it might be a bird, and then the lights went out.

Cook was sure he was dreaming one of those dreams where one tries to run or even move, but the feet have the weight of concrete, and the arms hang limp and lifeless like pieces of soggy wood. Yet, the pain between his eyes was real, and he remembered the bird, which somehow now didn't seem like a bird. The subconscious world retreated, and he opened his eyes, staring straight up into the clear blue sky of the hot afternoon. A blurry face, framed by long black hair, moved across his field of vision.

"Saulo. I can't move. What happened?"

"Sorry, you have me confused with someone else," Johnson said and pulled the gag up over the man's mouth.

Fully conscious now, Cook twisted from side to side. Bare chested, he was some distance from the cabin. Trees and several humps in the ground hid it from view. Unmovable, his arms and legs were staked down, his body spread-eagled on the earth.

"I just about have everything ready, and when I do, I'm going to ask you to call your partner out of the cabin," Johnson stated conversationally. Cook mumbled something unintelligible through the gag and shook his head in the negative.

"I was afraid you'd feel that way. So first I'm going to tell you a story, and then I'm going to give you one more chance to reconsider your decision. My Grandfather's people always considered women and children sacred, they were the most precious gifts of Mother Earth. To use one as a human shield was considered so cowardly that the perpetrator would be staked out on the earth, sort of like you are now, and in due time while he was alive, his eyes and genitals would be slowly and methodically eaten away by the little demons, the *Enigo*, sort of like your's soon will be unless you come around to my way of thinking."

Cook smiled slightly. This was all a bluff. Johnson's profile clearly showed him to be a quiet man without a trace of malice. He remained silent when Johnson removed the gag.

"You won't be calling to the man inside, then."

Cook chuckled. "You're pretty green at this. I, on the other hand, have played this game for most of my adult life, and you just don't have it in you. No, I'm not going to call Saulo out into your trap, and I don't believe you're going to summon little demons out of the earth either."

"Then I guess there's no point in continuing this conversation." He placed the gag over Cook's mouth again and moved out of his line of sight, yet continued talking. "You are certainly correct. I can't summon the bad spirits like the Old Ones. However, I do have an effective substitute." He reappeared and from Cook's own shirt, began dribbling something onto his naked chest. First it tickled, and then there was a slight pinch. Then Cook arched his back from a painful bite that left a burning sensation. "I have to admit, I exaggerated a bit," Johnson continued. "The *Enigo* aren't really demons. They're just biting ants." With that, he dumped the entire contents of the shirt on Cook's chest, and the swarming mass spread out in all directions. Panic flooded Cook's bulging eyes, as the ants made their way up his neck and onto his face, and under the waist of his pants. Though endurable individually, dozens were now biting, and his brain registered the burning sensation from nearly all over his entire body. "Oh, I better mention one other thing before I get another batch. Ants have a fondness for warm, dark places. Nasal cavities for instance, and ears. Later on, larger body openings, if you get my meaning."

Cook felt the ants spread across his face and into his hair. A few entered his nose, which he tried to snort out. He was nodding vigorously now, with his head and eyes, and a pleading look swept across his face. Johnson lowered his head down close to Cook's right ear, and spoke in a forced whisper. Gone was the easy conversational tone. "If anything happens to that girl, I swear I will leave you here buried in an ant hill and let them eat you one inch at a time." Unbridled panic now filled Cook, and as Johnson removed the gag, he immediately uttered a gurgling cry, simultaneously trying to spit several ants from his mouth.

Saulo finished testing the cameras and up-link and was beginning to wonder why Cook was taking so long in the latrine when he heard the call for help, and immediately his eyes focused on Cook's revolver and shoulder holster, which hung on the wall peg where he'd left them. The voice carried with it an overpowering sense of panic, which was completely out of character for the usually calm and calculating man, and it took several seconds for him to be completely convinced it was really his brother. He quickly drew his own revolver, and ran to the door, but stopped one step beyond the threshold. The man was screaming now, something like 'get them off me.' He quickly discerned the direction, and withdrew into the cabin. Moments later, he emerged with the girl in front of him, pushing her along. The duct tape and rope no longer bound her, but Saulo maintained a firm grip, left hand to left shoulder, with the weapon in the other. His brother's calls suddenly stopped, and he increased the pace, eyes sweeping back and forth around the trunks of trees, looking for the only man who could be responsible. At every sound, real or imagined, he fired off a round into the woods. The hell with the buyer and the money. This was going to end with a bullet.

Topping a low ridge just south of the cabin at a running pace, Saulo nearly tripped over the body of his brother, spread and staked to the ground. His face had moving red and black specks all over it, as did his bare chest and arms. Unable to speak with the gag, he nonetheless appeared to be desperately trying to say something, and shook his head back and forth. His eyes kept darting up towards his forehead.

Saulo knew he was trying to do too much, watching for the tracker, while at the same time wanting to remove the gag from his brother. Yet to do that he either had to set down the gun or release the girl. Whatever else she might be, the girl was insurance, and so he chose the gun. Slowly, he bent to set it on the leaves, and then swung his arm around towards his brother. He came close, but not quite.

From directly above a noose made of an inch thick vine encircled his neck. Johnson swung down with the wood firmly in his grasp, and as the tension increased over the thick branch, Saulo became suddenly lighter, standing on tiptoes, with hands clutching at the wood rope around his throat. Suddenly free, Jennifer stood confused, too bewildered to move.

"Jennifer, get the gun!" Johnson shouted. The vine was not a nylon rope, and as Jennifer began to come out of the shock, it suddenly broke sending Saulo stumbling for the weapon. He reached it a split second before the girl.

Saulo's first impulse was to shoot them both on the spot, but he realized the operation could yet be salvaged. His brother was still trying frantically to tell him something, but he ignored him. He'd finish this himself. Johnson and the kid stood stone still and silent. Then a twig snapped behind him, and he turned to face a man with shaggy brown hair all over his head and face, a silver tooth, red eyes, and carrying a high powered hunting rifle casually across his chest. His body was covered with standard army combat fatigues. Saulo breathed a sigh of relief.

"About time you showed up. You can help finish the job but you ain't getting any of our cut." Just looking at the red eyes made him nervous, and the weirdo kept petting the rifle like it was some kind of family pet.

"Ol' Bessie and I's just passin' through." He looked past Saulo to the man on the ground. "Looks like you boys is havin' a bit o' trouble."

"Nothing we can't handle. Cover them while I cut my brother free."

"Well, ya know I just can't do that."

"Why the hell not?"

"Like I said, I's just passin' through. Done my part. Just wanted to see how it'd all burn down. Looks like it ain't quite done yet."

Saulo pivoted around, and backed up several paces so he could cover all three, his .38 revolver now trained on Bullet. Cook strained at the stakes and vines that held him, sweat dripping from his body and ants forgotten, shouting something at his brother but only a muffled sound came through.

Jennifer finally realized Johnson was on her side and moved over to stand next to him. Johnson, however, watched the developing events with fascination, particularly the newcomer. So this was the man who hit the six-inch aspen tree dead center from over a hundred yards away. Even though he was standing at the wrong end of the barrel, Johnson couldn't help but believe something else was going down.

"Well if you won't cover them, then you cut my brother loose," Saulo ordered.

"You know I's just can't do that either."

"You know the rules of the business as well as anyone. You're either with us or against us. What's it going to be?" To emphasize his intended meaning, he drew the hammer back on the .38 with his thumb.

The newcomer's red eyes shrunk to thin slits, and his voice deepened.

"Have you ever seen what a two hundred twenty grain bullet traveling twice the speed of sound can do to a human body?"

Johnson immediately picked up on something that went over Saulo's head. Suddenly this man, this very strange looking man, had dropped the folksy southern accent.

"You forget. I'd get the first shot."

"A couple years ago in Dallas, a man took four slugs from a .38. Now maybe he was just lucky, or maybe it's the reason almost no one carries a .38 anymore, but this man then managed to walk four blocks to the hospital unaided. So if you think you can get four shots into me before I bore a four inch hole through your chest, you're welcome to try."

Saulo digested that for a few moments. "Just what is it you want?"

"Like I said. I's just passin' through." He turned to face Johnson. "You folks is all right. Most likely we'll meet again sometime. Just so's you know. I counted 'em all up. His .38 is empty."

He kept telling her it was all over but Jennifer McGraig would not release her hold on Charlie Johnson. She'd shed not one tear throughout the entire ordeal, but now as they were about to leave the cabin, the bottom fell out, and the release carried with it the pent up tears. He managed to free up one hand and dialed Bodeman's number.

"About time," Bodeman growled. "What's the situation? We're about to leave with the cavalry"

"Jennifer is safe."

"That's a relief. And you?"

"Fine. There's a couple men here you'll want to question."

"Thought you said there were three altogether."

"One managed to get away."

"You're slipping. Where are you?"

Johnson relayed the coordinates, and three minutes of silence passed as Robinson entered them into the computer to get the exact location.

"You're on a private forty out in the middle of nowhere owned by a Jackson Grayling from Minnetonka. Should be some kind of trail into it."

"I hit an ATV trail coming in. Appears to have been coming from the east."

"That's probably it. You're about two miles from County Rd 42."

"I'm going to leave immediately with Jennifer. A brave kid. Held up a lot better than most would in her situation."

"She OK?"

"Have an ambulance meet us. Nothing life threatening, but she's going to need some medical attention, and probably someone to talk to."

"Understood. I'll notify her parents. What about the two men?"

"They will be here when you get here."

"So how do we find them? GPS is not accurate to the inch."

"Oh, you'll know when you're close. Just listen for the screams."

* * * *

The woman threw the papers down on the desk for effect.

"Both had extensive bruising to the wrists and ankles. One had a savage blow to the forehead that resulted in a mild concussion. And both received several hundred insect bites, resulting in excruciating pain. Further, their legal rights were not explained to them." She pointed to a man who stood quietly in a corner of the cluttered office. "This man is a menace to society, and certainly has no place in law enforcement. Expect a lawsuit. I hold you personally responsible, Sheriff, for the condition of my clients."

"And what about the crime they committed against a defenseless young lady?"

"Alleged crime, Sheriff. Nothing has been proven in a court of law."

"I'm a bit unclear as to what you expect me to do at this point."

"I'm willing to waive the lawsuit, if we can come to some arrangement."

"Well, Ms. Beckworth. I'm afraid it's completely out of my hands. You'll have to see if you can manipulate someone else, say the county attorney, or maybe the judge who ordered them held without bail. Now the injuries you mentioned are easily explained. While I admit the ankle and wrist bruising was due to being tied up, it will clearly be shown Deputy Johnson was forced to result to those primitive measures for his own safety. The blow to Cook's forehead was due to a nasty fall tripping out of a toilet, and the bites, well this is, after all, northern Minnesota, land of a hundred billion mosquitoes. As to reading them their rights, I understand they were clearly explained; however, at the time they may have been somewhat distracted."

"You know damn well it didn't happen that way."

"You have your version. I have mine. Let's let the courts decide which is more credible. I'm fairly confident, however, that when a jury weighs the testimony of a battered and innocent child against the testimony of two men who have rap sheets longer than my arm, justice will be served."

"My clients have rights…"

"I hope they rot in hell, and you can quote, or in your case, record me on that."

The tall woman clenched her fists at her side, and her voice sputtered with anger. "You're insulting, rude…"

Bodeman gave her his back. "If you'll excuse me, I have work to do."

Audrey Beckworth turned abruptly on her heel, and marched out of the office, back straight, nose held high. Bodeman immediately turned to face Johnson, who was the first to speak.

"'Deputy Johnson?'"

"Well, officially you were. If it were up to me you'd get a medal for what you did. The McGraigs asked me to personally relay their deepest appreciation."

"Aw, shucks, Sheriff, it was nothing."

Bodeman picked up a white envelope and began tapping it absently on the desk. "As a friend, there is something I'd like to say."

"I really didn't know she was your daughter."

"Seriously."

"Go ahead."

"I'd like you to consider becoming a full time deputy, not a 'when the mood hits' kind of thing. Not a member of the tribal police, either, who I have the utmost respect for, but a county deputy. You've been a tremendous asset on occasion, and that's the point. With your heritage and all, you could do a lot of good."

Johnson waved off the suggestion. "I appreciate the offer, Forrest, but I'm not a joiner."

"OK, let me attack this from another angle. I know you don't accept any casino money, and what you make in a year is…is…"

"Pitiful?"

"I was trying to think of a kinder term."

"I don't need much. I sold my house in town to the county, and I still have Grandfather's house. And I'm not starving."

"I know you're into the natural food thing, but that doesn't make you indestructible. What if you get sick? You don't even have health insurance. You'd end up losing everything."

"I guess I'd just die."

"Dammit. I'm serious. You're one of the smartest people I know. Two college degrees before the age of twenty-one. Now you're thirty-odd years old, and yet you…you…"

"Haven't amounted to a damn?"

"I know you have your own…own…"

"Standards?"

"Do you always finish other people's thoughts?"

"It's a gift."

"It's also damn annoying."

"Just trying to help."

"There's also something else to consider. I know it's none of my business…" Bodeman opened his mouth to speak, but decided to leave the thought unsaid.

"So what about Bechworth and the lawsuit threat?" Johnson continued.

"She's just blowing smoke out the backside, doing her job. Speaking of jobs. There is something you can do for me."

"Does it have anything to do with the envelope you've been whacking on the desk for the last five minutes. I notice it's addressed to me."

"What? Oh this. No." Bodeman handed the piece of mail to Johnson. "It came in this morning addressed to you in care of the Sheriff's department. No return address."

Johnson tore off the end, extracted a single postcard sized piece of paper, read it quickly, and then placed it in his blue denim shirt pocket.

"Fan mail or hate mail?" Bodeman grinned.

"Seems I've been invited to participate in a contest."

"That would be a first."

"I just hope it isn't the last. So what is this job you want me to do?"

"The conservation officer stopped by wondering if you might hike in to Buck Lake and check on the family."

"No problem."

"Take Whitney with you. Maybe you can walk some of the sass out of her."

Five minutes later Johnson left the Emergency Services and Law Enforcement building. As he stood next to his decaying Ford pickup parked along the busy street, he removed the envelope from his pocket and read it again. Recent events made it clear this was not fan mail. Printed in bold one-inch type, the dozen words prompted a quick glance over his shoulder. They read: *You win round one. I wouldn't let it go to your head.*

Chapter 3

▼

It was hard going. Charlie Johnson's feet sank deep into the soft moss and grass, and the bog under him rose and fell with each step. Despite being in excellent physical condition, he stumbled forward, his legs giving in to fatigue. He rose to his feet again, and stopped momentarily to give his companion a chance to catch up. In brief seconds the water—that was stained brown from slowly decaying vegetation—rose within inches of the tops of his rubber boots.

A thorough dousing of insect repellent kept the hoards of mosquitoes at bay but did little to deter the biting deer flies, stable flies, and an occasional horse fly, that buzzed around them like vultures circling carrion. To fend off the flies, each wore a loose fitting long-sleeved flannel shirt and denim jeans, despite the fact that the temperature was near eighty degrees. Their hats were equipped with camouflage colored mosquito netting that covered all exposed skin above their shoulders. The only body parts left unprotected from the onslaught of insects were their hands, and they frequently suffered a stinging bite.

"'Let's go bog-hopping', he says. 'It'll be fun.' I should have known better than to trust your definition of fun," the young woman said as she struggled to Johnson's side.

"It's your boss who suggested this, not me. And I'd like to stop and chat a while, but, if you'll notice, the ground—and I use that term loosely—is rapidly subsiding under us." He immediately began to move away from the woman.

"How much farther?" she asked.

"There's a beaver lodge by the edge of the lake a hundred yards or so ahead."

"Have you seen them yet?"

"One of them. When you get a chance, look across to the south side of the lake. You'll see a big white spot against the green of the shoreline."

"Maybe later. Right now I'm more concerned with staying alive."

Buck Lake covered about ten acres, and was at most six feet deep. It was in stark contrast to its big sister. Leech Lake had beaches. Buck Lake had floating bog. In the summer a dense growth of lily pads turned the blue waters of the small lake green, and frogs could easily hop from one end to the other without getting their feet wet. Later in the season, the water lily's six-inch white and yellow flowers added their wild and fragrant beauty. Few people, however, ever hiked the two miles from the nearest road to see the flowers. No cabins or summer homes with neatly manicured lawns occupied the beach. There was no beach. The floating bog that surrounded the lake simply ended, and the lake began. Stepping from the tenuous footing on the bog to the lake would find the hapless hiker immediately in four feet of water. Under the water was another twenty to forty feet of soft muck, decaying vegetation that had been slowly filling the lake since the retreat of the continental glaciers twelve thousand years before. The muck had a sucking quality that would make quicksand seem like hardened cement in comparison. The locals had given the muck a name not found in any geology textbook, and without any logical connection to the organic material. They called it Loon Shit. Because of the shallow depth and high acid content of the water, the only fish that survived from year to year were minnows. There were also leeches up to eight inches long, and striped-back bloodsuckers with voracious appetites.

Hundreds of thousands of them. At times they could be seen swimming through the water in waves. They would certainly welcome any adventurous swimmer, but, of course, no one swam in Buck Lake, at least no one who had a choice in the matter.

Charlie Johnson and Lora Whitney literally crawled onto the beaver lodge, the first solid footing they had had for the last fifteen minutes. He looked at her now, this young woman who seemed to occupy his thoughts every moment of the day, and he found himself wondering how two people so different could actually stand each other's company. He was light brown skinned with long black hair, an outdoorsman to the bone, rugged looking, and even a mite antisocial. She was ten years younger than his thirty seven years, fair skinned with light brown hair, a little shorter than average height, with almost childlike facial features. Her appearance, he knew, was deceptive. There was a definite toughness there, and the few extra pounds she carried were not fat, but muscle. Several months before the McGraig kidnapping, they had been through hell together and survived, and that, he decided, had forged a bond that was, as far as he was concerned, unbreakable. They had very different mindsets—his logical but with a spiritual bent, and her's, structured and stubborn—yet had in common a bantering style of humorous interplay, and at times they fed off each other like a well-rehearsed comedy team.

They sat together, Whitney in front between his legs, and he put his arms around her. She leaned back into his supportive body, and temporarily removed her hat. Long light brown hair tumbled down past her shoulders.

"May I ask you something? Seriously."

"Since when did you ever ask permission?"

"I was wondering. You've never actually said how you feel about me," Whitney forged ahead.

"You don't beat around the bush, do you. I can't think of anyone I'd rather be with at this point."

"That's not exactly what I mean."

"I'll tell you this. I'll never leave without saying good-by. I know you would do the same."

"You're still evading the issue. Coward."

Johnson knew where the conversation was headed, and for reasons he couldn't quite explain even to himself, he didn't want to go there. The reason for their visit to the marsh saved him.

"Over there," he said pointing. "But I haven't spotted its mate."

"You can't get out of this conversation that easy," Whitney insisted, but Johnson remained silent. "Maybe on the nest?" Whitney said finally, resigned to the fact that she couldn't force Johnson to say anything he didn't want to say. It would have to come out of his mouth when he was ready, if he ever was.

"They'd be off the nest by now. But I suppose I could check. I'll call them in. Stay here."

"Gosh. Do I have to? I so enjoyed trudging through this swamp. I wouldn't want to end it now."

Johnson smiled. "I knew you were a wimp, but I won't tell your boss."

Sheriff Forrest Bodeman was the man ultimately responsible for their presence on the bog. He was repaying a favor to the local conservation officer, who had asked that he send someone in to Buck Lake to check on the health of its two very important inhabitants. Since Johnson knew every inch of the mostly forested area, he became the logical person for the job.

Johnson stood up on the beaver lodge, and searched for the best place to put his first step.

"Be careful," Whitney said seriously. "I have to tell you I've decided I don't much care for bogs."

"I like honesty in my women."

"It better be woman."

Whitney watched as Johnson made his way along the boggy shoreline for another fifty yards. He squatted down until he was barely visible amidst the scattered cattails, cupped his hands around his mouth, and produced a loud, low-pitched bugle-like sound. Within moments, the white spot along the south shore began to move in Johnson's direction. A smaller gray colored spot followed the white. Whitney watched in wonder. The two Trumpeter Swans, an adult and its offspring, were responding to Johnson's call, parting the lily pads as they approached. She recalled the fact sheet Charlie had given her earlier: Hunted to almost extinction in the late eighteen-hundreds, a wingspan of up to eight feet, thirty pounds, sixty inches long. The huge majestic birds swam up to Johnson without fear, and she could see him place the cracked corn he had brought on the moss at the water's edge. The two swans quickly began consuming the offering. Slowly, Johnson rose and walked back to Whitney.

"Both parents should be here," Johnson said, when he again was on the beaver lodge. "I'm thinking I should check the cove on the west side. The bog is not very stable over there so you might want to either wait here, or head back to high ground on your own. This could take a while."

"So the bog we just came through was supposed to be stable? Sorry. You can't get rid of me that easy. Where you go, I go."

"Suit yourself, but make sure you follow my footsteps exactly. Stay one step behind," Johnson cautioned.

"Yes sir," Whitney responded, and gave him an exaggerated salute.

"Take off your boots, tie the laces together, and carry them over your shoulder."

"What? No way. You're serious?"

"We're apt to be knee deep in loon shit before this is over, and two boots full of water would only complicate an already precarious situation."

"Not only that it could be dangerous," Whitney said, deadpan.

"I think I said that."

Barefooted, Whitney dutifully followed Johnson's footsteps, and the reason why he insisted she do so soon became evident. In many places the bog collapsed downward under the weight of a human, and soon both were soaked well past their knees. As they approached the cove on the western side, Whitney realized she had no business being there. In places the bog had broken apart leaving narrow gaps of open water. For Charlie Johnson, this was, indeed, fun, hopping from one hummock to the next, and his experience as a woodsman made it dangerous only to the point of excitement. Whitney was, however, completely out of her element, her legs considerably shorter, and soon found herself getting two and then three steps behind. She was not about to tell Johnson to slow down, however, and made a lurching attempt to catch up. In her attempt to match Johnson's step, she missed one of his footprints, stepped into what appeared to be a shallow puddle of water, and went down so fast she was completely submerged in less than a second. Instinctively, she tried to kick her feet to propel herself back to the surface, but from the knees down, she was caught in the unforgiving muck. She felt her body sinking, and panic gripped her. She struggled to find something solid to pull herself up to the surface. Her fingernails dug frantically into the underside of a submerged log over head, but slipped away. Desperately she grasped for anything solid but only succeeded in getting handfuls of soggy moss and plant roots. Finally she caught hold of something hard, but it did nothing to stop her downward movement. She opened her mouth to scream, and it filled immediately with water and decaying vegetation. Suddenly, she felt Johnson grip her arm, and a powerful force pulled her to the surface. She came up choking, fighting for oxygen, and with arms flailing at the air. Plant parts were tangled in her hair and hung from her shoulders. Brown muck caked her legs, and a leech had attached itself to her exposed neck. She held tightly to the object that she had grasped in desperation.

"Try to relax. Don't struggle," Johnson was saying. "Don't try to get up. Stay in the prone position on your side." He removed the leech, and a spot of red blood marked the place where it had been.

After a few minutes, Whitney could breathe normally. With her weight spread out over a greater area, she held her own against sinking.

Johnson watched over her, at first with a face lined with concern. Then, when he saw she was going to be all right, he began to chuckle.

"Follow my footsteps, remember," he said smiling. "How's the water?"

"You think this is funny? I almost drowned!"

"I knew exactly where I was going. You can thank me later when I conduct a more thorough search for leeches."

"When hell freezes over!" Somehow, this was all Johnson's fault. Whitney threw the object with a handful of plant roots and mud half-heartedly in his direction, which he deftly caught in his right hand. Maybe, in a year or two, she might see some humor in this.

"I hate to be the one to tell you," Johnson said inspecting the object, "but it looks like you're going to have to go back down."

"Over my dead body!"

"Not yours. His," Johnson explained, pointing to the object. He was about ninety percent sure the object in his right hand, though brown and slimy, was the femur of an adult human being.

Sheriff Forrest Bodeman, a middle aged man built like a professional football linebacker but with the creased and weather-beaten face of a seaman, carefully inspected the object, turning it over and over, and then returned it to the cotton filled box on his kitchen table. He looked past the two people who sat across from him, through the dining room windows, and at the blue waters of a Northern Minnesota lake so large he couldn't see the other side. There was something missing from his lakefront home, he knew, and it was the sound of his daughter's voice and his granddaughter's laughter. Both Nicole and Mary were visiting friends in the southern part of the state, had been gone for only a few hours, and already he missed them. He looked back at the two who sat across from him. Other than his daughter and granddaughter, they were as close to family as he had anywhere.

"Damn, Charlie. Where in the hell did you find that?"

"Buck Lake. Lora went for a little swim and came up with it. Is it what I think it is?"

"Well it sure isn't a deer leg. Something this size and shape? I'm no expert but I'd say it very well could be human." He looked at Johnson with an unspoken question.

"It's not Native American, at least not from a conventional mound, if that's what you're thinking."

"I know you of all people wouldn't desecrate a mound. Plus it doesn't appear to be that old."

"Lost hunter?"

"All lost hunters in the last twenty years around here have been accounted for."

"There may be more of the remains. Lora came up with only this one specimen, and I couldn't get her to go back in for the rest."

"Respectfully Sheriff, it will be a cold day in hell when I walk out on a bog again, let alone swim under one," Whitney stated firmly.

"I'll send it down to the BCA lab today for analysis…and get a crew into Buck Lake to see what else is there. If it turns out to be human, we're going to have to rely on the folks from St. Paul for a medical examiner, since Doc Brown is in Hawaii."

Johnson realized Bodeman's usual fire-breathing personality was absent, he seemed preoccupied, and Johnson suspected it had to do with the absence of his family. They were very close, had recently been through some harrowing times, and emotional aftershocks from that experience were undoubtedly weighing on his mind. The possible discovery of a human bone would have normally sent Bodeman into an investigative frenzy, but he seemed hardly interested. Johnson decided to stick his nose in where it might not be welcome.

"Something bothering you, Forrest? If there's anything I can do?"

"I've been doing a lot of thinking," Bodeman said, pushing the bone aside as if it were an empty soup bowl. "I might call it quits this year."

"Call it quits?"

"In a word, retire."

"But you're no where near retirement age, and I can't think of a soul who would vote against you in November."

"Oh, there's plenty. Our friend, Bechworth, is only the tip of the iceberg. You probably haven't heard," and he smiled at Johnson and Whitney. "It's no secret you two have been seeing a lot of each other. You've been preoccupied. There's substantial opposition out there this time."

"I can't imagine why."

"Do you want to hear the whole list, or the abbreviated version?"

"It can't be that bad."

"I'm too tough, too gruff, too insensitive, too bossy, and I swear too much, just for starters," Bodeman interrupted. "Many, especially the newcomers to the county, think a sheriff should be a kinder, gentler, more sensitive individual. Or a damn politician. Really, more of a psychologist than a lawman. They think I should give talks to the grade school kids, talk about drug abuse on the radio, be a sort of front man for law and order in the county. Don't get me wrong. These are good ideas, but that's just not the way my head's put together."

"You might be surprised. You might just make a startling impression on young people."

"Probably scare the hell out of them. Besides, I'm too set in my ways."

"You'd have to adapt, true, but I have to tell you I can't think of a better man for the job," Johnson replied.

"Sheriff, you've made a real difference in my life, and no one can argue against your honesty and integrity," Whitney observed. "I've learned more about law enforcement since I've been on the force...I can't imagine checking in to the office without you being there."

"Thanks, but I've been thinking maybe the opposition is right. Times change. Look at me. When I took this job I had wavy brown hair. Now its short, sticks out like a wire brush, and snow white. Maybe some new blood wouldn't be such a bad idea."

"Have you talked about this with your daughter, Nicole?"

"Not yet, and don't say a word to anyone. I'll sleep on it, and when the time comes, I'll do what I have to do."

"As you always have," Johnson observed. "Getting back to the bone, when do you expect to get the crew in to Buck Lake?"

Some of the usual fire came back to Bodeman's eyes. "Can we get in on ATV's? Wouldn't want to haul all the diving gear in by hand."

"No problem. Some wire mesh wouldn't hurt either, especially around the place where we have to work. The bog's pretty unstable."

Bodeman nodded. "I would contact the BCA lab in Bemidji but I know they're swamped with other cases so assuming I can get a medical examiner from the lab in St. Paul, we should be at the lake by early afternoon tomorrow."

"You may not find anything. In fact I can't figure out how Lora managed to get this piece. This bone was relatively near the surface, yet it should have sunk out of sight in the deep muck."

"Not necessarily," Bodeman said. "The body would have at first sunk to the level of the top of the muck, and assuming the person was dead before he went in, there wouldn't have been any struggle, and hence he probably wouldn't have gone any deeper. As a body begins to decay underwater gas builds up inside and causes it to rise to the surface again. In this case the surface was mostly covered with the floating vegetation, so he would have been held under there until such time as only bones were left."

"True. But the bones should have then settled back down, and the one Whitney found was not very deep. What would hold it up there? It's not logical."

"I might have the answer," Whitney offered. "There was a submerged log just off to the right of where I went down. I tried to grab onto it, but couldn't quite reach it. Maybe the body became hung up on top of it somehow, and I grabbed a piece when I went past." Whitney shuttered as she relived the incident.

"Quite possible," Bodeman decided. "Which means we'll have to be very careful not to disturb the log."

"Lora may have already disrupted the remaining body parts," Johnson speculated.

"Sorry, I was just trying to stay alive."

"If she did, you may never find so much as a vertebra. There's about four feet of water between the floating bog and the muck. Your diving crew will have to be very careful not to disturb the silt, or they'll be blind as a bat. I'd suggest you send down only your best man, and tie a rope on him just to be safe."

Bodeman nodded in agreement, and then Johnson continued, "Tomorrow, Lora and I will be there waiting for you and your crew on the west side in the cove so we can point out the location. A word of advice. Wear lots of insect repellant. The bugs are ferocious. The bog is very unstable so watch your step. And one other thing."

"Yes?"

"Try not to disturb the swans."

"Correction," Whitney interjected, as a couple parts of the conversation registered. "Charlie will be waiting in the cove. I'll be watching from high ground. And I think there is something both of you have overlooked."

"Which is?" Johnson asked.

"If the person was dead before he went in, and yet managed to get under the floating layer of vegetation…"

"Someone else must have put him there," Johnson concluded nodding in understanding.

"Homicide, or at least something very suspicious." Bodeman added. "Nice work, Whitney. While you're at it, mind telling me who did it?"

"Sure. It had to be the butler."

"And just why would you say that?" Bodeman asked.

"Because I always wanted to."

Using a pair of binoculars to satisfy her curiosity, Lora Whitney watched the group on the bog from a hundred yards away. She stood in a treeless clearing that had been a subsistence farm seventy-five years before. All that remained was the twenty-foot square low hump in the earth where the cabin had been. The crew on the bog rolled out several sections of aluminum mesh to keep from sinking through the unstable surface vegetation. She could see Charlie Johnson pointing, directing the diver to the place where she had fallen through. Bodeman, two other deputies, and Doctor Sarah Thomson, a special investigator and medical examiner from the BCA Lab were also present. The diver had a rope around his waist as Johnson had advised, and watching from Whitney's vantage point it was as though he suddenly disappeared into solid ground. A few minutes later, he came up arm first, handed something to Thomson, which she placed in a padded plastic container. Within the next half hour, he appeared several more times. Finally, he was under for a good ten minutes, and this time, she could see, he came up empty handed. Bodeman and Johnson then pulled the diver up onto the mesh. The group huddled together, looking in the box. They seemed to come to a decision, and then began making their way directly toward her, and solid ground. Johnson, who carried the box, was the first to reach her.

"What did you find?" She strained to see into the box, unable to contain her curiosity.

"Well, it certainly wasn't an accidental death," Bodeman said, as he joined them. Sarah Thomson, and the two deputies followed. Each carried some of the diving gear, and the diver brought up the rear.

"Wire," Thomson explained.

Dr. Sarah Thomson was almost five feet tall, trim almost to the point of being anorexic, an avid jogger, and of African American descent. Of them all, she seemed less fatigued by the struggle over the bog, partly because she was in excellent physical condition, and partly because she weighed scarcely a hundred pounds soaking wet. Her face was perpetually set in a serious expression, yet she looked much younger than her forty-two years.

"Wire?" Whitney asked, still trying to peek into the box, which Johnson kept just out of her sight. She couldn't tell if Johnson hadn't noticed her interest, or if he was just being a pain in the ass. Finally, she reached up and grasped the edge of the box with her right hand, and pulled it down to her eye level. Taking the hint, Johnson set it on the ground.

"Originally, the body appears to have been wired to the submerged log," Bodeman continued, "which makes suicide or a heart attack very unlikely," he added dryly.

Whitney studied the contents of the box. Somehow she expected the bones to be white, but they were brown, with streaks of green algae. "Looks like we're missing some pieces."

"We have the important ones," Thomson interjected. "Pelvis, skull and jawbone, some ribs, nearly one full arm, and the femur you found earlier. The rest of the pieces were not present on the log, and are probably lost forever."

"Important ones?" Whitney questioned.

"I can tell you from the femur you found that this person was not much over five foot tall. At first glance, there isn't any indication of disease in the ribs or arm bones. No arthritis. The skull shows no evidence of trauma, as from a gunshot wound or blunt object"

"The teeth look perfect."

"They are. Too perfect. They're implants. At more than a grand apiece, I'd say we have someone with cash to burn."

"And what about sex?"

"It should be obvious," Johnson interjected. "This person was a woman."

"How would you know that? And please don't say you took down her genes and looked at her."

"I have a degree in biology, remember."

"Don't quote me," Thomson continued, "but I'd say we have a middle aged woman, slight build with fine facial features, who, at least at some point in her life, was relatively well to do. I'll have our sculptor get to work right away putting a face on the skull. Also run it through the computer simulations." She produced a zip lock bag from her shirt pocket. "And get these fragments analyzed."

"What are they?" Whitney asked.

"With any luck, hair, which is the one thing that I don't understand."

"What do you mean?"

"Usually, there's quite a bit of hair left around a skull. Hair is very resistant to degradation."

"So you're saying we have a bald woman?"

"I'm just saying there should have been more hair. At this point, I don't know what it means."

"The skeleton was most likely picked pretty clean relatively soon after submersion, probably by leeches and snapping turtles, as soon as the body began to decay," Bodeman offered. He turned to Thomson." Any idea how long she's been down there?"

"Really hard to tell. But I'd say at least five years, and not more than twenty."

"Any idea on the cause of death?"

"None of the skeletal remains give a hint, at least to the naked eye. We might never know. Her killer may have simply wired her to the log and pushed it under the floating layer of vegetation. It could be something as simple as drowning. Best to put her back together and see where she leads us."

"Put her back together?" Whitney questioned.

"Her face at least, and DNA. She may not look like much now," Thomson said, gesturing towards the contents of the box, "but just wait until we get her makeup on. Getting a positive ID will be the next hurdle. After that it's simply a matter of Who-done-it 101."

"Who-done-it 101?"

"Determining who hated her the most, or who had the most to gain from her death."

"Whitney can save you the trouble. She already knows who did it," Johnson grinned.

"Really," Thomson stated skeptically. "And just who might that be?"

Johnson deferred to Whitney who made a mental note to herself to never make a flippant statement again.

"It was a joke. The butler," she said apologetically.

"In a novel, maybe. However, in real life the first place we look is within the family. If it turns out she was rich, then I can say with a ninety percent certainty monetary gain is somehow interwoven into the motive. We have a saying. Follow the money, and most of the time it will lead right to the killer's doorstep."

"Doesn't seem like much to start with."

"You'd be surprised how few reasons there are for someone to commit murder. Power, greed, or jealousy pretty much covers it. I predict we'll have a positive ID within a month, and a very sort list of suspects within two." Thomson glanced at the moist brown bones. "I have a feeling this person left a pretty big hole in society somewhere."

Chapter 4

Professor Bill Backus set the correspondence to one side and sighed in relief. He would yet again be able to bow out gracefully. Since his published work, *Telling Nature's Time in An Evolving Universe*, had hit the bookshelves he had been repeatedly challenged to defend his claims. His intent had been to write a book explaining, in layman's terms, how scientists determined approximate ages for natural phenomena. Using examples and some simple math, he showed how the age of ancient cave stalactites and stalagmites, some hundreds of thousands of years old, could be determined when the growth rate and the present volume were known. He reduced the principals of elemental radioactive decay to understandable English. The chapter on light went into extensive, yet understandable, detail on how rays of light actually allow scientists to see billions of years into the distant past. A chapter entitled *Layers* talked about tree rings, stratigraphy, lake sediments, and the annual layers of ice that formed on the great Greenland and Antarctic ice caps. These were of particular importance, he said, because they contained not only a way to count back tens of thousands of years, but also to actually 'see' into each year. Grains of pollen carried on the prevailing winds from hundreds of miles away gave hints about the ancient plant life; sealed pockets of air revealed the composition of the atmosphere for thousands of years into the past. He ended the book on something of a philosophical note, pondering man's unique place in the animal kingdom. We have a brain that is more than we need for survival, he said, and unlike any other animal, we have this vast limitless potential, and the question is 'why?' The book was unexpectedly successful, and helped relieve some of his domestic problems. If not him, then his wife would enjoy the financial reward.

As a scientist, he was very willing to listen to the logical criticism of his colleagues, but the correspondence he put aside contained a challenge that did not come from a fellow scientist. It came from a man of considerable religious influence who found much of his book in conflict with his beliefs. Bill Backus felt ill equipped to argue the nature of the spiritual realm with someone who made it his life. He had hoped to avoid the 'either you're with us or against us' mentality that was rapidly polarizing the nation and the world, but he was not the kind of person to dismiss someone who was willing to discuss differences in a calm, logical manner. The minister had assured him his intent was not to condemn, but merely to get a better understanding of scientific thought. Thankfully, he was off the hook for now. On the date suggested for the discussion, he would be happily stuck in a man-made ice cave doing what he loved doing most, getting his hands dirty indulging in real science.

His wife was not at all supportive. "Why would you want to go to Greenland, of all places," she had chided him. "Isn't Northern Minnesota cold enough for you? You're the boss, not some grunt. You don't have to be there."

He didn't even try to explain to her that Greenland was a geologist's dream. It contained the world's oldest dated rocks, approaching four billion years. Under the massive ice cap, which contained over ten percent of the world's fresh water—mostly in frozen form—was some of the oldest known subsoil. The northern reaches of the ice cap were millions of years old, little affected by the brief warm inter-glacial periods of the present ice age, and contained a record—literally sealed in ice—of the earth's climate for millennia past.

Most scientific research in Greenland focused on the great ice cap that engulfed most of the world's largest island. Several ice core-drilling projects were underway from various institutions. However, the project he led was somewhat different. They would not be sampling the ice sheet only. Instead, their goal was to drill through the ice sheet at a southern location where the depth of the ice was only about a thousand feet, and continue on into the bedrock below. Glacial ice was not static, it moved at different rates from a fraction of an inch to many feet in a year. The location selected had relatively stable ice, making drilling possible. They expected to continue drilling and bringing up core samples of ice and then the underlying rock until equipment or technical failure ended the mission. Or until they ran out of money. The financing was due in large part to a man named Jerry Koler, from the SciOgen research company, who had been able to convince the board of directors of that company as well as the National Science Foundation of the worthiness of the project.

The project had progressed 'steady by jerks,' as Backus was fond of saying, where just about everything that could go wrong did. Yet setbacks were standard issue for any scientific endeavor, and all had been overcome. Just hours before, the drill team had informed him via the satellite link that according to the charts they were nearly through the ice, and very close to whatever lay beneath. As project director and having shuffled back and forth from Greenland to the States for most of the mission, this was one event he didn't want to miss.

"Hey Lynn, would you come in here a minute," he called through the open door of his office in the Geology department on the Bemidji University campus. The campus was part of the greater Minnesota University system, but was not nearly as well known as the campus in Minneapolis, noted for its medical school, or the campus in Duluth, noted for its hockey team.

Quick with a smile, Backus made it a point to call everyone he knew by their first names, a habit that was not always appreciated by those who felt a proper title should come first. In his middle fifties and with a slight bulge around the middle, he didn't consider himself in any danger of attracting the many young female students that frequented his classrooms. Most looked up to him as a sort of father figure, and that suited him just fine. However, the Geology department's new secretary, Lynn Bergen, was a whole other ball game. She was a mature single woman in her thirties, and it just wasn't fair, he decided, that any woman should look so delicious. He had to keep reminding himself he was a married man.

"Yes sir," Lynn said as she entered the cramped office. Backus outwardly cringed.

"Nobody, I repeat, nobody calls me sir. And before you even start, I forbid you from calling me Doctor or Professor," he said with a hint of frustration in his voice. This was not the first time for this conversation. "For crying out loud, call me Bill. Please."

"Yes sir…I mean Bill…sorry."

"Permission to speak freely," Backus invited with an uninhibited smile that seemed to engulf his entire being.

"Yes sir. Oh shit! I did it again. Sorry. Oh no. Did I say shit?"

"Very clearly."

"It's just that I'm kind of nervous. I don't want to mess this up."

"No one here is going to bite you."

There was a moment of awkward silence, and then Lynn said, "Thanks."

"For what?"

"For making me feel welcome. I can see the student rumors about you are true."

"What rumors?"

"That you are…"

"Yes?"

"A nice old geezer."

"Ouch! That hurt."

Backus picked up the correspondence he had been reading and handed it to her.

"This man, the Reverend Luke James, insists on having a discussion or debate of some sort regarding my book, and I'm not in the habit of ignoring reasonable requests, although I wish this one would just go away. Contact him at the email address he provided, and set up something…lets see…sometime later this summer. I should be back from Greenland by then.

"Yes, sir," Lynn said.

"Bill," Backus corrected yet again. "Hopefully, I'm going to be gone for more than a few days this time, so I expect you to be my eyes and ears here. I will be in contact via satellite with you daily, and I expect to get a daily update from you on what's going on, and also to just have a contact on the outside."

"What about your wife?" Lynn mentally bit her tongue as soon as the words cleared her lips. She had been there long enough to know that Professor Backus and his wife had something of a strained relationship, and it was a subject she had been warned not to bring up.

"My wife has other interests," he said simply.

* * * *

The man mentally cursed. To do so out loud would have been disastrous. His assistant had handed him the message when he left the microphone and was heading back to his office. Bill Backus, the geology professor and author, had yet again postponed their meeting. This would be the third time. Maybe later in the month. The correspondence informed him that on the scheduled date, Backus would be in Greenland, an unlikely story at best. This meeting was something he had counted on. His ratings were slipping, and so was the inflow of 'love gifts' required to keep his television ministry going. A chance to debunk a scientist would go far in stirring the emotions of his viewers. Increasingly, there was a great deal of money to be made in the Christian movement. As people became more and more disillusioned with the often corrupt underpinnings of the modern world, they reached out for something, anything, to hold on to. In times of stress, religion had always enjoyed a resurgence of popularity. Yet, increasingly, as he saw it, religion had competition from scientific thought. To have a battle there had to be two sides, and he was determined to show that this man's book was nothing more than a very thinly veiled attack on religion. If he handled it right, it might just win back some of the undecided voters.

Luke James was a tall thin man in his early sixties with a long hawk-like nose, and neatly combed thin white hair. His ears were small and seemed glued to the sides of his narrow head. His dark eyes seemed never to stay focused on anything for more than a few seconds. His less than ideal appearance was more than made up for by his gift, the ability to convince people of his sincerity. His current office was located in a weathered red brick building in Bismarck, North Dakota. Bismarck was not exactly the center of the television universe, but with modern satellite technology, where one set up shop made little difference. Bismarck was only the latest of a string of cities that had welcomed him with open arms. He had a rule, however, which he followed religiously. Never stay in the same place for very long. Make an impression, reap the harvest, and then move on. From the Deep South to the Canadian border, from the Atlantic to the Pacific, the harvest had been bountiful.

The red brick building where he currently conducted his ministry was shaped like a cube, three stories high, and had once been a bank, then converted to rental units, and finally vacated. Located just off State Street, it was less than a half-mile from the North Dakota State Capitol Building. The entire front was overgrown with green vines, and the postage stamp untended lawn had long ago gone natural. The building and lot had been a gift to him from the city fathers, and free was always good. He had remodeled what he needed, mostly the first floor for his ministry and living space, and largely ignored the rest. Two satellite dishes were mounted on the roof for communication and transmission.

He had only two full time employees, a studio technician who handled the audio and visual, and a personal assistant to handle the 'details.' Both were young stable family men. He planned to let them go very soon, as it was, again, time to move on. For more involved projects, he had hired a television crew that worked for the local TV station, and free-lanced on their own time. Most of his ministry, however, was conducted from inside the brick building, with a few well-chosen audience members who would shout Amen on cue, and speaking directly into a TV camera. He appeared to live a pious lifestyle, kept to himself, had no known vices, and the citizens of the communities where he settled grew to know and respect him as a man who lived the message he preached. No one suspected that there was yet another side to Luke James, a side that he had buried deep in his past.

With some of the tax-free money from his ministry, he had recently purchased a property called the Retreat in Northern Minnesota, a vast secluded acreage on a picturesque lake. He also owned rural land in Tennessee and Florida, which had a much more hospitable winter climate then the Upper Midwest. All properties were isolated and remote. The Retreat didn't even have a road access. The end, he believed, was coming and he planned to have a place to hide when it did.

Not that James worried about the end in the biblical sense. God's horrifying judgments in Revelation were simply something useful to scare the folks into parting with ten percent of their income. The Hebrew god was often portrayed as merciful, but he found its wrathful side served his purposes best. James' concern about the end came from a far more human source. Someday, he expected, a part of his past would come back to haunt him. He never anticipated, however, that it would be today.

The Reverend Luke James, a name he had adopted to sound more biblical, entered the dark confines of his office, which had once been the walk-in vault, and closed the door. Automatically, his right hand reached for the light switch, and in the suddenly glaring light saw the one thing he feared most. A short unassuming man with red hair and almost feminine features sat in his padded office chair with his feet on the desk. He wore gray slacks, a white shirt, and black spit shined shoes. A peculiar lopsided grin turned his lips, one side up, one side down, and a lighted cigarette hung from the drooping corner.

"Hello, Dad. How about a big hug for your long lost son?" the intruder asked, the voice laced with sarcasm, and he smashed the cigarette directly into the wooden desktop.

"Maclin," James said with certainty as his eyes adjusted to the bright light, even though he hadn't been face-to-face with his son in years. "This is a pleasant surprise."

"Right. Just like finding horseshit in your Cheerios. Admit it. To you, I was never more than a handicap."

"Your mother felt it necessary to return to old Wrightham, and believed you would be better off going with her, since you would have a brother to grow up with."

"And you've been crying all the way to the bank ever since. But not to worry. I'm going to give you a chance to make it all up to me."

"And just how am I going to do that?"

"You can aid me with a project that's in the works. I understand you have a meeting coming up with a college professor."

"How do you know about that?"

"I have my sources. We need to use it as a distraction for more important business."

"We?"

"My partner and I."

"No doubt something illegal. I understand you became quite successful running a research company until you tried to kill off some board members who didn't agree with you. From what I read you're wanted for a great many crimes including attempted murder. I even heard there's a reward."

Maclin Ethek shrugged. "You don't need to know the details."

"I read also that you somehow managed to get your leg blown off."

"Just my foot."

"So you have a wooden leg?"

"Actually mostly composite, with some steel and aluminum."

James considered for a few moments. "So, what if I say no?"

"You won't."

"What I want, and what I'm going to get, is you out of this building and out of Bismarck immediately, or, son or not, I'll turn you in myself."

"Now are you finished?"

"For now."

"I'm going to tell *you* how it is," Maclin stated, and jabbed his finger into the older man's chest to make the point. "You won't turn me in because on my way down, I'll scream this fine upstanding man is dear old dad, who humped my mother repeatedly for ten years while she was married to someone else, and while he was supposedly on a crusade for God."

"I'd deny it and no one would believe you."

"You really need to subscribe to some science magazines. Ever heard of DNA matching? A simple blood comparison would prove with a one in a billion chance of error that you are my father. Now just what would a revelation like that do to your little scam, and don't give me the holier than thou routine. I was there, remember, when you and Mother started this, and you've been giving honest Bible thumpers a bad name ever since."

James' worst nightmare was coming true before his eyes. The one part of his past that could destroy him was standing facing him. He should have drowned the little bastard when he had the chance. He could quit the evangelist business. He had enough money, but it was beyond money at this point. It was a matter of principal. And lately he even had the faint notion he was actually doing something important. "What do you want?" he said quietly.

"I didn't quite catch that," Ethek said, cupping his right hand to his right ear in an exaggerated gesture of victory.

"If any of your story leeks out, I will destroy you."

"Is that any way to talk to your son? Where's all that brotherly love you preach on cable? Yes, I've caught your show a time or two. Pretty good act. At least you forgo all the fake sets and glitter of some of your colleagues. And yes, I do want something."

"I'm listening."

"When I was in control at the research SciOgen facility, I discovered the key to an unlimited fortune, unlimited power, and I had it in my hands."

"Dream on," James said sarcastically, and skeptically.

"Please don't interrupt. It may save your life."

"I'm still listening."

"It was all taken from me by a backstabbing double cross, and a back-woods hick. I made a vow to make them pay, and I plan to."

"You're serious."

"Deadly."

"This is ultimately about revenge."

"Of course."

"So you're asking me to become an accomplice to murder?"

"Who said anything about murder? Really, Dad. What kind of a man do you think I am? Just think of it as a contest with winners and losers. It's just that in this particular case, the losers sometimes die. So I think you can see that choosing which side you want to be on is critically important."

"I'm still unclear about my role in this."

"My partner and I need a place to draw certain people together, that's all. You needn't know more than that."

"You mean here?"

"We were thinking your property in Tennessee would be perfect, but for certain logistical reasons have decided on your recently acquired acreage in Minnesota. The Retreat, I believe it's called. No road access, quiet and secluded."

"I have to tell you. I don't have a clue what you're driving at."

"The great debate, of course!"

"The great debate?"

"Your upcoming discussion with the college professor. I'm thinking your rural property would make a wonderful setting. Don't you?"

On the surface Luke James was as calm as an evening pond, but piranha were chewing his insides, and he'd come to one inescapable conclusion; his son was psychopathic, and should be in prison somewhere.

"We'll make a great team, again, Dad. Just like when I used to follow you and mom around to all those houses, selling the Good Book for charity, only the only charity involved was your pocket book."

"Sure, why not."

"Just remember one thing. Don't do anything stupid, like suddenly getting an attack of conscience. It would be totally out of character, and could have serious consequences. Just set up the discussion, do your thing, and forget we're even there."

"I...I don't have a problem with that."

Maclin smiled his strange crooked smile, and stuffed another cigarette in the corner. "Each of us holds a bomb over the other. Mutual assured destruction. I like that."

"Mind if I ask who your partner is?"

"Of course not, Dad. It's Big Brother, who else?"

Chapter 5

While the surface conditions often fluctuated rapidly and unpredictably from almost livable to blizzard, the temperature within most of the tiny system of rooms and corridors carved out of the ice remained at a steady forty-two degrees. Most of the heat came as a by-product from the fifty-eight horsepower four-cylinder diesel engine that powered the core drill, and kept the deep storage batteries charged for the lighting. The walls of the rooms were insulated, not to keep the interior warm, but to keep the limited warmth of the interior from melting the surrounding ice. Piping for both exhaust and intake for the motor were routed to and from the surface, but the heat remained. The first thirty feet of drilling had been done from the surface, but the operation had moved below as soon as the operation rooms were complete.

At first the interior temperature had seemed cold, and each man started each day with several layers of clothes. Yet they soon grew accustomed to the less than ideal temperatures, shed most of their artic clothing with the mandatory increase in physical activity, and often worked with the sleeves of their long underwear rolled up to their elbows.

For the sake of the research, the temperature in the cave was perfect, if not a little warm. The coolness gave the crew adequate time to remove the ice cores from the drill pipe and get them to the 'cold' room before they began to degrade. Every third day the support crew came on snowmobiles pulling a specially designed sled to take the cores to the base laboratory on the Greenland coast, bring in fresh supplies, and to take out the garbage. They worked steadily and methodically every day except Sunday. Sunday was supposed to be a break from the routine, a time to catch up on accumulated emails, and generally relax. However, by the end of the eight-hour 'day' the men usually found themselves huddled around the computers with cups of coffee discussing technical glitches or equipment problems. The research project and their lives became as one.

Backus knew he couldn't have selected better, or more different men, and they were certainly not the roughnecks typical of drilling crews. They included Jack Reagon, a mechanical engineer who made sure the equipment held together from day to day, Erich Vander, an electrical/computer engineer who kept the computers and communications up and running, Peter Nordeen, a meteorologist/climatologist who had previous experience with ice core drilling, and Ben Atwauter, a psychologist who was there just because he wanted to be. Their ages ranged from thirty-eight at the youngest to Backus who was fifty-six. All were in excellent physical condition, and after two weeks Backus was pleased to see his own extra padding around his waist starting to melt away. Backus figured he had the most highly educated drilling grunt crew of all time, because, their education and expertise aside, their primary duty was to bring up cylindrical shaped rods of ice four inches in diameter and eight feet long.

Making up for lost time, Backus became immediately immersed in the project. While the others had frequent contact with their families on the outside, his wife had made no attempt to contact him. He felt it strange that that fact did not disturb him, and then finally admitted to himself, there was no bond to maintain, no bond at all. His link to the outside world had continued to be Lynn Bergen, and she faithfully sent him a cheerful hello at least once in every twenty-four hour period. At first their messages had been impersonal, if polite, exchanges of data, but gradually personal information began seeping in between the weather reports and expedition progress. Unlike his wife, Lynn wanted to know everything about his work, what motivated him as a scientist, and even his views and strategy on the upcoming discussion with the tele-evangelist. He remembered his wife's parting comments at the airport. "Why can't you just be a normal college professor?" It was refreshing and even exciting to talk to an intelligent, sensitive, woman who seemed on the same wavelength he was, and in a matter of days realized he knew more about Lynn Bergen than he did about his own wife. He had to make a conscious effort to keep thoughts of a more intimate nature from creeping into his consciousness. His own marriage was a mess, but he and Lynn were just too different to ever have more than a professional connection. She was a young, vibrant woman and he was just…well, a nice old geezer.

There had been the equipment problems, hardware problems, software problems, personality conflicts, an attack of a flu-like illness, tainted food; literally everything that could go wrong did, proving once again Murphy's Law, but the overriding scientific goal kept the project moving forward.

The ice cores were strikingly similar, and the men looked forward to the occasional dark bands in the otherwise opaque ice that most likely were indicative of a volcanic eruption somewhere in the Northern Hemisphere in the distant past. They were only guessing, of course, since they did none of the actual analysis of the samples on site, and it would be in university laboratories around the world that those determinations would be made. At first the ice layers, which reminded Backus of tree rings, were clearly visible. But as they drew cores from greater and greater depth, the bands became increasingly blurred, crushed and tortured by the tremendous weight of the overlying ice. However, at over nine hundred feet Backus could no longer even pretend interest in the ice cores. The soundings had said nine hundred forty two point eight feet. He waited expectantly for the first core that brought up terra firma, good old-fashioned dirt.

"Pay dirt!"

Bill Backus knew the moment had come, though most people would not have noticed the slight variation in the sound of the diesel engine. It was working just a bit harder, powering the carbide tipped drill head through something harder than ice. The carbide bits, good for ice but impractical for continous drilling in rock, would be replaced with diamonds as soon as they extracted this core. He looked at the section of drill pipe as it entered the nearly thousand foot deep hole, and checked his clipboard. The soundings that had measured the depth of the ice sheet had been off by six inches. Just less than three feet of the new section had disappeared, which meant this core sample should be three feet of ice and five feet of whatever lay beneath. His heart pounded with excitement. This is why he was here. To bring up the first ever samples of earth and bedrock that lay beneath the great mass of ice. He looked at his crew. They looked like cave men, heavily bearded, and badly in need of haircuts. They, like him, had noticed the change in the sound of the engine, and they, like him, were grinning from ear to ear.

"Pay dirt!" Backus repeated.

"I wouldn't break out the champagne just yet," Jack warned. "Let's wait until we have the bird in hand."

"Party pooper," Backus replied. He focused on the drill pipe, watching it slowly grind its way downward, a millimeter at a time. When it finally reached its limit, the engineer disengaged the clutch, released the drive coupling, and activated the winch that would retrieve the core from nearly a thousand feet below. The core was enclosed in a tungsten steel extraction tube that fit inside the drill pipe. The winch cable engaged a mechanical clamp at the lower end to keep the sample from sliding out of the case on the way up. Ever so slowly, the cable wound on the drum bringing up its precious cargo. All five men were silent now, watching the drill pipe for the first glimpse of the core.

The steel tube arrived on schedule. The engineer detached it from the cable as he had done over a hundred times before, and all five carried it carefully to the cold room, as if it were thousand year old china. Once in the cold room, the core was gently slid from the extraction tube into a long narrow clear plastic bag, which they immediately sealed at both ends. It was only then that the scientists stood back to view their handiwork. The first three feet were ice, tens of thousands of years old, there was a narrow band of dirty ice, and then the grayness of compacted earth and solid rock completed the eight-foot section. Backus removed a hand-held magnifying lens from his shirt pocket, and slowly began inspecting the section beginning with the ice. When he reached the earth, he suddenly straightened, frowned slightly, and then looked again.

"What's the matter, Bill? Never seen rocks before?" the engineer joked.

"What? Oh. Rocks. Of course. I'm going to turn in now," Backus said abruptly. "I mean, probably we should shut everything down and take a breather. This has been enough excitement for one day."

"I thought for sure you'd want to keep going."

"Tomorrow," Backus insisted, and left the men standing by the drill rig.

"You're the boss," the engineer replied, and turned the key that stopped the flow of fuel to the engine's injectors. The engine shuttered, its cylinders starved, and abruptly stopped turning.

Backus was late getting to the drill rig after the required eight hour rest period. When he arrived the diesel engine was silent, and the engineer had just delivered a powerful blow with a pipe wrench to the cylinder head.

"What's wrong?" Backus asked.

"This piece of shit just won't go. I've checked everything. There seems to be plenty of fuel, compression and timing's OK. It should start, but it won't."

"Check the muffler bearing?"

"Very funny."

"Maybe it's bad gas."

"No, I feel fine," they both said together. It was the standard joke when things didn't go as planned.

"You want more time or should we call it in?"

"I've checked everything there is to check. I'm at a loss." He turned to Erich Vander, the communications expert. "Better let base know."

Backus suddenly slumped forward slightly. Reagon reached out to steady him, and couldn't help but notice drops of moisture on his forehead. "You OK?"

"I think the bug came back for me," Backus admitted. He had avoided the illness the first time around. "Turned my stomach inside out last night. There was a little blood, and I'd be lying if I said I wasn't a little worried."

Reagon turned back to Vander. "Make your call. Better tell them we're sending Backus out too."

"Not so fast," Backus protested. "I can't leave just when things are getting interesting."

"No arguments. We aren't prepared for a real medical emergency."

"I suppose you're right. Can't hurt to have a doctor give me the once over. I'll get a few things packed, and hit the cot until the support crew gets here."

"Don't worry. Without the motor, we aren't likely to make any major discoveries until you return."

Bill Backus nodded, and slumped away. He knew full well he had no intention of coming back any time soon.

A cascade of events closed the expedition down. The diesel engine was replaceable, communications and computer problems were solvable, but Backus' sudden illness, which led to his return to the States, was a sea the crew just couldn't cross. He dropped out of the project, no warning, no explanation. His drive and enthusiasm had been the wind in their sails, and without him, the project simply wilted and died. It was when the last of the ice cores were being removed from the cold room that the final tragedy was discovered. The final core with its ice and rock sample had somehow rolled off the shelf bursting the plastic wrap, and shattered pieces of ice and rock littered the floor. The pieces were meticulously and painstakingly put back together in the hope of salvaging some scientific data, and when all was as good as could be expected under the circumstances, a startling fact emerged. The eight-foot long core was about one foot short.

Bill Backus arrived home much earlier than expected, and unannounced. He thought afterward he should have called his wife before he left the Bemidji flight terminal. This would have at least given her enough time to get Jeffery Winkope, their next door neighbor, out of their bedroom before he walked in. As it was he was treated to a display that would have been outrageously humorous under any other circumstances. As he entered the bedroom Jeffery was doing his best from the reverse angle, but his wife, who was buck-naked on her hands and knees on the floor, kept saying, "I don't feel anything." They were too preoccupied with the business at hand to even notice him, and Backus quietly closed the door and went to the one place that was truly home, the Geology department on campus. He suddenly looked forward to a conversation with Lynn Bergen.

The Geology department was virtually empty, however, when he arrived. He checked his watch. Most of the other professors who accepted summer school duty would be in class. He entered his office, and found Lynn Bergen sitting in his chair. She looked up from her work, clearly startled by his sudden appearance.

"Bill! What are you doing here? I mean why aren't you in Greenland? Nobody said anything. Why didn't you let me know you were coming? I wondered why you hadn't been in contact the last couple of days."

"Something came up. Mostly my lunch. Had a nasty case of the flu, but I'll live. Not that I care, but you never told me you had adopted my office. What are you working on?"

"Working on? Nothing," Bergen said nervously, and quickly folded the notebook on the desk.

"May I see?"

"What?"

"The tablet, or is it some deep dark secret?"

"It's none of your business," Bergen stated firmly, and seriously. She stood up quickly, too quickly, bumped the spiral bound booklet with her left hand, sending it to the floor. Backus picked it up and started to hand it back to her, but pulled it back when he saw the heading on the front cover. His own name was printed in small letters in the upper right hand corner.

"Give me that," Bergen demanded. "It doesn't concern you."

"Maybe it does, maybe it doesn't, but since it has my name on the front I think I'm entitled to at least take a peek." He was teasing her, but at the same time extremely curious. Bergen twisted her hands together nervously, as he opened the notebook to the first page. In the left hand margin were dates, and across from each date were hand written observations. He briefly skimmed through several paragraphs, and immediately became deeply interested. It was a condensed version of the conversation they had had the day he left for Greenland. He flipped a couple of pages. It suddenly became clear the entire notebook was a record of everything, professional and personal, he had ever said to her. He turned to the last page. It was dated just two days before, and said, "Mentioned his excitement. Last core before they hit solid rock. Getting his thoughts together for his discussion with James. Not looking forward to it. Said he misses me."

Bill Backus felt stunned, hurt, and confused. He turned his attention to Lynn. "I don't understand…why?"

"Like I said," Lynn said coldly, "It's none of your damn business." She grabbed the papers from his hands, and ran from the room. He couldn't help but notice the tears streaming from her eyes as she rushed past.

Backus didn't try to stop her, and placed his heavy duffle bag on the desk before him. He sat down heavily in his chair. It was still warm from Lynn Bergen's body heat. "Women," he said in exasperation, "are just too damn much trouble."

Chapter 6

▼

The two men, one with red hair and one with white, waited quietly in the rear seat of the plush compartment of a sleek black stretch limousine in the pickup lane of the Minneapolis International Airport. White leather framed the interior, and mauve seats were arranged in a semicircular fashion around a miniature conference table. A view screen and communications council occupied the area just behind the front seat. The privacy window between the front and back was retracted. The uniformed driver, a slight man with a pudgy face, stepped out and waited by the rear door.

Every few minutes, like clockwork, airliners thundered overhead. Parents with young children, grandparents, college students, businessmen and women, and foreign visitors turned to gawk at the obvious display of wealth. Soon, a lone man in his late thirties and wearing a thousand dollar blue suit and snow white tie approached the limousine. He carried a briefcase, but no one would mistake him for a salesman. His dark sunglasses and bearing projected an aloof personality. He walked briskly and purposefully, and nodded to the driver.

"Thank you, Alfred," he stated politely, as he entered the limousine. Alfred took his position behind the wheel, and the vehicle glided forward as smoothly as a sled on snow.

"Is this the best you could do?" Wrightham asked, immediately addressing the red haired man, and placing his briefcase on the table. "I haven't ridden in one of these since…I don't remember when."

"Nice to see you, too." Maclin Ethek gestured toward the man sitting next to him. "I don't think you've ever met dear old dad face to face. Dear old dad, this is Big Brother."

The man turned slightly and briefly glanced at Luke James. "Mr. James," he said as he began to remove white gloves a fraction of an inch at a time. "I'm Jonathan Wrightham, your son's half brother. I already know all there is to know about you. You have quite an upstanding, if manufactured, reputation. Let's hope it will hold together long enough to accommodate my needs."

"Pleased to meet you," James said, extending his hand, which Wrightham ignored. "You know, from the side, your face looks remarkably like your mother's, although I'd have to say Maclin is a dead ringer. How is she by the way?"

"Unknown. She headed off to Europe years ago with a young stud. Said she didn't want any part of the business as long as the checks kept coming. And Maclin's resemblance to our mother is probably the only reason Father kept him around. He was your kid, and Father could have easily booted him out." He glanced over at Maclin who merely shrugged.

"You may find this hard to believe, I know Maclin does, but there was a time I truly loved your mother. Maybe still do. I'd really like to see her again," James continued sincerely. "Perhaps, with old man Wrightham out of the way for all these years, you could arrange a meeting between Morgan and me."

"Anything is possible."

"So what part am I supposed to play in your little drama?"

"You have center stage, but the details shouldn't concern you. Just make sure your discussion with…"

"Bill Backus."

"Whomever...gives us enough time to take care of some things. I have something for you that just might help. Some ammunition as it were." He opened the briefcase, and extracted its contents, a brown, spiral bound notebook with the name, Bill Backus, on the front cover. "This should give you an idea of the kind of man Backus is."

"What's in the notebook?"

"From what I can get out of it, everything you want to know about a pathetic middle-aged man with two going on three failed marriages, a lustful desire for a much younger woman, and someone who obviously couldn't make it in the real world."

"Have you read his book?"

"There's nothing there that would interest me."

"Well, it's obviously an attack on the Written Word."

"Why Mr. James. If I didn't know better, I'd say you're starting to believe some of that mumbo-jumbo you deliver to your flock. Let's get one thing straight. The only thing that matters is this." Wrightham pulled his wallet out from a breast pocket with his right hand and smacked it in his left. "Money is all that matters, or more correctly the ability to use money to control your domain."

"I have amassed a considerable..."

Wrightham interrupted with a snicker. "You have nothing of consequence. You know how I know that? Because you're here being led around by the ring in your nose. If you had any real power or influence, you would be doing the leading."

"I can see you and Maclin are pretty much alike."

"We think the same, after all we had the same mother and upbringing, but unfortunately Maclin is only half as smart. I must, therefore, assume those genes came from your side of the family."

Maclin Ethek smiled his curious smile. "If that is so, dear brother, then how is it you are here, where I have led you?"

"You led me! That's rich. This cleanup operation is just a sidebar. The real reason I'm here is much more important. A man is coming to meet me at the lodge. A man who is going to change my life forever, and if you're good little boys I may throw you a few crumbs."

"And just who is this figment of your imagination?" Maclin asked.

"No less than a representative of the Family. I have made the necessary arrangements for membership."

Maclin roared with laughter. "What have you been smoking? You really think you have a chance?"

"I have the money."

"This I have to see."

"You will. You both will."

"So that's why you left your hundred room shack in California," Maclin continued. "To become a demigod?"

"That and to make sure you don't foul this up like you have everything else in your life, including your miserably botched attempt at ridding us of Johnson."

"That freak, Bullet, that was supposed to be so wonderful, let Johnson just walk away. Didn't even try to help Cook and Saulo, who were staked to the goddamn ground. Just how was I supposed to know he was going to shit out on us?"

"As always, I have to take charge and bail you out of your misery. However, my main interest is the meeting with the Family, and as far as the cleanup operation goes, don't expect me to get my hands dirty. In fact, I don't know either of you. Understand?"

"As far as I'm concerned you've already done your part. Provided the capital to make it happen. But I don't like loose ends. This Bergen woman for one. How do you know she won't have a change of heart and confess everything to Backus?"

"Mother's teaching just never sank in, did it? It's about power, and who has it and who doesn't. I control Bergen, and own someone she would do anything for, even die for."

Luke James sat quietly listening to the conversation, unclear about what he'd gotten himself into, but sure he'd made the wrong decision to be part of it.

"What about Alfred?" Maclin asked, nodding toward the man behind the steering wheel. "Can he be trusted?"

"Alfred? He's been with the family since we were kids. He's about the only person I completely trust." He turned his dark eyes towards James. "Tell me everything is a go with the professor."

"Everything is set for the meeting…finally. It will be at my new property in the northern part of the state. It's a hundred sixty acre retreat with two small dormitories…"

"I know the place better than you do," Wrightham interrupted.

"When were you ever there?"

"Satellite photos and blueprints. Just get there and do your part."

"Of course."

"What worries me most is that you'll turn out to be as incompetent as your son, Maclin. Bad genes tend to run in families. However, if the two of you don't screw this up, we can all gain something here. You, James, get a boost in your ratings and cash inflow, Maclin gets his revenge and a step closer to a whole lot of cash, and I get the chance to prove my worth to the Family. However, right after this business is taken care of, we all go our separate ways. No offense, but you're simply not in my league."

"No problem," Maclin interjected. "After this you may well never see me again."

"I hope that's a promise." Wrightham dismissed father and son with a turn of the head and directed his attention at Alfred. "Did you install the necessary electronics?"

"Yes sir. Everything is set." He extracted a tie clip from his pocket and handed it to his employer, who immediately attached it just above the 'V' of his suit coat.

"What if something goes wrong?" Maclin asked, thinking of how recent events at the campground had started out so well, only to fail miserably at the end.

"Nothing will go wrong."

"How can you be so sure?"

"Simple. There are no flaws in my plan."

The narrow, paved road shone black in the evening sun. The driveway wove around the trunks of mature oak and jack pine, even though construction would have been much easier had they been removed. The ribbon-smooth driveway ended at the entrance to a four-stall garage, which was attached to a three-story log structure that looked more like a hotel than a home. Three homes had once occupied the property, each valued in excess of a million dollars. Franklin Wrightham had bought all three, brought in the bulldozers, and razed them all to ground level to make room for his new home. In order to insure his privacy, he had thirty foot spruce and red pine planted in much of the open space left by the demolished homes. He had to have several replaced, as transplanting such tall and mature trees was difficult. The end product, however, was a three-acre park around a country mansion that overlooked the clear blue waters of Leech Lake.

"Looks like you have company," Maclin laughed, as Alfred parked next to a used sky blue Chevy Blazer. "Somehow, judging by that vehicle, I have a feeling your company is not representative of the most powerful people on earth."

A look of concern briefly crossed Wrightham's face.

"A break in?" Alfred offered from the front. "Want me to check it out?"

"Go ahead."

Alfred left the limo, and walked up the split fieldstone walkway. The door should have been locked but it swung inward when he turned the bronze door handle. Without hesitation, he entered the building and came back out within seconds.

"All clear," he called from the doorstep. "They've been expecting us."

"Who?" Wrightham wondered.

"Probably some long lost relative looking for a handout," Maclin laughed again. "There are no flaws in your plan? I can't remember when I've had this much fun."

"Well, if it isn't who I think it is, we'll just have to get rid of them, won't we dear brother?"

"It's your house, even if it should have been half mine."

"You never quit do you?" Wrightham reached forward and activated the communications console. He turned to face Maclin, adjusting his tie as he did so.

"How do I look?"

"Like a pimp, as usual."

"Do me a favor. Keep your mouth shut. If you spoil this for me, you won't see your next birthday."

"I wouldn't think of it, and I just can't wait to see who's been sleeping in your bed."

"They're in the sun room," Alfred said as he led the others through the interior of the house. Even though Jonathan Wrightham and Morgan, his mother, had inherited the lake lodge with the rest of Franklin's fortune, they had rarely used it. It smelled old, musty, and unused. Except for an occasional summer vacation, it had remained essentially vacant, it's only occupants the visits from utility personnel, grounds men, and housekeeper. There was something sad about that, a sadness that was lost to its present occupants. Heavy purple drapes covered all the windows, except for the huge rectangular shaped thermopanes that filled the lakeside of the sunroom. One man, his back to Wrightham, sat on a brown sofa that faced the lake. Another man stood near the windows looking out over the whitecap crested waves. Neither looked in Wrightham's direction until he spoke.

"You may remain with the limo, Alfred." Alfred nodded politely, an unspoken message passed between them, and he returned to the vehicle. "Now just who the hell are you?" Wrightham began angrily, addressing the intruders. "And what are you doing in my house?" Maclin Ethek and Luke James stood several steps behind him.

The man on the sofa stood and turned to face him. He was old, in his late seventies Wrightham guessed, or even early eighties. There was no sense of urgency in his reaction, no startled look. In fact, his deep blue eyes looked out from a face set in an expression of complete calm. A light blue plaid shirt, and brown slacks covered his slender body. Everything about him said this man was ordinary. His partner by the window, however, was not ordinary. His plain gray suit hung loosely on his six-foot muscular frame. He turned from viewing the lake and Wrightham saw that his tanned face was hard and angular, as if chiseled from stone. His shaved head shown in the afternoon sunlight that streamed through the massive windows. One of his ears had a half-inch 'v' shaped notch at the top from a past altercation. His dark eyes seemed to catch everything in a glance, and Wrightham felt immediately uncomfortable. Luke James was instantly terrified of the man and involuntarily took a step backward. There was something about him that wasn't right. His expressionless face and demeanor said this man was capable of anything.

The older man smiled a faint smile, nodded to his partner, and began in a voice so low Wrightham had to make a conscious effort to hear it. "I prefer you do not use the coarser verbiage, but I will allow you that one lapse. You may call me Mr. Parish, and this is Mr. Bell."

"Obviously not your real names."

Parish merely shrugged. "We are responding to your invitation and request."

"You don't expect me to believe you represent...dressed like that...in a vehicle like that?"

"We are representatives of what has become known in some circles as the Family. We are here to determine if you qualify for our select group." Up until this point, the old man had ignored Ethek and James, but now addressed them. "I anticipated your presence. You may stay or leave, the choice is yours, but this conversation is between Mr. Wrightham and myself. Any interruption and Mr. Bell will immediately remove you forcefully from these premises. Is that clear?"

Both Maclin Ethek and Luke James nodded enthusiastically. Ethek went to find a chair, but James backed up against the wall, then slid down until his butt rested on the rust colored carpeting. Wrightham remained standing.

"I find it difficult to believe that someone like you—if you are who you say you are—would dress like that and drive a vehicle like the one outside," Wrightham insisted.

"Who else would know about your desire to join our family? And frankly you're already losing points. You obviously believe you have to prove to everyone just how wealthy you are. Your clothes, your transportation reek of bad theater and conceit. They say, 'Here I am. Look at me. I'm rich.' The truly wealthy have nothing to prove to anyone. They wear overalls, blue jeans, work boots or whatever they feel like, drive ordinary cars or custom-built cruisers, live truly comfortable lifestyles. It is only the wannabes that buy the latest Paris fashions, or pay ten dollars for a cup of coffee. If you fall into that group, perhaps there is no point in continuing this conversation."

"But what's the point of being rich if you can't…"

"Make a foolish spectacle of yourself? Wealth buys anonymity, Mr. Wrightham, and the freedom to do whatever you choose to do."

"Like what?"

"Like anything. Paint, climb mountains, join a circus, develop the perfect rose, seek enlightened conversation, or nothing at all. Really, it's like being a child again, and the entire world and everything in it is the sandbox. The point is, after a while, even you would get tired of counting your gold coins."

"Quite frankly that all sounds rather boring. My ambitions tend toward politics."

"And power," the old man concluded.

"Is there something wrong with that?"

"Nothing at all, if that's what you choose. But be forewarned. We monitor our own. We watch, but do not interfere, unless one falls from grace, then it is the wrath of the Family one must face."

"How do I begin?" Wrightham asked sincerely.

"I have several questions. Please be honest. Most of the answers I already know, but I need to hear them from your own lips."

"I understand."

"Good. First, in round numbers, what was the greatest return you've enjoyed at one time and what strategy did you employ? Interest income doesn't count, nor does the sale of personal property."

"Fifteen million dollars or so," Wrightham reflected. "I invested in twine."

"Continue."

"Nothing glamorous. I arranged to buy most of the imported twine, largely from South American countries. This was the kind of twine farmers and ranchers use for baling hay or whatever. I cornered the market in ports from San Francisco to New York, from New Orleans to Duluth. The going rate was six dollars a double roll. I paid seven, and everyone thought I was crazy. Instead of offering it for retail, however, I had the entire inventory stored in warehouses, and let only a miniscule amount out. The laws of supply and demand took over, and soon demand drove up the price. I released my cache for thirty-five dollars a double roll. My profit, minus some minor storage expenses, was over fifteen million dollars. Not much, I suppose, according to your standards, but a tidy sum nonetheless."

"A sound business venture, indeed. But then what did you do with the proceeds?"

"Invested it in the market."

"Where you promptly lost most of it in junk bonds. Most people would have been very happy with fifteen million dollars. You gambled it away."

Sitting backwards on a borrowed kitchen chair, Maclin Ethek couldn't contain himself and started to laugh. For once it was good to see someone take Big Brother down a peg or two. Parish looked in his direction, and then at Mr. Bell. Bell's malevolent stare wilted Ethek's joyful mood. James, who squatted next to Ethek on the floor, sat fearfully mute, uncertain what was going on but confident he should have run like hell when he had the chance.

"I'm very sorry," Maclin blurted. "It won't happen again…interrupt, I mean."

The old man turned back to Wrightham. "How much money did investors lose in the junk bond collapse?"

"I don't know," Wrightham said honestly. "Billions for sure."

"And where do you think those lost investments went?"

"I really don't…not you?"

"Some people try to predict the market from the inside. I, and other Family members, subtly control the world market from the outside. It's a lot like the weather. Predictions are unreliable. Better to make it rain where one chooses. Understand that with just a word the Family can send stock or bond prices tumbling and just as quickly build them up again. Some people still have the quaint notion that it is politics or the military that controls the world. However, governments are transitory and generally irrelevant, and wars merely business opportunities. It is economics that rules the world, Mr. Wrightham, and whomever controls the economics of the world controls the world."

"I understand economics. The Fed blinks, and the market goes into a freefall."

"I think you're missing the point. Who do you think controls the Fed?"

Wrightham remained silent, contemplating his next statement. His response must sound conciliatory and sincere, he knew, or any hope of joining this ultimate club was forever lost. He knew his marks at this point were poor.

"I know I have a lot to learn. I'm willing to do whatever you ask of me. How may I prove myself to you?"

The old man considered for over a minute, and Wrightham began to wonder if he would answer at all. Finally he seemed to come to a decision, but did not go where expected. "What country do you think I'm from?" The question was obviously another test. The answer would most likely be a determining factor in his quest to become a member of the Family. The obvious answer was that the old man was American, as he had no noticeable foreign accent. But was he? A riddle from ages past surfaced in his mind. Something about a small bird concealed in the fist of a magician. Is it dead or alive the magician had asked. Immediately, Wrightham knew the correct answer.

"It is as you wish it," he said and knew he had passed on to the next level.

"Very good," the old man said approvingly. "Maybe there is some hope for you, after all. You're beginning to see the bigger picture. I can be a citizen of America today, and of Nepal the next, and have when the desire arose. My country is the world."

"So where does that leave me?"

"I understand your ambition is to become a US senator. From California, I believe?"

"That's true. However, I missed the window last year due to unforeseen circumstances. With the elections only a few months away, I wouldn't have enough time to prepare, let alone get on the ballot."

"The Family has decided that will be your test."

"But the next election after this won't be for some time. I would rather not wait that long."

"Of course not, and that wouldn't be much of a test anyway. Elections are simply the vaudevillian theatrics of the near rich. So we have added a bit of a challenge. If, in fact, you can pass this test, I will recommend to the Family that you be placed on probationary status."

"Probationary?"

"We all begin that way, Mr. Wrightham. Just in case things don't turn out appropriately."

"I am honored you would consider me," Wrightham quickly added. "What would you have me do?"

"You have three weeks to become a US senator…"

"That's impossible! The elections…California…"

"…from Minnesota."

"What! That's ridiculous. In case you've forgotten, elections are in November. This is summer time. Also, even though I own this house, I'm not a Minnesota resident."

"Because of the recent death of Senator Petterson, there is a vacancy that the governor has not as yet filled."

"Still…"

"If I can change my citizenship in a day, surely you should be able to change your residency. In three weeks the Reverend James has his meeting with Professor Backus. Yes, I know all about the impending discussion, and your intention to clear up some unfinished business. That would also be a good time for the official announcement."

"Even if I could arrange Minnesota residency, there is still the problem of getting the appointment."

"I'm sure you will think of something, if you want this badly enough."

"So I have to become a Minnesota resident, and then somehow get the governor to appoint me to that vacancy. All to be accomplished inside of three weeks and announced at some back woods hoedown?"

"You have summarized the task very well."

"Pardon me, but even Moses had to ask God to part the Red Sea. What you've asked would take a miracle of nearly equal magnitude."

Wrightham was beginning to feel the physical effects of standing for so long a time, and had to marvel at the old man. He continued unaffected and relaxed. Both Ethek and James had remained wisely silent, merely observers to the unfolding drama. Mr. Bell, too, watched, unemotional and detached, but obviously ready to carry out whatever directive the old man should give him.

"There are no such things as miracles, Mr. Wrightham. Only cause and effect. It is up to you to design the cause to obtain the desired effect. You, however, seem ready to give up before you've even tried." He turned to his partner, and began to move towards the outside entrance. "I think our time here has been wasted." Jonathan Wrightham might have let them go, later for a few brief seconds would wish he had, but he saw his half-brother looking at him with an ear-to-ear grin. Maclin Ethek was enjoying seeing him fail. He was not about to let him get the last laugh.

"I accept," he blurted. "What have I to lose?" he added flippantly.

"Quite a lot, actually," the old man stated.

"How?"

"If you cannot pass this test, I'm afraid your fortune will not survive the fallout."

"Since when did my holdings become part of this deal?"

"From the moment you accepted my test. Once you did so, there was no way out but to succeed. If you do not succeed, your fortune will be absorbed. You now have another powerful incentive to become one of us. Your very way of life. Maybe even your life. You must further realize that we reserve the right to end this test at any time we feel it is not progressing in accordance with our own standards."

"You make that sound like some kind of threat."

"Make no mistake, Mr. Wrightham. It is most definitely a deadly threat, and one we may well carry out. This is not a game. This is reality, and the stakes are very, very high. I will also expect a one million dollar cash gift to cover my expenses when we next speak." Mr. Bell extracted a piece of paper from a side pocket of his suit coat and handed it to the old man. "Further, this is a partial list of people you must control or remove, in order of importance. They include the governor, Sharon Wrightham—your wife, Charles Johnson…"

"Charlie Johnson?"

"Because of your earlier dealings with him in California and the recent botched attempt on his life, he may well pose a threat to our test. He knows you. More importantly, he knows what you're capable of doing. Anticipate problems, and deal with them. Further, you must realize that we are essentially observers, but will not hesitate to step in if we feel our own way of life is threatened."

Jonathan glanced over at Maclin. "The screw up on Johnson was not my doing. My incompetent brother was supposed to take care of him."

"My sources told me of the failed attempt to lure the woodsman into the trap. It was certainly very stupid to pick the forest, where he is an expert."

"We have been planning a lesson of sorts for a few troublesome individuals. Johnson is at the top of that list."

"Whatever works. A word of advice, however. In ancient biblical times it was common practice by all sides to deal harshly with the defeated. They killed their enemies, and then they killed their enemies' families all the way down to the newborn child. Even the Hebrews considered this cleansing necessary to prevent a surviving enemy relative from extracting revenge at some later date. This was accepted practice, and culturally ingrained. This brutality was only marginally effective for various reasons, only one of which was the martyr syndrome. It was also why the new commandment to love thy enemies was so hard to swallow. Remember that you are dealing with mere common folk, and that you have many tools at your disposal. Do not rush to a violent solution. Should you feel compelled to go that route, I am placing Mr. Bell at your disposal. He is very efficient. However, violence is merely one tool, and although occasionally a necessary one, it is overworked. It is often more advantageous to mold a person to your way of thinking. Be creative. You may find it is more profitable in the long term to buy an adversary, or exert some other means of control."

"I get the idea, however, you've resorted to the violent solution on occasion."

"For the record, never, but off the record, more times than you could imagine. Sometimes one has to do what one has to do." The old man looked down and continued reading from the list. "Maclin Ethek, Luke James..." Both Ethek and James responded with equal looks of astonishment.

"Why me?" they both said at once, forgetting the order of silence.

"Because," the old man said, "you both elected to stay, just as I knew you would." He turned to Wrightham, and handed him a white card with a phone number. "I'll check back in with you in one week's time to evaluate your progress, which, I presume, will be duly noted by the press. If you feel you need Mr. Bell's services before then, here's a number where you can reach us. You needn't know where we will be staying, but rest assured it will be close by. Remember the million-dollar gift. I realize it is a trivial amount, but the gesture will create a positive impression with my associates."

Jonathan Wrightham stood just inside the doorway of the rustic log home and watched the blue Chevy Blazer disappear from view down the driveway. He waved to Alfred, who had remained in the limo, and removed the innocuous looking clip from his tie. Alfred exited the vehicle and approached the house carrying a laptop computer under his arm.

"Well?" Wrightham said as Alfred came through the doorway.

"Every last word, sir, and good quality video."

"Perfect. Set it up in the sun room."

Alfred set the computer on the hardwood table, and moved to stand next to the log wall. He stood there at semi-attention, blending into the woodwork, waiting for instructions on what to do next for Jonathan Wrightham.

"What have you done now, dear brother?" Maclin asked suspiciously.

"You don't really think I was going to let that old fool have the upper hand, do you? Watch and learn, Maclin. Maybe someday you'll finally get it right. Everything that just transpired was recorded, sound and pictures."

Luke James slowly rose from the floor, and the thick carpeting showed clearly the indentation from his buttocks. His face had been white and drawn, only now regaining color. Wrightham noticed his fearful condition and laughed.

"You're a real piece of work, James. A coward to the core. I just hope you didn't soil my rug."

"That man Bell. Didn't you see his face? And his ear? He's not…right. I thought we were all dead."

Ethek ignored his father and nodded to his half-brother in approval. "I have to give you credit for the surveillance camera. Something I would have done. So what's the plan? Something tells me you're thinking beyond the senatorial position."

"Oh, I'll go through the motions on that. Plant a few news stories in the papers to make it look like I'm actually interested."

"Then you don't intend to go though with it?"

"Maybe just for laughs. It really wouldn't be that hard to do. As for the governor, I could always throw a nude hooker or two into his lap with cameras flashing. His ultra-conservative friends wouldn't approve should the pictures be released. The residency thing would be just a matter of predated paperwork. Cover it all with a couple hundred thousand dollars, and it's a done deal."

"But you made it sound like it was an impossible task," James interjected.

"Strictly for the old man's benefit."

"I don't know. He was old, but still didn't seem like someone you could cross."

"He won't touch me. Not with this recording. There's enough on here to make his life a living hell, should the press get it, not to mention the legal implications. Didn't you pick up on his weakness? He might be able to buy anything or anyone he wants, but with this tape I can destroy what he values most. Anonymity."

"Blackmail," Maclin observed.

"I prefer to call it leverage."

"What are you going to ask for?"

"Quite simply, everything."

Exactly seven days after the meeting with the old man and Mr. Bell, the same blue Blazer parked behind the Wrightham vacation lodge. Mr. Bell exited the driver's side, and moved to open the passenger door. He extended his arm to his partner, but the old man waved it off, and exited the vehicle entirely on his own. Alfred came down the walkway to meet them.

"May I be of assistance?" Alfred offered.

"I'm not dead yet," the old man answered. "Where's Mr. Wrightham?"

"Inside waiting. I so hope you haven't eaten. We have secured a very attractive seafood buffet."

"Afterwards maybe, if I still have my appetite, and Wrightham his britches."

Alfred saw movement from within the Blazer. "What about your pets. Anything for them?"

"They already eat too much. Let's get on with it."

Jonathan Wrightham emerged from the house, and a broad welcoming grin spread his lips. "Welcome. Come in." Instead of his expensive suit, he wore a plain brown cotton shirt and casual slacks. The limo was notably absent and had been replaced with a Ford crew cab blue pickup truck.

"Before we begin, I will assume possession of your stipend to the Family," the old man said as soon as they were within the house.

"Of course," Wrightham stated, as Alfred handed a black briefcase to Mr. Bell.

"You may count it if you like."

"At this point your word is not something we're concerned about."

"I appreciate your confidence in me."

"That remains to be seen. However, I do see you've made some improvements. Your mode of transportation, for one"

"Yes, on your advice, of course. Please. Take a seat in the sunroom. How about a hot cup of chamomile tea? May Alfred fix you a plate? We have steamed clams, fresh lobster, crab legs…"

"Later. Maybe," he said as he sat down on the same brown sofa he had the week before. Bell came and stood directly behind him, and Alfred moved to stand away from the group, but close enough to respond if his services were needed. "My presence here is purely business," Parish continued. "What progress have you to report? I did read in the Minneapolis Tribune of a possible sex scandal in the governor's office. Your work, I take it?"

"Who, me?" Wrightham said with faked innocence. "It seems our born-again governor has a fondness for hookers, and it just so happens I have the pictures to prove it. I'm thinking they should be worth at least a senatorial appointment."

Parish studied Wrightham for several seconds. "I may have underestimated you. You seem to have things well in hand. Perhaps this meeting…" The old man began to rise from the sofa, but Wrightham motioned him back down.

"Before you leave, there is something I'd like to discuss with you."

"Yes?"

"In private, if you don't mind."

"This is against procedure," Bell interjected. "I don't approve."

"Very well. In private then. Please leave us, Mr. Bell." Bell nodded and moved toward the exit, holding the million-dollar briefcase firmly in his right hand.

"You too, Alfred," Wrightham said.

"Where are your two hangers-on?" the old man asked after they were alone.

"James and Ethek? Out on some errand."

"So, Mr. Wrightham, what is so important that we must speak in private?"

"This so called test of your's…"

"The Family's."

"Whatever. It really is pretty Mickey Mouse, and totally unnecessary."

"Unnecessary?"

"You're going to make me a full-fledged member of the Family regardless. I've had enough of this initiation crap."

"I am? Just why would I do that?"

"Because if you don't, I'll put your face on the front page of every newspaper in the world."

The old man sat very quiet, and stared directly at Jonathan Wrightham. His slightly sad expression caused Wrightham just a moment of pity. He was too old, his mental ability too crippled, to stand up to a much younger man.

"You seem to have me at a disadvantage."

"I recorded our earlier conversation, complete with audio and video. There are now multiple copies. If you do not ensure my membership, I will distribute them to various news organizations world wide." Wrightham expected the old man to be shocked or angry or show some emotion, but his calm expression never changed.

"Blackmail, Mr. Wrightham? You are very desperate. And I know why. Your recent financial losses have reduced your holdings by nearly ten percent. Too many poor investments, too many unnecessary risks."

"Irrelevant at this point, wouldn't you say? Once inside your inner circle, I will be unstoppable."

"You have embarked on a very dangerous journey," the old man continued in his low quiet voice. "However, you have also shown considerable cunning and creativity. For that you must be given a great deal of credit. Perhaps, in your case, we can make an exception. I will relay your demands to the rest of the Family, along with the million dollars to show your sincere intentions. I'm sure the proper reward will be forthcoming. May we shake hands to finalize the arrangement?"

"Of course," Wrightham said, and he extended his right hand. The old man grasped it, and Wrightham was surprised at the strength of the grip. For a brief moment he was startled at a bit of pain, like a pinprick, but it quickly passed.

"Did you hear about the Messiah?" the old man continued in a soothing voice, "They say he walked on water."

Just beyond the swinging door into the kitchen, Alfred listened intently to the conversation between his employer and Mr. Parish. Protection of the Wrightham fortune was his promised duty. At this point, that fortune appeared to be in jeopardy. As he listened to Mr. Parish drone on, he realized this duty was going to be tested yet again. He chanced a quick glance at the two. Wrightham seemed to be almost asleep, probably disinterested, as Parish quietly spoke. Then the true nature of their conversation registered, and he quickly realized that what was being said was something he could use—in case Jonathan Wrightham failed—to save the Wrightham fortune.

CHAPTER 7

▼

Charlie Johnson reached to shake the man's hand as soon as he stepped out of his restored brown '79 Ford pickup. Coincidentally, it was the same make and model as his own; however, his was beyond help. The truck's owner was a tall man with thick black hair, an open and honest face with large features, and warm green eyes framed in smile lines. With his faded blue jeans, denim shirt, well worn western style boots, and deeply tanned face, he could have just come off the range after a cattle drive, but had, in fact, just five hours before left a corporate boardroom. Many years before, he had been a transplant to Minnesota from Kansas and still retained a residue of the distinct Kansas accent. Though he regularly attended the Lutheran Church with his wife in LaCrecent, Jerry Koler was a man who made honesty his religion. Those he dealt with on a regular basis, corporate executives, did not always welcome his absolute adherence to that conviction. Most believed in 'truth modification,' which meant unpleasant facts could be discarded or distorted if the bottom line, or their ass, was at stake. He was, however, respected as someone who would always tell it like it is. Johnson had come to know him during recent turmoil in the SciOgen Corporation, where Koler was a member of the board of directors. Jerry Koler was the one man responsible for getting the dollars, both from the National Science Foundation and his own company, to fund

Professor Bill Backus' research in Greenland. Koler had also been the one who saved the SciOgen research company by exposing its corrupt leadership, most notably the former CEO, Maclin Ethek.

"Charlie," Koler said with a wide grin. "Good to see you."

"You're looking pretty good for a man who rose from the dead," Johnson replied, firmly shaking the man's hand.

"And I have the scar to prove it," Koler laughed. He parted his hair on the left side of his head with his right hand revealing a four-inch long line the width of a pencil where no hair grew.

"I'd show you my scars, but I'd have to undress, and would probably get arrested here on Main Street."

"Please don't," Lora Whitney advised as she walked out of the restaurant behind them. She was in uniform. "I would have to arrest you. Hi Jerry. You're looking good for a man..." Koler interrupted with a laugh. "What?" Whitney said confused.

"It's just that, as always, you and Charlie seem to be on the same wavelength. I'd give you a hug but it looks like you're on duty."

"Oh well. What the hell," Whitney answered and wrapped her arms around the much taller man. "It is good to see you."

"OK, you two. Break it up," Johnson said, pretending jealousy. "Come on in. Professor Backus is probably wondering where we went."

The three friends entered the café that faced the main street of the community located on the southern shore of Leech Lake. Though the small town was the county seat, its main source of revenue was from summer vacationers, and dozens wandered up and down the sidewalk, casually gazing into shop windows, trying not to look like tourists. The inside of the café was filled to capacity and the dozens of different conversations were going on at once and reminded Johnson of the noisy clamoring of a hundred hungry geese. A multitude of odors from the kitchen blended together in one enticing fragrance. The three threaded their way around tables, around customers coming and going, and busy waitresses, to get to a corner table where a lone man sat waiting for them. He rose as they approached. Koler reached to shake Backus' hand, while Johnson and Whitney excused themselves to get cold liquid refreshments at the service counter.

"Hello again, Jerry," Backus said. "I want to thank you yet again for getting the funding together to make my work in Greenland possible."

"The pleasure was mine. I'm just sorry it had to end on such a negative tone. There were, and still are, a lot of rumors flying around."

"There are a lot of folks, including the college board of trustees, who were not happy with the way things ended."

"Perhaps, if you could enlighten me. From your perspective. To help me understand."

"I wish I could, but not at this point in time. Perhaps one day. You of all people have a right to know the facts." Backus hesitated and then shifted the focus of the conversation. "Nice of you to show up for the discussion. How did you get wind of it?"

"Special invitation," Koler stated. "I assume you sent it."

"No. Not me."

"What about Charlie's invitation?"

"No again. I only just met him, and Miss Whitney. I thought you set up this meeting."

"This is your show, Bill. I just assumed the invitations came from you," Koler stated.

"Well this is puzzling. I wonder who's responsible? Could have been someone in the department," Backus speculated, "but I can't imagine who or why."

Johnson and Whitney returned with a tall glass of ice-cold lemonade for each.

"As I understand it," Whitney said as she slid onto the bench seat next to Johnson. "This meeting between you and…"

"Luke James."

"…is supposed to be a discussion about your book. Is that correct?"

"Yes."

"Nothing more?"

"Not that I know of. Why do you ask?"

"I talked to Forrest, Sheriff Bodeman, and he said he was asked to provide extra security at the Retreat, since it is in this county. I'll be going out there with a couple other deputies. Most people are coming in by boat, but apparently there are some coming by helicopter and light aircraft."

"What are you talking about? What helicopters? What light aircraft?" Backus interrupted. "What people are coming? This is supposed to be just a friendly discussion between two people who look at the world a little differently."

"I think you may have been slightly misled," Whitney surmised. "The people who requested the extra security…"

"Yes?"

"…were from CNN."

Some forty years before, four businessmen from the Twin Cities of Minneapolis and St. Paul decided to purchase property in the northern part of the state. It was to be their private hunting ground, with a lake access, and inaccessible by road. Two years later, one of the men was in divorce court, another had died of lung cancer, the third was transferred to Japan, leaving only the fourth who loved the country, but whose wife couldn't quite overcome mall-withdrawal. They camped out on the property one time, were eaten alive by mosquitoes and deer flies, and upon his return to the Cities, the fourth partner promptly put the property up for sale, and it quickly sold. The new owners were members of the Fellowship Missionaries, a Christian group looking for a secluded place completely isolated from the outside world. Originally there were no phones, no electricity, no indoor plumbing, although all, except phone service, were added as soon as the wives took an interest. Working as a volunteer group, they cleared a four-acre plot of underbrush and small trees, constructed two plain brown brick dormitories, and happily set up nature and Bible classes for young people. It worked out very well, was very popular for a time, until finally, with the collapse of NASDAC, its financial backers pulled out their support, and it again changed hands. The new owner was a man who promised to continue with the spiritual goals of the previous owners, a man who was well known in religious circles, the Reverend Luke James.

Armed with nothing more than the knowledge in his head, Bill Backus stood at the entrance to the clearing, which was the Retreat. During his trip across Marion Lake in the johnboat with Jerry Koler and also the hike up the path from the boat landing—which was crowded with boats of all sorts—he had met no one. He now knew why. They were all here waiting for him. Perhaps a hundred people milled about in the open area in front of the dormitories. Many, he realized, were reporters or technical support people scurrying about with microphones and shoulder-held TV cameras. A group of men and women stood visiting in the shade of a Norway pine, and the focal point of the group seemed to be a man with long wavy brown hair, wire rimmed spectacles, and a white collar. Next to the edge of the clearing two helicopters were at rest in full sun, and farther on, at the end of the narrow grass runway, yellow nylon ropes held several light aircraft firmly to the ground. One forest green airplane sat on the end of the runway, and appeared ready to take off.

A neatly mowed concave shaped hill rose just to the east of the dormitories forming a natural amphitheater, and several large Norway pines provided some shade. Camera crews were setting up their equipment on the gentle hillside, focusing on the empty place at the bottom. A man appeared with two blue padded folding chairs and placed them at the focal point.

"My God, Jerry," Backus gasped. "What have I gotten myself into?"

"I don't know. It seems, however, that someone has placed a lot more importance on this discussion than you ever anticipated."

"I want to turn and run, but my knees have turned to jelly," Backus said only half-jokingly. He scanned the open area from one end to the other. "They say everyone gets their shot at fame. This must be mine."

They made their way through the crowd looking for someone who might be in charge. Finally they corralled a young man with a speaker under each arm, and he directed their attention to the front of one of the dormitories. In the doorway stood a man with thin white hair, and a long nose. He wore a bright blue suit with a white ruffled shirt. From a picture attached to one of the emails, Backus recognized Luke James. He threaded his way through the crowd and introduced himself.

"Luke James? I'm Bill Backus."

"Hello," James replied. "And I am quite aware who you are. I am pleased you had the courage to come."

"Perhaps you might explain to me just what the devil is going on," Backus blurted. "This is hardly the 'friendly chat' you requested in your email. What are all these people doing here?"

"You can still back out if you wish. Of course, I'd have to make a statement to the press saying you were unable to defend your position in your book."

"Defend my position. What position? It's scientific fact. There is no position."

"We will see, won't we? A couple of people were here looking for you earlier. A Mr. Johnson and Officer Whitney. They said one or the other would wait for you in the foyer of the other dormitory. See you in…" James checked his watch. "…about twenty minutes. Oh. One of the television people wanted to know if you wanted makeup."

"Makeup?"

"Yes. You know. To hide any facial flaws, and reduce shadowing. You wouldn't want to look like you have two black eyes. Television cameras tend to exaggerate such things." James hesitated and then continued. "I have to get my notes together. I'm sure your friends are anxiously waiting for you." With that Luke James turned and entered the building. Bill Backus was too overwhelmed to say anything.

"It's called blindsiding," Koler offered.

"What?" Backus asked after several seconds.

"You've been blindsided. Set up. Lured into the trap."

"I get the picture," Backus interrupted. "I don't mind speaking to a crowd. I do that on a daily basis in class. But this is…is…"

"I know how you feel. Believe me, I've been there."

"It's just that I wouldn't have expected a spiritual man to pull a stunt like this. I am totally unprepared. Off balance."

"That's the point of a blindside. Get in the first psychological blow. You have one advantage, however."

A smiling young woman approached Backus with a makeup kit. He waved her off.

"Tell me quick, before I really panic."

"People who have to resort to tactics such as this have a hidden agenda. You don't throw a swarm of bees at someone unless that person is a threat. This Mr. James is probably not exactly what he seems."

"I'd never even met the man until just now. What could I possibly have done to him?"

Koler shrugged. "Want some advice?"

"At this point, anything."

"Old Chinese Proverb. When strong, pretend to be weak. When weak, pretend to be strong.…"

"…and when scared, mess your pants. I've heard that one. But I get the point. No use throwing in the towel just yet. Who knows? Maybe I'm just overreacting." Backus watched as a popular newscaster of Asian descent walked by with her secretary. "Then again, maybe not."

A loud squeal was immediately followed by a male voice over the PA system. "Will Professor Backus and Reverend James please take their seats. We begin in ten minutes."

"Did you hear that? A director, no less. It would have been nice if I would have received an agenda at least," Backus said.

"Just speak from the heart, or in your case, the head. Remember, most of the people here don't really care about the topic. They're here to cover a story. You're a teacher. Get in there and teach."

Backus smiled and nodded. "Thanks coach. I needed that."

The three story brown brick dormitories were twins, the builders having accepted the adage 'Why build only one when you can build the second for half price?' Each had gray cement steps that led to the entrance door that opened up onto a central hallway on the second floor. Steps then led up to the third or down to the first from that level. One could continue walking straight down the hallway and exit through the back door. The front and back of the buildings were identical. Each floor contained six living spaces three on each side of the hallway. The apartments were not glamorous by any stretch of the imagination, but were of adequate size to accommodate a family of four, and came complete with a kitchen, bathroom, two bedrooms, and a living room-dining room area. They bore the unmistakable smell of infrequent human habitation, or more correctly the lack of human odors. Phone service was notably absent, having been banned by the previous owners, but with modern cell phones the lack of wall connections was only missed by someone wishing a hard wire Internet connection. With the development of wireless service, that, too, was becoming increasingly inconsequential.

Charlie Johnson stood on the top of the cement steps, and surveyed the rapidly increasing crowd of people who had come for the discussion. He looked for a tall, dark haired man, Jerry Koler, as did Lora Whitney. She had elected, however, to kill two birds with one stone and mingled with the crowd to advertise her deputy presence. She expected no trouble, but it wouldn't hurt to reassure the media that law enforcement was available should some unforeseen incident occur. Charlie had just made up his mind to join her, when someone quietly called his name. He turned to see a tall blonde woman standing in the shadows of the doorway, holding the door open for him to enter. Streaks of darker brown flowed through her hair, framing a perfectly dimensioned face. A one-piece blue denim jump suit with embroidered yellow butterflies on the sleeves followed the curvature of her athletic body. Immediately, he recognized someone he had met a year before in

California." Sharon?" Johnson began somewhat taken back. "What are you doing here?"

"I'm like a bad penny I guess. Please come in. Hurry." Lines of concern dented her face, and Johnson noticed the faint beginnings of horizontal wrinkles across her forehead. He followed her through the hallway and out the back door. She stopped a few yards farther on by the edge of the woods. As soon as they were alone and out of sight of the rest of the crowd, she turned and threw her arms around his neck with such force Johnson thought he might fall over backwards.

"I'm so happy to see you," she said, and the sudden radiance emanating from her face clearly indicated the emotion was genuine. "I don't have much time. I can't let Jonathan see us together."

"Your husband is here, also? I really didn't think he'd be interested in science or religion."

"He's not. There is something else going on. Something sinister."

"Like what?"

"I don't know the specifics. Are you a pilot?"

"As in airplane pilot? Afraid not."

"Do you know anything about flying? Please, this is important." Johnson noted she kept looking about nervously, as if expecting a pack of wolves to burst from the trees.

"I started taking lessons once. I can keep a plane in the air, make gentle turns, and maybe even take off, but don't ask me to land on my own. Why do you ask?" He didn't mention the fact that in three of the four lessons taken, he'd ended up with his head in a bag.

"Don't go near a plane, I beg you. Trust me. Your life may depend upon it."

"What's this all about? You're shaking like a leaf."

"Remember when you were in California last year I said Jonathan controls not only me but my family?"

"Yes."

"I only have one surviving family member. We're the last of our line."

"And he has threatened to harm him?"

"Her. But not just harm. If they even knew I was talking to you, she would not survive the day."

"They?"

"His half-brother, Maclin, is here, too. He's in on this. Jonathan has never forgotten the time you hit him in the nose and knocked him unconscious. And, of course, you helped in bringing Maclin down. They're planning something and it has something to do with airplanes. That's why I'd hoped you had some flying experience. Please, just leave now while you still can."

"I can't do that."

"For the love of god, why not?"

"I have friends here. Jerry Koler for one. If Maclin is here, then Jerry is most likely in danger also. While I played only a minor part, Jerry is directly responsible for Maclin's humiliating fall from power." Johnson considered for a few moments. "Does what's going on have anything to do with the discussion between Professor Backus and Reverend James?"

"I don't know. Maybe. I know Jonathan came to Minnesota a few weeks ago. Then just a few days ago, he had Alfred fly me here in the Corporation helicopter. Jonathan said he was going to make a major announcement today, probably since all the media is here already for the debate."

"Announcement?"

"I don't know what he's going to say. Listen. I have to go. I'll do whatever I can to help you. I just hope it's enough."

"Maybe it's time you just left Jonathan."

"You just don't leave men like Jonathan. He's above the law, or at least he thinks he is. He makes his own rules. For the sake of my family, I'm stuck here."

"If there's anything I can do…"

"You told me once life's a circle. That someday we'd meet again. I never forgot that, and kept hoping it would come true. Seeing you now, I wish things were different. That we'd be free to see each other. Maybe later."

"Maybe. Life is a circle."

Sharon circled her arms around him again, and kissed him hard on the lips. She held him for several moments, and then drew away slowly, finally letting her fingers part from his. Quickly she turned, ran up the cement steps, and disappeared into the dormitory.

From the shadows of a third story apartment window, a well-dressed man turned to his companions.

"I think we have to make room for one more."

Charlie Johnson and Lora Whitney had split up in order to try to find Koler and Backus when the call came over the PA system. The discussion was about to begin. Whitney suddenly spotted Koler by the west dormitory, waved to get his attention, and shouted, "Stay where you are!" Koler waved back in understanding. Now that she had located Koler she looked around for Johnson, who should have been standing on the cement steps. He wasn't there, however, and she couldn't locate him in the crowd, even standing on an available folding chair. She circled the crowd without success, and continued on behind the east dormitory. She immediately noticed two people with their arms wrapped around each other. The woman had her head on the man's right shoulder, and several locks of long blonde hair with streaks of darker brown streamed down the man's back. Whitney quickly glanced away to allow them their moment of privacy. She started to leave, but stopped at the sudden recognition. She looked back just as the couple separated. The strikingly beautiful woman backed up slowly, holding onto the man's hands until the last possible moment, and then entered the rear door of the dormitory. The man turned sideways as he watched her leave. Whitney blinked her eyes in disbelief.

Hoping upon hope that there was some rational explanation for Charlie's encounter with the woman, Whitney headed back to the main crowd. Normally, she would have confronted Johnson directly and immediately, that was her style, but lately her emotions seemed to overwhelm her—one moment in complete control and the next near tears, and for no apparent reason. She had taken only a few steps, however, when Johnson came up beside her.

"There is something going on here," he said quietly, and looked intently ahead.

"So it seems," Whitney answered, thinking of the blonde woman. "Want to tell me about it?"

"You remember me telling you about Jonathan Wrightham?"

"Of course. From California. He wanted you to help him become a US senator."

"Anything else."

"Well, you hit him in the nose when you met him, I remember that—for which you could have been arrested I might add."

"He brutally struck his wife. What was I supposed to do?"

"Chivalry is not dead after all," Whitney said with not a little sarcasm. "So what does that have to do with here and now?"

"Sharon is here."

"Sharon?"

"Wrightham's wife. I just talked to her."

"So that's what they call it now. Talking. It looked more like foreplay to me."

"What! You saw? We're just friends."

It was coming again, that unreasonable impulse to break down in tears, and Whitney was thankful that Jerry Koler appeared out of the mass of bodies.

"Something is not right here," Koler said immediately. "Backus has been set up, for what possible reason I don't know, but this…this circus," and he waved his arm indicating the crowd, "is not what he and James had agreed to."

"You're correct. I just met with Sharon Wrightham. She warned me that there was some kind of plot unfolding, but couldn't be more specific. She also said her husband, Jonathan Wrightham is here, and also Maclin Ethek. We had only a few moments together…"

"It seemed a lot longer to me, and you should have been talking instead of fondling each other," Whitney interjected.

"…since she didn't want her husband to see us together," Johnson finished ignoring Whitney's comment.

"Wrightham and Ethek are here?"

"Apparently, although I haven't seen them."

"What would a multimillionaire be doing here? I can't imagine Wrightham would be interested in a philosophical discussion concerning the nature of time."

"It may all be nothing. However, Sharon seemed to think we were in some kind of danger. Wanted us to leave. Said an airplane had something to do with it."

"I doubt we'd be in danger in broad daylight, and surrounded with TV cameras. What could possibly happen?"

"There is a warrant out for Ethek's arrest," Whitney interjected. "If I can verify he's here, I'll call for backup. How's Professor Backus handling this change of plans?"

"He's pretty shocked," Koler responded. "Can't say I blame him."

The crowd had grown noticeably more quiet and subdued, and again the PA system squealed. The three made their way back to the natural amphitheater, and stood off to the side where they could see both Backus and James sitting on the blue folding chairs. A technician clipped tiny microphones to their collars, and then moved away to check the speakers. Three TV cameras focused on the pair. Several reporters with open pads or hand-held tape recorders waited expectantly for the discussion to begin. Beyond them a semi-circular crowd of people completed the audience. The same young makeup woman who had approached Backus was doing a last minute touchup on James. He appeared unperturbed, joking with the woman, but Backus looked clearly concerned, clutching the arms of the folding chair like it was a life raft. He looked around the crowd, caught side of Koler,

Whitney, and Johnson, and when Koler gave him the thumbs up, he smiled broadly and noticeably relaxed.

A young man appeared behind the trio, said something to Whitney and quickly exited.

"I have to go," she said.

"What's up?" Johnson asked, only half-listening.

"There's a blonde out back who's taking all her clothes off."

"OK. Sounds interesting." Johnson heard the sounds but not the words, his attention focused on Bill Backus.

"You know sometimes you can really be an insensitive ass."

Johnson responded by shifting his position to get a better view.

"What's really going on?" Koler asked, noting Whitney's increasingly testy mood.

"Some kind of scuffle out back," she said, shifting to Koler. "Better check it out. That's why I'm here."

"OK. Later then." Johnson did not turn as Whitney headed toward the rear of the dormitories.

Chapter 8

The crowd, which now numbered over three hundred people including news people and observers, grew silent as the director said some words directly into the television cameras. All three operators gave him the thumbs up, signifying all was in working order. He introduced the speakers to the assembled group, and then, realizing he had a captive audience, droned on for another twenty minutes about his own personal battle with a drug addiction. Finally, he moved out of the camera angle, and nodded to the two men. James cleared his throat, and didn't waste any time getting to the heart of the discussion.

"You have written a most interesting book, Professor Backus."

"Call me Bill," Backus said. It was an automatic reflex. He followed it up with a warm smile, also standard procedure. The interruption seemed to trip James up for a second, but he quickly recovered and continued.

"You have written a most interesting book, Professor Backus," James began again, not allowing Backus the first points in the discussion. "Isn't it true that it is nothing more than a thinly veiled attack on the Word of God?"

"It is science, and has nothing to do with God," Backus said frankly.

"Do you know you use the word 'evolve' over eighty times in the book, and yet nowhere could I find the word 'create.'"

"I'm just glad you read my book. Would you like it autographed?" A murmur of laughter rippled through the crowd. Backus felt more at ease. It was a long time since his college debate class, but he suddenly remembered the first commandment. Follow up a question with a question. Keep your adversary on the defensive. He waited patiently for James to continue.

"Do you believe in God, Professor Backus?"

"Do *you* believe in God, Reverend James?" Again a murmur of laughter.

"You're cleverly evading the central issue, which is, if I might speculate, that your book's intent is to discredit the Written Word. Your assertions that the Universe is billions of years old, that the stars and planets somehow 'evolved,' and that life on earth, including people, arose out of some kind of primordial sludge directly contradicts the Written Word. How do you respond to these charges?"

"Guilty on all counts, except it was not my intent to discredit anyone."

"And frankly, I don't understand at all this light thing. It really makes no sense whatsoever. How does light relate to the age of anything?"

"Since you've read my book, you know that light travels at a fixed rate in a vacuum, and hence, the deeper we look into space, the farther back in time we are seeing. A simple example would be our own sun. When we look at it we are not seeing it as it is but as it was approximately six minutes before, since it took that long for its light to reach us. Light takes a while to get from place to place. When we look out into the Cosmos with powerful telescopes, we see the most distant galaxies billions upon billions of miles distant. We are not seeing these distant galaxies as they are, but rather as they were billions of years in the distant past. In the real time of the present, they may not even exist."

"I can answer that easily enough," James said confidently. "When God created the Universe he created everything in motion, the light in transit to earth. The Universe only looks old."

"Do you believe God is deceitful?"

"Of course not."

"Then why would He create the Universe in the way you suggest, when all the clues He has left us say differently?"

James sat silent for several moments, collecting his thoughts. This was not going as he had planned, and he realized why. Backus had fallen back upon what he did best, teach. The people in the audience had become students, and listened with undisguised interest to Backus' remarks. James quickly decided to drop the age of the Universe subject entirely and begin on a different front. He reached down and took something from a duffle bag, but kept it hidden in his hands.

"In your book you talk a lot about the different periods of time on earth, dinosaurs, coal beds, and such."

"Yes."

"You maintain, for instance, that the coal beds formed millions of years before man ever walked the earth."

"That is correct."

"Then how do you explain this?" James uncovered the object in his hand. It appeared to be arrowhead about four inches long embedded in a black lump of coal.

"May I take a closer look?"

"Certainly, but do not try to destroy this evidence."

Backus studied the object carefully. Before he could offer an explanation, James continued, extracting an eight-by-ten photo from his bag.

"And the dinosaurs were extinct long before man?"

"Yes again."

"But as you can clearly see in this photograph, these fossilized human footprints are side by side with dinosaur tracks on this riverbank in Texas."

Again Backus remained silent studying the photograph.

"You are undoubtedly a logical person, Professor Backus. Is it not true that it only takes one contradictory piece of evidence to prove a proposition false? For instance, if I assert all dogs have four legs, and you produce a dog with only three legs, my claim is refuted."

"That is essentially correct."

"Then if man was not present when the coal beds formed or when dinosaurs walked the earth, how did this arrowhead come to be eighty feet below solid ground in a coal bed, and how did human footprints come to be side by side with dinosaur tracks? Wouldn't you say this evidence disproves your theory? I'll wait for your answer."

"Without further analysis of your evidence I have no answer."

"Don't you trust your own eyes?"

"Not usually. There could be other explanations."

"Like what?"

"The first thing that comes to mind is the evidence could be faked."

"Oh come on Professor. You're grasping at straws."

"And without closer examination, I have no idea what made the tracks in your photo. They undoubtedly just look like human prints, and are, in reality, from some other animal. I will give you this. This certainly is interesting, and warrants further study."

"Well, that's the typical answer, isn't it? Let's do further study. Why can't you just admit the Earth, the entire Universe, is only thousands, not billions, of years old?"

"Because everything around me tells me differently. There is a scientific explanation for your evidence, I know, because the overwhelming evidence says coal beds were long formed and dinosaurs long dead when man finally evolved." Backus had avoided the 'e' word out of consideration for the Reverend, but at this point there didn't seem to be any point in trying to be tactful.

"In other words, you don't know."

"I don't pretend to know everything."

"Well, thankfully, I do. And it's all in the Good Book. Everything else is irrelevant."

"Everything like science?"

"Not all science, but certainly most of it."

"Let me ask you this. Probably you know some people who accept parts of the Bible, but reject others that are an inconvenience to their lifestyle."

"Certainly. They're nothing but hypocrites."

"Yet you select the part of science that fits your needs—for instance, all the broadcast technology that's all around us at this moment, all derived from the scientific method—and discard that which doesn't agree with your own personal bias."

"I have a right to pick and choose as I believe."

"That you certainly do."

"I'm missing your point."

"I'd *never* call you a hypocrite, Reverend James, but you can't have it both ways. You paint science as evil, yet you use all that the scientific method has given us to further your own agenda."

"I only use science so that I can get the word out. How else am I supposed to reach the people?"

"Maybe from the back of an ass."

"What kind of gibberish is that?"

"While I do not pretend to know as much about spiritual matters as you, I do know one thing. In science I can't prove my proposition correct by proving a differing view wrong. Likewise, you can't prove your faith by attacking the beliefs of others, whether they are scientific or spiritual. Faith is unprovable; otherwise it wouldn't be faith. If yours is the true path, then by your righteous example others will see the truth in it, just like if my scientific discovery is correct, others will be able to verify the truth in it. In this way the basis of both science and religion is the same. Yet, science does not claim to have all the answers. It is simply one path to finding them. No, I am not perfect, but if there is a twig in my eye, then there is a log in your own."

"Very clever. Using Christ's own words to try to mock me. But it is you who are mocked, because for all your science, you are clearly wrong."

"Why does science scare you so much?"

"It doesn't scare me at all."

"Maybe 'scare' is too harsh a word. For some reason it does, however, threaten your beliefs."

"The truth of the gospel is my belief."

"Perhaps there is more than one path to the truth."

"Not likely."

Both men sat quietly for several moments, the crowd also noticeably subdued. The director gave James a questioning look, and he continued.

"You make another interesting statement at the end of your book. You say, and I quote, 'We have a brain that is more than we need for survival, and unlike any other animal, we have this vast limitless potential, and the question is, why?' Care to elaborate on that statement?"

"Sure. To date millions of species of animals have arisen and gone extinct on earth. Millions exist today. Yet in all that time and all those species, only one has attained self-awareness, and the realization of its own mortality. It is us. Intelligence is clearly not a prerequisite for survival, yet here we are, smarter than we have to be, but probably a lot dumber than we think we are." Again laughter followed Backus' comments.

"I couldn't have said it better myself. Your own statement proves we are well above the rest of the animal kingdom, created for some special purpose."

"There is a possible scientific explanation for this extra brain power, and I fully admit it is an educated guess."

"I can't wait to hear."

"The age of ice."

"I don't follow."

"The human race was forged out of ice. Our development has paralleled and was almost certainly driven by the present Ice Age. When the great sheets of continental glaciers periodically covered much of the earth, on average the climate was much colder, far more brutal. Only the very cleverest, the most innovative, and certainly savage, early humans survived. Yet, they also had to learn to cooperate with others to hunt and build structures, and share and trade. Savage carnivores could easily kill a lone human, but a group working together could drive off or even kill the predators. Early humans that didn't measure up became saber-tooth cat food. There was a powerful evolutionary force at work, which in the case of humans heavily favored intelligence, since we have no other survival gear. We have no protective hair to amount to anything, no fangs, no claws, no body armor. Only intelligence. There is genetic evidence to suggest we just about didn't make it. All of humanity may have arisen from as few as a few hundred proto-humans."

"So you're saying a group of apes woke up one morning and decided to be smarter?"

"That's not how natural selection works."

"Then I guess you'll have to explain it to me."

"In every species there are subtle genetic variations among individuals. This is not by choice but by accident. Those individuals that have accidental variations favorable for survival survive to reproduce, and those that don't, die. These include physical as well as behavioral changes. There is no conscious will at work. Just, well, survival of the most able for the environmental conditions present. Using and comparing genetic codes, we can see today the vast changes that have occurred over millions of years. A specific example is the hippopotamus whose closest living relative is the whale which indicates a common ancestor somewhere in the far distant past."

"That's preposterous."

"Genetics is not a figment of someone's imagination. It is not a theory. It is real nuts and bolts science. As scientists map an ever increasing number of the genetic codes of earth's living species, they are merely confirming what evolutoionary scientists proposed decades ago. And I'm sorry if your beliefs are so narrow and fragile as to exclude the truth of our existence."

"That's rubbish. The truth is that we've been given a special place on earth."

"On that I agree. The question is: What are we going to do with that special place? If we take an honest look at what we've destroyed so far, it appears the earth has not been left in the best of hands."

James' confrontational style suddenly turned friendly. "I understand you recently returned from a scientific expedition to Greenland."

"We were taking core samples from the ice sheet that covers most of the island," Backus offered.

"I have evidence that you may not be as truthful and forthcoming as you seem."

"You have me at a disadvantage."

"I have been told that the ultimate sin in the world of scientific investigation is tampering with the experiment."

"Sometimes we have to insert the 'fudge factor,'" Backus said jokingly. "But, yes, altering the results of an experiment is tantamount to treason."

"So why did you do it?"

"I don't follow."

"There is someone here who you know quite well." James focused on one section of the audience. "Would you stand up please?" A bearded man stood and brushed the grass from his backside. It was someone Backus knew very well. "I'm sure you recognize Jack Reagon from your crew. He has shared an interesting story with me. Apparently he believes quite strongly that you removed part of a core sample, I believe he called it. Actually, 'stole' would be a better term."

All eyes were now on Backus, and the only sound was from the birds and insects in the nearby forest. Like the rest, Backus sat silent. So this is what this was ultimately about. He would offer no explanation for the missing piece. He felt it ironic, for like the man from Galilee, he would remain silent before his accusers. James, however, was not about to let the subject drop.

"If true, and if this were a court of law, the attorney would now suggest to the jury that you cannot be trusted. This one piece of evidence casts considerable doubt on your entire testimony. How do you respond to the allegations Mr. Reagon has made?"

"I will not respond," Backus said simply. "There is no point in continuing this." Backus rose from his chair, and walked directly toward the place where he had last seen Jerry Koler. No reporter rushed to him with a question. In fact, his departure seemed little more than a footnote. The reporters were still intent on the Reverend Luke James, who was fully engaged in the animated and emotional voice of a true salesman, delivering his wind up. When Backus arrived at where Koler had been standing, however, only empty space and footprints in the grass remained. The crowd again grew quiet, and Backus turned to determine what had caused the silence. A handsome man in his late thirties was standing under the suspended microphone, and looking directly into the television cameras. He was dressed like the stereotypical Minnesotan, with a long-sleeved red plaid shirt and faded blue jeans. Holding a hand-held microphone, the director was in the process of introducing him. "…and without further ado, I give you Jonathan Wrightham." A polite applause followed. The man nodded graciously to all present, raised his right hand to silence the onlookers, and smiled warmly.

"First, I'd like to convey my condolences to Senator Petterson's family for their recent loss. It was a loss that must also be born by all the residents of this great state. However, Senator Petterson would be the first to insist the fight for decency in government must continue. I am therefore deeply moved by the governor's recent announcement that I am a final contender for the Senatorial position. Although a relative unknown to most Minnesotans, I have always worked hard for the betterment of the folks in our fine state. I share your conviction for a return to basic moral values; God, family, and country. I only hope I can in some small way fill the void left by the tragic loss of Senator Petterson. I pledge to you this day and on my honor as a Minnesotan and before the Almighty, I'll give the residents of this great state every ounce of energy I possess in order to make Senator Petterson's dream a reality. He was truly a hero. Thank you so very much. I will be briefly available for questions."

Total silence followed Wrightham's brief statement. Then far to the rear of the crowd one lone observer began to clap. Another joined in, and then another. Within seconds the applause built to a deafening roar, and Jonathan Wrightham beamed in the spotlight.

"I could get used to this," he muttered to himself.

Jack Reagon made his way through the now boisterous crowd and confronted Backus. He held a white envelope in his hand.

"I'm sorry about this," Reagon began, and had to raise his voice to make himself heard. The applause gradually subsided.

"It turned out to be quite a spectacle," Backus said, motioning toward the crowd.

"I meant this," he said, indicating the letter. "They voted to send it to you, but I wanted to present it to you personally."

"What's in it?" Backus asked as he accepted the envelope.

"A chance to get things straightened out. I'll be frank with you. I don't know for sure if you took part of that last core or not. Hell, if you had asked for it they probably would have given you the whole damn thing. All I know is part of it is missing, a damn important part, you had the best opportunity to take it, and well, stealing is stealing."

"I wish there was something I could say."

"Just tell me what the hell is going on."

"I can't. For now. You'll just have to trust me on that."

Sadly, Reagon shook his head. "They've given you a week," he said, and walked away.

The discussion between Backus and James had barely started, when the fine hair on the back of Johnson's neck began to tingle. His gut feeling, his intuition, was not something he discarded out of hand, and had served him well in the past—when he took the time to listen. He turned to Koler.

"Where did Whitney say she was going?"

"To check on some kind of fight behind the dormitories, I think."

"A fight. Here. Over what, I wonder? I think I better check it out."

"Want me to come?"

"No. You stay here for moral support for Backus. I'll be right back."

Johnson made his way to the rear of the dormitories expecting to find Whitney, but she was not there. There was no one there, in fact, as all were watching the discussion. No one seemed to be by the helicopters or light aircraft, and the green airplane was still parked on the end of the runway. He checked the back doors of the dormitories. Both were locked. He went back and stood next to Koler.

"She's not there," Johnson said, and concern sounded in his voice.

"Probably in the crowd somewhere," Koler guessed.

"Could be. But a deputy uniform should stick out like a sore thumb. I can see the other two Bodeman assigned to baby-sit, but not Whitney."

"And why wouldn't she come back to join us?" Koler said, feeling a bit concerned himself.

"She might be somewhat upset with me," Johnson realized.

"Upset. Why?"

"No big deal really. She just caught me in the arms of another woman."

"You think? You were also somewhat distant when she was attempting to explain where she was going."

"I admit I was preoccupied but…"

"Rule number one. Never take a woman for granted."

"I explained the woman was a friend. Why would she get upset over a little thing like a hug?"

"Was it?"

"Was it what?"

"Just a hug."

"Of course, at least to me. And a kiss."

"You don't have much experience with the opposite sex, do you. When it comes to courtship, women are very competitive, much more so than men."

"Lora means everything to me."

"When was the last time you told her?"

"Well, never actually. I just assumed she knew."

"Rule number two. Never assume anything."

The same man who had appeared earlier suddenly appeared again.

"I'm supposed to tell you your friend is in trouble. She doesn't know how to fly." He turned quickly and disappeared into the crowd.

"What was that all about?" Koler asked.

"Not a clue, but I don't like the inference. I'm going to get a closer look at the airplanes."

"I better come too."

"What about Backus?"

The crowd was laughing at something Backus had just said.

"Look's like he has everything under control. Let's go."

Besides the two helicopters, five other light aircraft sat neatly in a row next to the grass runway. There were two high-winged Cessna's, a two-place one-fifty, and a four-place one-eighty. Two were low-winged Piper Cherokee's, and the last was a maroon colored classic nineteen forty-seven Stinson tail dragger.

The green aircraft that sat on the end of the runway was a high-winged Piper Tripacer, affectionately called the Flying Milk Stool by the older generation of pilots, because of the short wingspan and sturdy assembly that held the two main wheels and the nose wheel. Built in the nineteen fifties and when equipped with a one hundred fifty horsepower Lycoming engine, it could easily carry four people. Unlike the other aircraft, it was not tied down with ropes, and appeared ready to take off. From a distance, Johnson couldn't see anyone in the aircraft, and after a closer inspection, neither Johnson nor Koler could find anyone in any of the aircraft. It appeared the message had nothing to do with these airplanes. They turned to walk back to the crowd, and immediately were confronted by two men who walked directly toward them. Both were smiling. Johnson recognized small caliber automatics with silencers in their hands. The men stopped about ten feet away. They wore gray suits, could have easily passed for businessmen, and were generally clean-shaven. One, however, had a neatly trimmed pencil thin mustasche.

"Get into the aircraft," the one with the mustache ordered.

"Sorry, I don't like to fly," Johnson said "I get airsick."

"What's this all about? Who are you?" Koler asked.

"Get into the aircraft if you ever want to see the policewoman again." The one with the mustache seemed to be in charge, and did the talking.

"Where is she?" Johnson asked, and edged closer to the men.

"Somewhere safe and sound. No one will get hurt as long as you do as you're told. We can do this the easy way or the hard way. The easy way is for you to get into the airplane. The hard way is for us to put you there." He focused on Johnson. "And don't try anything stupid. Your reaction time is no match for a bullet."

"Well, looks like it's going to be the hard way." Johnson began, but Koler grasped his arm to get his attention.

"Whitney," he advised. "Perhaps we better do as they say. We can't help her if we're…"

"Smart boy," the man said. "Now get in or I may put a couple slugs in your legs just for fun. Take the back seats."

Koler opened a door of the Tripacer, placed his foot on the step and entered. He pushed the yoke of the dual controls all the way forward, tipped the seat forward and climbed into the rear seat. Johnson hesitated for a moment, mentally searching for a way to overpower the two, but knew it would be a suicidal attempt. What in the world had

Whitney gotten herself into this time, he wondered? He entered the aircraft behind Koler, and took the seat directly behind the pilot's position. The man slammed the door closed, locked it, and without another word both men turned and walked away. Johnson began to laugh. Surely they didn't believe a fabric-covered aircraft would make a secure prison cell. He watched as the men departed, and suddenly they disappeared into a gray fog that seemed to be enveloping everything.

Backus made his way out of the crowd, found a friendly tree some distance from the rest, and sat down, resting his back against it. It was past midday and he was hungry, but mostly he was homeless. He had no desire to go home, face his wife, and pretend everything was okay. The memory of her on the bedroom floor with their neighbor was not something he was likely to forget. It bothered him greatly, not so much because of his wife's infidelity, but because of his own lack of outrage. He should be hurt, or angry, or numb, or something, but he just felt empty. Also, he had no desire to go back to his office on campus and face Lynn Bergen. Her actions where baffling, and it was as if she had suddenly mutated into a completely different woman. When he thought about it, that's how all the women in his life had turned out. He certainly didn't want to face any more reporters. One moment of fame was more than enough. He would, he decided, go back to the tiny room he had rented in Bemidji ever since his return from Greenland, if he could catch a ride with someone. It was quite possible, he realized, his wife didn't even know he had returned.

Despite their very different views on existence and the Universe, Reverend James had been right on target about at least one thing, and if he had been more perceptive and less narrow minded, may well have guessed the complete truth. There were things out there that he now had to question, things that were just too shocking to present at this time even to the scientific world. Science had always been his religion, the one thing that gave his life meaning and a sense of purpose. Now, it seemed that faith was being put to the test. Still, there had to be a logical answer.

Backus' thoughts swirled around in his head like the storms on Jupiter, and he realized a good part of the reason for the turmoil was a splitting headache. He looked at the white envelope in his hands and absently tore it open. He already had a good idea what would be contained inside. He opened the folded piece of paper and read the heading, UNREQUESTED LEAVE OF ABSENCE, crumpled it up into a ball, and tossed it away. Reagon's comment was now clear. He had a week to get his personal effects out of his office. His life, he realized, was coming unglued before his eyes.

"You had him going for a while," a male voice said interrupting Backus' thoughts. "But toward the end you seemed to lose your way. Overall I'd give you a B minus. May I join you?"

The intruder was the last one Backus would have expected. He was in his forties or well kept fifties, Backus guessed, above average height, with a deeply tanned face, long wavy brown hair combed back over his ears, and athletic build. A broad and welcoming smile spread his lips. Wire rimmed glasses hung on a slight hump on his nose. It wasn't his physical appearance, however, that caused Backus to wonder. It was the white collar around his neck, beneath a brown plaid work shirt.

"Sure."

"Name's Michael Malley. You can call me Mike," the man said as he squatted down next to Backus.

"You're a…"

"Priest? Depends on whom you talk to. I'm without a flock at this point."

"I don't follow you."

"I also have a wife and a child."

"Oh."

"I realized one day after meeting my future wife I could live without sex, but I couldn't live without her. I also can't live without my faith."

"So without a flock, as you put it, and without the blessing of your church, what do you do for a living?"

"I grow rare red roses, and I'm also a carpenter. Pretty ironic, isn't it. My inspiration started out as a carpenter, I ended up as one." He extracted a business card from his shirt pocket and handed it to the professor. Backus gave it merely a cursory glance and set it to one side.

"And yet you wear the collar."

"I know I'll probably go to hell for it," the man said smiling, "but I find I get a lot more respect when I wear it. People are a lot nicer, keep their language in check, and go out of their way for me. I can't give up the perks, even if the Pope won't let me dole out any penance. Pretty selfish, wouldn't you say?"

"Who? You or the Pope?"

"Take your pick," Malley laughed. "I like you already. Mind if I call you Bill?" He extended his right hand.

"Bill is good," Backus responded, shaking his hand. Mike's grip was strong, his palm and fingers calloused, a worker's hand. "What can I do for you?"

"I'd like to continue the discussion that you and Reverend James were having, if you don't mind."

"As long as the camera crews don't show up."

"Promise. And you're free to end this conversation at any time." Malley waited a moment and then continued. "I have to ask. Are you a believer? I already know about James, and even though you did so flippantly, questioning his beliefs was entirely appropriate."

"The honest answer is no."

"It takes a lot of courage to deny the existence of a supreme being."

"I didn't say I deny the existence of a supreme being. There may be millions of alien species out there that we would regard as supreme. But a white haired old man who controls every aspect of creation is not something I can swallow."

"What about the Written Word?"

"Mostly stories, moral lessons, and Jewish history, told mainly from their point of view, which would be considered biased by any scientific inquiry, or court of law."

"True. True. Very biased. But you know, there is some really good stuff in there. Miraculous stuff to get a man thinking."

"But many of the so-called miracles have been scientifically explained. If similar events happened today, and they have, we wouldn't give them a second thought."

"True again. Even the Pope has conceded there is something to be said for the scientific method."

"A lone voice crying in the spiritual wilderness," Backus said without sarcasm.

"Most Jewish scholars will tell you there are many levels of understanding in the Testament. There is what appears on the surface for those, perhaps, who are disturbed at the prospect of deeper thought, but who still need guidance. There is, however, a much deeper level for those who have the courage to search their souls for it."

"I'm not quite sure I follow."

"The real meaning is not necessarily what's on the paper. That's the guide. It is something else, unspeakable, a feeling. Most people would call it a connection, or love for lack of a more precise term, but it's more than that. It is something that is definitely there, yet just beyond our reach. The Native American people called it the Great Mystery."

"Let me tell you something about love. I've loved three women, would have done anything for them, and each time they used my love as leverage against me." Backus picked up a pinecone and tossed it away. "Anyway, all you've stated is explainable without a creator."

"This is not about creation; this is about living. And the fact that the women in your life didn't accept your love doesn't diminish the fact that you offered it."

"Where did it get me? If I'm honest with myself, I'd have to say empty and bitter. I don't blame anyone, not even my wives. Calling my personal life a failure would be charitable, and now I have to accept the fact that the one thing I always wanted, children of my own, will never come to be. If I thought it would help, I might even pray, but at this point I can't be that hypocritical."

"Let me tell you something. When I first started my own spiritual journey, I had this very practical problem with the whole idea. It seemed a bit like believing in Santa Claus. Then I discovered an answer for this dilemma. It is the Quaker philosophy that asserts there is a bit of the divine—whatever that might turn out to be—in each of us, which makes us all equal, worthy, and connected. In the language of your scientific world, we might call that the First Postulate, the common ground from which we might all begin." Both remained silent for a time and then Mike continued. "I have to apologize. I'm not really a priest anymore. I shouldn't be preaching."

"And I suppose I shouldn't be confessing." Backus laughed. "I have to say you're one poor liar. But I think I like you anyway."

"And you're one sorry excuse for a scientist who didn't strike me as the kind of man who would sulk away licking his wounds. You're searching for the Truth, and whether you know it or not, you're doing His work, much more so than Reverend James. A true believer welcomes the search for the truth in whatever direction it may take him, because the truth must lead him closer to, not farther away from, this Great Mystery of life."

"And if it doesn't?"

"Then perhaps he is following a false god. Look around. There is a crisis in the world today. And you know whose fault that is? It is not, as Reverend James would assert, the work of the devil. It is because of those of us who claim to be believers, but have grown so narrow that we have lost sight of the Message. We see the world faith eroding and look for something to blame—the devil, science, greed, the political system, other belief systems—when it is our religious institutions that are rotting from the inside. My god, we believe we have God on our side and we still can't get it right. We are supposed to be setting the example, yet what thinking person can excuse the blatant material excesses or sex abuse by some our most trusted leaders? We excuse men like James because, we say, at least he is spreading the Word. Yet men like James dine on the lonely, selling salvation for so-called love gifts like it was their's to offer, and then drive away in Cadillacs. Never mind some grandmother in Chicago went without decent food or heat for a month to help purchase it. In their sick minds, they believe—if they are even believers—that the Divine has smiled on them for all their good deeds, and that they somehow have earned and deserve the material rewards. In the end, that is all they will have, and it will be decidedly insufficient."

"Where will it all end, I wonder?"

"Sometimes a person has to hit rock bottom in order to begin again. It may well be the same for the human race."

Backus looked at the man who spoke his convictions with passion and intensity. He couldn't help but smile. "You know, you're awfully radical for a man of the cloth."

"A nice compliment. Thanks. So was my teacher. I'm even thinking of starting my own church."

"What are you going to call it?"

"The Church-of-Heaven-Help-Us has a nice ring to it. What do you think?"

"Maybe you better stick to growing roses and carpentry."

Chapter 9

The crowd was breaking up, the event over, and television support crews were packing their equipment in what looked like oversized duffle bags. Backus made his way toward Luke James, and even from thirty yards away his sky blue suit stood out like overalls at the ballet. Several reporters still surrounded him, and one held a microphone inches from his mouth. Backus waited until they left, and then approached James with an outstretched hand. Reluctantly and suspiciously, James shook it.

"I look at life as a learning experience, Mr. James. This event certainly qualifies. For that I have to thank you."

"Thank me?"

"Sure. How else would I…?" Something familiar in Backus' peripheral vision caused him to look towards the aircraft that were tied down at the end of the sod covered runway, and he lost all interest in James. "I'll have to get back to you on that."

Backus had to look closely but it was definitely Lynn Bergen being escorted by a man in a gray suit. The man had his arm around her waist and he smiled broadly at her. A boyfriend, Backus thought, and felt undeniably envious. He realized Lynn must have been present for the show, having flown in with her boyfriend, and was now preparing to leave. There was something peculiar, however. Lynn didn't seem to be smiling. Even from a distance, Backus could see her face contorted into a profound look of sadness. He hesitated, wondering if he should involve himself in something that might be as simple as a lover's quarrel. Lynn had very clearly told him to mind his own damn business. He decided he should do just that, but when she looked in his direction, he realized it was not sadness that contorted her face, but distress. Without a conscious thought, he began to move purposefully in their direction. His scientific mind calculated the correct angle and speed to intercept them at their apparent destination, a green single engine aircraft parked on the end of the runway.

Deputy Lora Whitney had checked behind the dormitories, but either the scuffle was already over or it had moved to a new location, because there was nothing there but green grass and trees. Instead of immediately returning to Koler and Johnson, however, she decided to make her presence known, and again walked slowly and purposefully through the crowd. If there were a few folks with an attitude, a clearly visible police uniform might just provide the necessary deterrent. The other two officers also hovered at the fringes of the audience, sweeping their eyes over the sea of heads.

During the debate, which seemed a lot shorter in duration than she had anticipated, Whitney completely circled the group, and then walked the quarter mile path back to the boat landing. All was well there, with a half-dozen people sitting on the long aluminum dock splashing their bare legs in the water. After the boat landing, the only thing left to check was the aircraft, and Whitney decided to take a short cut through woods to the runway. If she judged the direction correctly, she would intersect the runway near the parked aircraft. She continued on, avoiding the poison ivy, and slapping at the occasional mosquito. Then, very clearly, she heard the distinct sound of an aircraft engine starting up. It seemed to idle for a few seconds and then suddenly revved to full throttle. She came out of the woods just in time to see the green Piper Tripacer gathering groundspeed as it passed directly in front of her. While she had only a brief moment to view it, two disturbing thoughts immediately registered in her mind. Charlie Johnson's head was clearly visible against a rear passenger window. He appeared to be sleeping. This made no sense whatsoever, because unless her eyes were malfunctioning, there was absolutely no one flying the aircraft. The other thing that disturbed her was the blonde head of hair that seemed to be resting on Charlie Johnson's shoulder. She watched as the flying machine sped down the runway, and for a moment she was sure it would never leave the ground and crash into the trees at the north end, but at the last possible moment, it broke free of the earth, and rose into the blue sky.

A few hundred feet from the airstrip on top of the western most dormitory, two men's attention was focused on a computer monitor. One of the men sat directly in front of the screen, which displayed the forward view of a rapidly moving vehicle. He manually operated a control lever. "Now! Now!" the other man said, as he watched from behind.

"They're heavy. Have to get as much groundspeed as possible, or they'll never get off."

"We don't want the thing to crash right here!"

"It won't. Please remain quiet and let me concentrate." He focused even more intently on the video image, and moved the joystick steadily backward. The aircraft lifted off the ground, and cleared the bank of trees at the north end of the runway by inches. The video image now showed a moving panoramic view above the tops of green trees.

"You cut that pretty close."

"They're over the weight limit. Good thing there's only a few gallons of fuel on board, or it never would have made it."

"How much time?"

"Thirty four minutes."

"You sure?"

"All the computer simulations put engine failure at between thirty-two and thirty-three minutes. Well within the target area."

"What's the chance of a passenger taking control?"

"Zero, unless they can fly an airplane in their sleep. Your work here is done. The show over. From now on we let the program do its job."

The man with a long hook-like nose and with ears that seemed glued to the side of his head turned to leave, but then hesitated. He turned to a third man who sat sipping ice tea on a blue folding lawn chair some distance away, and who seemed uninterested in the video images. "I'd still like you to arrange a meeting for Morgan and me. It might be hard for you to understand, but I really did…do love her. I still wake up at night and see her sleeping next to me."

"Of course," Jonathan Wrightham said, "if I knew exactly where she was. Want to stay and watch the final ending of our little production?" James turned back to the monitor, which continued to display video of the forward view of an aircraft in flight.

"I'll pass. As you stated, my part in this is done. I have to admit I'm not exactly clear on what you're trying to accomplish here. What do you intend to do when you get them to the target area?"

"Shake them up a little, that's all. They're set to come down in a big open meadow and they should regain consciousness just in time to get the scare of a lifetime."

"A lesson they will most likely never forget. I just hope…"

"You've seen the technology. Nothing will go wrong. No one is going to be seriously injured, except maybe their pride."

"My one concern is Backus. He wasn't supposed to be on that plane."

"It was unavoidable. Don't worry. You'll get another chance to humiliate him. I have Alfred's assurance, and he is never wrong about people, that this episode will make it clear everyone is vulnerable."

"What do you get out of all this?"

"My goal has always been to increase the Wrightham fortune. This means I have to set an example from time to time. And impressing the Family can't hurt."

"Speaking of the Family, what ever happened to Mr. Parish and that man Bell?"

"We came to a mutual understanding. Parish went back to the Family to make arrangements for my admission. Nothing to concern you. Mr. Bell is now in my employ."

James nodded, took one last glance at the screen and entered the doorway to the stairway. Wrightham waited for only a few minutes, smiled faintly, and rose from his lawn chair.

"Record everything, Alfred. I want absolute confirmation."

Without bothering to check the screen himself, he left Alfred with the computers doing their work. Alfred was like a second set of eyes, completely trustworthy and loyal to the Wrightham family to a fault.

Alfred switched on another adjacent monitor. The second display was divided into four separate images, each of a different view of the interior cabin of the four-place single engine aircraft. Two men and one woman were crammed in the tiny rear seat. Both men had black hair, and their heads rested on opposing windows. The blonde woman sat more on them then between them, and her head rested awkwardly on one man's right shoulder, and face turned away from the camera. Head thrown back, a third man sat in the front right seat, and a fourth smaller man with reddish hair sat slumped over in the pilot's position. All appeared to be resting comfortably. The dual aircraft controls, the yoke and rudder pedals, one set on each side, seemed to move by themselves, compensating for moderate air turbulence on the sunny August afternoon.

Jonathan Wrightham thought about how events would now unfold. The computers would continue to control the aircraft and record video until the plane's impact with the ground destroyed the onboard cameras. The tragic end of the doomed flight was something he felt it necessary to conceal from James. If Alfred had read him right, and Alfred always read people right, James was on the verge of a fit of conscience, and that was something that would put everything in jeopardy. Only afterward would he reveal the truth. By then it would be too late.

As Wrightham descended the stairs, his mind played out the last minutes of the doomed flight. The aircraft would be cruising at four thousand feet above ground level, the engine would sputter a few times and then die. A relatively minor explosive charge on the right aileron control was set to detonate as soon as the engine stopped turning, instantly locking the aircraft in a left bank. Without active control, the short wingspan of the Tripacer would provide little gliding capacity, the nose would drop like a rock, and the green aircraft would plunge earthward in a rotating death spiral. The carefully selected point of impact was a vast expanse of forest and marshland, a mostly uninhabited wilderness area dotted with potholes. The occupants of the aircraft would be sleeping soundly. The drug in their system would completely dissipate after fifty minutes from the time of exposure. Should their bodies be found intact, no forensic genius would ever find the slightest trace.

The ELT, the emergency locater transmitter for the aircraft, would be of no help as it had been removed and now rested at the bottom of Marion Lake. Of course, to make an effective statement to certain people, the tragic accident would have to come to light eventually. He estimated it would take the locals a week to make the discovery.

Without aileron control or power and according to the computer simulations, there was only a one in ten thousand chance of a survivable crash. Maclin's plan for revenge had fit nicely into his plan. Maybe, given enough time, he might be able to find some subordinate role for his bastard brother once again. The accident would send a clear message to Mr. Parish and the Family. He was someone to be reckoned with. The plan was nearly complete. He only briefly regretted the one passenger, Bill Backus, who was not supposed to be on board. His appearance had delayed the takeoff, but not long enough to draw the attention of any nosy onlooker.

Mr. Parish's earlier threats had turned out to be nothing more than the whimpering of an old man. It appeared the Family was going to meet his demands, and he wisely refused to hand over all copies of the recording. To maintain one's health, it is often desirable to have a good insurance policy.

Wrightham reached the main central hallway, and entered one of the second floor dorm rooms. His two aides were there waiting for him. In spite of Backus' unexpected appearance, getting the necessary people into the old Piper Tripacer had seemed to go without fault. Both men rose from well-worn yellow kitchen chairs when he entered.

"Good work, gentlemen. Any problems?"

"None," the one with the thin mustache responded. "The Indian and Koler went in like babies, as soon as we mentioned the woman deputy."

"What about the blonde woman?"

"Funny thing about her. She went willingly. We were expecting trouble, but it wasn't until Backus showed up that we had to give her the shot. You said 'No witnesses' so we persuaded Backus to join the party."

"You did the right thing. You may leave now. Your bonus is waiting for you at the designated location. Your service has been…what the devil!"

Wrightham rushed over to the window to get a clearer view, and then turned back to his henchmen. "What kind of scam is this? How much did she pay you?"

The two men stood speechless and confused. Finally, the one with the mustache spoke. "What are you talking about?"

"My wife! I just saw her walk past outside on the back lawn. The wench was supposed to be on that plane."

"An attractive blonde woman, just like you said. We had no trouble finding her. Who could miss someone who looked like that?"

Realization dawned, and Wrightham drove his fist into the wall in frustration. "Lynn Bergen," he said. "It had to be." It would be the first error of several in his otherwise perfect plan.

Built more like a tractor engine than an automobile engine, the hundred fifty horsepower Lycoming power unit in the Tripacer thundered through the air. Dual magneto's provided spark to two sets of spark plugs increasing the efficiency of mixture burn, and adding a measure of security should one magneto fail. Even the most reliable engine, however, will not run without fuel, and at the twenty-six minute mark into the flight, the first hint of imminent engine failure manifested itself as a 'hiccup,' a misfire. The needle on the tachometer, which had stayed steady at twenty three hundred RPM's, flickered briefly.

Charlie Johnson opened his eyes, and moaned. The only thing he hated more than being in a hospital was riding in the back seat of a single engine aircraft. He was going to be sick.

Confused and disorientated, he adjusted his right leg to better support a blonde woman who sat with her head on his shoulder. He tilted her head so he could see her face, but it was not Sharon Wrightham as he suspected. Jerry Koler sat next to him, and the woman also occupied a good part of his lap. Across from him in the front seat, Bill Backus sat hunched over with his head thrown back, eyes closed and mouth open. A bit of red hair showed ahead of Johnson in the pilot's seat, but it was obvious this person was not flying the airplane.

"What do you make of this?" a voice called above the roar of the engine and prop noise. Johnson turned to see Jerry Koler rubbing his eyes.

"It can't be good," Johnson answered. "We seem to be pilotless, but steady at the moment. You know anything about flying?" Something about the question caused him to wonder, and it suddenly occurred to him Sharon Wrightham had asked him the same question not long before. Although he'd taken a few lessons, the flying bug had never really hit. She had warned him against flying. Now he knew why.

"I am a private pilot, and I'd feel a lot better up there. Who's in charge of this boat?"

"You won't believe it unless you get a good look yourself."

Koler moved the woman fully onto Johnson's lap. Only when she was out of his line of sight could he see the man in the pilot's seat. "What the…. it's Maclin Ethek!"

"Talk about strange bedfellows," Johnson quipped. "The last time I saw him he was doing his best to kill me, and after the events at the campground, I have the distinct feeling he still is."

"But why would he be up here joy riding with us?"

"I haven't the faintest notion. We were all drugged. That much is certain. You and I must have received the first dose, so we woke up first."

"You have any idea what to do next?"

"You're the pilot. You tell me."

"We seem to be in level flight, but I assure you this old timer didn't come standard with automatic pilot. I need to get behind the controls as soon as possible, and there isn't much room in here to maneuver."

As if to emphasize the extreme urgency of the situation, the engine noticeably faltered, then seemed to clear itself and continued to run smoothly. Quickly, Koler slid over the seat, and Johnson pulled Ethek to the back, working around the woman who sat unconscious on his lap.

"Something is fighting me," Koler shouted back to Johnson as soon as he took control. "The controls are really heavy. And if the fuel gauges are accurate, we're running on fumes. I better call in a mayday." He unhooked the old style microphone from just beneath the firewall, and realized immediately there was no trailing cord. "I have a bad feeling about this. I think we're on our own."

"Better find a place to land," Johnson advised, and moved the woman onto Ethek's lap.

Koler nodded, and pulled back the throttle until the tachometer registered just over five hundred RPM's. He banked the plane into a sharp left descending turn, and let gravity do its work. The altimeter registered a steady descent.

"Looks like a small field directly below us," Koler said with relief as he brought the plane out of the turn. "It might be a bit bumpy but I think we're going to be OK."

"I hate to spoil your day," Johnson called back, "but that isn't a field. It's a marsh, complete with cattails, and floating bog. Trouble is, there's nothing else to choose from."

"This could get ugly. Better buckle everyone in as best you can."

Koler searched the ground below for anything that looked solid, but from their altitude it all looked like a grassy meadow, dotted with islands of evergreen trees, and water-filled potholes. "The book says for an emergency landing pick a place and stick with it. Straight ahead looks good."

"If you say so. Let me know how it all turns out," Johnson said, his stomach about to revolt against the bumpy ride.

Koler laughed briefly. "Nice to see you haven't lost your sense of humor."

"Who's joking?"

At five hundred feet above the ground, the engine sucked up the last of the vapors from the wing tanks, and the pistons coming up on compression abruptly brought the engine to a halt. For a few seconds an unnatural calm filled the cabin. A pop like a firecracker sounded, and then all was quiet, except for the sound of moving air over the wings. Abruptly the plane lurched to the left.

"I've lost aileron control!" Koler shouted, as he turned the yoke as far as it would go to the right. He glanced hurriedly out the right and then left window.

"Lost aileron control? What does that mean exactly?"

"I have positive control of the left aileron only. The right one seems to be locked in a left turn. I have to hold the yoke over in a hard right just to keep us level. The ailerons are now acting like wing flaps, braking our air speed. I have to keep the nose down, or we'll stall."

"Forget the technical explanation. What are you trying to say?"

"We're bound to crash land, and will probably die."

"Don't try to sugar coat it. Just give it to me straight."

"We're…" Koler glanced back quickly at Johnson. "Never mind."

"How likely is this type of equipment failure?"

"As far as I know, it's never happened before. The small explosion we heard…"

"I'd say Ethek was responsible, but then why is he here? Someone really doesn't like us very much."

"If we hadn't regained consciousness when we did, right about now we'd be a two inch layer of mush on the ground."

"Can you get us down?"

"If not me, then we can always count on gravity. The left and right ailerons are canceling each other at the moment. There's no way I can make a controlled turn. Most I can hope for is to keep us straight and level. It's safe to say where we come down is now out of my hands. Maybe a more experienced pilot could make it work, but…"

"Anything I can do? The ground is coming up awfully fast."

"Brace for impact. It looks like we've opted for the treetops."

Charlie Johnson watched with fascination as the plane rapidly approached the dark green tops of an area of black spruce. He was only dimly aware of Koler sitting directly ahead of him struggling to keep the plane level. Bill Backus and the blonde woman were unconscious, but Maclin Ethek was now wide awake, and stared with undisguised horror as the ground rapidly came up under them. "This can't be happening," he shouted. "The bastards did it again!"

"Oh no!" Koler shouted suddenly.

"What now?" Johnson called back.

"I forgot to buckle up!"

The tricycle landing gear struck a treetop, and Koler pulled back sharply on the yoke, forcing the airplane into a stall. The airspeed dropped almost immediately, the nose pitched downward, and the plane fell like a rock into the trees.

The Tripacer plunged into the evergreens, which caught the fabric-covered aircraft like a web catches a fly, and the impact ripped the left wing completely from the fuselage. The plane neatly sheared the first few treetops, but as it continued downward the trees bent with the plane absorbing the incoming blow.

Unrestrained by a seat belt and thrown forward by the force of impact, Koler's head struck the firewall, and blood streaming down from a gash on his forehead painted the instruments red. Dazed and confused and hanging by his seatbelt, Johnson accepted that as a good thing. Dead men don't bleed. He absently surveyed the others. They lay misshapen and haphazard, unmoving. There was no sound, no sound at all. Almost straight ahead and straight down, he could see the forest floor, perhaps forty feet below. A branch snapped, and suddenly the ground was coming up to meet him. Something was wrong with that, he knew, but what? Probably if he could just get some rest, his stomach would stop churning, and everything would become clear. He closed his eyes, and slept.

Wearing casual slacks and a ten-dollar shirt, an elderly man sat very still on the soft spongy ground with his right arm outstretched and fist clenched. He was still a relatively strong man, even at near eighty years old, but he knew he couldn't hold his arm steady for more than a few minutes. He wouldn't need to. He already heard his friends approaching. He opened his fist slightly revealing yellow kernels of corn, and a gray animal with a bushy tail climbed up his back and ran along his arm as if he were a tree. It stuck its nose in the tiny space between his thumb and first finger, looking for the meal that was concealed there. Slowly, he lowered his hand to the ground, spilling the grain between his legs. Another gray appeared, made threatening movements toward the first, and the first retreated a few paces, and waited.

"Don't worry. You'll get your dinner. Not much for a couple grays to eat in a forest of spruce, is there?" he said, and then looked towards a sound in the distance. "Not much longer now."

There had been a time in his youth when he would have immediately concealed himself from a low-flying aircraft, but after the many intervening years, it simply didn't matter any more. Still the sounds of war echoing in his head were impossible to forget. The engine noise stopped abruptly and he glanced back at his friends, as close to real friends as he had anywhere. Then there was a sound like the wind through the wings of an eagle gliding overhead, and it grew in intensity. Suddenly, he heard evergreen treetops shattering, and broken limbs raining to the earth. After a brief walk in the direction of the accident, he came upon the green monster that hung suspended in the forest canopy. Suddenly, more branches snapped, and the aircraft continued straight down colliding nose first on the earth. After the brief wait they'd come to him at last, right where they were supposed to be.

Chapter 10

Jonathan Wrightham and Alfred sat at a plain yellow pine desk in a drab dormitory room at the place called the Retreat. The walls had once been a lighter shade of green, but had faded into a chipped and peeling yellow. Together, they watched recorded events unfold on the laptop view screen before them.

"Just fast forward to the last couple minutes. That's all that concerns me."

"I have viewed the entire recording. There appear to have been no survivors."

"I will verify with my own eyes if you don't mind."

"Very well." The thin man with the round face scrolled forward until the embedded clock said thirty minutes. "This should do it, sir. The cameras failed at the thirty three minute mark." The action was frozen, waiting for Alfred to engage the program.

"There is only one image? What happened to the other three cameras?"

"No signal. I don't know why. They quit half way into the flight. This one is from the firewall looking back at the occupants. You will notice the pilot is fully awake and attempting to regain control of the aircraft."

"An unexpected development. Proceed."

The images on the screen suddenly came to life. Most of the camera view was of the pilot, with only unrecognizable parts of two other passengers visible. The Pilots lips were moving, but there was no sound.

"It would have been nice to have audio."

"Unnecessary. As you'll soon see."

The pilot suddenly lurched forward striking his forehead just inches above the camera aperture. For a moment a convoluted mouth completely filled the view screen. He slumped to one side and the image filled with the contorted forms of human bodies. None appeared animate. The image suddenly shook, the pilot's face again fell over the aperture, and then the picture grew dark, as if a shade had been pulled over it. Another few seconds, and static filled the screen.

"Looks pretty conclusive," the man agreed. "Anything from the forward navigation camera?"

"It went out as soon as the nose hit the ground. They came straight down in evergreen trees."

"Did you get a fix on the location?"

"Yes. An exact fix. Well within the target zone. Are you going to verify?"

"No hurry. In a day or two we'll swing by with the chopper. I assume the dark matter that blotted out the screen just before the end was blood from the pilot."

"Most likely." Alfred hesitated. "What about Mrs. Wrightham?"

"I've known she was a traitor for nearly a year, and then when I saw her and Johnson together, I knew it was time to end our relationship."

"Yet, by some stroke of luck she didn't end up with the others. Perhaps it is best for now."

"The hired help mistook Bergen for her. At first I was mad as hell, but then I realized Bergen knew too much anyway. I'll have to deal with Sharon in other ways."

Alfred nodded, and watched as Jonathan Wrightham stood up and left the room, leaving him alone with his thoughts. He had done something he had never done before, withheld information from Jonathan

Wrightham. He had taken action to conceal the true outcome of the accident, deliberately deleted the data from the other three onboard cameras. He had been completely loyal to the present Wrightham family, but that was secondary to the promise he'd made to protect the Wrightham fortune. Jonathan was just too reckless, and it appeared as though he was going to have to use his own judgment once more. He felt sorry for Sharon, Mrs. Wrightham, and made a mental decision to do what he could while he could. Soon she would discover her own sister had been among the victims of a plane crash, but he knew the time would come when he'd have to set his personal feelings aside.

The door opened and the tall blonde expected to see her husband coming back, but instead it was her guard. His demeanor exuded malevolence, and she had quickly made it a point never to be alone with him. This time, however, she was caught, as he closed the door behind him. His face, really his entire hairless skull, looked like it had been chiseled from stone, and seemed always set in an unreadable expression. His slightly large ears matched his face perfectly, but she shuddered when she looked at the one with a notch. His face was not an ugly face by any means, and she wondered what he would look like if he ever smiled. Probably his face would crack. He reached into his suit pocket, clearly grasped something, and walked steadily towards her. She didn't know whether to scream or run, but, in fact, could do neither as fear muted her tongue and kept her rooted firmly to the chair.

"In less than five minutes, you're going to receive a phone call from a man whom you do not know," he said in a flat, monotone voice. "That will give you some time to collect your thoughts." He removed a cell phone from his pocket and placed it next to her on a kitchen table that should have been firewood long before.

"My thoughts? What does the man want?"

"It is not my business to interfere in his business."

The admission was ludicrous, as Mr. Bell seemed fully capable of interfering in whomever's business he chose.

"A hint would be helpful."

"I can only tell you this. It would be wise to pay very close attention to whatever he has to say. His name is Mr. Parish."

"Thanks for the advice. I think," she said and managed a weak smile. For just a second she thought she saw something else in his eyes, another emotion, maybe just a hint of humor. Perhaps he found it entertaining to frighten the hell out of people. She decided to take a very dangerous chance, and stood to face him, straightening the folds in her blue jump suit with her hands. She turned slightly sideways, and put on her most seductive smile. Her long blonde hair fell in a wild jumbled mass upon her shoulders.

"I don't suppose there is anything I could do for you. I mean something that would get you to, well, leave your post for a few minutes so I might leave? Really, anything at all."

Briefly, a broad smile turned Bell's lips, and then his rock-like face crumbled into one of thoughtful understanding. The transformation was shocking, as, momentarily, he looked like a totally different person. From head to toe, his eyes traced her well-proportioned youthful body. A forced look of indifference quickly replaced the brief smile. "A most tempting offer, ma'am, but I think not," he said. "I'll just wait by the door should you need anything." He moved to stand at the entrance, then turned to face her, his stone face reset. Embarrassed, she nodded politely and attempted a smile. Her husband had picked the right man to watch her. Someone who would not bend to temptation.

Since early morning Jonathan had been overly friendly, even promising to let her leave as soon as some exercise was behind him. Something about unfinished business and an initiation. She, however, was not stupid. He had no intention of letting her walk away with the information she possessed. His hired help kept her a virtual prisoner. It was only a matter of time, she knew, and he would decide to rid himself of her company. However, when she thought about it, two could play that game. The hard blank face of Mr. Bell filled her mind, and when the time came she wondered if his would be the last face she'd ever see.

The sound of the cell phone interrupted her thoughts, and Bell nodded, an unspoken order for her to answer it.

"Hello," she said tentatively. "Mr. Parish?"

"Listen very carefully. I'm going to ask you some questions, you will answer them truthfully and carefully, and then, if your response is satisfactory, we may be able to find some common ground. Do you understand?" The voice on the other end sounded old, yet there was also toughness and resolve.

"I guess."

"My first question seems all too obvious, yet I must ask it. How badly do you want to remain alive?"

Bill Backus gradually awoke from a terrible nightmare, one of falling without end. Now an annoying buzzing sound filled his head, and it felt as though dozens of tiny needles were penetrating his body. Shafts of sunlight filtering through the spruce forest canopy shone directly into his eyes, and he turned his head to one side to avoid the glare. The buzzing and the needles, he quickly determined, was a cloud of mosquitoes foraging on his warm body. There was little he could do but attempt to ignore them. A woman with blonde hair lay unmoving next to him on the ground. He remembered her name. Lynn Bergen. He shook her gently with his right hand, without getting a response. He tried to prop himself up on his elbows, but his left arm collapsed under him, and he nearly passed out from the excruciating pain. A piece of bloody bone protruded from a rip in his shirtsleeve, and he realized with an almost clinical detachment that his arm was severely fractured.

Backus tried desperately to remember just how he had come to be in the depths of a spruce forest. He remembered approaching Lynn Bergen by a green airplane, and he remembered her telling him to mind his own business, and leave her alone. Her face had been distorted with fear, and he had refused to leave. He remembered the man that was with her, or were there two? It was at that point his memory failed.

"Lay back down," a voice instructed. "You have some serious injuries."

"What happened?" He turned to see Charlie Johnson. He seemed to be peering over an obstacle, and it occurred to him it was the body of Lynn Bergen.

"Plane crash."

"Plane...I don't remember...where are we? Is Lynn OK?"

"She's alive, but unconscious."

"Who else?"

"Koler and I, you and Lynn, and one other man were on that plane," Johnson said indicating the wreckage several feet away. The plane sat on it's flattened nose, one wing ripped completely off, doors open. The surrounding trees held the fuselage in a vertical position. "You and Lynn were unconscious when we crashed."

"Unconscious? I don't understand."

"Drugged. It looks like someone didn't want us to survive. We'll discuss it later. You need to take it easy."

"And the rest of you?" Backus persisted, holding his left arm with his right hand. His body ached, but his mind was now clear.

"Koler is still out with a severe blow to the head. I was also unconscious, but seem to be OK with only a headache. I don't know where Ethek is. Maybe still in the aircraft. I haven't had time to look."

"Ethek? Why do I know that name?"

"Maclin Ethek. The former CEO of SciOgen, the corporation that helped fund your Greenland project. He's now wanted for multiple crimes including conspiracy to commit murder."

"I'm confused. Why was he with us?"

"A good question for which I have no answer."

"Also if the plane is over there, how did we get here?"

"Also unknown. Certainly we didn't walk over here. I can't imagine Ethek pulling us over here either. But I may have the answer. I do vaguely remember someone saying something."

"What?"

"I know it sounds crazy but something like, 'I'll help you. Just please don't eat the grays.'"

"Some kind of joke? That makes no sense whatsoever."

"Agreed. However, it does seem to indicate we have a guardian angel." Johnson hesitated and then began to get up. "I better check on Ethek, and then we have to do something about your arm."

Johnson stood, attempted to take a step, and his legs promptly gave way under him. He fell face first into the moss and brown spruce needles on the ground.

"You OK?" Backus asked with concern.

"I think my legs went to sleep. I can't seem to feel anything from my waist down."

On the forceful insistence of Lora Whitney, the Minnesota Civil Air Patrol conducted an extensive search of northern Cass County, and then extended their search outward for a fifty mile radius using the Retreat as the center point. Even though there wasn't any evidence of a crash, no mayday message, and nothing to indicate trouble of any kind, the object of their search was a forest green Piper Tripacer. All airports in the northern half of Minnesota with duty personnel were asked to report the aircraft, should it land. Whitney finally realized the effort was a waste of time. There were dozens of airstrips with no one in charge. There were also acres of fields and miles of back roads where a decent pilot could land a plane unnoticed. None of that was of any consequence, however. Dreadfully clear intuition told her the plane had crashed. After twenty-four hours of an extensive search, the Air Patrol abandoned the effort.

Sitting at her desk in the Emergency Services and Law Enforcement office for Cass County, Whitney reviewed the facts yet again. Charlie

Johnson, and an as yet unidentified woman, took off from a private airstrip at a place known as the Retreat, and promptly disappeared off the face of the earth. Also missing were Jerry Koler, a member of the board of directors for SciOgen Corporation, and Bill Backus, a professor at a local university. She searched her memory of the green aircraft that passed in front of her on the grass runway. She was certain there hadn't been anyone in the pilot's position, unless that person was awfully small, but there could have been others in the plane. An airplane equipped with dual controls, she knew, could be flown from either side, and there may have been someone in the right front seat. That was the only explanation. How else would it get off the ground? When she thought about it, she had to admit the blonde head of hair on Charlie's shoulder had captured her complete attention.

* * * *

Sheriff Forest Bodeman opened the back door to his lakefront home to admit a diminutive African American woman with a briefcase in one hand and a white box in the other. She held the briefcase over her head to ward off marble sized raindrops from an afternoon thundershower. The distance from her car to the back door was only a dozen steps. Still, she entered the house wet and running. Lightning cracked and thunder rattled the windowpanes.

"Thanks," she said, looking up at the huge man who was over a foot taller and two and a half time her weight. "It's not nice out there. Hope the donuts are still dry."

"Donuts?"

"Cop food. At least in my department. I didn't want to come empty handed. You'll notice there are a couple missing. My office in St. Paul is two hundred miles away, and, well, you know." Although her voice sounded good-natured, Sarah Thomson's expression remained serious. The corners of her mouth turned slightly downward giving her a perpetual look of sternness. Her dark hair was tied back in a bun, and she wore a light brown pants suit. "You sure it's OK for me to bunk in with you? With the state facing a billion dollar shortfall, lodging expenses are now considered a frivolous luxury."

"No problem. You can use my daughter's room. She's visiting friends, and won't be back for several days."

"I appreciate it. My presence here isn't going to create a problem for you, is it?"

"What problem?"

"I understand you're up for re-election. A live-in woman at the sheriff's home probably would be headlines in a small town gossip column. It certainly would where I come from."

"Oh that. Forget it. I'll just tell everyone you're my cousin."

"Like that would work. In case you haven't noticed, there is no family resemblance."

"Pardon me for being nosy, but I thought that Thomson was a Scottish name."

"It is."

"Then how…?"

"A couple generations back there was a white guy in the woodpile."

Bodeman gave her a questioning look, then chuckled. "I had that coming. As far as staying here, I don't give a damn what the electorate says. I'm thinking of retiring anyway."

"Really? Why? I've heard nothing but good things about you."

"Let's just say the list is long."

Bodeman led her into the dining room, where a young woman in a deputy uniform sat at the table sipping black coffee. Dr. Thomson nodded a hello to Lora Whitney.

"What do you have for us?" Bodeman asked.

"A very nice looking lady," Thomson said as she extracted several eight by ten pictures from her briefcase, which also contained a laptop computer. "I could have emailed these to your office, but decided that since I will be meeting with the rest of your people tomorrow, I might just as well deliver them personally." She laid the photographs on the table side by side. "Using the skull as a base we used a computer program to digitally overlay the consecutive layers of tissue," Thomson explained. "We also had our sculptor do basically the same thing manually with clay. I prefer to use real photographs of our sculptor's finished product. Better resolution, and there is something to be said for the artist's touch, although in this case artist and technology came up with virtually the same finished product. We can, therefore, be reasonably confident that this is what the bog lady looked like while alive." Bodeman gazed down at the pictures and Whitney came around to get a better look. "Recognize her?" Thomson asked.

"Can't say as I do," Bodeman said. "What about you Whitney?"

"She does look familiar. You sure about the hair color?"

"I'm afraid not. The tiny sample we examined was definitely hair, but the most we can say is that it was very fine in texture. We're reasonably confident it was human hair, but couldn't even be one hundred percent sure on that. It literally fell apart, almost as if it had been exposed to some type of chemical. We're still working on that. We're also trying to get a DNA profile, but that will take a while. Since we really couldn't say for sure about the color, we gave her a nice light brown. What do you think?"

Whitney studied the pictures. It was of a face molded out of sculptor's clay onto the human skull found in the bog. It was almost lifelike, but had the blank look of the dead. It was sad and disturbing to realize that the skull, and the other bones secured from the bog, had once been the framework for a living, breathing woman. "You have something?" Bodeman asked.

"I have definitely seen this face before," Whitney said matter-of-factly. "And recently."

"You sure?"

"Positive. Probably within the last year or so. I'd swear to it."

"I don't think so," Thomson interjected. "More likely someone who just resembles her. Our analysis suggests these remains are at least ten years old."

"Are *you* sure?"

"About ninety percent. Believe me, in the cold water where we found her, her remains would have been totally, well, different after only one year. There would have been remnants of soft tissue, primarily cartilage, probably even some bone marrow, and a lot more hair."

Whitney felt a shiver go up her spine. "I'm not disputing your work. I just know what I know. Call it a gut feeling."

"I think some of Charlie Johnson is starting to rub off on you," Bodeman said, intending the statement as a joke. Whitney didn't smile, and Bodeman immediately regretted his words. "Sorry," he said. "Charlie was…is…."

"I heard about the missing plane," Thomson said. "Friends of yours?"

"I think it crashed," Whitney stated firmly. "But I can't seem to get anyone else," and she looked directly at Bodeman, "to take me seriously." Two tears formed in the corners of her eyes. She quickly glanced to one side, brushing them away. "I don't know what's wrong with me lately. I don't usually get weepy."

"More than friends, I take it," Thomson surmised. "What's the story?"

"Whitney believes—and I'm not trying to make light of her account—that an unpiloted green Piper Tripacer took off from a private air strip with her friend Charlie Johnson and a blonde woman on board. Coincidentally, two other people disappeared the same day from the same location."

"I don't believe in coincidence," Whitney nearly shouted.

"Nor do I," a voice answered from the direction of the front door. "Pardon the intrusion. I'm looking for Sheriff Forrest Bodeman. I assume that is you, sir."

Bodeman turned towards the intruder. "Don't you believe in knocking?" he started to say, but stopped short. "Sorry Father. What can I do for you?" The man was dressed in blue jeans and a blue denim long sleeved work shirt, covered with a gray rain jacket. Long brown hair combed back covered his ears, and he wore wire-rimmed spectacles. The white collar around his neck betrayed his vocation.

"Name's Mike Malley," the man said as he slid his rain jacket from his shoulders.

"Well Father Malley…"

"Please, just Mike." He turned to Whitney. "I recognize you from the Retreat. You were one of the officers on duty."

"I'm Lora Whitney. And this is Doctor Sarah Thomson, from the Bureau of Criminal Apprehension."

"How may we help you?" Bodeman asked. As he spoke, Thomson gathered up the pictures of the dead woman into a single pile.

"I've been following the news reports on the missing plane. I went to your office, but they said you were here. I thought I might be able to help you."

"How?"

"I saw it take off."

"So did Whitney. She seems to think no one was flying it."

"There were at least two people on board."

"We know that," Whitney interrupted impatiently. "Charlie Johnson and a woman. Probably Sharon Wrightham, but I have not been able to confirm that."

"A woman, yes, but the man was Bill Backus."

"I distinctly saw Charlie sitting in the rear seat. Of that much I'm certain."

"The back seat? That explains it. Mr. Backus and I had just concluded a conversation when he went to talk to the Reverend James. I was thinking about our conversation and absently followed his movements. He spoke briefly with James and then walked hurriedly over to the green airplane. I saw both Bill and the woman get in. Well, actually they were helped in. There was a man with the woman, and then another man showed up as soon as Backus joined them. From the way the men carried themselves and were dressed, I remember thinking they looked like FBI agents. The woman seemed to trip or maybe faint, I remember, and then one man helped her up in the plane."

"And Backus?" Whitney asked.

"After the woman was in, the two men and Backus walked around to the other side."

"Was he also helped in?"

"I can't be sure. Now that you mention it, it does seem suspicious. However, the plane was facing away from me and most of it blocked my view of the men. I lost interest and shifted my focus to people watching. However, not long afterwards, I'd say maybe fifteen minutes, the plane started up and took off."

"That explains what happened to Backus," Bodeman said.

"How much do you want to bet Jerry Koler was on that plane, too?" Whitney interjected.

"I'm not following your reasoning."

"Charlie Johnson, Jerry Koler on a doomed..." Whitney began, but Bodeman rolled his eyes. "Hear me out," she continued. "Who was directly responsible for exposing Ethek last year? Charlie and Jerry. Both on an airplane..."

"We don't know Koler was on that airplane."

"...with no one at the controls!"

"What are you suggesting?"

"Revenge. Rumor had it Ethek swore he'd get even. The cops never caught him, and he's still at large."

"Let me get this straight. You think Ethek somehow placed Charlie and Koler on that airplane, an airplane that managed to take off by itself, in order to deliberately crash it? Do you know how farfetched that sounds? Just how would he go about it? And who was the blonde woman, the stewardess? What was Backus doing on board? He had no connection to the Ethek case. A Tripacer isn't exactly an airliner. I don't even know if you could get all those people to fit in it."

"I admit some of it doesn't make sense."

"And don't you think they'd put up some resistance? I can't imagine Charlie going quietly into the night."

"I don't know. Maybe they were drugged somehow. Mike did say the woman had to be helped into the airplane."

"You're trying to build a case out of nothing."

"Well, where is the damn airplane!" Whitney shouted at her boss.

Bodeman threw up his hands, and shouted back. "I don't know!"

Mike Malley had listened silently to the exchange. "I'm on Miss Whitney's side on this one. What can it hurt," he suggested quietly, "to assume she is correct? That the plane was deliberately sabotaged."

Bodeman hesitated, and then nodded. "Sorry Lora. I didn't mean to yell. I want to find Charlie too." He waited expectantly for a few seconds. "Now this is the part where you're supposed to say you're sorry."

"I may have some of the details mixed up, but this whole thing is clearly wrong. And every second we stand here wasting time over apologies could be spent trying to find that missing plane. I'm sorry, Sheriff, but I can't be sorry for trying to get the lead out of everyone's ass!"

Whitney braced herself for a sharp rebuke, but Bodeman merely grinned. "I knew you would be trouble the moment I hired you."

He walked into the kitchen, extracted a folded piece of paper from a drawer filled with assorted hand tools and hardware, and then spread out the map of Minnesota on the dining room table. He looked at it carefully for a few moments, and then put his finger directly on the location of the Retreat. He turned to Malley. "To the best of your recollection, what direction did the plane go after it left the runway?"

"After it was airborne? I really don't know for sure. North I'd guess."

"And you Whitney?"

"The runway was to the northwest, but after the plane was out of sight…west maybe…"

"Definitely north," Malley added. "I'd swear to it."

"Whitney?" Bodeman asked.

"Could have been."

"If you wanted an airplane to disappear up here," Thomson asked, "where would you want it to come down?"

"A lake, maybe. Both Upper and Lower Red Lake are in a somewhat northerly direction, along with many smaller ones. But the plane was a classic fabric covered Tripacer. Unless it came straight down, it would take quite a while for it to sink entirely, and even then some of the pieces would probably float."

"The forest?"

"More likely, simply because there's a lot more of it. Millions of acres. The Civil Air Patrol did an extensive search of the immediate area and found nothing. Frankly, that didn't surprise me. If the plane did crash, it will most likely be found after the leaves drop this fall. More than once a grouse or deer hunter has stumbled onto more than he bargained for."

"All aircraft are supposed to carry an emergency beacon," Thomson observed.

"That's right!" Whitney shouted yet again. "An Emergency Locator Transmitter. That would be the first thing whoever set this up would remove beforehand so the plane couldn't be found."

"Or it simply hasn't been activated," Bodeman added, "for whatever reason, and maybe there wasn't any reason to activate it."

"If we assume the plane did turn north as Father Malley suggests, what type of terrain would it be flying over?" Thomson asked.

"Take a look," Bodeman said, pointing to the map. "Except for an occasional farm and lakeside cabin, there's pretty much nothing but woods, lakes, and bogs all the way to the Canadian border. Hell, all the way to the north pole."

Whitney came to a decision. "Sheriff," she said firmly. "I want to be re-assigned to the missing plane case. If you won't do that, then I am requesting two weeks of vacation immediately. If you won't do that, then I will resign from my position."

"Whoa!" Bodeman cut in. "I suppose it wouldn't do any good to remind you that it's not a good idea to become emotionally involved in an investigation." Whitney simply folded her arms across her chest and shook her head. "I didn't think so. Better that you keep the uniform on instead of free-lancing all over the state. What do you want to do?"

"Hire a local pilot familiar with the area, and search a northerly sector with the Retreat as the starting point. I realize some of the area has already been searched, but I'd continue where the Air Patrol left off. Another pair of eyes can't hurt. While I'm doing that, you need to determine who was likely on board. See if anyone else is missing with connections to Ethek. I've tried to locate Sharon Wrightham with no success, which only strengthens my belief she was on Charlie's...was on the plane. We also need to determine if it's possible for a plane to take off and fly without a pilot."

"I can answer the last part," Thomson offered. "The answer is an unqualified yes. The military has been doing it for years with drones. The pilot sits behind the controls on the ground or in another aircraft and is linked remotely to the drone. It can even be done entirely without a pilot with the right computer program. With the right equipment, it would be a simple matter."

"A simple matter?" Bodeman asked skeptically.

"At least taking off and flying would be simple, as long as there's a line of sight connection."

"Line of sight?"

"Unless they're using satellites, there can be no major obstacles between the controller and the aircraft, at least during the takeoff phase."

"What about the satellite link?"

"Once in the air that would be fine, but not during take-off, where every moment is critical for a small conventional aircraft. Using satellites to forward take-off instructions would create an unacceptable time delay. You've probably noticed this delay on CNN when the anchor speaks with a correspondent in another part of the world. They're bouncing their conversation off a satellite, and that takes a while. Having said that, however, large commercial carriers do have computer guided take-off, approach, and landing programs, directed primarily by GPS location sensors. But I can't imagine anyone putting that much sophistication into a fifty year old private aircraft."

"So you're saying whoever controlled the aircraft was probably able to see it at least until it was airborne?"

"Not necessarily with his own eyes, but there was more than likely a line of sight connection between his equipment and the airplane. After take-off it could have been controlled via satellite, a computer program, or even by some sort of old-style automatic pilot. However, there would be a problem."

"What problem?"

"Taking off and in-air maneuvering is a cinch to handle without a pilot. Landing an airplane remotely, hands off as they say, is the real challenge. If the military loses a drone here and there, it's no big deal. There are no lives at stake. With a civilian aircraft it's a different story. That's why we have pilots. To deal with unexpected air turbulence, and the myriad other problems that are impossible to predict. To make sure the plane gets back down in one piece."

"If I'm right," Whitney said, "then getting the plane down in one piece is the last thing someone wanted to do." She turned to Bodeman. "I know there could be other explanations, but can't you see how this all fits? What can it hurt to try to find the truth?"

"If you don't mind me butting in," Malley said, "I'm still with Miss Whitney on this one."

Bodeman considered for only a few moments. "OK, Whitney. I'm putting you in charge of it. You aren't going to be any good for anything else anyway. You will want to contact the FAA investigator out of Duluth and let him know what you're up to. Also touch base with the NTSB. You will keep me informed on a daily basis as to your whereabouts and intentions."

"Is that it?"

"Except for a piece of advice."

"Yes?"

"Approach this investigation with an open mind."

"What do you mean. I am."

"You've already decided Ethek is the guilty party. While he may well be, don't get obsessed with proving him guilty. Let the chips fall where they may. The answer to this is probably something no one has thought of."

Whitney nodded. "Be logical."

"Exactly. Like our good friend Charlie Johnson."

"Mind if I tag along?" Malley asked. "Having met Bill Backus, I feel somehow connected to all this."

Whitney looked to Bodeman who merely shrugged. "It's your case. It's up to you."

"Sure, why not."

"Do you have a pilot in mind?" Malley asked.

"There's a semi-retired man I know who hangs out at the Aitkin airport who is excellent, and works cheap. Gene Turk, but everyone calls him Lucky."

"A pilot called Lucky? Is it too late to withdraw my offer to help?"

"I know for a fact he can fly an airplane in his sleep."

"Is he that good or that old?"

"That good. I'll contact him and see if he can work out of the Remer airport for a few days since it's a lot closer to the Retreat. If this storm moves through and he isn't busy, I can get him up here in an hour. Are you up for some flying?"

"You don't waste time, do you, but sure."

"We should be able to make one trip to the Canadian border and back before dark."

"Just one more thing, Whitney," Bodeman said, as he handed her a picture of the dead woman. "You will also need to be available in case something turns up on the bog lady, even though it is a separate case. Show this photo around. See if you can get a hit. Are you OK with this?"

"Yes sir," Whitney stated, as she folded the picture in half and placed it in an inside pocket of her deputy jacket. "And Sheriff?"

"Now what?"

"I just want to say I'm sorry for yelling at you."

"Apology accepted. But now I'm thinking Sheriff Whitney has a nice ring to it."

Mike Malley looked confused. "I must have missed something," he said. "Who's the bog lady?"

Chapter 11

Charlie Johnson sat with his back up against a windfall and considered their situation. They were into the third day of their exile, and food in the form of whole wheat bread, peanut butter, and fresh water had miraculously appeared at night to keep them going. They had immediately built a signal fire, but had generally been in mental shock the first day. It was on the third that it finally registered in Johnson's mind that these people expected him to lead them to safety. As a woodsman, he was their logical choice. If only he could walk more than a few paces without falling on his nose. Yet, he knew it was time to try to determine where they were and seek help. From the rising sun, the cardinal directions were easy enough to determine, but which way to go was the problem. The lack of human-made noises, traffic and the like, indicated they were far from any road or community. Still, deeply imbedded in the natural noises of a forest night, there had been the hint of something alien, possibly a vehicle on a distant highway.

Johnson decided it was time to stop feeding the mosquitoes. If they couldn't walk out under their own power, which was becoming increasingly likely, then they'd have to find a way to get someone's attention. The signal fire had been the logical solution, but he was beginning to realize unless it was very large, it would most likely be ignored by anyone searching for them. Campfires and the accompanying wood smoke were not an uncommon occurrence in the north woods.

He breathed a sigh of relief at his own condition. A pronounced tingling permeated his right leg, which meant permanent paralysis was unlikely. Probably just a pinched nerve. Feeling was definitely coming back, and he wiggled his toes. His left leg, however, still felt like an attached piece of cordwood. He wasn't going to be sprinting any time soon.

Off to his left, Backus sat with his back against the scaly bark of a black spruce. The blonde woman, who Backus had said was his colleague, Lynn Bergen, was re-wrapping his broken arm with strips of the fabric cut from the crashed plane. With Jerry Koler's help, she had begun immediately to set his arm as soon as she regained consciousness and understood the situation, but there was something odd about their interaction. In the three days since the crash, Backus and Bergen hadn't said a word directly to each other; in fact, they refused to even look at each other.

Bergen had come through the crash injury free, and had, apparently, been in the drug-induced state through the entire ordeal. Maclin Ethek had disappeared immediately, but it was too much to hope for that he would actually be seeking help. It was also doubtful he knew anything about navigating through the woods. Koler, with a piece of white cloth circling his forehead, was rummaging through the crumpled remains of the airplane, studying a particular piece, discarding it, and moving on to something else. For the last two days he had been over every inch of what was left of the aircraft a dozen times.

Two plump grays had appeared from time to time, and seemed totally unafraid of them, and their antics provided some comic relief. Their mysterious benefactor, however, had not appeared, although Johnson knew exactly where the person was standing. He, if it was a he, hung back in the shadows, and even though they had called to him on several occasions, he refused to come any closer. When Koler had walked towards him, he simply disappeared into the undergrowth. If it hadn't been for the food the recluse provided, it would have been easy to conclude this man didn't have their best interests at heart. Koler abruptly discontinued his investigation and walked over to join him.

"How you doing?" Koler asked.

"I'll live. Starting to get feeling back. Probably just a pinched nerve."

"Or a cracked spine?"

"I don't think so."

"Still, stay put for a while."

"And you?"

"Other than a couple fainting spells, I feel…terrible," he admitted. "At least now there are no longer two of everything."

"When you have a minute, see if you can find some kind of forked stick for a crutch. We've laid around long enough. Time to start figuring out how to get help. We can't continue to count on the nightly manna from heaven to keep us going."

"What about the signal fire? Eventually someone has to see it."

"Probably lots of folks have already seen it. The trouble is wood smoke is not an oddity in Northern Minnesota. Thankfully, the weather has been good, but that could change at any time. Looks like some rough weather to the south of us right now. Did you find anything over there?"

"It's what I didn't find. I've searched everywhere in a hundred foot radius. No ELT."

"ELT?"

"Emergency transmitter in case of an accident. Once activated it would have sent out a signal that would have pinpointed our exact location. However, it just isn't there."

"After what we've been through, that's no surprise. Anything else?"

"A lot of my blood all over the firewall, and something else that's most interesting. A transceiver of distinctly modern design, which seems to be tied into the aircraft control surfaces."

"Which means?"

"Someone was pulling our strings as we suspected. I can't imagine it was Ethek since he went down with us, but someone with a lot of technical knowledge, and access to a ton of money. The aileron control was definitely sabotaged. Someone wanted to make sure we weren't going to make it. Also, I found a smashed video surveillance camera mounted in the firewall. There may be others. Someone not only wanted us to crash, but also watch it happen."

Johnson decided he had been keeping a concern to himself long enough. "You hear about the kidnapped girl?"

"Sure. It made all the Twin City stations. Even saw where they tried to interview you. Seems like you kept deferring to Sheriff Bodeman."

"Figured he needed the publicity more than I did. Hopefully, he'll forgive me for that eventually. Anyway, whoever set it up had video cameras mounted in the hunter's cabin so they could watch the final execution."

"Pretty sick. To harm an innocent girl…"

"She was just the bait. Apparently, I was the intended victim."

"You sure?"

"Not at first, but afterwards I received a warning from an unknown admirer, who made it pretty plain that the game was still ongoing."

"Game?"

"To someone, all this is just a contest of sorts. I was reasonably sure it was Ethek. Me against him. Of course, you had been omitted from his Christmas list also, which would explain why you are here. But why Backus and Lynn? And why would Ethek tag along to end up in what he must have known would be a demolished airplane?"

"I can't imagine Ethek being innocent of anything, but maybe…" His voice trailed off as he looked again at the mangled aircraft. "We were extremely lucky. Do you have any idea where we are?" It wasn't the first time he'd asked.

"Not the vaguest idea, but probably the person who's been watching us for the last couple of days can tell us precisely where we are."

"Our guardian angel?"

"Yes, and I know exactly how to get him to reveal himself."

"How?"

"As soon as I can stand up, we're going squirrel hunting."

Bill Backus watched as Lynn Bergen changed the wraps on his broken arm. She and Koler had done a rather crude job of setting the bone, but at least the jagged fracture didn't stick out through the skin anymore. The dull ache seemed to flow from the broken bone to all parts of his body. He could only stand a glance. His arm was hideously discolored and swollen. They had applied what little disinfectant there had been in the medical kit in the plane, but with each passing minute the increasing pain was consuming his mind.

He had a hundred questions to ask Bergen, but remained silent. She'd made it clear that whatever was going on was none of his business. Although he felt that crashing together in a single engine aircraft clearly made it his business, he decided to wait until she was ready to talk. He was tired of the taste of his own foot in his mouth.

"This won't do," Bergen said suddenly.

"Pardon me?"

"Your arm. I've done a poor job. It's badly swollen, and black and blue. You need to get it set right by a doctor, and soon. There's a good chance of infection."

For the moment, however, Backus wasn't thinking about his arm. "Maybe I'm just an old fool," he said looking directly at her, "but I thought we were friends."

"What?"

"Your correspondence was a godsend when I was in Greenland. I anticipated and relished your cheerful notes every day. It reached the point, as I read the words, I could actually hear your voice. I really thought we had connected on some meaningful level. While I never expected, or even hoped, for more than friendship, your actions were…upsetting."

"The notebook? I had to do what I had to do. I don't owe you an explanation. I tried to keep you out of this, but you couldn't listen."

"Mind my own damn business?"

"Yes."

"What's this all about? Why are we all here?" Backus asked directly.

"I don't know what you're talking about."

"I'm asking you, as a friend, to tell me the truth. I know you know."

"It's all a big mistake." Lynn said, and her attitude cracked just a bit.

Backus realized the time for politeness was over. He rose unsteadily to a standing position, took her by the arm, and led her over to where Johnson and Koler were talking.

"It's time for a little soul searching," Backus said sharply. "And I think Lynn should go first." He released the grip on her arm, a grip that had been as much to keep himself from falling over as is was to direct her to the others. "Now please tell us in your own words, what the devil is going on."

"We were in an airplane and it crashed."

"You know what I mean. Someone tried to kill us all."

"Nobody wanted to kill you. You just couldn't mind your own business. I was the only one who was supposed to die."

"What about Charlie and me?" Koler asked.

"I don't know anything about you."

"Who's responsible?"

Bergen remained stubbornly silent.

"Why were you supposed to die?" Backus persisted.

"I know things. No one said anything to me directly. I just overheard a conversation."

"You're not making the smallest amount of sense," Backus stated. "How come only you were supposed to die? You sound like you volunteered to be some sort of sacrificial lamb."

"Don't you see? I traded my life for another life. Someone they can hurt. Only they lied. They said the rest of you would be left out of it. Just scared somehow."

"Don't *you* see? We were all supposed to die. Even Ethek. You have to tell us all you know."

Lynn Bergen struggled to understand how events had placed them all together. It wasn't supposed to happen this way. But, she realized, her executioners probably thought she was dead, and, therefore, at least one person was safe.

"My sister," she said finally. "I went for my sister."

"Who's your sister?" Johnson asked, and suddenly realized what the answer would be.

"Sharon Wrightham," Lynn said quietly.

"And her husband, Jonathan Wrightham, is somehow mixed up in this," Johnson guessed.

"What did you overhear?" Backus pressed. "What happened? If what you say is true, your sister is still in grave danger. Maybe we can help, somehow."

Bergen suddenly caved in to the pressure, and the release felt good. "Jonathan had Sharon fly in from California after he arrived at the Retreat."

"Hold it. Fly in?"

"You remember the black expensive looking helicopter parked near the end of the runway. That belongs to Jonathan Wrightham. Sharon came with Alfred, their family servant."

"OK, continue."

"She called me before she left and we managed to get together in one of the dorm rooms just before your discussion with Reverend James. I overheard Jonathan talking to men next door as I was leaving. He said he needed to get rid of someone. Said she was expendable and replaceable. When he began to describe the woman to the men, I realized he was talking about Sharon, and also realized they had never met her. Later they mistook me for her, since we do look a lot alike."

"So you went along with them to save your sister?"

"Yes."

"Knowing you might end up dead?"

"Yes."

"You're lying," Backus stated firmly.

"It's all true."

"You know they could still eliminate her."

"I'm hoping she'll be able to get as far away as possible."

"Backing up a bit, who hired you to keep the diary of our conversations when I was in Greenland?"

"Nobody…"

"The truth!" Backus shouted. Koler put his hand on his shoulder to calm him down. "The truth," he repeated quietly, almost pleadingly.

"Jonathan Wrightham," she confessed.

"Why?"

"He said he wanted to know what kind of man you were. Where your weaknesses might be. How you thought."

"I meant why would you do that to me?"

"He threatened my sister. I had to do it to protect her."

"You must really love her."

"More than that. I need her. The two of us are the last of our family line."

"I know this," Johnson said changing the subject. "Koler has a severe head injury and can't take more than a few steps without getting dizzy, I figure I can barely hobble along with a crutch, Backus is on the verge of gangrene, and Ethek is long gone. The only completely healthy person among us is Lynn. She might just be our only choice."

"Choice for what?" Backus asked.

"Survival."

The low winged Piper Cherokee rolled to a stop in front of the single gas pump at the end of the three thousand foot grass runway, just north of the small village of Remer. The passenger side door—the only door in the airplane—opened, and a man immerged, yawning. Lora Whitney and Mike Malley, each carrying a pair of binoculars, walked over from the parked squad car.

"Hi, Gene," Whitney said, as the man jumped down from the wing step. Of average height and build, the sixty-year-old man was surprisingly agile. A full mustache completely covered his upper lip, and his tanned face was creased with smile lines. He wore the old style black aviator's pants, with a brown leather jacket. He took off his army hat, and ran his hand over his salt and pepper crew cut hair.

"Hi Lora. Nothing new on the lost plane, I take it."

"Nothing. Glad you could make it. Are you up to a trip to the Canadian border and back before dark?"

"No problem. Weather's cleared up nicely. Who's your sidekick?"

"This is Mike Malley. Father Malley actually. Another pair of eyes."

"Just Mike," Malley said. "I have to ask. Can you really fly an airplane in your sleep?"

"Managed to get a nice half hour nap on the way up here."

"You're kidding."

"Never."

"You must have automatic pilot."

"In this old girl? Not likely."

"So how?"

"Ten thousand hours."

"I'm not following."

"You'll see." He turned to Whitney. "You want to run some kind of grid, or just wing it? Just so you know. I forgot to bring the GPS receiver."

"Just wing it this first time. We're looking for a green Piper Tripacer or possibly some sort of signal. Maybe a fire. We'll head north from the Retreat, and investigate anything that catches our eye."

"Best you sit up front with me. You'll have a good view over the wing."

"I'm looking at three hours in the air on the first go. Keep track of your time. If I can't get the county to kick in, I'll pay you out of my own pocket."

"Half the people I know owe me money. Why should you be any different?"

The Retreat compound was completely empty except for a sleek looking helicopter that, with its shiny black color, could have come right from the set of *Airwolf*. A tall muscular man with bare arms leaned up against it. A short pencil thin mustache adorned his upper lip. He had discarded his suit in favor of a tight fitting gray shirt and combat fatigues. He had thought his job over, had been ready to leave with his partner, when Wrightham offered him another five thousand for a couple hours work. He'd said his regular help, a Mr. Bell, had left several hours before without so much as a good-by. If Wrightham was willing to give money away, he was very willing to take it. Several people approached from the direction of the dormitories. He recognized Jonathan Wrightham and his wife, their manservant, and Luke James.

"Have you entered the co-ordinates, Mr....?" Wrightham began.

"Smith."

"Yes, Smith. Why do I keep forgetting?"

"Course plotted and laid in, sir."

"We'll let Alfred take the stick. He's very capable. You fly backup and man communications and navigation. Can you handle that?"

"No problem."

"The rest of us will buckle up in the back."

Smith took Sharon by the arm, squeezing it hard. She looked up at his unreadable expression. It did nothing to comfort her.

"Why am I here?" James asked, somewhat confused. "I was all packed for Bismarck."

"We're out for a little bonding experience," Wrightham explained. "Something that will tie us all neatly together, should anyone decide to get righteous."

"I don't know if I can do this."

"Of course you can. Get in," Wrightham ordered.

"I have trouble with enclosed spaces. I get sick."

"No problem. We'll leave the door open," Wrightham laughed. "I'm afraid your only other alternative would be a most unpleasant encounter with Mr. Smith."

James quickly glanced at Smith, and he felt his knees grow weak. The man was like ice, with not so much as a shred of projected feeling. He looked even more menacing than Mr. Bell.

"But…"

Smith took a step toward him.

"Where are we going?" James added hastily, and took a step toward the helicopter.

"To see the fruits of our labor," Wrightham said.

From the moment the Piper Cherokee reached level flight at three thousand feet, Gene Turk rested his head up against the side window, and closed his eyes. His feet rested on the rudder pedals, and his left hand lightly gripped the yoke, but by all appearance he was fast asleep. Sitting in the back seat, Mike Malley tapped Whitney on the shoulder. "Is this safe? I mean, look at the man. Maybe he died." To avoid having to shout above the normal aircraft operational noise, Turk had provided each with headphones and voice-activated mics.

"Not dead dead, but definitely dead to the world. Not necessarily FAA approved but, yes, it's safe, as long as we keep our eyes open for other aircraft. It'll take about fifteen minutes to get over the Retreat. I promised to wake him then. Don't worry. I have control."

The distinct and steady noise of the engine and prop filled the interior of the cabin, and produced a measure of confidence in the occupants of the aircraft. The familiar and comforting sound rapidly becomes an ingrained part of every pilot, a sound that is so well known that even a minute variation is immediately noticed. The engine is the heart, beating on with precise regularity, and even one misfire is grounds for immediate concern. The engine in the Piper Cherokee had droned on evenly for several minutes, when Malley again spoke.

"So you're a pilot, too?" he asked.

"Ah, no. But I'm learning, and do know how to keep us straight and level. Not much to it, really. Remember Gene mentioned ten thousand hours?"

"Yes. I didn't catch his meaning."

"That's a very conservative estimate on how much time he's spent in the air as a pilot. Believe me, if this plane so much as twitches in the wrong way, and for whatever reason, he'll compensate immediately. You fly much?"

"Counting this time, once, at least in a single engine plane. The view is really amazing from up here. So many deep blue lakes, winding rivers, and forests of different shades of green."

"Charlie Johnson could tell you what species of trees there are down there just by the color of their leaves. All I know is the lighter greens are usually deciduous and the deeper greens are the usually the coniferous, the evergreens." She searched the area ahead. "Look there," she said pointing. "About two miles ahead just to the right of the nose."

"What am I supposed to see?"

"Two brick buildings in a clearing. The place where we start. The Retreat."

"We have company," Mr. Smith said via his headset to the other occupants of the chopper. "Just came up on the screen. Another aircraft is coming in from the east, slightly behind us."

"What is it?" Alfred asked, from the pilot's position.

"One moment." Mr. Smith keyed in a command on the console. "Configuration confirms it's a low wing single engine aircraft, probably a Piper."

"Destination," Wrightham asked from his place in the back.

"Unknown. At the moment it's heading is 270, and will pass above and to the south of us. Wait a minute. It's turning to straight north." A minute passed as Smith watched the display. "At its current airspeed, about one hundred ten, it will be parallel with us in minutes."

"How far away?"

"Two miles give or take."

"Maybe we should abort," Wrightham suggested.

"I wouldn't," Smith said, thinking that if they did he might not get his full five thousand payment.

"You're the expert. What is your assessment?"

Mr. Smith looked over at Alfred, who nodded back. "We have a ways to go to the target. Nothing we can't handle. I suggest we proceed. We can always do a little misdirecting, if it comes to that."

Gene Turk took over complete control of the Cherokee as soon as they were directly above the Retreat. Whitney and Malley began searching the ground below with their binoculars, and Gene pitched the nose forward slightly, throttled back the engine, and began a slow but steady descent. He leveled off at eight hundred feet, and pointed the plane straight north for the Canadian border. They had searched diligently for several minutes before Whitney spoke.

"The Tripacer was a deep green color, a lot like the evergreens down there," she observed.

"Like looking for a needle in a haystack," Malley realized. "I'm beginning to see why Sheriff Bodeman felt this was a hopeless task. Luckily, I don't believe in hopeless."

"Nor do I," Whitney added.

"Another aircraft," Turk cut in. "On the same heading, maybe a half mile west, and a little above us. Better give him a hello."

Turk unhooked the mic from the firewall, depressed the send button, and spoke slowly and clearly into it. "This is Cherokee Alpha Niner Niner Zebra calling the aircraft flying about thirty miles north of Marion Lake. I'm a half-mile east of you on a similar heading. Do you read? Over."

"We see you. State your business," came the terse reply.

"Search and rescue. We're looking for a downed aircraft."

A long pause followed and then, "We saw smoke in the forest maybe ten miles east of your position. Want us to call it in?"

Turk looked to Whitney for some direction, and she took the mic. "This is Officer Lora Whitney with the Cass County Sheriff's department. Did it look like a signal fire, a crash site, or just someone out camping?"

"It was definitely a big fire, and black, the smoke was black."

"Roger that. We'll check it out. Thanks. If you see anything else, please report it immediately."

"Of course. Out."

"Friendly sort," Whitney said, as she returned the mic to its holder.

"Where to, Boss?" Turk asked.

"Let's have a look. I don't want to leave any obvious stone unturned."

An atmospheric haze formed by water vapor rose from the earth as the afternoon sun began to evaporate moisture from the earlier thundershower. Visibility dropped from unlimited to ten miles, which was still excellent. But something was bothering Gene Turk, and his face twisted in thought, as he banked the plane onto the easterly heading.

"You'd think we'd have seen it," he said finally.

"Seen what?" Whitney asked.

"The smoke."

"What do you mean?"

"Ten miles may seem like a long way, but from three thousand feet and in even these weather conditions, that plume of black smoke should have stood out like a sore thumb. We should have seen it on the way here."

"We weren't looking," Whitney stated, "and you were asleep."

Mr. Smith continued to watch the view screen as the second aircraft began to veer off on the new heading. He keyed in a command and a topographical map appeared. A blinking arrow marked a static point, and a moving arrow marked their position. On the screen the two arrows were separated by the width of a pencil. Alfred eased the chopper down to five hundred feet, and slowed to fifty miles an hour. "Should be just ahead," he said. "Looks like it came down in the trees."

"See anything," Wrightham asked from the back.

"No smoke and no movement on the scope," Smith stated.

"Take us down to tree top level for a visual, Alfred," Wrightham ordered. "I want to verify with my own eyes."

The coordinates provided by the GPS system marked the plane crash with an accuracy of fifteen feet. It was far more accuracy than necessary. The treetops looked like they could have been broken by a strong wind, and it would take someone who knew exactly what to look for to spot the wreckage of the green Tripacer. From overhead, the occupants of the chopper could see the crashed plane, patches of forest floor, and four bodies that appeared to lie lifeless on the moss and needle covered ground.

"Perfect!" Wrightham exclaimed.

"What do mean perfect!" James shouted, and sudden panic turned him cold. "You said you only intended to scare them."

"And that I'm sure I did, at least if they were awake when they hit the ground. As you can clearly see, you are now an accessory. I've made my point. We can go home now Alfred. That is, as long as we're all in agreement. However, if there is someone who has a problem with any of this, they can, well, get out and walk." He waited several seconds for the implications to sink in. Sharon sat rigid in her seat, seething on the inside. Although it was impossible to tell for sure from their altitude, it suddenly occurred to her the woman with blonde hair lying on the ground could be her sister. Another person might be Charlie Johnson. If she spoke up and expressed all that was on her mind, she'd no doubt suffer the same fate. It was only her intense anger that kept her grief in check. The next time she had even the slightest chance she had to get away. Jonathan Wrightham began to laugh, a maniacal sound that gurgled out of his throat. James' face drained of color, he began babbling incoherently, and then wet himself.

Wrightham sat back in his seat confident in his victory. Perhaps old man Parish had been correct. He glanced at Sharon and then James. It was sometimes better to crush people into a usable mold, rather than simply dispose of them. The loose ends were being tied up nicely, he was going to be a US senator, and much more importantly, he would soon be a member of the most powerful family on earth.

Lying on his back on the ground, Charlie Johnson opened his eyes and watched the helicopter that seemed suspended in midair less than a hundred feet directly above him. He was thankful now their signal fire had burned down to coals, and produced no smoke. At first jubilation filled their camp at the sound of the approaching helicopter and possible rescue, but then when a clear view revealed it was as black as night, caution replaced the moment of joy. They had mere seconds to decide what to do, and had prudently decided to play dead. Lynn Bergen quickly identified it as belonging to Jonathan Wrightham, and it became immediately apparent it was not a rescue chopper. After the occupants had finished assessing the situation on the ground, the nose of the chopper pitched forward, it quickly gained airspeed, and slowly the vibrations of the rotor chopping the afternoon air grew faint, until the usual commotion of the forest completely smothered the sound.

Chapter 12

▼

Bill Backus lay very still on the ground. Within just the last hour, it seemed, he felt his condition steadily worsen. His rapidly increasing fever, he knew, was due to infection in the compound fracture of his arm. All normal feeling was lost in the swollen appendage, and yet any accidental bump generated immediate and excruciating pain. His fever-corrupted thoughts were becoming increasingly dreamlike and bizarre, and he fought hard to concentrate. It was only a matter of time before he would lose consciousness, and lapse into delirium. He knew Lynn Bergen was sitting next to him, knew she was talking to him, yet her voice seemed to be moving away, growing faint, and he had not the energy or inclination to respond. His Greenland discovery, he realized, would die with him. Probably, it was just as well.

Koler and Johnson motioned for Lynn to join them, and she left Backus' side.

"Lynn. It's up to you," Johnson said.

"What do you mean?"

"You're the only one who has a chance of getting help. You're going to have to try to make your way out of here. Our lives, certainly Bill's, depend on it."

"I'm not much good in the woods. I get lost easily. Please don't ask me. I have no idea which way to go."

"Neither do I, but we're about to find out."

"How?"

"I set a little trap. Very soon our savior is going to come busting in here to save his friends. He's going to be headed directly for Jerry. It's going to be up to you to make sure he doesn't leave."

"How?"

"Jerry salvaged about ten feet of insulated wire from the wreck. See the end of it near my left foot?"

Bergen looked down and nodded.

"All hell is going to break loose here in just a couple minutes. You have only one job. When I yell 'Now!' grab the loop on the end and pull as hard as you can."

"What do you mean 'All hell is going to break loose?'"

"Don't think. Just do it. No matter what. Trust me. You have to do it. The rest of us are just too unreliable." Johnson looked past her into the forest. "Get ready. Here they come."

From the first sight of the two grays three days before, Johnson knew something other than their natural surroundings must have been keeping them there. Their natural habitat was mature hardwood forests, preferably stands of oak, and although they might occasionally stray into a spruce forest, it was not their preferred habitat. The strange voice that he remembered, the apparent fearlessness of the animals, and their generally rotund shape convinced him these were someone's well-fed pets. Whoever the man was, he would no doubt know where he was, and would know the fastest way to reach a road, farm, or lakeside cabin. Johnson suspected he was a decent person, yet in hiding, some kind of hermit. The whole wheat bread that appeared every morning was evidence of a good man, and yet his refusal to show himself clearly indicated his desire to remain anonymous. That was all about to change. He nodded to Jerry Koler.

"Got 'um!" Koler roared, displaying two gray animals. They looked out from between the wooden bars of a makeshift wooden cage. "Looks like we have supper."

"Don't let them get away. I'll get the knife," Johnson shouted back.

"Sure are fat little buggers," Koler continued, poking at them through the bars with a stick. "Should keep us going for a while."

"Noooo!" a voice wailed, and an elderly gentleman stumbled into the tiny clearing. His deep blue eyes shown from a face twisted in distress. "You can't do that!" He rushed up to Koler and grabbed the wooden cage, just as Koler stepped back.

"Now!" Johnson yelled. "Now! Now!" Lynn Bergen pulled hard on the wire, and a camouflaged loop sprang from the ground encircling the man's legs as he turned to hastily leave. The snare tightened around his ankles, and he fell face first to the ground. The cage flew from his hands and shattered several feet away. The two animals raced to the nearest tree, and disappeared in the dense branches above.

Charlie, Lynn, and Jerry Koler moved to stand in a circle around the fallen man, as he struggled to remove the tightened wire. Lynn knelt down by his side.

"We mean you no harm," she said reassuringly.

"You were going to eat my friends!" The man was clearly distraught, as tears rolled from his eyes. "How could you do that? I asked you not to. I gave you bread and water."

"We would never have harmed your pets," Johnson said. "We just needed to talk to you and this seemed like the only way to get you to show yourself. Please believe me. We desperately need your help."

The man on the ground had expected some attempt at communication, but not this, and not now. It was too early, much to early, to divulge his true identity. A bit of theater was in order.

"I won't go back! You can't make me go back!"

"We won't make you do anything you don't want to do. We just need you to tell us which way is the fastest way to get help." He motioned toward the prone form of Bill Backus. "Our friend is dying.

You're our only hope. If you lay still, Lynn will help you remove the wire. No one is going to hurt you or your friends."

The old man looked at the three faces that surrounded him. "What about the helicopter?"

"It's gone," Charlie confirmed. The old man nodded, and a brief smile crossed his face. Johnson couldn't help but think the man's mind was not altogether intact.

"You're not here to take me back?"

"No. Whatever your secret is, it's safe with us."

"Promise?"

"Promise."

The gray haired old man smiled widely, displaying a mouth full of surprisingly clean teeth, and the two shook hands. "Name's Rolland Woodlove."

"Charlie Johnson."

Bergen removed the wire, and helped Woodlove to his feet.

"Highway six," Woodlove said.

"Where?"

"A mile or two into the rising sun."

"Straight east," Koler said with relief. "That's not all that far."

"Not an easy stretch," Woodlove continued.

"Any floating bog, or streams?"

"Not that way. Mostly swamps, spruce, and rip gut."

"Rip gut?" Koler inquired.

"It's a marsh grass with sharp edges. It can cut exposed flesh," Johnson explained.

"Do you have any idea how far it is to the nearest town?" Koler asked the old man.

"Don't know for sure. I know Big Falls is up the road a ways."

"How can you survive here all alone," Bergen asked, clearly concerned. "I mean, what do you eat? How do you stay warm in the winter?"

"I have a cabin, and I do alright. Best collect my friends now and get going."

"One other thing," Koler said. "There was another man with us when we crashed. A short red haired man. Do you know what happened to him?"

"Hit the ground running."

"What do you mean?"

"Ran off into the woods."

"Was he injured?"

"Limped some, but seemed to get on all right."

"And you pulled the rest of us out of the plane?" Koler continued.

"That I did. Least I could do."

"Thanks for your help," Charlie said shaking the man's hand. "A man's word is an oath. Your secret is safe with us. No one is going to make you go anywhere. However, I'd like to give you my address and phone number. If you should ever decide to leave here, I want you to know I'll be there to help you."

Woodlove stared at the man with the long black hair for several moments. "Thanks but no thanks," he said sincerely. "You're a good one. I'll remember you. Mind if I take a quick look at your injured friend?"

"I suppose it wouldn't hurt," Johnson replied, yet confused as to why he would want to do so. The old man walked over to Backus and knelt down by his side, his back to the others. He briefly placed his hand on Backus' chest.

"So this is the great William Backus," he muttered.

He rose, whistled sharply, and two grays came bounding down a spruce trunk. He turned and disappeared into the forest, his friends following closely behind.

When the old man was out of sight of the others and under cover of the dense forest he stopped and removed a cell phone from the inside pocket of his yellow windbreaker. He punched in a memorized number and waited several seconds.

"Everything is taken care of on this end," he said in perfectly clear and calm tones, and without a hint of mental impairment. "There's a total of four survivors on the ground, including Backus. He's not doing well, and could certainly die. I've done all I dare do under the circumstances. We've already contaminated this project beyond acceptable limits, so we must sit back now, simply let events unfold, and see what happens. Perhaps it is simply not yet time for the world to know."

The occupants of the Piper Cherokee soon realized they had been misled, although the reason for the deception was unknown. Either that or the fire that the other aircraft had reported had been put out. They passed over widely scattered farms and rural homes, dense forests and blue lakes. Long straight lines marked the roads that cut through the greenery. Both Whitney and Malley alternated between searching with and without their binoculars, and both had found no evidence of a fire. After fifteen minutes of a futile search, Gene Turk began to nod in understanding. Whitney broke off her search and looked over at him.

"Looks to me like we've been had, or the fire's been put out," Turk said. "Reach in the side pocket and dig out the map."

"You lost?" Malley asked from the rear seat.

"Not lost. Just don't know where I am."

"There's a difference?"

"The difference is I know which way to go."

"All I can find in here is a regular road map," Whitney said. "Is there supposed to be some kind of aviators map?"

"Nope. Just my IFR map."

"Nothing in here for instrument flight either," Whitney stated, recognizing the abbreviation for Instrument Flight Rules.

"Not instrument flight," Turk laughed. "It's the bush pilot's version. It stands for I Fly Roads. We're northeast of Lake Winnie. That should be Hwy 46 off in the distance to our left. A northwest heading should take us directly to Hwy 71, and almost straight north of the Retreat."

Whitney studied the road map, and nodded. "Who needs GPS navigation?" she said. "However, straight north from the Retreat will take us almost directly over Upper and Lower Red Lake. If they came down in the water…"

"Someone most likely would have seen them. There are always sport fisherman out on Upper, and the folks on the Red Lake Reservation would most likely have spotted it if it came down on Lower. They keep a pretty close eye on their domain. What else is up there?"

"Not much. No roads, other than Hwy 71, and only one river that I can see, the Sturgeon. The area is mostly inside Pine Island State Forest."

"The other aircraft we saw was on that general heading," Turk observed. "Do you suppose there was something there they didn't want us to see? How about we make a loop over the state forest, and come back along Hwy 6? One trip won't make much of a dent in what we need to cover, but it's a start. That'll just about use up the available daylight."

Whitney nodded and looked back at Malley, realizing he had been strangely quiet. He smiled courageously, but his drawn white face betrayed his condition. She looked at Turk. "Mike seems to be a little sick."

"Focus on the distant horizon," Gene advised. "We'll be straight and level for some time. It'll pass. However, if it doesn't there is a cache of plastic bags just under your seat."

"Thanks," Malley said sheepishly. "Sorry about this."

"No apology necessary. Don't let anyone kid you. It happens to everyone on occasion. The biggest, meanest guys barf just like the rest. Can't tell you how many times I've tossed my cookies. My fault. I should have had you take a couple pills beforehand. Just try to relax. Air turbulence will diminish as we get later into the evening." The pep talk was meant to be encouraging, but Turk knew full well that a complete cure for airsickness usually required two feet planted firmly on terra firma.

Johnson leaned his crutch against a tree, steadied himself, took Lynn Bergen by the shoulders, and pointed her straight east. "This is going to be a crash course in how to navigate a straight line in the woods without a compass when the sun is shining," he began. "First decide which way you want to go, in your case east. Then take a minute and memorize your relationship to the sun. Notice it is over your left shoulder. Look at your shadow ahead of you. You'll want to walk just to the left of it to maintain the proper heading. Do you understand?"

"I understand. Make an angle. But what about bears and wolves?"

"What about them?"

"Am I apt to see one?" she asked nervously. "Get…get…"

"Attacked?"

"It could happen," Bergen insisted.

"You have a better chance of being struck by lightning. Deer flies and mosquitoes are a bigger threat." Johnson hesitated, contemplating whether or not he should include an additional piece of information, and then continued. "You may hear a scream."

"A scream?"

"It won't be from a human. But certain wild cats…"

"Mountain lions?"

"Not likely. But bobcats and lynx are common. Don't worry. They won't harm you. However, a wildcat's cry can be quite bone chilling. You probably won't hear one, but I thought I better warn you."

"I know you probably think it's foolish, but I've always had a fear of the woods. I don't know if I can do this."

"At this moment, our survival is in your hands. I can barely walk, Jerry could black out at any time, and Backus is clearly in trouble."

"I know. I know."

"Good. Now walking through a forest with a dense under story is not like a leisurely walk in the park. You're going to encounter a tangled mass of low brush, waist high ferns, swamp grass that can cut your skin like a knife, branches and windfalls. Even though you've only a mile or two to go, it's going to take a while. Maybe over an hour. This is important. Every twenty steps stop and line up with your shadow just as you are now. Look for a tree in the direction you are heading, and walk toward it. Whatever you do, don't panic, or you'll end up walking in circles."

"I don't see how I could."

"As long as you keep a clear head you won't. But I've helped find people that were lost. They often get hysterical, and do very strange things."

"Like what?"

"Like tearing off their clothes. Scream. Inflict pain on themselves. Once I tracked down a lost camper out in Colorado who had left his campsite to gather firewood. When I found him four hours later, his clothes were in shreds, and he still carried an armload of kindling. When he saw me coming, he turned and ran the other way. Later, when he calmed down, he said he thought I was the devil coming to get him."

"My god!"

"Don't worry. You'll do fine. Just remember the simple rule. Every twenty steps verify your heading. When you get to the highway, flag down the first motorist you see."

"What if no one will stop?"

"Do whatever you have to. More than likely we're in Koochiching County. Call 911 immediately. You can do this. Remember, twenty steps. Now get going."

"Twenty steps, twenty steps," Bergen repeated, and headed off into the dense forest.

As Gene Turk predicted, the moderate afternoon air turbulence dissipated as the sun fell towards the western horizon. The clear air couldn't have come any sooner for Mike Malley. He had filled one of the plastic bags with his half-digested lunch and Whitney had suggested they abort the mission. He refused to give in, however, and was now certain it had been the correct decision. Although uncertain for a time, he was now confident he would live. They were approaching the thin blue line on Turks IFR map that represented the Sturgeon River. This was as far north as they would go this day, and Turk began a gentle wide turn to the east. Malley knew it was for his benefit. Several minutes later, they passed over the village of Big Falls, and Turk again initiated a wide turn, this time back to a southerly heading.

Lora Whitney, her earlier enthusiasm defeated, sat back in her seat resigned to the fact that this trip had been a failure. She had to admit to herself she had not fully comprehended the enormity of the task. So much forest, so many lakes, so much of raw nature to cover, and then there was the distinct possibility that they weren't even looking in the right place. Perhaps it was a reaction to Malley's airsickness, but she, too, felt nauseous. Again there was the barely controllable urge to cry. She mentally cursed herself for being weak. What was happening? This was not like her. Her body, her mind, seemed to be turning against her. She looked across at Gene Turk. He was not asleep, and continued to scan the ground below. She looked back over the right wing, and rested her head against the window. It was hopeless. Bodeman had been correct, and it had been as a friend, not as her boss, she suddenly realized that he let her try. Tears began to roll down her cheeks, but she stubbornly refused to let her gaze stray from the green earth that passed under her.

Struggling through the tangle of brush, ferns, and swamp grass was an ordeal by any standards, and fifteen minutes into her journey Lynn Bergen was already lost. Not more than a minute or two before the sun had been over her left shoulder where it was supposed to be, and now it was fully in her face. She was almost ready to believe the sun had somehow moved from its designated celestial place just to confuse her. She tried hard to recall every word of Johnson's crash orienteering course, but all she could remember was something about a man running hysterical and naked through the woods. "Don't panic," he had said, but what else? Something about twenty paces. It had all been so clear, but now the trees were closing in on her, blocking her thoughts.

Very close, an animal snorted and ran crashing away through the undergrowth. Just for a moment she sighted a white tail moving away. She was startled and frightened by the encounter, just as the deer, but the incident was the jolt needed to effectively reset her mental processes. "Twenty paces," she said aloud. "Every twenty paces stop and verify your direction." She turned until the sun was again over her left shoulder, and then set out for a broken aspen tree directly in her line of sight. She began to count out the paces aloud, and the sound of her own voice gave her confidence. She stopped at the base of the broken aspen, again made sure her shadow was as she remembered it at the crash sight, and located another marker ahead. The process became easier each time, and soon she picked up the pace to a disciplined jog. She was only dimly aware of the limbs and brush that slapped at her face. She began to anticipate the highway that was directly ahead.

Suddenly and without warning, a high-pitched scream shattered the stillness of the evening forest, and instinctively and fearfully she froze. Again the scream sounded, this time much closer, and was followed by the sound of breaking branches. The approaching animal, she quickly realized, was not a light-footed wild cat, but something much bigger. She wondered if bears scream. It screamed again, seemed almost upon her, and she dove for cover in a thicket of willows and marsh grass. She lay very still, her heart pounding in her chest, afraid to look up at what might turn out to be the last thing she'd ever see. She bit down on her own right hand to keep from crying out. Again the scream, like a terrified woman, then the sound of irregular footfalls hitting the earth, and the sound of an animal gasping for breath. Hidden from view, she stared wide-eyed through the foliage at the animal that was now almost close enough to touch. Its upper body was covered with red scratches. It's red hair hung in a tangled mass. It screamed again, and clumsily moved on, half dragging one leg. Lynn Bergen curled up in the fetal position, blood seeping from her self-inflicted wound. She was certain Charlie Johnson was prophetic. The animal had been a man.

Bush pilot Gene Turk saw the tears that flooded from Lora Whitney's eyes. He had never met Charlie Johnson, but knew of him, and also knew that he and Whitney were more than friends. Her earlier optimism and stubborn resolve had melted away, and now she sat with shoulders slumping, looking like a child wearing an adult's deputy uniform, a child who had just had her heart broken. He knew when they set out that the chance of finding the missing aircraft was exceedingly remote, even if they were to fly directly over it. It is often left to fall hunters to stumble upon the remains of lost hikers, accident victims, or the surprising number of people who find a secluded spot in the forest to end their own life. There were still millions of acres to cover, but he doubted he would be coming back again. Forrest Bodeman had called before he left, even before Whitney had called, to explain the situation. The flight had been arranged for Lora, to help her come to grips with the futility of the search. It appeared, in that regard at least, the flight had been a success.

"You know the last thing I said to Charlie?" Whitney said suddenly. Turk glanced back at Malley. This was something a priest would be better suited to deal with, but Malley merely nodded back, and remained silent.

"What?"

"I told him he was an insensitive ass, and walked away."

"Why...?"

"Anger, jealously, I don't know. It was stupid. I know he..."

"Cares about you?" Malley interjected from the back seat.

"I thought...I don't know...maybe. I'm used to dealing with things directly. I'm no good at this emotional stuff." She took a deep breath, seemed to draw from a reserve of inner strength, and continued. "Charlie's gone. I have to face that."

"You don't know for sure."

"I know. We made a deal. We were sitting on a beaver lodge on Buck Lake just before I found the bones of the bog lady. Neither would ever leave without saying good-by. It's been three days. He would have contacted me if he could. Something terrible has happened. I know it, and I have to accept it."

"You're right," Malley agreed. "Probably we should just face the facts. Charlie's dead. This entire trip was a waste of time."

Whitney whirled around to face him. "A waste of time! What kind of priest are you? I won't give up until…" Whitney stopped short noting the broad grin on Malley's face. "Very clever. You knew I'd get angry."

"I just couldn't believe anyone who would stand up to the likes of Sheriff Bodeman would just give up. I had to find an alternative method to get you back on track. Or as we used to say on the farm, there's more than one way to slop the hogs."

"I know if the situation was reversed, Charlie would be doing everything he could to find me. I just feel so helpless and frustrated."

"Some advice from a friendly priest?"

Lora merely shrugged.

"Hope is a funny thing. Without conflict, stress, or pain it is not needed; it doesn't even exist. Therefore, hope is born with adversity, opposite twins you might say. I don't think that's a coincidence. It's a terrible thing to lose hope. I know. To stand at the grave of a loved one is…is…" Malley reached forward and placed his hand on her shoulder. "I know this sounds like the standard line, but with hope there are always possibilities." He hesitated and withdrew his hand. "Sorry. I shouldn't be preaching."

Lora smiled faintly. "That's OK. It's your job."

"I gave it up once, but some habits die hard."

"One thing for sure. You're not like any priest I know."

"That's because I'm not really a priest," Malley said with a wide grin. "I'm a carpenter, and can drive a nail with the best of them."

In spite of the situation, Whitney laughed out loud at the man's strange sense of humor.

Just as suddenly as the screaming began, it ended. Birds and insects, frogs and chattering squirrels again contributed their notes to the deep wood's symphony. Lynn Bergen was unable to appreciate any of it. She ran, stumbling, falling, rising again, panic stricken. Her dirt stained clothes caught on hawthorn spikes that ripped the fabric as she struggled past. One foot caught in the branches of a deadfall, and she left one shoe there to rot away with the wood. When she realized it was missing, she found that amusing, and briefly laughed.

She remembered nothing clearly of the hideous screaming creature except his eyes. The body was of a man, but the eyes were those of a wild animal, devoid of humanity, wide with terror and viciousness and yet at the same time pleading—exuding a pathetic helplessness. They had cried out to her unseen form with primordial emotion, with all consuming fear and panic. It occurred to her she might have tried to help the man, but her own fear had been too great for the thought to have even entered her mind. Now she moved through the woods as in a nightmare, no more counting steps, no more caution, running headlong into her shadow. It was the only thing that seemed right.

Chapter 13

It had been several minutes since Leroy Olson had last seen a vehicle, a red pickup with a white overhead camper, and it simply reinforced what he already knew. This was one lonely stretch of road. That didn't necessarily make it safe. As evening shadows lengthened, deer came out of the forest to forage in the narrow strip of tender green grass that grew along the shoulders. The highway department had made one pass with a mower on each side a month earlier, and now the lush regrowth drew deer like a magnet. Beyond the single mower pass, weeds, willows, and stunted evergreen shrubs filled the remaining ditch. Beyond them, green spruce trees, punctuated with the white trunks of mature aspen, marked the forest's edge. Never mind safety, Olson thought. The half-assed mowing job was simply an effort to save money. Deer could and often did run unexpectedly out onto the highway from the cover of the unmowed area, much to the surprise of both deer and motorist, and much to the delight of local auto body shops. In his entire life of twenty-three years, Leroy Olson had never so much as nicked a deer. Driving his girlfriend's restored yellow Mustang convertible, he didn't intend to begin now.

A quarter of a mile ahead, Olson noticed something move up out of the ditch and onto the highway, and immediately began slowing from his cruising speed of seventy miles an hour. He realized it was a person wearing what appeared to be a red shirt, probably looking for a ride, or maybe a jogger. Just minutes before, he had passed one wild-eyed and apparently deranged individual. The person appeared to be half naked, and waved at him frantically with a white flag as he sped past. He didn't intend to stop for anyone. Once, when he had been in high school, he'd made the mistake of stopping for a hitchhiker. She had been attractive, even seductive, and looked entirely harmless. Once stopped, however, he quickly found himself looking at the business end of a revolver, and a big ugly man suddenly appeared by her side. Luckily, they only wanted his car. From that time forward he had made it a habit to raise his middle finger at all hitchhikers.

With arms spread wide, the person ahead moved to the middle of the road, effectively blocking both lanes. As he drew near, Olson decelerated with the intent of going around the living obstacle. At the same time, it occurred to him this person might actually need assistance and against all good sense he made up his mind to stop, but only after reaching a safe distance past. To his horror, it became suddenly clear this was not a person that blocked the road, at least not like any person he'd ever seen. More like a wounded animal, red with scratches and dragging one foot. It lunged towards him snarling, and he veered onto the shoulder to avoid a collision, and then stomped the accelerator all the way to the floorboard. The rear wheels threw grass and gravel fifty feet behind but didn't gain the necessary traction in time. The man leaped onto the seat next to him just as the Mustang regained the highway. Quickly, the frantic driver opened the door and rolled out of the vehicle onto the grassy shoulder. The creature slid behind the steering wheel, and continued on, weaving back and forth and finally settling on the wrong side of the road. Sitting on his buttocks in the green grass, Olson thought it must be the phase of the moon that was bringing all the crazies out of the woods. It occurred to him watching the mint Mustang move farther and farther away that his girlfriend was never going to buy this story.

Lynn Bergen's relief at finding the highway soon turned to anger. First a red and white pickup camper had passed her and despite waving her arms frantically and shouting 'Help!' as loud as she could, the motorist cruised on past without so much as a sideways glance. Next a young man in a yellow convertible approached and she removed what was left of her tattered white blouse and waved it to get his attention. Instead of stopping, however, he waved her off with his middle finger and continued on. She had nothing to do but wait for the next motorist and hope she'd have better success. This stretch of road held little hope of that happening any time soon. The shadows lengthened and sun sank ever closer to the western horizon. Darkness would soon descend, and the thought of the creature from the woods once again brought an immediate wave of panic.

She turned to face the faint sound of a vehicle approaching from the north, and stared at the ribbon of asphalt for the first sight of the vehicle, but it was not an automobile but an airplane paralleling the road that produced the sound. From her vantage point the aircraft looked like a small dark bird in the distance. There was little chance that its occupants would see her on the highway.

In spite of Mike Malley's pep talk and optimism, Lora Whitney felt herself sliding steadily back into despair. Long shadows on the ground made it impossible to discern anything but the largest objects clearly, and she had nearly given up. Absently she focused on the only clear image below, Hwy. 6 that cut a clean swath through the northern Minnesota forest. There was very little to see, as traffic was virtually nonexistent. Even the highway soon disappeared from view as Gene Turk let the moderate east wind push the plane to the west side of the road. She thought about protesting, that there was still some daylight left, but realized it was pointless. She closed her eyes against the tears. It was doubtful a crashed Piper Tripacer would go unnoticed even on an infrequently traveled road for three days. When Turk asked to borrow her binoculars, she absently handed them to him, without turning or opening her eyes.

"There's someone running along the pavement up ahead," Turk advised. "Can't be sure, but I think it's a woman."

"Kind of risky for a woman jogger out here in this desolate area all alone," Whitney stated, grateful to occupy her mind with other thoughts.

"Wild animals?" Malley interjected from the back seat.

"The kind with two legs," Whitney said. "She should know better. Let's go down for a closer look."

Turk handed the binoculars back to Whitney and began a descending 'S' turn that would again place the woman in Whitney's field of view. "Have a look," he said.

Whitney focused the binoculars on the woman below as soon as she came into view, and her heart raced.

"I don't think it's a jogger," she said and had to fight to control her excitement.

"Why not?"

"Because she's waving wildly in the air with a white flag and looking directly at us."

Officer James Marshall drove the maroon Crown Victoria highway patrol squad car out of the infrequently used logging road access, and back onto the asphalt. He had waited long enough. Apparently the Olson kid was not making his regular evening run. He had clocked him at eighty-nine miles per hour the week before, but had to abort the traffic stop for an emergency. It had been a disappointment, since this was probably the most boring duty he had ever drawn, and it would have broken the monotony, if only briefly. Nothing of consequence ever happened along this stretch of Hwy. 6, which, he had to admit, wasn't altogether a bad thing. He glanced at his watch. His shift was about over. A fifteen-minute drive would get him to the Corner Store in Big Falls and a cup of coffee with home made sweet rolls. It appeared his speed trap would go unsprung this day.

He barely reached cruising speed at the crest of a hill, when the familiar yellow Mustang convertible suddenly appeared directly ahead of him, and in the wrong lane. He had just enough time to pull the steering wheel hard to the right, and the two vehicles scraped paint at a closing speed of over a hundred forty miles per hour. He continued on into the willow filled ditch, pressed hard on the accelerator, and plowed a path for fifty yards. A loud 'bang' on the undercarriage indicated he'd met mister rock, just before he was able to climb the shoulder and regain the highway. Steam erupted from the engine compartment, the motor abruptly quit, and sparks flew from the instrument panel. Adding insult to injury, he leaped out of the burning squad car just in time to nearly have his head taken off by the artificial wind generated by a landing airplane.

Gene Turk brought the Cherokee within five feet of the centerline, and then continued to utilize the ground effect to float for another half mile. Fortunately, traffic was light, although he was aware of a vehicle almost directly beneath him when he first came in on final approach. A low winged aircraft restricted a pilot's vision directly downward, and he'd once read where a pilot attempting an emergency landing on a freeway and flying a Cherokee had inadvertently set the plane down directly on the flatbed trailer of a semi truck. Apparently he had missed the vehicle, but since it was traveling in the same direction it would no doubt catch up to them in short order. The wheels on the Cherokee protested briefly as they made contact with the pavement, and after a rollout shortened by applying the brakes, the airplane came to a full stop, completely blocking the highway. His concern, however, at the moment was the half dressed blonde woman who came running to meet them. He shut down the engine—mixture lean, magnetos off, master off—before letting Lora get out of the plane.

Lora was certain the woman would be Sharon Wrightham, the other woman, and sudden disappointment drowned her earlier enthusiasm when she realized it was not. Probably, she realized, this woman had nothing to do with the missing plane.

"Twenty paces, every twenty paces," the woman began hysterically when she saw Whitney's uniform. She began backing away as Whitney approached.

"What happened to you?" Whitney asked. "I won't hurt you." The woman had put her white blouse back on as best she could but it was ripped to shreds. Red scratches covered her bare skin, her blonde hair hung in a tangled mass, and she was missing one shoe.

"It was horrible. Screaming over and over."

"What was screaming?"

"A crazy man. A crazy man in the woods."

"You're safe now," she responded as if it happened all the time. It was obvious this woman was not completely rational, and had probably been lost. Malley and Turk walked up next to Whitney. The bush pilot immediately took off his worn leather flight jacket and wrapped it around the dazed woman's shoulders.

"Twenty paces. Sun over my left shoulder."

"Who said twenty paces?"

"There was an old man…"

"Why don't you just sit quietly by the side of the road until we can get an ambulance? You need help." Whitney removed her cell phone from a jacket pocket and turned it on. She moved in a complete circle holding the device at arms length. "No signal," she said. "What a time for the battery to go dead!" Whitney looked at Turk. He nodded in understanding, and went back to the plane to call in the emergency on the NavCom.

"No! No! You don't understand," the woman said suddenly. "We crashed! We crashed! Dear God, we crashed!"

"A plane crash?" Whitney asked, barely able to maintain a normal voice.

"Yes. Yes. We crashed in the trees."

"Where exactly?"

"Charlie said walk east…"

"Charlie Johnson is alive?"

"Yes. We all survived."

"Who is all?"

"Charlie, Jerry Koler, Bill Backus…you have to get help immediately. Bill's arm is broken, and it's getting infected."

Something the woman had said made no sense, and it finally registered.

"Why did Charlie send you? Surely he…"

"He hurt his back in the crash. He can't walk."

Gene Turk came back from the airplane. "I contacted the highway patrol. They said there should be a patrolman on duty on this highway and should be along shortly. They're notifying the Koochiching county sheriff's department. When I told them what county you were from, they said they would also contact Forrest Bodeman. He's probably already on his way." He looked north and south along the road, and saw traffic approaching from both directions. "Looks like we're going to have company, and I'm blocking the road."

"They can wait," Whitney stated. "I'm going back in to find them."

"No way. You have only an hour or so of daylight, and could end up lost yourself."

"Maybe not." She turned to the woman. "What's your name?"

"Lynn Bergen."

"Miss Bergen. How long did it take you to get here?"

"It seemed like forever. Maybe an hour. Maybe more. But I was turned around a couple times."

"Did Charlie build any sort of signal fire?"

"It went out, but they were going to start it again."

"Let's hope they did." She again addressed Turk. "I'm heading straight west from here. I need you in the air above me to try to spot the signal fire. If you find it, keep circling that location."

"Once you get into the woods, I won't be able to see you."

"I know, but I'll be able to see you. Just keep circling until it gets dark, and you have to give it up."

"The darkness isn't a problem. It's fuel, and getting to an airport with a lighted runway. I'm guessing it would be either be Bemidji, International Falls or Grand Rapids."

"Can you make it?"

"I'll have to."

Six cars were now backed up on either side of the Cherokee, and several curious motorists approached the woman deputy. A highway patrol officer, gulping air to catch his breath, burst through the small group, and faced Whitney directly.

"Place the maniac who's flying this plane under arrest," he ordered.

"Why?"

"Because he darned near took my head off, that's why."

She ignored his demand and turned to Turk. "How much highway do you need to get in the air?"

"A quarter mile would be nice."

"Officer…"

"Marshall."

"Officer Marshall. This is an emergency. There's a downed aircraft just west of here. Get these cars off the road, and set up a roadblock a half-mile to the south. Gene needs a clear…"

"I can't set up the roadblock," Marshall interrupted. "My unit's out of commission."

"Well improvise, dammit! I have to get going." Without further explanation, she jogged down into the ditch and disappeared into the woods. One of the motorists approached Officer Marshall. The heavy-set man wore a multicolored Hawaiian shirt and pink shorts.

"Officer. I picked up a hitchhiker just a ways back. Seems he has something to tell you." He turned to the young man who stood behind him. "Get up here boy. He won't bite."

Marshall looked at the young man with a look of total confusion. It was that damn Olson kid. The one who had just run him off the road.

By the time Gene Turk was in the air and circled back to where the woman had come out of the woods, he could see the flashing lights from police and emergency vehicles approaching from the north. The climbing turn brought him to five hundred feet, and he maintained that altitude on a westerly heading. With dense green foliage and long evening shadows, it was impossible to see Whitney on the ground below, and instead he searched ahead for the smoke from a signal fire. The woman had said she'd gotten turned around a time or two, so her exact heading was an educated guess. However, within seconds, he noticed a thin white veil in the distance ahead. The easterly breeze had died completely, and the smoke seemed to rise up out of the trees. Without knowing what to look for, Turk realized the smoke could have just as easily been mistaken for the birth of evening fog. A minute later, he passed directly over the smoke's origin and noted the broken treetops. He banked the Cherokee in a hard left turn, and looked nearly straight down into the spruce forest. Partially visible, a broken Tripacer rested on the forest floor. In the dim shadows he could also see at least two people waving their arms wildly in the air.

For half an hour the plane continued to circle overhead, and Charlie Johnson realized it was acting like a homing beacon, probably directing a rescue party to the crash site. Help couldn't come too soon, as Backus' condition was deteriorating steadily. His own condition seemed to be improving. His right leg now seemed completely normal, and his left was close behind. Koler had taken charge of keeping the signal fire going, and came out of the undergrowth pulling a ten-foot dead aspen blowdown. Backus lay on his back, and wandered in and out of a disturbed consciousness. Suddenly, he called out a name, Lynn Bergen. Johnson threw the crutch to one side, and moved haltingly to his side.

"Help is on the way," he said reassuringly. "Hang in there."

Backus looked towards Johnson, and his eyes focused in recognition.

"How do you feel?" Johnson asked. It was a stupid question, he realized, but was for some reason what everyone said to someone who obviously felt like shit.

"I've been better."

"Lynn made contact. You're going to be just fine."

Backus didn't seem to hear. "Tell Lynn I really appreciated her friendship, and wish her the very best. Tell my wife…tell my wife…" Backus slumped back to the ground, and lapsed into unconsciousness.

As soon as he spotted the people on the ground, Gene Turk immediately switched to the emergency channel on the NavCom and made contact with the emergency personnel on the highway. Officer Marshall had taken charge of the scene, and maintained a nearly continuous running dialog with him. Four different services responded to the emergency call—the Koochiching county sheriff's department, the Minnesota Highway patrol, Northland Ambulance out of International Falls, and the Little Fork/Big Falls volunteer fire department. Turk and Marshall briefly discussed getting a chopper to airlift the accident victims out, but quickly realized it would be dark long before it would arrive. Instead, Turk kept circling providing a focal point first for Deputy Whitney and then the crew of twenty volunteers who made their way through the dense forest to reach the accident site. Fully aware they would never get back out in daylight, the last member of the string of emergency workers ignited a signal flare at regular intervals. John Thurber, a retired logger and member of the volunteer fire department, fervently hoped that in the process of the rescue, they wouldn't accidentally set the woods on fire.

The deepening shadows reduced visibility to mere yards, as Lora Whitney pushed her way through a dense alder thicket. Wood smoke filled the air and she knew she was close. The easterly breeze had died away, however, becoming light and variable, which meant the signal fire could be in any direction. She had only one alternative.

"Hello," she called out loudly and cupped her hands around her mouth to form a feeble megaphone.

"Hello yourself," came the immediate reply, from perhaps twenty or thirty yards away. "Keep your voice down. You're scaring the wildlife."

Lora ran directly for the voice, burst into a small opening in a spruce forest, and rushed headlong into the arms of Charlie Johnson.

"I just can't seem to get away from you," Johnson said, after several moments of a mutual embrace. Whitney released her grip and took a step back. She glanced over at the remains of the demolished airplane.

"Your first attempt at a landing? Not bad, but aren't the wheels supposed to hit the ground first?"

"Any landing you can walk away from…"

"Is a good landing."

Jerry Koler appeared out of the woods with an armload of broken branches.

"Lora! You are a sight for sore eyes. And none too soon. Backus is in bad shape."

"There should be a crew coming in right behind me. Start calling out a hello to let them know where we are." Koler moved several yards away and called out. In the distance, a call came back to him. Again he called, and again there was an immediate response.

"How did you find us?" Johnson asked, suddenly realizing Leech Lake and Whitney's usual stomping grounds were over a hundred road miles away.

Whitney thought back over the unlikely string of events that had brought her to this place. All the right turns, all the right guesses.

"I had a lot of help," she realized. "A lot of people were willing to let me…were willing to help me…"

"Bodeman?"

"Yes, and a man you don't know, Mike Malley. Someone who wouldn't let me give up hope."

"I'd like to meet him."

"You will. I'm sure he's coming in with the emergency crew."

"So where's he from?"

"I really don't know," Whitney realized. "He was at the Retreat, maybe you saw him in the crowd, and then just showed up at Bodeman's house. Said he knew Backus, and wanted to help. I was ready to give up, but he wouldn't let me quit."

"For all of us, I'm grateful he wouldn't."

It took less than five minutes from the time the emergency workers entered the clearing until five of them disappeared back into the forest darkness with Bill Backus firmly secured to a stretcher. Beams from powerful flashlights lit the clearing as the teams systematically went about their business of examining each victim. Despite his head injury, a probable concussion, Koler refused to be carried out and set out with several other volunteer workers. Within fifteen minutes the crash site was nearly vacant, with Charlie Johnson, Lora Whitney, Mike Malley, and three of the emergency responders remaining. John Thurber also remained, intending to be the last man out. At this point he was examining the remains of the aircraft, inserted his flashlight beam into various places to get a better look. Finally he realized these people were not going to leave anytime soon, and headed back towards the highway. Someone else was going to have to worry about the flares.

Johnson stood off to one side resting his shoulder against the trunk of a spruce tree, watching the proceedings. He realized the FAA and the NTSB weren't going to be happy with the way the crash site had been corrupted. Koler had dug around for clues, strips of the aircraft fabric covering had been cut away for various emergency projects, and then Thurber had attempted to satisfy his curiosity.

Smoke from the smoldering signal fire and the darkness of night now obscured all but the most obvious objects. Though slightly irritating, especially for the eyes, Johnson welcomed the smoke as it kept the mosquitoes at bay. Like Koler, he had also refused to be carried out, and seemed near one hundred percent. Whitney was giving last minute instructions to the last of the emergency workers and then led Malley over to him. She carried a battery-powered lantern, and hung it from the nearby broken limb of a tree. Light from the lantern illuminated a fifty-foot hemisphere around the cluster of human forms.

"Father Malley," she began. "This is Charlie Johnson."

"Hello. Lora tells me you had a lot to do with finding us," Johnson said as the two shook hands.

"Call me Mike, please. And Lora is the one you need to thank. She was the driving force. Without her stubborn resolve, none of this would be happening."

"I have to give Sheriff Bodeman credit. He let me try."

"You should have seen her," Malley reflected. "She's one fiery gal, when she sets her mind to something."

"Not this mild mannered woman I hang out with," Johnson joked. "I would have liked to have been there for the discussion."

"She did you proud," a voice called from the direction of the newly formed path. Sheriff Forrest Bodeman came plowing through the underbrush like a tank, breaking trail for the diminutive woman that followed. Immediately, he saw the wreckage of the airplane. "Jesus!" He unhooked his portable and spoke loudly.

"We're in."

"Any problems?" came the reply.

"None. The flares are still active, and after all the traffic in and out, even I could follow the trail."

"I'd appreciate it if you'd put up the accident scene tape."

"Will do."

"One other thing."

"Go ahead."

"After this I'd appreciate it if you'd keep your mess in your own county."

"Roger that. See you in an hour or so."

Bodeman noticed the assembled group had been listening in on the conversation.

"That was Sheriff Ed McNeal, my counterpart from Koochiching County, out on the highway. Now he's a real modern sheriff. Does all the right things, says all the right stuff, and wouldn't say shit if he had a mouth full."

"Hope you don't mind me butting in," Thomson said to Whitney as she stepped from behind Bodeman's massive body, "but I happened to be in the neighborhood. Actually Sheriff Bodeman and I were in the office reviewing some new information when the emergency call came through, and I just couldn't resist tagging along."

"No problem," Whitney said slightly confused. "But I…"

"This is still your case, Whitney," Bodeman advised. "What's next?"

"Thanks Sheriff, but I'd appreciate a little help at this point." She looked up at Charlie, who stood firmly next to her. "I found what I was looking for."

Bodeman nodded and turned to Johnson. "What happened here?"

"The plane was rigged to crash from the start," Johnson stated. "Unfortunately, we happened to be out cold and in it."

"Out cold?"

"Some kind of drug. Koler and I came to just in the nick of time, and Koler managed to get us down alive. Believe me," he said, gesturing toward the demolished aircraft, "if not for Jerry, it could have been a lot worse."

"I passed him on the way in. He said he was going to head back home to LaCrescent to see his wife, after the medics checked him out. He looked pretty peaked. He said you should be on your way to the hospital. Something about being paralyzed from the waist down?"

"As you can see, that was clearly an exaggeration."

"But you were."

"True. But I'm a fast healer. Other than feeling like I just barely survived a plane crash, I never felt better."

Bodeman looked at Johnson skeptically, but continued in a different vein.

"So how did you come to be here picking pine needles out of your butt cheeks?"

"Ah spruce, Forrest, spruce needles." Johnson grinned momentarily, and then continued seriously. "Jerry is convinced someone or ones were controlling the plane remotely, were running it on a very limited fuel supply, and it crashed pretty much exactly where they wanted it to. Just to make sure, the flight controls were also sabotaged. Without Jerry's flight experience, we would have nosed in at a couple hundred miles per hour."

"So who's at the top of the list of people who hate you?"

"First we were certain Ethek was behind it, since Jerry and I helped foil his plans last year. But that didn't make sense for two reasons. First, Bill Backus and Lynn Bergen, who were also on board, had nothing to do with the SciOgen scandal."

"And second?" Bodeman pressed.

"Ethek was with us on the plane."

Bodeman didn't seem at all surprised and merely nodded. "That fits with what I know, but continue."

"He disappeared shortly after we crashed. Then, through information we extracted from Lynn Bergen, we thought Jonathan Wrightham was responsible."

"How?"

"Unknown at this point, but Wrightham's helicopter did show up earlier and gave us the once over."

"And?"

"We played dead, and he left."

"So you don't actually know who was on board."

"True. It could have been the Pope, but I sincerely doubt it."

"There always has to be one wise ass."

"Just stating the ridiculous to support the obvious. Anything new on the bog lady case?"

"Only this," Whitney said, extracting the photo from her jacket pocket. "Sarah brought the results of forensics, specifically the reconstruction of the woman's face."

Johnson took the piece of paper, unfolded it, and then moved to stand directly in the lantern's light to get a clearer view.

"Recognize her?" Whitney asked. "I know I've seen her before. But I can't seem to make the connection."

"The resemblance is striking," Johnson stated. "I wonder."

"So you've seen her, too? Who is she? Her identity has been driving me crazy."

"Well if you cover up the long hair and look just at her face."

"Go on."

"It looks remarkably like an old friend of ours."

"Are you going to tell me or do I have to beat it out of you?"

"Well, it looks very much like…"

"Yes?"

"Maclin Ethek."

Whitney grabbed the picture from his hands and studied the face intently. "I guess you were right, Sara. It was just someone who reminded me of the woman. An unfortunate coincidence."

Mike Malley had been content to listen to the discussion, but now spoke up. "I seem to remember another part of the conversation at Sheriff Bodeman's home. I clearly remember you saying you don't believe in coincidence."

"We can't ignore the possibility of a connection, however unlikely," Johnson observed.

"There's a better chance that the Pope really was in the chopper," Bodeman added dryly.

Whitney turned to Bodeman. "What did you find out about the crash on your end?"

All eyes focused on Bodeman. "Immediately after our discussion at my house—and following your expressed orders—Sara and I did some digging, trying to find anyone suspicious with connections to Ethek.

We discovered something interesting. Maclin Ethek and Jonathan Wrightham are brothers…well half brothers actually. They had the same mother but different fathers. Wrightham's father was Franklin Wrightham, a rich ex-banker who seems to have made most of his money foreclosing on Midwest ranches during the farm crisis."

"And Ethek's father?" Johnson pressed.

"Someone you will not believe."

"For crying out loud," Whitney exclaimed. "You're as bad as Charlie. Just tell us."

"Luke James."

"You're kidding. The preacher?"

"I said you weren't going to believe it."

"That is interesting, but what does it prove?" Johnson wondered.

"Maybe nothing, but they were all together at the Retreat, like one big happy family reunion," Bodeman continued.

"Also present was your friend, Sharon Wrightham," Whitney stressed for Johnson's benefit. She vividly recalled the two holding on to each other like a couple love-struck teenagers.

"Not quite all of the family were present," Thomson interjected. "Missing would be Franklin Wrightham who is deceased, and Morgan Wrightham, Maclin and Jonathan's mother."

"Where's she?"

"Unknown at this time, but we're trying to get a picture and location."

"There is still another missing piece," Johnson reflected. "Maclin Ethek. If he managed to find the highway on his own and hitched a ride he could be anywhere."

"I let the FBI in on what was going on. Ethek's case is still very much open at the federal level. They said they would get their people working on the whereabouts of Morgan Wrightham, and just about everyone else I could think of who's even remotely connected to all this. And it's probable that Ethek did make it to the highway. Someone driving a yellow Mustang ran the highway patrolman assigned to Hwy

6 off the road earlier. He thought it was some local kid, but the kid showed up right after Whitney headed into the woods. The kid told this wild story about a crazy man stealing his car. Turns out it was probably true. Lynn Bergen also encountered him on her way out."

"So Maclin survived again. One has to give the guy credit. Any word on the yellow Mustang?"

"Found abandoned near Deer River. No idea where he went from there. He has one foot missing and wears a prosthesis, and was, according to the kid and Miss Bergen, pretty beat up and hysterical from being lost. There's an APB out for him, but I believe we can safely say he didn't cause this crash, which could very well have ended his own life."

"Still," Johnson said, "he might have a good idea who did."

"Which leads us back to his half-brother," Thomson interjected. "According to our reports the two brothers had no love for each other after Jonathan ended up with a good piece of the family fortune and Maclin virtually nothing."

"But what possible motive would Jonathan have for eliminating Maclin?" Whitney wondered. "He already has all the money. If anything, it should have been the other way around. Maclin should have been the one out for revenge. It seems we are still missing a lot of the pieces."

"There are certainly more players yet to be identified unless we pin everything on Wrightham," Thomson concluded. "But again, we run into the motive problem. It wouldn't make sense for a multimillionaire to risk his fortune on a stunt like this."

Bodeman came to a decision. "The bog lady case is pretty much at a standstill until we can get an ID, so I'm dropping that and putting all our horses on this plane crash. Further, since it's getting late, I suggest we meet at my house in a couple days. I would suggest my office, but it's hardly bigger than a rat hole. That will give the FAA and the NTSB a chance to investigate the plane for sabotage—we may be able to get at least a preliminary report out of them by then—and it will give the FBI a chance to see what they can come up with on Morgan Wrightham."

"It might be a good idea to get a search warrant for the Retreat," Johnson suggested. "That's where all the action started. With the debate underway, James has an air tight alibi but someone must have hired the muscle that forced Koler and me into the Tripacer."

"They were probably the same two I saw with Bill and Lynn," Malley volunteered.

"I intend to get the warrant immediately," Bodeman confirmed, "and also bring in Reverend James for questioning, despite his alibi. Also Sharon Wrightham."

"Who-done-it 101," Thomson said thoughtfully.

"I'm not following," Johnson questioned.

"It's simple detective work," Whitney stated, getting Thomson's drift. "Who had the most to gain from Ethek's death? Who hated him the most?"

"I can safely say the list is long," Johnson confirmed.

"This is starting to make sense!" Whitney exclaimed. "Kill off all heirs to the Wrightham estate—Jonathan and Maclin—and who gets the entire pie? Logically, with both brothers out of the way, the entire fortune falls to Jonathan's wife, your friend Sharon Wrightham."

"The chain of heirs is certainly worth a check, and if what you say is true," Thomson said thoughtfully, "then it is possible this entire elaborate plane crash was simply an attempt to kill off Maclin, and the rest of you were there for some sort of cover story."

"I'm not buying any of that, and you've jumped over a lot of mountains to get there," Johnson stated. "Jonathan Wrightham is alive."

"Is he? Has anyone seen him since his senatorial speech at the Retreat?" Whitney stated.

"Good point," Thomson said.

"Well, Maclin is still…" Johnson began.

"It could very well be Sharon Wrightham," Whitney cut in forcefully.

"Pardon me for talking while you're interrupting," Johnson said sharply. He turned back to Thomson. "As mother to both Jonathan and Maclin, Morgan Wrightham could also lay claim to the estate."

"And isn't it funny no one knows where Morgan is either," Whitney observed.

"If Sharon Wrightham is behind this then Jonathan is now the one in danger," Bodeman concluded.

"Have you people been smoking dope?" Johnson asked, and didn't attempt to hide his growing irritation. "I'm hearing a lot of 'ifs,' with not so much as a shred of actual fact. A moment ago you were all sure Jonathan was the guilt party."

"Just exploring all avenues. You have to concede it's a possibility," Whitney pressed.

"Anything is possible but I can't believe Sharon…"

"You're letting your emotions get in the way of your logic," Whitney interrupted yet again. "Sharon may well have seen this course of action as her only way out of a bad situation. You told me yourself Wrightham struck her. That she felt trapped. Maybe she had enough and decided to go for all the apples."

"You don't know her like I do."

"I guess not," Whitney said, and couldn't conceal the sarcasm. It was so very obvious to her, Charlie had been totally taken in by this woman.

"Let's pick this up again at my house," Bodeman said, sensing a rift developing between two good friends. "I don't think there'd be a problem if you stopped in also, Mike. If something classified comes up, we can always kick you out."

"I'll be there," Malley said.

"I don't think I can make it," Johnson stated.

Whitney studied his expression, and knew what was on his mind. "You're not going home are you?"

"Not right away. I want to check on something first."

"Well, a week then," Bodeman continued. "Say one week from today, at one in the afternoon? That will give all concerned a chance to sift through all the unanswered questions. Maybe we might even come up with some damn answers."

"Sounds good," Johnson stated.

"What are you going to do now?" Whitney asked. "Seems I can't let you out of my sight and you're getting into trouble."

"I'm going to follow the trail of a couple grays, and see which tree they climb."

Chapter 14

In June at night the sounds of the northern forest can be almost deafening, with several species of frogs, and dozens of species of birds calling for mates or staking out territory. Loons call out their mad laughter. Owls whooo. Coyotes yip and cry, and occasionally the deep-throated howl of a timber wolf echoes. Bat's wings flutter. The buzz of insects, primarily crickets and mosquitoes, provides a continuous background choir. Fireflies provide specks of moving light. And behind it all is a very real and dramatic life and death struggle to survive.

By late August the forest night is much more subdued. Birds have raised their young, become less vocal, and the mosquito population has tapered off. 'Tapered off,' however, is a relative term. Warm, unprotected bodies still attract hundreds. The insect attack is relentless and fearless, they exist only to get the warm red fluid to reproduce, and the death of millions does nothing to deter the one. They have, quite literally, on occasion driven men to the brink of madness. Perhaps the only place where mosquitoes are more numerous is the north slope of Alaska, where millions draw as much as a quart of blood per week from individual reindeer.

In what would become northern Minnesota, early European settlers used primarily smoke to keep the hordes at bay. Smudges made of slowly burning moist grass and wood produced copious amounts of gray smoke and were often used inside settler's cabins. Occasionally, the smudges erupted into torches, and turned both building and occupants to ashes.

Despite enduring three nights of mosquito bites and remaining sane, Charlie Johnson was thankful Forrest Bodeman had been kind enough to relinquish his aerosol can of bug dope. It allowed him to sleep comfortably through the night with nothing more than an extra white covering cloth provided by the rescue workers. Now, with the morning sun lighting the tops of the spruce trees, he intended to find the old man, Rolland Woodlove, and perhaps persuade him to return to civilization. He was not opposed to living a life apart from society, he had done so himself for two years, but the old man had clearly seemed confused, and perhaps even a bit senile. The hermit had watched them for three days from just outside the crash site, which indicated he had a base camp relatively close by. When captured by the wire snare, he had mentioned a cabin. Johnson pictured in his mind a black tar paper shack with years of accumulated human refuse. For the old man's well being it was worth a try to get him to go to a retirement facility, or to at least determine if he had relatives on the outside.

As confusing as recent events were, it was also possible Rolland Woodlove was not exactly what he seemed. His clean-shaven face, respectable clothing, and well cared for teeth did not exactly match the stereotypical description of a recluse. And how was it possible for him to be exactly where they crashed, then pull them all out of the wreckage, and finally provide them with processed food to sustain them for three days? A coincidence was a possibility, but simultaneous events, no matter how unrelated they might seem, were always suspect. He had come to accept his grandfather's view: All things are connected. Moreover, the strange, pathetic old man was a curiosity he just couldn't ignore.

Sheriff Bodeman and Mike Malley had been the first of their group to return to the highway the previous evening. Bodeman had also put up the crime scene tape, which, given the general overall corruption of the site by nearly thirty people, was probably a waste of time. Lora Whitney had volunteered to stay, but Johnson convinced her that her deputy uniform might just be enough to frighten the old man away. Johnson felt he and the old man had connected on some level and that connection, he hoped, would be trust. Lora had seemed somewhat distant, and he wondered if their disagreement over the possible guilt of Sharon Wrightham would qualify as their first fight. He wasn't about to hold it against her, no matter how utterly wrong her assumptions had been. In the end she had given him a quick peck on the cheek without emotion and as if she were simply fulfilling an obligation, and left the crash site without so much as a backward glance. She left her cell phone so he could contact someone when he was ready to return to Cass County. She hadn't volunteered to pick him up. But her last words, 'Be careful,' remained imprinted in his thoughts.

Johnson rose from the carpet of brown spruce needles, stretched his frame out to its maximum length, and sucked in and expelled the maximum amount of air his lungs would hold. That, he realized, would be as close to breakfast as he would get. When he had lived alone at a remote lake, he had maintained a survival kit that included emergency provisions. His return to civilization, however, had made that unnecessary, but at this point he would have welcomed dried wild mushrooms, pulverized cattail roots, or acorn flour. There was little natural food to eat in a spruce forest. There was the prospect of finding a late ripening patch of blueberries, but that thought only served to frustrate an already voracious appetite.

Johnson put all thought of food aside, and paced a hundred yard circle around the crash site. Except for the path crushed into the forest floor by the emergency workers, the modest distance put him outside the range of human activity. Within fifteen minutes he located another well-traveled path that led directly north, the same direction Woodlove indicated his cabin was located. That part of the hermit's story appeared to be true, and Johnson studied the bent and broken stems of forest ferns carefully. They were still green, which indicated this path was of recent use. This was not a trail that Rolland Woodlove had used before the crash.

Johnson followed the meandering trail to an aspen covered ridge that gradually rose sixty feet above the lower and flatter spruce forest floor. He continued on for another fifteen minutes, and was suddenly overwhelmed by the enticing aroma of frying bacon. The odor hung in the morning air like fresh bait before a black bear. Rolland Woodlove, it seemed, was about to have breakfast.

The white trunks of aspen and tangle of hazel brush gave way to larger and taller red pine on the sandy ridge. While the spruce forest had a dense understory composed of willow, alders and red brush, the stand of pine was essentially pure. Johnson quickly determined why. The scaly trunks grew in straight lines, like rows of corn, while high overhead the green crowns restricted the amount of light that reached the ground. This was one of hundreds of tree plantations in northern Minnesota that had been planted during the CCC days of the Depression. Roosevelt's plan to put men back to work was now bearing fruit. The red pine in this plantation were of marketable size, and Johnson noticed occasional deteriorating stumps indicating thinning had already begun. No hermit's cabin, however, graced the pine forest. Instead Johnson was surprised to see a trailer camper about the same length as a pickup truck sitting at the very top of the ridge and overlooking the spruce forest below. A blue used Chevy Blazer was parked next to the camper. This was hardly the tarpaper shack he expected to find, and he realized this was most likely not the home of the hermit.

After at first politely knocking, and then finally pounding, Johnson opened the unlocked door slightly and called out a hello. He could hear the bacon sizzling, so swung the door open completely, and stepped inside. To his right, a lone bunk lay unmade, straight ahead was the propane stove and a countertop refrigerator, and to his left, a round table was set with a single setting of dinnerware. To his immediate left, a tiny sink held several clean white plates and some silverware.

Everything else was colored various shades of brown, and the walls were covered with birch veneer paneling. Except for the bed, everything was neat and clean. The owner, however, was not at home, and Johnson turned the knob on the stove stopping the flow of propane. It was not a good idea to leave cooking bacon unattended. He left the trailer and had taken two steps from the door when a man's voice stopped him.

"May I help you?"

Johnson turned to see a man approaching from the south, and along the same path he had followed. He was elderly, but fit, clean-shaven, well groomed, and casually dressed. He wore a yellow windbreaker to repel the morning dew. His low voice carried with it a quiet confidence.

"Good morning, Mr. Woodlove, or whatever your name is."

"Good morning, Mr. Johnson. And a beautiful morning it is, too."

"How did you get here?"

"I drove in on the plantation access road just to get away from the highway and enjoy some privacy when I accidentally found this place. Take a look at the view," he said. "I can see for miles out over the spruce forest beyond. The tree tops look almost like a lawn from here."

"So you just accidentally stumbled onto this place? Just who are you?"

"My name is Mr. Parish, or just Parish if you like."

"What is your connection to the crash, and don't tell me you just happened to be in the neighborhood enjoying the view."

"What you really want to know is am I friend or am I foe?" He spread his arms wide from his body. "Look at me. Totally unarmed."

"Then why do I get the feeling you're the most dangerous man I've ever met?"

"I could be, Mr. Johnson. I could be. However, not today. But where are my manners? Come in. Come in. It's not often I get to share the morning meal with anyone."

"Truthfully, the smell of the frying bacon drew me like a bear to honey."

Caution turned to curiosity, and Johnson followed the old man into the trailer.

"Anything I can do?"

"Oh no. Just take a clean plate from the sink and make yourself comfortable."

Johnson seated himself on a bench by the table while the man began gathering covered plastic bowls of fruit and an unopened carton of orange juice from the refrigerator. He placed several strips of crisp bacon on a paper towel, drew whole wheat bread from a drawer under the countertop refrigerator, and systematically began heaping the table with the morning bounty. By the time the man sat down across from him, there was enough food for a half dozen people.

"Just help yourself," the man said, as he began heaping his plate. "We don't stand on ceremony around here." For fifteen minutes both ate in silence and then Perish pushed his plate aside. "I know you must have a great many questions, which, unfortunately, I cannot answer. However, I will answer one question, but only one. Perhaps you'd like to know something about Lora Whitney, or who did cause the plane to crash, or maybe how I'm involved in all this, or…"

A sudden scratching on the outside of the door prompted Parish's neutral expression to change into a wide grin, and he rose from his seat.

"Pardon, me. I have to let in my friends."

Johnson was not at all surprised when two well-fed grays came bounding through the open door. Parish placed a dish of unsalted peanuts on the floor, and the two guests immediately began helping themselves. They sat back on their haunches and manipulated the peanuts in their mouths with their front feet. The obvious parallel to human hands was striking.

"Let's be perfectly candid, shall we?" Parish said as he again took his seat across from Johnson. His calm voice had a soothing quality that reminded Johnson of his old sixth grade teacher. It was, however, usually the calm before the storm. "I make it a habit to know as much as possible about the people I deal with. You are something of a paradox, Mr. Johnson. An educated man, obviously intelligent since you earned two college degrees—Biology and forest ecology I believe—by the time you were twenty-one. But also possessing something of an anti-social personality, which has left you essentially a loner."

"I don't get out much, if that's what you're driving at."

"But when you do, you seem to make an impact on people's lives. I knew you'd come, of course. It's all in your profile. Curiosity, strong moral character. I'm rather touched, actually. That's why I'm still here. I wanted to meet you personally and without the theatrics, just to see what I might be up against."

"Up against?"

"In case we come down on opposite sides. Now, having met you, I rather hope we might be on the same side."

"Of what?"

"Do you really want to waste your one question on something as trivial as that? Search your soul, Mr. Johnson. I know a great deal about a great many things. There are even some who believe I can see ahead in time"

"Like some kind of prophet?"

"Nothing so biblical. It's really not that hard to predict the future when one has a clear understanding of the past. This is your chance to answer the one thing you would give your soul to know. But you have to ask."

"It's personal."

"Of course it's personal. The really important questions are always personal."

"You couldn't possibly know the answer. The only one who knows for sure is..."

"Your grandfather?"

"Did you know my grandfather?" Johnson asked surprised.

"I know of him. I'm essentially an observer, that's my gift, and as I stated, in my many years I've come to know a great deal about, well, everything."

"If it were somehow possible, I'd like to know for sure what happened to him. Is he really…dead?"

"I was hoping you'd ask that question, because, quite frankly, it's about the only one I can answer."

"You know what happened to him?"

"Not precisely. But you do."

"I wish I did."

"Forget your head, and think with your heart. What does it tell you?"

For several moments Johnson stared into past, remembering the overturned canoe, then the search and rescue people who spent days dragging the frigid waters of the lake, and finally his futile search for tracks along the shoreline. Tears formed in the corner of his eyes and rolled down his face, but he continued to hold his head high, unashamed.

"In my heart I know he's alive, but I don't know where to look."

"He doesn't want to be found. Yet, when the time comes, he'll find you."

Johnson's head again took control, and he looked at Parish suspiciously.

"Just what kind of sick game are you playing with the lives of innocent people?"

"Believe me. This is no game."

"Backus damn near died. And might yet."

"A fine team of doctors reset Mr. Backus' arm, and he is responding very well to antibiotics at Northland hospital in International Falls. It's quite likely he'll be transferred to the Bemidji hospital in a few days to be closer to his wife."

"How could you know that?"

"Do you believe in supreme beings, Mr. Johnson?" Parish continued calmly.

"Do you mean God?"

"Well lesser gods, actually, but supreme nonetheless. Your profile indicates you are a very open minded individual."

"If you're talking about supreme people, the answer is no."

Parish studied Johnson's face for several seconds before he spoke. "In time, you might well have believed, Mr. Johnson." Parish extended his right hand to Johnson over the table and turned it palm up. "Do you know the origin of the handshake?"

"It is an ancient custom believed to have originated in Europe."

"Clasping the hand of another was a way to verify to both parties there were no concealed weapons hidden in the palms. It was a sign of trust."

Johnson slowly extended his hand and grasped Parish's firmly. He felt he should thank him for the insight into Grandfather's disappearance, or at least breakfast but remained silent.

Parish nodded a polite acknowledgement to his unspoken words. "You're quite welcome, Mr. Johnson. Just so you know. There are some who have regretted ever shaking hands with me. It will certainly be interesting to see how this all plays out."

Johnson paused briefly in the doorway, looked back at the old man, and then continued out the door. As he began walking eastward along the plantation access road to the highway, he retrieved Whitney's cell phone and attempted to dial a memorized number.

"Figures," he said disgusted. "Battery's dead."

Parish stood on the carpet of brown pine needles near the entrance to his camper and watched Johnson's back as he walked away. He turned to his two companions, who had followed him outside.

"What do you say? Time to pack out the trash?"

After Johnson was out of sight, a man appeared from behind the Blazer, and walked to Parish's side.

"Everything go alright?" Mr. Bell asked.

"Fine. He's a decent man. I was never in any danger. And you?"

"When the emergency reponders headed out, I simply melted into the woods. Everyone was too focused on the situation to notice. Where to from here?"

"Looks like one's in and one's out. I suppose we should extend our congratulations."

"And the crash?"

"I think it's fair to tell Wrightham the results weren't quite what he expected."

Chapter 15

Engrossed in a conversation, Charlie Johnson and Mike Malley walked up the ramp of the Bemidji hospital and were nearly overrun by a blonde woman who ran directly into them. The lines of concern on her face gave way quickly to surprise.

"My fault," she mumbled, and then recognizing the two quickly added, "Charlie, hello. Sorry. I wasn't watching where I was going. Father Malley."

"How's Bill doing?" Malley asked.

"Ok, I guess."

"What do you mean?"

"I couldn't get past the nurse's station. He doesn't want to see me."

"I don't understand."

"I tried to warn him, but the fool just wouldn't listen. Now he blames me. Trouble is, he's right."

"We're going in to see him. Would you like me to relay a message?"

"Just tell him I'm sorry." A drop of moisture rolled down her left cheek, and she hurriedly brushed it away. She pushed her way past the two without further explanation.

Johnson and Malley continued into the hospital, and after some questioning, located Backus' room. As they approached the doorway, a huge woman stepped directly in their path and the sergeant's expression on her face told them that she was going to have it her way. No arguments. She stood in front of them, arms folded across her barrel chest, and tapped one foot threateningly on the floor. In several places her nurse's uniform was stretched to the point of imminent rupture.

"Only one visitor at a time," she insisted, "and I won't hesitate to throw you out if I think you're disturbing my patient. Is that clear?"

"Absolutely," Malley said.

"You go in first," Johnson said. "I'll find a phone and call Whitney. See if the meeting at Bodeman's home is still on for tomorrow."

Malley nodded and smiled lovingly at the no-nonsense woman who hadn't moved from her place in the hallway. "May I?" he asked politely.

"Remember, don't get Professor Backus excited. I don't care who you are." She stepped aside and Malley walked quickly to Room 112. He knocked gently on the door, and it swung open, revealing a sterile two-bed hospital room. Backus, however, was the lone occupant. Dressed in gray slacks and a white shirt, he sat propped up with several pillows reading a blue hardcover book. His left arm was encased in a plaster cast. Backus closed the book as soon as he recognized Malley.

"You come to break me out of here?" Backus asked hopefully.

"Not after I met your bodyguard. I value my life." He pulled a chair closer to the bed and sat down on it backwards, resting his arms across the backrest.

"That's Irene Latala, one tough woman, and one of most kind-hearted people I know."

"A bit overprotective, wouldn't you say?"

"I was able to help her two kids get through college."

"And she feels she owes you?"

"I hope not. All I did was recommend them for some part time employment on campus to help with the bills. Great kids, hard working. As I recall, one's an engineer, and the other went into music."

"So when do you get out?"

"If I can sneak past Irene, the doctor says tomorrow."

Malley studied the patient for several moments. "Why do I get the feeling you're not that excited about leaving?"

"I was just thinking. I never realized how much my job was my life. Without it, I don't know what I'm going to do next. I have nowhere to go, no one to see." He shifted his body on the hospital bed to help relieve the soreness, and turned away.

"Want to talk about it?"

Backus stared out the only window in the sterile off-white hospital room. It was merely a delaying gesture, since the view was of a solid red brick wall. A lone wild sunflower plant, whose seed had no doubt blown in on the April winds, grew light starved in the narrow space between the buildings, and a single yellow flower was the only reward for its valiant efforts.

"My first wife—sounds like the beginning of a bad joke doesn't it—and I were married in Vegas, literally in a sexual fever. Man, were we hot for each other. But then all the romantic dust settled and reality set in. Other than sex I don't think we had a single thing in common. Her life went one way, and mine another, and after ten years of bickering and no children, our mutually exclusive life styles became the irreconcilable difference that ended our relationship."

Malley listened intently, but offered no comment.

"My second wife was a professor of Economics here at the University. Joan Franks. Very smart. I think that's what attracted me to her. Things were great at first."

"But then?"

"Joan had been raised in a fundamentalist faith, but had abandoned that as too restrictive. After about a year I realized why. She had a drinking problem."

"A drinking problem? As in alcoholic?"

"Yes. I had the naïve notion I could get her to change, and finally convinced her to join AA, although she never would fully admit to having an addiction."

"Most people won't."

"For two glorious, wonderful years she remained completely sober. I wanted to love her to death. She began to exercise, take charge of her body, and became a kind of health nut for a while. I truly thought the beast inside her was dead."

"What happened?"

"The inevitable, I suppose. She started drinking again. A glass of wine here. A martini there. She stopped going to AA. I saw what was happening and briefly convinced her to stop drinking again."

"How?"

"Bribery. I bought her a new car as a reward."

"But that didn't work."

"Her dark side quickly realized she could get what she wanted from me simply by promising to stop drinking. The last was a beautiful home on the shores of Musky Lake, just north of town."

"It's called enabling. Where is she now?"

"At our, actually her, lake front home. Retired. She's not well. Only fifty-nine years old and battling diabetes, high blood pressure, and the early stages of heart disease. I'm sure liver problems are just around the corner. Such a waste."

"It is obvious you still care about her."

"Of course. I cling to the memory of the two years when she was alcohol free. I still go over and help her with the yard work. Funny thing. She will invariably offer me a drink to show her appreciation. After all this time, it still hasn't sunk in. I do care, and that's always been my problem."

"Has your present wife been to see you?"

"She stopped in right after I was transferred in from the Falls. You know why? She wanted to know if I was hiding any extra income. What income? I'm broke, with no job. What I get from the sale of my book is not really an income. More like a stipend." Backus hesitated, and again faced Malley directly. "I've always loved life, loved kids, loved teaching, but I have to tell you I'm beginning to wonder."

"Yes?"

"If its all worth it. Maybe I'd be better off..."

"That's not the answer."

"Well, then you tell me what is, because my life, my experience has come up short."

"I can't offer you any magical solution. I can only tell you it's very important you don't give up. I know there's something you have to do."

"Like what?"

"We all have a purpose. It sometimes just takes a while for it to dawn on us." Malley reflected a moment and then continued. "I met your friend, Lynn, on the way in. She wanted me to relay a message."

"I left definite orders with Irene at the nurses' station. I don't want to see her."

"She seemed quite upset."

"The common denominator in what laughingly might be called my personal life is me. She's better off staying as far away as possible."

"She seems to think you blame her for something, and she also said she was sorry."

"I certainly don't blame her for anything. It's just that she needs to put this entire mess behind her and get on with her life, with people her own age."

"Good friends are hard to come by, and so I would think an age restriction would be counter productive."

"I appreciate what you're trying to do, but maybe you should save your breath for someone who has never taken a psychology course. I, too, know all the right things to say. All the verbal tools."

"I came because you are a friend. I would expect you would do the same for me."

Backus held up his good arm as a signal of surrender. "Sorry. I guess I'm just feeling sorry for myself."

"Did I ever tell you I was raised on a farm," Malley asked, and a broad smile caused crow's feet to appear at the corners of his eyes.

"No. I don't think so."

"You learn a lot growing up on a farm. I remember once we had this sick cow. Dad couldn't figure out what was wrong, so we penned her up to keep an eye on her. Pretty soon we figured it out. Invariably, right after she'd take a drink, she'd turn right around and crap in the water bucket, then take another drink."

"There's a moral to this story, I take it."

"Sometimes we can be our own worst enemy. Quit beating yourself."

Backus' face cracked into smile. "As I said once before. You're one poor liar. My guess is you've never set foot on a farm. However, your bedside manner is certainly unique."

"That's why I'm really a carpenter, and the priest thing is just a disguise."

The door opened, a man entered, and then hastily closed the door behind him.

"How did you manage to get past Irene?" Backus asked.

Charlie Johnson merely shrugged. "I told her she was needed at the front desk, and the rest is history."

"Glad you made it. I understand there's going to be a meeting at Sheriff Bodeman's home to try to determine the reasons behind the crash."

"That's correct. Tomorrow, to be exact. He's also working on a separate case."

"The bog lady?" Malley asked.

"Yes."

"I want to be there," Backus stated.

"You can ride with me if you like," Johnson volunteered. "If you don't mind riding in an old pickup."

"No problem. It's either that or thumbing it. So what does Bodeman hope to accomplish?"

"He's looking for answers, as are we all. He provided a federal agent he has worked with before, Aaron VanHorst, a list of everyone even remotely connected to this case, and he will have the results of the background checks."

"Like who?"

"Parish or Woodlove—whatever his name is—from the crash site, the Wrightham family members, people who were at your debate with James, James himself, those of us who were in the Tripacer…"

"Wait a minute. Why us? We were the victims."

"They're just looking for connections. It doesn't mean we're guilty of anything. Even the pilot who flew Lora up to find us, and, you, Mike, are on the list."

"Should be interesting," Mike interjected. "Count me in."

Backus was suddenly thoughtful. "I suppose they'll get all the dirt on the Greenland mystery. From everyone's point of view but mine."

"I wasn't going to bring it up," Malley said. "But I remember at the Retreat, it was at the point in the discussion when James brought it up you seemed to lose your way."

"There's nothing more I can add."

The door suddenly flew open with such force it crashed loudly into the wall. A woman who looked as cross as a bull burst into the room. Her narrow eyes focused squarely at Johnson, and she looked ready to drag him away by the scruff of his neck. Backus, however, saved the day.

"Irene. These are two good friends of mine."

"They better be. But now they both have to go."

"Why is that?"

"You have a female visitor, and sure as Moses I'm not going let all three in here."

"I told you. I don't want to see her."

"It isn't that Lynn woman. She's come and gone. It's wife number two, I think. With you it's hard to keep track. Joan Franks is her name." Bill Backus had to bite his tongue to keep from asking if she was sober.

"I guess that's it then," Malley said rising from the chair. "In case something comes up and we never meet again, the best of luck." He turned to Johnson. "And take care of Lora. You have a good one."

"I know," was all Johnson could think of to say as Malley exited the room. A slightly overweight woman of average height immediately replaced him. Her smooth silver hair curled up at her shoulders, and framed a pleasant, if somewhat drawn, face that was set in a weak smile. Her plain yellow dress was about a half-size to small. She looked directly at Backus, whose face registered concern.

"How did you know I was here?" Backus asked. The woman glanced at Irene, who spoke up immediately.

"I let her know. Couldn't let that blood sucking wife of yours be your only contact with family."

"That's quite alright, Irene. Charlie, I'll see you tomorrow. Now, if you don't mind, I'd like to talk to Professor Joan Franks alone."

Charlie Johnson immerged from the hospital expecting to find Mike Malley waiting for him. Instead, the cab of his faded and failing red Ford '83 pickup was empty. Malley had struck him as a loner much like himself, and someone who seemed to have his head screwed on pretty well. He was also secretive, and seemed to pop in and out of the flow of events at the most opportune times. It occurred to Johnson he didn't even know where Malley lived. Perhaps, since he was a priest, he resided within the rectory attached to St. Joseph's church in town. His idle curiosity about Malley faded as he noticed a piece of paper on the driver's side on the seat. He never locked the old truck so getting inside would not have been a problem for anyone. He retrieved the note, and slid in behind the steering wheel. He unfolded the paper and read:

Charlie, I must speak with you alone. You are the only one I can trust. Meet me at the Shoreview motel at six this evening. Room 19. Knock four times in quick succession. The motel is on old highway two just south of town. Please come. I need you. Sincerely, Sharon Wrightham

The hair on the back of Johnson's neck bristled. The handwriting was clearly by a practiced hand, neat and flowing and without flaw, which seemed peculiar for someone who might be under a great deal of stress. He recalled a lesson he had learned a long time before from his grandfather. "It is easy to catch an animal," the premier woodsman had said, "when you have the right bait." He couldn't shake the feeling he was the animal and Sharon Wrightham was the bait.

Absently he watched a red squirrel run up the trunk of a nearby oak tree and then disappear into a four-inch hole about six feet above the ground. It reappeared moments later and returned to the ground. Two college age women came by engaged in an animated conversation about the inebriated antics of someone named Lee, and the animal retreated to the branches. His thoughts again returned to Sharon. It had taken him a while to figure it out but Lora had clearly been jealous of her. He had to admit that if one went strictly by looks, Sharon would be very difficult to beat. He also had to admit his feelings for her were not entirely limited to friendship. He remembered the clock on the wall of the waiting room in the hospital. It had said five o'clock. He had an hour to decide what to do.

Deputy Lora Whitney sat quietly at her desk and stared blankly out into nothingness, a look that did not go unnoticed by Pam Calway, who worked the main desk of the Emergency Services and Law Enforcement center for Cass County. At the moment only an emergency operator, Calway, and Whitney occupied the room. Of Native American descent, Calway had over time adopted Whitney as her own, since Lora had no knowledge of her biological parents. Lora's relationship with Charlie Johnson was no secret, and it didn't take a psychologist to realize there was trouble in paradise. Johnson had just called from the Bemidji hospital to determine the status of an upcoming meeting at Sheriff Bodeman's lakefront home. She told him it was still a 'go,' and then asked if he wanted to speak with Lora. He had said 'sure,' but Lora declined, saying she was in the middle of a pile of paperwork, a gross exaggeration since the only thing occupying her desk at that time was a sleeping computer. It troubled Calway to see two of her children being so incredibly foolish. She left her place at the front desk, walked through an open door at the end of the open room, and into mass chaos, Sheriff Bodeman's office. She looked around with obvious bewilderment at the piles of papers, open cabinet drawers, and then closed the door behind her.

"Don't even think of flying into one of your cleaning moods," Bodeman ordered, looking up from the paperwork on his desk. "I finally have everything exactly where I want it and changing just one thing would throw my entire system out of whack."

"If there's a system here, I fail to see it."

"Don't start. What's up?"

"It's Lora. First she comes in late this morning. Some kind of flu she says. Since then she's been moping around all day."

"Maybe I better send her home."

"The end of her shift is not far off, and what she needs right now is not at home anyway."

"And what is that?"

"Charlie Johnson."

"Help me out here. Since when is playing cupid in my job description? Anyway, I thought the two of them were, well, you know, inseparable."

"Since you're obviously too old to remember how it goes, let me refresh your memory. Two people meet, they fall in love, everything is wonderful and they live happily ever after."

"Right. In the movies."

"I know. After the initial burst of excitement, usually one or the other or both start to have second thoughts. Rather than discuss their differences openly with each other, they let them fester inside, and often a tiny crevice becomes a deep canyon just too wide to cross."

"Exit romantic excitement. Enter reality. End of relationship. I've been there."

"Not necessarily. A relationship sometimes just needs a little help."

"OK. I give up. What are you driving at?"

"I'm going to tell you a secret, which must remain a secret, and then I'm going to ask a favor of you."

"I know what you're going to say, but go ahead. I'm not that old."

Pam Calway emerged from Bodeman's cluttered office with a smile and a white envelope. She glanced over at Whitney who sat exactly as she had for the last hour. Calway made her way around several workstations, and placed the white envelope in front of her. Whitney seemed to stir from a waking dream, and looked up at Calway's face.

"What's this?"

"Something has come up on a very important case."

"The crash?"

"Well, yes, actually. Sheriff Bodeman needs you to run this up to Johnson right away. He's at the Bemidji hospital visiting with that man Backus that was in the plane crash with him."

"Why not just give the hospital a call?"

"It's only a forty minute drive."

"Still. Is it something important?"

"Don't ask me. I just work here."

Johnson parked the pickup in the empty place reserved for Room 19, and stared at the motel ahead. The long low building was painted an atrocious shade of yellow, and the paint was peeling away in several places revealing the previous color, an even more atrocious pink. A piece of rusty metal with the number nineteen painted on it hung slightly askew on the varnished wooden door. A brown shade on the inside of the window prevented anyone from seeing into the room. The motel rested just feet from the continuous whining traffic of Old Hwy. 2, and Johnson wondered how many people actually spent an entire night there, or ever intended to. At this early evening hour, however, business appeared to be booming as a row of perhaps twenty cars lined the front of the building, and the red neon sign flashed 'no vacancy.'

This present endeavor, Johnson knew, was not a logical course of action. Just as important, his instincts told him not to proceed, that this was almost certainly some kind of trap, and his decision to proceed, in the final smelting, was a matter of trust. Despite what Whitney had proposed concerning Sharon's possible motive for eliminating her husband and Ethek, he couldn't bring himself to believe she would betray their friendship. In his mind he could hear her speak the words she had written on the paper, and he was ready to stake his life on the assumption the words were sincere.

Twice Charlie Johnson repeated the four knock staccato with no response. He tried the doorknob, found it unlocked, and slowly pushed the door inward. It occurred to him that that was backwards. An exterior door should always open outward for a fast exit in case of a fire, or whatever. The inside of the room was dim, and smelled of stale cigarette smoke. There was one double bed, a nightstand with a phone, and a dresser with a television set on top. One corner of the room was boxed off forming a six-foot cube, and the tiny compartment was undoubtedly what contained the bathroom. There was no luggage, no evidence of habitation, and Johnson suddenly felt relieved. He had fulfilled his self-imposed obligation to respond to Sharon's request, and now he was within his rights to simply turn and go. Except he couldn't. He knew he was at least fifteen minutes early, and could not, in good conscience, leave until the six o'clock time passed. He sat on the foot of the bed and felt suddenly awkward, like a nervous virgin waiting for his first prom date. He was considering returning to his pickup, when the faint grinding sound of a turning doorknob captured his complete attention. He looked closely at the outside door, and it suddenly occurred to him that the sound came from within the room, from the bathroom. He fully expected someone to appear with guns blazing, and was happily mistaken.

"Hello, Charlie," Sharon Wrightham said softly. She looked just as she had at their meeting at the Retreat, long blonde hair spilling over her shoulders, and she wore the same light blue denim jump suit with embroidered yellow butterflies. "I'm so glad you're alive. I knew you'd come." She sat down next to him at the foot of the bed, an arm's length away.

"Your request. How could I stay away? How did you get here?"

"Alfred. He seems to be on my side, at least for now."

"What can you tell me about the plane accident? I'm guessing your husband was somehow involved."

"It wasn't an accident. Maclin set it up."

"That doesn't make sense. He was on the plane with us. He took off on his own right after the crash."

"What? I don't understand…see how that's possible. Unless…"

"Yes?"

"Unless Jonathan decided to get rid of him. There was no love lost between the two."

"So Jonathan did at least know about it."

"I know he provided the money to make it happen, and afterwards, he took me to the crash site."

"The black helicopter."

"Yes. I saw you and my sister. I'm so thankful you're both alive."

"Lynn Bergen?"

"Yes. I was supposed to be on that plane, and my sister went in my place."

"So she said. She must care for you a lot."

"We are very close."

"Where is Jonathan now?"

"Reveling in his Senatorial appointment. I think he suddenly realized I could be an asset rather than a liability. I've been given a reprieve. He plans for us to stay at the lodge on Leech for now. That's where I'm headed when I leave here."

"I saw your sister earlier at the hospital."

"She's going to stay in town for a while, but out of sight. Jonathan thinks you all perished in the plane crash."

"Doesn't he watch the news? The rescue has been on all the Duluth stations, and in most of the papers."

"He doesn't concern himself with local activities. It's beneath him."

"Surely, he must have someone."

"In California, sure, but here, only Alfred."

"What do you think he'll do when he finds out?"

"I don't know. Probably nothing for now. Other than a few witnesses, he has no direct link to the crash. It would be nearly impossible to convict him of anything. Really only his brother, Maclin, could put him away, and possibly Luke James."

"You realize your testimony might be enough."

"I won't testify. Please don't think badly of me. He could easily finish what he started. There has to be another way. Please keep this conversation just between us, until I can figure some things out."

"Take this," Johnson said as he handed her a white card from his pocket. "It's Whitney's cell phone number. Just in case you change your mind." Johnson hesitated a few moments and then continued. "There is another angle to consider. There are those who think you might have had a hand in all this. That you are trying to eliminate the Wrightham heirs to claim the estate for yourself."

"I don't know what to say to that except it's not true. I just want to be free, to get my life back. You are the only one I can completely trust. I need you, Charlie, to be on my side, to be at my side, forever."

Johnson found himself getting lost in Sharon's captivating, almost hypnotic presence, and had to turn away to keep from losing himself in it.

"I will always be your friend," he said.

"Your true feelings betrayed you at the Retreat," she continued, and moved closer.

"I don't recall…"

"You told me if there was anything you could ever do."

"Sure. Anything to help. I still mean that."

"Good." She stood, and looked down upon his face. "Please excuse me for just a moment." Sharon returned to the tiny restroom and Johnson sighed in relief. He wondered if she realized how overpoweringly attractive she really was. Her comments seemed to put some sense to recent events, at least as to who was behind the crash, but there were still many unanswered questions. Maclin's involvement could probably be chalked up to revenge, but why would Jonathan get involved, how did Parish fit in, and why had Maclin ended up among the unfortunate passengers on the plane?

"Sharon, I was wondering..." Johnson called out, but stopped in mid thought. "Oh my god," was all Johnson could manage to say as someone reappeared from the restroom. She turned to face him directly. Sharon Wrightham, with flowing blonde hair with streams of darker brown cascading about her shoulders, stood just feet away wearing only a nightshirt made of some kind of fabric mesh. The white garment clung to her perfect curves. The sole purpose of the widely spaced interwoven threads was to stimulate sexual excitement, which at this point, was not going to be a problem. Her youthful breasts struggled against their prison bars and Johnson steadfastly refused to let his eyes stray any lower. In the dimness of the room, she looked like a goddess with a beauty beyond reality. There was absolutely nothing he could do to prevent the normal sexual masculine reaction, or force his eyes from the figure before him.

"How...why...oh boy," Johnson said groping for words.

"I know you care about me," Sharon said seductively.

"I do, but..."

"You're the only man I know who has ever helped me without expecting something in return. What you see before you is all I can offer you."

"Please. You don't have to do this."

"I want to do this. I think I love you."

"I...there is someone..."

"Lora Whitney?"

"Yes."

"It is natural for a man to love more than one woman. Look at the Bible. Look at the Mormons. I would understand. I could share you with another, as long as I knew you loved me." She took a step forward, just inches from Johnson, and the intoxicating scent of sexual desire drove all other thoughts from his mind. What she was saying suddenly made perfect sense. Even Grandfather talked about the old Indian ways when a man might have more than one wife. It was natural. There was something else, however, tugging at his conscience, something that he must also consider. It haunted the fringes of the overwhelming sexual reaction, a wisp of a notion that was disturbing in its honesty. There was someone who would not understand this 'perfect sense.' That she might never know was beside the point. A betrayal of the heart was a betrayal of the soul.

Lora Whitney turned off the four-lane onto Old Hwy. 2 just a couple miles southeast of Bemidji, and continued on towards the south end of town. It hadn't occurred to her until she was halfway there that she had no clue where the Bemidji hospital was located, and intended to stop at the first gas station and ask for directions. She turned north at the junction of Hwy 2 and Hwy 71 and began watching for a gas pump. The flashing no vacancy sign for the Shoreview Motel caught her attention and she remembered the rumors about the place, and its nicknames, Skinview for one, and several of a much cruder nature, and parked clearly in view in front of the building was a familiar faded Ford pickup.

Sharon Wrightham moved very close to Johnson and rested her hands on his shoulders, as he remained sitting on the edge of the bed. Her warm fingers gently but firmly kneaded his neck muscles, and then began moving down his chest.

"This is all I can do well," she whispered in his ear. "I can bring you to the brink a dozen times before you…"

"Sorry, but I just can't," Johnson said and couldn't believe his own ears.

Light suddenly cancelled the dimness of the room, and both Sharon and Charlie turned to see Deputy Lora Whitney standing in the open doorway. Her uncomprehending expression gave way quickly to one of disbelief. Very slowly, she drew her revolver from its holster, but let it hang at her side. Johnson's mind suddenly filled with the countless movie plots that shared a similar theme. Jealous lover finds the significant other in the arms of someone else. Looking at her revolver reminded him some had a most unhappy ending. He rose to face her directly, and Sharon sat down on the foot of the bed, drawing the blanket around her. Suddenly, the room felt chilly.

"This is going to take some explaining," Johnson began.

In circumstances such as those, some might break down in tears, some might fly into a rage, some might simply turn and leave, but Whitney's despair went yet another way.

"What's to explain?" she said, returning her firearm to the holster. "It's not like we're married. What you do on your own time is none of my business. I wish you both the best."

"We didn't do anything," Sharon said.

"You mean you didn't do anything yet. But in another couple of minutes this would have been a real triple X show."

"We were discussing the plane crash," Sharon offered.

"Right. Dressed, or should I say undressed, like that?"

"Are you willing to at least listen to an explanation?" Charlie asked.

"Hey. No explanations necessary. I'm sorry I intruded. I'll leave now and you can finish what you started."

Sharon took Johnson by the arm and he turned to face her. "Go now. Let me talk to Lora alone."

"Are you sure?"

"Positive. You'd be bored anyway. Woman talk."

"Lora?"

"Suit yourself. I promise not to shoot her," she added sarcastically.

Whitney stepped aside as Johnson left through the open door. He noticed the parking lot was now mostly empty, and he wondered if Whitney's squad car had anything to do with the sudden loss of business. He sat for several moments behind the steering wheel of his old pickup, and thought, if he was a drinking man, he would now go out and get as shit-faced as possible.

"You are a very lucky woman," Sharon Wrightham said, as she emerged from the bathroom fully dressed.

"I don't follow," Whitney said suspiciously.

"Nothing did happen, and wasn't about to. It was over before it started."

"Why should I care? Take him. No skin off my nose."

"I would in a heartbeat, if I could. But he's committed to you."

"Committed?"

"I said committed because it's a matter of honor for him. He won't let you down, no matter what. Not until you tell him to leave."

"Since when are you the expert?"

"I am an expert on only one thing, and that's men. You will also notice I didn't say he loved you. I said he was committed to you. There's a difference."

"Which is?"

"You'll have to figure it out. And you'll have to decide which of the two, if either, represents your feelings towards him?"

"I'm not good at feelings," Whitney admitted.

"I can tell you this. You better get good. Or you're going to lose the one in a million man out there who would jump off a cliff for you. And I'll lay it out so even you can understand. The moment you let him go, I'll be there to catch him."

"You could have any man you wanted," Whitney observed.

Sharon laughed. "You don't know what it's like to be really beautiful. Everyone stares at you like you're some kind of freak. Women are jealous, and don't hesitate to stab you in the back. Men mentally undress you with their eyes. You're a target for every pervert on the street. You can't go out in public without a bodyguard or covering your face. In a strange way, it's a lot like being truly ugly. Only a very few want to get to know you for who you really are. Few can see past the exterior."

"Am I supposed to feel sorry for you?"

"No, but understand me. And understand this. You're an even bigger fool than I thought if you don't realize what you have. My guess is you knew once how truly unique this man is, but you're letting him slip away, or worse yet, you're driving him away."

"As I said," Whitney said quietly. "I'm not much good when it comes to feelings."

"It would be worth your while to learn. Remember. Commitment or love. You decide. If neither, then tell him good-by." A faint knock sounded on the frame of the open door, and Sharon nodded to the slight man who stood there. "One moment, Alfred. I'll be right there." She turned back to Whitney. "Just so you know, this little discussion was to level the playing field. From now on, you're on your own."

Lora Whitney sat alone on the bed where Charlie had been sitting a few minutes before. She realized full well she had spoken the complete truth to Sharon Wrightham. She was no good at feelings. It wasn't that she didn't have them. The massive jumble of thoughts and emotions in her mind at this point was clearly something. It was just that all her life she had met events head on, perhaps not always with the required tact, but always honestly and openly. Emotion really didn't have much to do with it. She also knew Sharon was correct. Somehow, after a wonderful start, her relationship with Charlie was slipping away, and what hurt even more was that she didn't have a clue what to do about it. They had seemed completely compatible at first, bantering and playing off each other like a well-rehearsed comedy team, only it wasn't rehearsed. It just came naturally. It had been wonderful to keep things loose, fun, and uncomplicated. The sudden appearance of Sharon Wrightham at the Retreat seemed to be the turning point in their relationship, and his dedication to her was maddening. It was at that point that she began to doubt his feelings for her. He always had been good at evading the issue, but then, she quickly concluded, so had she. One thing was for sure, however. She sure as hell wasn't going to change for any man. This is who she was, and if Charlie couldn't accept that, then, well, Sharon Wrightham could have him.

"Oh shit!" she said out loud, remembering the envelope she was supposed to deliver to Johnson. She pulled it from her inside jacket pocket. Pam Calway's handwriting on the front said: *For Charlie Johnson.* "What the hell," she mumbled, and tore open the end. Johnson was gone, and now it might be up to her to complete whatever task Bodeman had requested. She opened the folded note, and read the two printed words several times before their full implication finally sank in. It was, she realized, merely a confirmation of something she already suspected. Suddenly, her jumble of emotions came together at one focal point. She crumpled up the piece of paper, and flung it against the wall.

"What are we going to do?" she said. "What are we going to do?"

Chapter 16

▼

September one dawned clear and chilly with the temperature settling in at thirty-eight degrees, and a few weather stations reported scattered frost in some low-lying areas. The power of the sun, however, quickly warmed the air, and by one-thirty in the afternoon the mercury hit eighty-two degrees. The not uncommon wide range of temperatures made morning clothing selection something of a gamble. The light jacket and sweater cheerfully selected in the AM would be soon discarded, as they became a burden in the afternoon heat.

Parish noted the new black Cadillac that was parked next to the blue crew-cab pickup, as Mr. Bell parked the used Chevy Blazer at the Wrightham summer lodge, and also the black helicopter that occupied a small open area of the manicured lawn. He waited patiently for Wrightham's manservant, Alfred, to acknowledge their presence. Soon he appeared in the doorway, and then approached along the split-stone walkway. He opened the passenger side door, and Parish slowly stepped out.

"Thank you, Alfred," he said.

"Mr. Wrightham awaits you in the sunroom."

"Very good. Mr. Bell, a little help please. I seem to be feeling my age today."

Bell came around from the driver's side and took the old man's arm.

"Lead the way," he said, and walked stiffly next to Bell. He glanced in the direction of the house, and noted Wrightham watching through the door window. It was not Wrightham who greeted them as they entered, however, but Wrightham's wife, Sharon. She acknowledged him with a polite nod, but noticeably shrank from Bell's cold stare, and disappeared immediately into an adjacent room. Alfred led them to the sunroom where Wrightham sat staring out over the blue waters of the lake and then exited into the kitchen.

"I've been expecting you," Wrightham said abruptly. "What have you to report from the Family?" The old man looked tired and feeble, and Wrightham wondered why the most powerful group of people on earth would send such a misfit.

"May I sit?"

"Whatever suits you. Seems like the last time you preferred to stand."

"Arthritis." With Bell's aid, he lowered himself onto the sofa. Bell then moved directly behind him, arms folded across his chest.

"Whatever."

"If you don't mind my asking," Parish began in his low quiet voice, "how are your projects progressing?"

"On track. No doubt you've heard about the unfortunate fatal airplane accident."

"No, actually I hadn't."

"Surely, you...never mind. You will. And except for the official swearing in ceremony, the senatorial appointment is a done deal."

"Really?"

"The important thing is why are you stalling on your end? With just a word, I can release your face to the world with very serious implications for not only you, but the Family."

Again Wrightham couldn't help but feel sorry for the old fool. But business was business. The old man had spent most of the conversation looking at the floor, but now he noticeably straightened, and looked directly at Wrightham. "You don't get out much do you?"

"I've been exceedingly busy with the senatorial…"

"It would be advisable for you to pay greater attention to the local events."

"What possible interest would I have with the hicks around here? As soon as everything is finalized, I'm heading back to civilization in California."

"In case you haven't heard, Congress convenes in Washington, not LA."

"Whatever. I'm sure I'll put in an appearance now and then. It's not like I need the work," Wrightham laughed.

"I'd like to share some information with you if you're not too busy. Information that you may find quite shocking."

"Nothing shocks me."

"First, the Governor is reconsidering your appointment."

"What? How would you know?"

"I know most everything, Mr. Wrightham."

"Why would he do that?"

"It seems two of the young women who were in the compromising pictures are willing to testify it was just a scam. While he has no direct evidence against you personally, he is, how do they say, dropping you like a hot potato."

"No matter. What's a mere senator to being a member of the Family?"

"No comparison, of course. But then there is also the matter of this plane crash in which you endeavored to prove yourself in some way that yet escapes me."

"What about it?"

"All survived."

Wrightham noted that the fragile old man that had entered his home was no more. Parish seemed to gain strength with each word.

"I don't see how that's possible. I saw the crash. All four bodies."

"Four? That event was staged, I believe, for your benefit."

"But we did the computer simulations. There was only a remote chance of failure."

"Yes, I'd been advised of your simulations just before the event occurred. We ran one of our own, and it predicted a seventy eight percent chance of a survivable crash. About the only thing you had right was the crash site."

"How is that possible?"

"A simulation is only as good as the information you feed into it. Yours was decidedly incomplete."

"That's unlikely."

"You forgot to include the fact that Koler was a pilot, and, therefore, the sabotage was ineffective."

"It shouldn't have mattered. They were supposed to be unconscious." Wrightham remembered reviewing the replay and seeing the pilot fighting to maintain control. The final seconds, however, seemed conclusive.

"You see, that's where the wild card comes in. Professor Backus. His concern for Lynn Bergen delayed the take off, which enabled both Koler and Johnson enough time to regain consciousness."

"How do you know all this?"

"As I said, Mr. Wrightham, I know most everything. The point is, however, these are all things you should know."

"Again, it's irrelevant."

"Where are your people?"

"What do you mean?"

"Those that rode with you in the helicopter to confirm the crash."

"Well, James is back in Bismarck, I think, and my wife and Alfred are right here."

"You're missing someone."

"One of the hired help. Mr..... I can't remember his name...Smith, I think. He had a thin mustache."

"Where is he?"

"Unknown. I paid him off and he disappeared."

"You have great potential, but you're sloppy, Mr. Wrightham."

"That's getting annoying."

"Pardon."

"You keep saying my name. I know who I am."

Parish ignored his concern. "You're sloppy, Mr. Wrightham, and that concerns me. You've let yet another wild card loose."

"I suppose you're going to tell me where he is."

"He has been secured. Other than that, I don't know."

"I thought you were invincible. That you knew everything."

"The rich feed off the middle class. We feed off the rich. There's always a bigger shark. To make it all work, there cannot be loose ends. From the very beginning of this project, you've left many strings dangling."

"All of this is irrelevant. I have the tapes, and am prepared to release them."

"Now I must tell you the hard truth," Parish continued. "Your threats to expose me to the world are worthless."

"And just why is that?"

"Each member of the Family knows he's expendable. Rarely, but occasionally, one of our own falls from grace, and is written off, disposed of as a liability."

"You mean murdered?"

"Murder, never. Execution, of course."

"There's a difference?"

"We are our own country. We write our own laws, and we dole out punishment to the occasional few who break those laws. Our executions are no different from the gas chambers, lethal injections, electric chairs, or occasional hangings of this country."

Wrightham glanced over at the menacing figure of Mr. Bell. "He looks like he might…"

"Mr. Bell has occasionally helped with these unpleasant tasks."

"A hired killer?"

"Hardly. He is no more guilty of murder than the man who trips the gallows. He's merely doing what our society has determined is appropriate under the circumstances."

"So where is this 'country' of yours?"

Sadly, Parish shook his head. "You still haven't gotten the picture. We are a nation of people not restricted to any borders, or geographical location."

"And you just kill off those who…"

"Kills or leads to the death of one of our own. We live by the old view, an eye for an eye, and we observe that rule from the highest to the lowest level. We do not make war on other nations, we do not execute world leaders. And we do not generally involve ourselves with the suffering masses, except to observe and occasionally accept new members. We encourage activities that are advantageous to us and discourage those that are not, which is no different than any other country, or religious institution. We are not murderers, Mr. Wrightham, and, in fact, there are crueler things then executions."

"If there are, they escape me."

"To be shunned, discredited, and condemned to live out one's life apart from the group in abject poverty."

"So much for Family loyalty."

"Be not deceived by the name. We like to say we are a family of gentle sharks, and to ensure our survival, even we have been known to turn on our own."

"So where do I stand?"

"Your threats are empty. Worse yet, your handling of this matter has been poor. You do not make a fit member of the human family, let alone the Family."

Wrightham sat silently studying the man, looking for a sign of weakness, but could not find the slightest trace in his sober expression.

"Why do I get the feeling you're about to make some kind of a deal?" Wrightham speculated.

"There is no deal, and I'm here to tell you need to maintain control over your people, Mr. Wrightham, by whatever means. Your poorly executed plan aside, there is one member of your group who has been, how shall I put this, freelancing on her own."

"Sharon," Wrightham said without hesitation.

"Did you know she had a secret meeting with Charlie Johnson?"

"Well, no."

"I wonder what they were talking about. The beautiful Minnesota weather perhaps?"

"She's dead," Wrightham said with conviction. "Or soon will be."

"You have learned so little. As I said once before, do not rush to a violent solution. Only after all other options have been exhausted."

"I'm exhausted!"

"Well, we'll see, won't we? Seems like the last time you tried, you couldn't tell the difference between her and her sister."

Wrightham studied the old man carefully. What had happened to the meek old fool that had entered his house just minutes before? His voice had quickly grown in intensity and then never faltered, and gave not the slightest hint of his apparent age.

"To protect my own interests and the interests of the Family, I'm forced to help clean up the mess you've created," Parish continued. "The FAA will not determine the reason for the crash."

"Why is that?"

"Bad fire," Bell said. "Burned upon impact."

Sharon Wrightham appeared from the kitchen of the Wrightham summer lodge carrying a tray with assorted hors d'oeuvres, and a fresh pot of tea. Bell watched her carefully as she approached. A beautiful specimen of a woman. The butterflies on her blue jumpsuit reminded him of his own wife, a lover of flowers and nature. He quickly buried her memory under a ton of reality. Wife and child were gone, lost in a senseless tragedy, and it had been a chance meeting with Mr. Parish that saved him from following them into oblivion. He'd lost count of the years he'd taken assignments for the Family through Mr. Parish.

The first had been a deserter of sorts, an important businessman who thought he could double cross the most powerful people on earth, steal millions of dollars, use a pathetic legal system to his advantage, and get away with it. For many years, he'd been part of Parish's Family, and while he owed Parish a debt he could never repay, it was all about to change. His time was nearing an end, his mission nearly complete.

"We're having a private meeting here," Wrightham snapped, as Sharon was about to set the tray on the round wooden end table. "Get that crap out of here. And don't you have anything to wear other than your butterfly suit?"

"That's very thoughtful of you, Mrs. Wrightham," Parish interrupted. "And much appreciated. Please join us."

"She's not important." Wrightham insisted.

"And what's your assessment of all this?" Parish asked Sharon, while ignoring Wrightham.

"All of what? I'm afraid I've been preoccupied with the hors d'oeuvres."

"The mess your husband has gotten us all into."

"I don't really have an opinion."

"We have an arrangement," Wrightham interrupted. "I do the thinking. She provides the entertainment."

"Let me put it this way, Mrs. Wrightham," Parish continued, and seemed to choose his words carefully. "Your honest opinion. Just yes or no will do. Shall we simply let events unfold?"

Somewhat confused, yet knowing her own life could very well be on the line, Sharon considered for some time before she spoke. "I guess," she said finally. "I don't see any other alternative."

The occupants of the Bodeman home were occupied in casual conversation, enjoying cold drinks, in anticipation of forensics expert Sara Thomson, who had not yet arrived from her office in St. Paul. Forrest Bodeman was about to start without her, when the familiar diminutive form pushed her way into the house carrying a large briefcase.

"Thought we'd have to start without you," Bodeman said, as he took the briefcase from her hands. He looked out through the open door to the driveway behind his house. "I thought the Feds were going to send an agent up with you."

"Something urgent came up and VanHorst couldn't make it. However, he did brief me on some interesting information that he uncovered. Quite startling even."

"Yes?"

"It's all in the briefcase. Let's just say I brought along a couple bombshells. Could I talk you out of a drink before we get started."

"Pick your poison."

"A tall glass of ice water would hit the spot."

"There's a pitcher in the fridge. Help yourself. I'll get the crew together around the dining room table." Bodeman turned and addressed his three guests. "Listen up. This meeting is hereby convened."

Charlie Johnson and Bill Backus, his left arm in a huge white cast, came to the table first, followed by Lora Whitney. Bodeman noticed the two friends had barely looked at each other, and had, as yet, to share more than a polite hello. If the note that Calway had sent to Johnson had been meant to bring the two closer together, then it was evident it had been a total failure. He considered saying something, but thought better of it. He was no damn cupid, and meddling in someone else's personal life was something he swore he'd never do. The best of intentions quite often created a worse outcome. This was an investigative meeting concerning the crash of a single engine aircraft, not the lonely hearts club, and he was sure all present would treat it as such. However, if Johnson was to ask him for advice, that would be a different story, and he'd likely give it to him with both barrels.

Thomson took a chair on one long side of the table, with Backus and Bodeman directly across from her. Whitney and Johnson sat on opposite ends, Bodeman noted, as far as they could get from one another as possible. He wondered if they knew how obviously ridiculous they were acting. Thomson opened her briefcase and pulled out a handful of papers. Before she could begin, the sheriff posed a question.

"Anyone hear anything from Father Malley? I though he wanted to be here."

"Nothing," both Johnson and Whitney said together. They looked directly at each other, Johnson managed a weak smile, but Whitney looked away.

"I doubt if he'll be here," Thomson offered.

"And just why is that?" Bodeman pressed.

"Because there is no such person."

"What are you talking about?"

Thomson retrieved a printout from the pile of papers and scanned the contents. "VanHorst found sixty seven people in the country with the name Mike Malley. However, none were from Minnesota, none were priests, and none matched his description."

"He must have missed something, somehow."

"He did all the standard checks. Military, social security, IRS, federal and state records, criminal records, and even People Find on the Internet. He couldn't get a match."

"You visited with him as much as anyone, Whitney. Did he give a hint as to where he was from?"

"Not that I recall. I just assumed he was from around here. Who'd ever question a priest?"

"He said he was really a carpenter, and even that he was married with a child," Backus interjected. "He always said it sort of tongue-in-cheek and I really thought he was just joking."

"We may be making a lot more of this than there is," Johnson observed. "Not everyone is on a government list."

"Since when?" Whitney cut in. "Maybe if he was some kind of alien…"

"As in from another country or outer space?" Johnson shot back.

"Whichever," Whitney replied sarcastically, and immediately turned away.

Bodeman was on the verge of telling them both to go to their rooms when Thomson continued.

"VanHorst ran background checks on fifty four people related to this case, and no one other than Malley and Maclin Ethek sent up a red flag."

"What about Wrightham?" Johnson asked. "Sharon indicated…" He suddenly remembered her request to keep their conversation confidential and continued. "…that there might be something there."

"Nothing criminal or even suspicious. Just your average multimillionaire taking advantage of whomever he can."

"And the easy ones twice," Bodeman finished.

"Was he able to find out anything about our friend from the crash site, Rolland Woodlove, alias Mr. Parish," Johnson asked. He had described his encounter with Parish to both Bodeman and Whitney immediately upon returning to Cass County.

"There are hundreds of Parish's in this country, and so without more to go on that was a dead end. He did say he'd try his overseas contacts, and get back to me, but the name, Rolland Woodlove, was apparently made up as there is no such person anywhere in this country."

"Not surprising."

"Anything to support my theory that Sharon Wrightham was behind this," Whitney asked.

"Will you give it a rest already," Johnson interrupted. "Just because you're jealous of her…"

"Of her! That poor, defenseless, spoiled, Barbie doll."

"Enough!" Bodeman roared. "I liked you two a lot better when you were playing kissyface. You two have been taking shots at one another since you arrived here and I'm getting damn sick of it!" Whitney mumbled an apology, but Johnson was sorely tempted to get up and leave, and probably would have except that he knew Bodeman had a valid point. This was no place to discuss Lora's obvious jealousy problem.

"Sorry," he said sincerely. He turned to face Whitney directly. "You were saying?"

"I was just wondering if VanHorst turned up anything that would lend support to my theory?"

"Well, maybe," Thomson said, with a hint of drama. "I have to admit, I saved the best for last."

"Yes?" Bodeman pressed.

"It seems our investigation and the Feds' crossed paths, and we were able to determine the whereabouts of Morgan Wrightham, Jonathan and Maclin's mother."

"So where has she been hiding for the last dozen years?"

"Apparently resting comfortably under a floating bog."

Following Thomson's startling disclosure that the bog lady was almost certainly Morgan Wrightham, the group huddled together on Thomson's side of the table. They compared the various pictures VanHorst had provided with the results of the forensics analysis and the resemblance left little doubt that the pictures were of the same woman. After several minutes they returned to their places. Whitney felt that one more chip had fallen in favor of her theory, but Thomson quickly took it away.

"I've tended to support your hypothesis about Sharon since she had everything to gain from eliminating the Wrightham heirs, but this present development presents something of a problem."

"Which is?" Whitney asked.

"Morgan Wrightham met her fate long before Sharon was ever a part of the Wrightham household. She couldn't have known her."

"So we're back to determining who had the most to gain from her death, and the death of Maclin, and the death of the others on the plane," Bodeman said. "Assuming there is a connection between them all."

"Logically, we're back to Jonathan," Johnson stressed, and looked over at Whitney, who would not look in his direction.

"VanHorst also ran a check for the 'line of heirs' for the Wrightham estate," Thomson continued. "At least as much as he could determine. Seems it's all pretty secretive."

"Find anything?" Bodeman asked.

"He's still trying to get a copy of Franklin Wrightham's original will, but from what he can determine so far, through some sort of contest, Jonathan and Morgan ended up with his estate. Maclin was left out in the cold."

"So it is conceivable that Jonathan did arrange for the elimination of his mother in order to have the entire pie."

"It is possible, certainly I'd say of all known suspects he had the likeliest motive; however, according to what VanHorst dug up, that assumption is tenuous at best. Morgan apparently had no interest in running the estate, and turned all the business dealings over to Jonathan. She seemed quite content to spend money, and hired several male escorts to take care of her more personal needs. Having said that, however, the Wrightham family did in fact make a trip to Minnesota from California at about the time Morgan seems to have dropped out sight, no pun intended. At least she was no longer socially visible."

"Did anyone ever report her missing? Jonathan, for instance, or Maclin?"

"Maclin was essentially booted out of the family not long after their first trip to Minnesota, and, no, there was never any missing person's report filed by anyone."

"That seems rather strange."

"The super rich pretty much isolate themselves from the suffering masses, and there was never any indication of foul play. For all anyone would know, she could have been traipsing around Europe for the last twenty years."

"What about Maclin as a suspect?"

"Although he surely would have had a motive for murder, Jonathan would have been his logical target, not Morgan."

"This is one hell of a mess," Bodeman admitted. "Throw in the plane crash, and there's more loose ends than at an octopus convention. Speaking of the plane crash, the FAA came back empty handed. Seems the entire area was reduced pretty much to ashes."

"It must have been Parish, alias Woodlove," Johnson speculated. "But why?"

"Well, whoever it was clearly intended for all evidence of a sabotaged plane to be obliterated."

"If Wrightham is involved, that probably means he and Parish are connected somehow, or at least share a common goal."

"Or maybe lightning struck," Whitney suggested. She intended the statement as a joke, but her voice lacked any indication of humor, and the rest merely stared at her.

Bill Backus had remained silent during most of the conversation, but now spoke.

"I'm having a hard time trying to figure out how I tie in to all this."

"Maybe you just happened to be at the wrong place at the wrong time," Johnson stated. "I have come to believe you are responsible for saving all of us."

"How's that? One minute I was walking over to see what was going on with Lynn, and the next I was laying flat on my back under some spruce trees with a broken arm."

"It's likely your appearance was not anticipated, and delayed the take off. That bought the necessary time for Koler to wake up and take control of the aircraft."

"Where's Koler now?"

"Back home with his wife in LaCrescent, still undergoing treatment for his head injury, which turned out to be more severe than he thought."

"And Lynn?"

"Last I heard she was still in Bemidji trying to see you."

Backus nodded, frowned slightly, and then continued on a different front. "There is something else to consider."

"Yes?" Bodeman asked.

"If it's true we were all supposed to die, then someone out there is not happy, and might very well try again."

Johnson sat silently contemplating what to say next. Sharon had indicated her husband was most likely a co-conspirator in the crash, along with Maclin. He felt he had an obligation to bring up her suspicions at this meeting, but also there was the promise to her to keep their conversation between them.

"I don't think we're in any immediate danger," he said finally.

"Another of your gut feelings?" Whitney asked, and this time her voice was sincere, something that did not go unnoticed by Johnson.

"Trackers have a saying. Pick a set of tracks and follow them to the end. Don't get sidetracked by a cross trail. Don't lose focus. Unfortunately, there is a set of tracks in all this that none of us have picked up on."

"At this point in time," Thomson concluded, "Jonathan Wrightham would seem to be the primary suspect in the death of Morgan Wrightham, and possibly the plane crash. However, there is no direct evidence, merely a very flimsy connection, and that falls well short of probable cause."

"I think that's where we have to focus our investigation," Whitney added. "Try to determine a common link between the victims of the plane crash and Morgan Wrightham. As Charlie has stated, there must still be a missing thread."

"You're still officially in charge," Bodeman advised. "What do you want to do next?"

"I don't…as I stated…I'm in over my head."

"Not long ago we sat at this same table, and your stubborn, obstinate character led to the discovery of the plane crash. You have good instincts, if a little misdirected at times."

"Yes sir." Whitney suddenly felt ashamed for her earlier performance. She couldn't blame it all on Johnson. Bodeman might jump on her one moment, but it was not meant to be taken personally, and just as quickly he would offer her a compliment. He was just bluntly honest, and didn't know any other way to be. "But my instincts at this point are a little confused," she admitted.

"You and Charlie make a good team, at least you used to. I suggest you two shake hands and come out fighting for the same side this time." It suddenly occurred to Bodeman he had done exactly what he swore he wouldn't do. Play cupid.

Johnson looked across the table at Whitney.

"I think I can handle that."

"For the good of the investigation," Whitney added.

"Well, put your heads together and get back to me."

Both recognized that as a not so subtle hint to leave, and both walked towards the exit. Whitney left first, but Bodeman spoke before Johnson was out the door.

"And Johnson?" he said.

"Yes."

"Make peace with Whitney before you two drive me crazy, and break Calway's heart."

Chapter 17

On the trip back to Bemidji after the meeting at Bodeman's home, Johnson and Backus remained silent in the old Ford pickup. Johnson had picked him up earlier in the day at the entrance to the hospital, thinking it might not be a good idea to go inside and provoke Mrs. Latala any further. On the way to Bodeman's home and the investigative meeting they had chatted about a wide variety of topics, but now both were occupied with individual thoughts. Finally, Johnson turned off the four lane onto Old Hwy. 2, and five minutes later pulled in behind Backus' tiny apartment. Backus sat silently staring at the door for several moments, as if in indecision as to whether he should go in or not, and finally nodded a thank you to Johnson.

"Kind of hard not to notice you and Whitney aren't on the best of terms," he said as he exited the pickup. "Hope everything turns out all right. I'd give you some advice, but given my success with women, you'd be well advised to do just the opposite."

"Thanks. Whitney and I are meeting tomorrow morning to go over some things. Are you going to be OK here?"

"Yes, and there is actually somewhere else I could go, but…"

"But?"

"My second wife invited me to stay with her at her home on Musky Lake, but watching her self-destruct would be worse than living alone. Hey. Don't worry about me. I'll be fine."

"You still have my number?"

"Yes, and Officer Whitney's."

"Let me know if there's anything I can do. Don't hesitate to call."

"Thanks."

Well after the headlights from Johnson's pickup had faded in the darkness, Backus remained standing outside his hovel, staring at the door. Its spartan amenities were perfect for a couple of college kids, but they were not exactly what he would consider sufficient for home sweet home. After earning three post-graduate degrees and two doctorates, and having taught for over twenty years, all he had to show for his efforts was a one-bedroom flat that smelled like old tennis shoes. He was broke, shunned by his colleagues, and alone. The only people who treated him as a friend were the people he had just left in the Bodeman home, and that was merely because they were not privy to the workings of the college board who could, quite literally, end his career. If he explained everything concerning the Greenland incident to his peers, it would still not be enough. He would certainly be called a liar and a charlatan, since at this point they would have only his word to go on. It was ironic. It was quite likely he'd end up doing what he always told his students not to do—flip burgers for minimum wage for the rest of their lives. Finally, he dug deep in his pocket and extracted the key to the lock, and it was at that point he realized the door was slightly ajar. He stepped slowly over the threshold, and was momentarily startled by a familiar voice that came from deep within the darkness of the room.

"Hello, Bill." Backus immediately recognized the voice of Mike Malley. "Please close the door, and don't turn on the lights. I seem to be having some trouble with my eyes, and the bright light is very painful. There are a few things I need to discuss with you."

"But I can hardly see you."

"Bear with me on this."

If it had been almost any other person, Backus would have been suspicious, but Father Malley was someone he completely trusted.

"Sure. So what is it you want to discuss?" Backus asked as he settled into the only other chair he owned, a brown kitchen chair with padding starting to escape from the seat. He could just barely make out the dim outline of the other man, who was perhaps only fifteen feet away. He seemed to be wearing some sort of tight fitting covering over his hair. "Another farm story?"

"No," the man chuckled. "I'd like to but I don't have the luxury of the extra time."

"Then what?"

"I know what you brought back from Greenland."

"You do? How?"

"Not important. But what you don't realize is that in some strange way you didn't find it, it found you."

"You lost me."

"What are the chances of drilling a four inch hole a thousand feet deep through solid ice on a glacier bigger than Texas and finding a piece of metal one inch in diameter?"

"About one in several billion," Backus admitted.

"Do you know what it is?"

Backus hesitated. He'd kept his discovery a secret, but it would be a relief to share it with someone. He couldn't think of anyone more appropriate than Father Mike Malley. "An ancient artifact from an unknown civilization," Backus speculated.

"And yet at the debate at the Retreat, you couldn't bring yourself to admit that."

"No scholar on this earth would believe me. It would be on par with the arrowhead in the lump of coal that the Reverend James produced at the Retreat. An obvious fake. An advanced civilization a hundred thousand years old is beyond belief by itself, and for it to be located in southern Greenland is even more preposterous. And even if I could somehow get the scientific community to accept the artifact as valid, it would throw a monkey wrench into what scientists believe to be true about the origins of modern man. Do you remember hearing about the Ice Man?"

"Of course. The five thousand year old corpse that was found intact in the Alps."

"There were a great many scientists who considered the find a hoax for sometime, because the man carried something that no one from that time period should have had."

"Which was?"

"A precision copper artifact."

"And that was noteworthy because…?"

"People of the time weren't supposed to have that level of technology. There is still considerable debate over where he might have acquired it. Perhaps you haven't heard, but there is growing evidence the Egyptian civilization could be ten thousand or more years old, not a few thousand as currently believed. Men in ancient times appear to have acquired a vast amount of knowledge, even secrets of the Universe unknown to us today."

"I have heard. So what happened to this knowledge?"

"A huge repository of knowledge was stored at the great library in ancient Alexandria. Unfortunately, there was another movement afoot that found that knowledge heretical."

"The Christian movement?"

"A zealot mob stormed the library, and literally stripped the flesh from the woman proprietor, and then burned as many of the scrolls as they could find. Only a tiny bit of the original material survived to modern times."

"That explains some things."

"Like what?"

"Your aversion to religion."

"Maybe. Most people I know who claim to be religious are so narrow minded they can't see past their blinders."

"There's a vast difference between religion and faith, and maybe, after nearly two thousand years, you might forgive them."

"Established religion has always bucked change and new discoveries because it threatens the established buearuocacy."

"That is absolutely true, and was what Christ, himself, was up against."

Neither man spoke for nearly a minute, and then Malley continued.

"So how does all this relate to your discovery?"

"The base age of the ice where we conducted our drilling in Greenland is over a hundred thousand years old, and at that time men—at least as far as we know—had barely harnessed fire, and certainly should have known little about advanced metallurgy. What I found required a sophisticated knowledge and tools comparable to modern times. All that I know about history tells me it's just plain impossible."

"Yet, there's the artufact, proof of something beyond known science."

"You want it, don't you?" Backus suddenly realized.

"We did at first. That's why I'm here."

"Why the change of heart?"

"We are essentially observers. Are you familiar with what's known as the observer's paradox?"

"Of course. Essentially it says the outcome of an experiment or observation is corrupted by the mere presence of the observer. It invalidates the idea of ever knowing a pure truth. There is always error, and the overriding goal of scientific discovery is to minimize that error."

"We have corrupted the outcome of this observation."

"I'm not following."

"Put simply, the error, as you put it, has not been minimized."

"You lost me."

"A simple observation involving a millionaire, an airplane, and a checkered past went completely out of whack because of one man. You."

"Me?"

"As my boss has stated, you truly were the wild card."

"I don't know. Am I supposed to say I'm sorry? And who's your boss?"

"Someone who probably saved your life. An old man who provided food and direction."

A brief silence filled a space and then Backus continued. "You know I just came from a meeting where you were pronounced a non-person. It seems there is no Mike Malley answering to your description in this country."

"That's understandable since I changed my name, and only use Malley when I'm being a priest."

"And when you're being a carpenter?"

The man stepped forward, his wire-rimmed glasses were absent, and the dim light reflected off the smooth skin of a bald head. Even in the meager light, Backus could detect a hardness to his face that had never been there before, and a small notch at the top of his right ear. Without the long brown hair, this man bore no resemblance to the priest he had met at the Retreat.

"I guess I'm confused." Backus confessed. "Just who the hell are you?"

"My real name is James Edward Bell."

"No I mean, *who* are you?"

"Definitely not a priest. In fact I've done things that are so horrible you can't imagine. Yet, like the others inside me, he is real."

"Sounds like you have multiple personalities."

"Don't we all? The difference is I let mine out."

Bell extended his right hand. Backus hesitated a moment, and then offered his.

"Keep searching, Bill Backus, for the truth is in the search. Cling with all your strength to your friends, and to the artifact. The time is coming when *your* faith will be put to the test."

"So where do you go from here?" Backus asked after several moments of silence.

"After tomorrow, back to carpentry, I suppose, and my rose bed." He hesitated a moment and then continued. "Everything looks different in the morning. Tomorrow you will dismiss what I've said as ridiculous."

James Edward Bell nodded a good-bye and quickly exited into the evening darkness. Backus closed the door and sat quietly in the worn overstuffed chair in the gloom of his tiny apartment. He considered turning on the light, but suddenly felt so completely exhausted he didn't bother. His mind couldn't quite digest the fact that the man who had just left was the friendly priest he'd met at the Retreat. He closed his eyes, and in minutes his regular breathing indicated he was asleep. Some time later, a soft knock on his door jarred him from the dream of a happier time, and reluctantly his mind returned to reality.

"Be right there," he called out as he made his way to the door. He stumbled over the kitchen chair he had occupied while conversing with Bell, and cursed under his breath. He was still mumbling when he opened the door.

"Hello, Professor, I mean Bill. I'm sorry to bother you at this hour but I'd very much like to talk to you…if you will…"

"Of course. Come in. I wanted to speak with you anyway. I wanted to thank you and apologize."

"Not necessary," Lynn Bergen said, as she entered the apartment.

"Take the good seat," Backus said indicating the dilapidated parlor chair, and then turned on the light. "I'll use the kitchen chair. I know standard etiquette says 'ladies first' but I want to say something before you start."

"You don't…"

Backus held his hand up, a signal for Lynn to let him continue. "As you are well aware, my days as a teacher are probably over." Backus hesitated and then struggled on. "I hope you don't mind me being blunt, but it's very difficult for a man and woman to have a close friendship. Almost inevitably sexual considerations begin to find their way into the thoughts of one or the other, and that changes the entire set of parameters. It creates a certain amount of tension."

"Yes?"

"Tension that can lead to…"

"Continue."

"You're just going to let me keep digging a deeper hole, aren't you," Backus said with a smile.

"Certainly don't stop now. It was just getting interesting."

"What I'm trying to say is you saved my life and I'm grateful, and I'd like to continue to be your friend."

"Only if you'll forgive me for not telling you about the notebook."

Both sat quietly for several awkward moments before Bergen continued.

"Something is about to happen."

"Like what?"

"I don't know for sure. Sharon has been getting messages to me when she can. Some sort of deal Jonathan had going fell through, and he's extremely angry. He also found out that we all survived the plane crash. Sharon warned me to hide. She didn't know what he might do next. I had nowhere else to go. Would you mind very much if I stayed here? It would be just for a couple days until I can figure something else out."

"You and Sharon need to just break away before he does something violent."

"It's not that simple. Jonathan could find us where ever we'd go."

"Go to Sheriff Bodeman."

"That's just it. Other than the plane crash, which no one can prove, he hasn't actually done anything to harm us. Just thinly veiled threats, and innuendo. A threat is not the same as breaking the law. The police can't do anything until we come in with bruises, broken bones, or in a body bag. I only hope that I'm not putting you in danger by just being here."

"I don't think so."

"So I can stay?"

"They don't call me a nice old geezer for nothing."

"What about sleeping arrangements?" Lynn said looking around.

"You take the bed. I'll camp out on the chair."

"Thanks."

"You probably won't thank me in the morning. The bed is an old army cot I used in Greenland."

"I'm sure it will be fine. If you don't mind, I'll get my suitcase now and turn in."

"Your suitcase? You know me pretty well."

"I know you better than anyone I've ever known," she smiled. "After all, you're the only man I ever kept notes on."

Backus couldn't help but wonder what wife number three was doing—probably entertaining their neighbor. He struggled for a moment to even remember her name.

Jonathan Wrightham sat on the right side of the brown leather sofa in the sunroom of his mansion and looked out over the blue waters of Leech Lake. Only the top half of the late afternoon sun was visible above the level of the water, and it appeared to be sinking steadily into it. A thin layer of blue-black clouds provided just enough light absorption so that he could look directly at the radiant display for a few seconds without diverting his eyes. Northern Minnesota, he decided, would be a beautiful place to live, if it wasn't for the bugs, the too-short summers, the cold winters, the snow, and the fact that there was very little to do if you weren't into casinos, crafts, or outdoor activities. With fall rapidly approaching, his northern California home was drawing him like a magnet. He had, however, a few things to take care of before he could leave. His troublesome wife for one. After a very limited discussion, Mr. Parish had assigned Mr. Bell to keep constant watch over her. At the moment she was in one of the guest bedrooms with Mr. Bell posted outside. Parish had indicated it was up to him to deal with her, and Wrightham had contemplated several ways to end the problem. To prevent revenge, he would probably also have to deal with her sister, Lynn Bergen. However it was to be done, it had to look like an accident. Out on the lake, white caps were forming on the incoming waves, and he knew what form that accident would take.

He had sent Alfred into town for frozen crab legs, the best he could do under these primitive living conditions, and it occurred to him how fortunate the family had been over all those years to have someone as dedicated as Alfred. He was a cook, chauffer, butler, pilot, and advisor, all rolled into one. With the guaranteed two hundred thousand dollars he received each year from the estate, he could have easily retired long before, but still he continued to watch over the family and provide counsel. He did virtually everything that was asked of him. What he might have done before his acquisition by Franklin Wrightham was unknown, but once on board he never seemed to have the slightest interest in pursuing a life beyond the walls of the Wrightham fortune. It was the world's loss, and the family's gain.

Footsteps sounded from the direction of the door, and Wrightham turned expecting to see Alfred returning with dinner. Instead, a haggard and dirty wretch of a being right out of a Charles Dickens story stood staring at him. Only after it spoke did he recognize it as his half-brother. Maclin Ethek repeatedly wiped his left hand on his dirty brown shirt, and his eyes seemed not to focus on any one thing for more than a moment, as if he expected some animal to jump out of the woodwork and grab him. His red hair, complete with twigs and bits of grass, hung in a tangled mass. His face was covered in several days worth of beard growth.

"What the hell happened to you?" Wrightham asked, clearly startled by Maclin's ragged appearance. "You look like death warmed over."

"You know damn well what happened to me. You tried to kill me with the rest of the peasants."

"Kill you? I wouldn't waste my time thinking about it. You're nothing more than an annoyance, and not worth getting my hands dirty."

"You lie! Who else would do it?"

"A person as well loved as you? Take your pick."

"So you're saying you didn't dope me up and put me on that rattletrap of an airplane?"

"The what? You mean you were on the plane when it crashed?"

"Your acting job might get you an Oscar, but it's going to take a lot more to convince me you had nothing to do with it."

"I swear I never knew, otherwise I would have certainly aborted the mission."

"Like I really believe that."

"I don't care what you believe. But this does cause me to wonder. There is another player in all this that up until recently I've taken entirely for granted."

"What are you talking about?"

"Maybe," Wrightham said thoughtfully, "I've been underestimating my dear wife."

"I thought you took care of that."

"The pair of thugs I hired screwed up and put her sister on the plane instead. Didn't you see her?"

"Hey, when I woke up we were already in the trees, and I didn't take the time to introduce myself. Damn lucky I survived at all."

"You do look somewhat worse for the wear. How did you get here?"

"Grabbed a car, then walked here at night, and stayed under cover during the day. Stole some clothes from a cabin, and food from some gardens. I don't remember all of it." Maclin considered, and then continued. "If you weren't behind this, then who the hell was? And don't expect me to believe your bought and paid for wife would set this up. Other than slap her ass a few times, I hardly know her. What possible motive would she have?"

"Unknown, but no matter. Very soon, it will all be taken care of." Wrightham looked with distain at his pathetic brother. How, he wondered, had he come out such a misfit.

"Did you get your big promotion into the Family?" Maclin asked.

"No. The deal went sour."

Maclin Ethek began to laugh, a strange hysterical sound that caused a shudder to race up Wrightham's spine.

"What's so funny?"

Ethek doubled over with a mirth born of madness and the satisfaction of seeing his half-brother fail. "How soon we forget. You said there were no flaws in your plan."

"Careful, my dear brother," Wrightham said seriously. "It's not like I couldn't squish you like a roach if I really wanted to. Now go clean up. You look like a bum."

Chapter 18

The brown-skinned man with the long black hair looked up from the dishes in the sink and out the open window of his home towards the pavement of Hwy 200 a hundred yards away. His home was a plain white square building that had belonged to his grandparents. His grandmother now lived with his parents near Duluth, and his grandfather's whereabouts were shrouded in mystery. Until recently, and even though the body had never been recovered, he had accepted the fact that his grandfather had drowned on a cold November day. Now he wasn't so sure. A strange old man had given him reason to hope.

A year before he had moved into the vacant house. The pine trees he had helped plant in the front yard when he was a child were now slender poles nearly fifty feet tall. His grandmother had pruned the lower branches when they were small, and now the dense crowns overhead prevented sunlight from striking the lower needles, and the underlimbs hung there, misshapen and dead. The wind stirred the crowns high above, and Johnson couldn't help but think that Indian spirits slept peacefully there.

A silver colored SUV 4x4 turned off the highway, and came to rest next to the footpath that led to his front door. Lora Whitney stepped out, closed the door, and stood there for several moments, as if contemplating what to do next. She was not on duty, wore her favorite clothes—a faded pair of blue jeans and red plaid shirt together with military type combat boots—and was unarmed. Most of her light brown hair was corralled under a hat that advertised Red Demon gunpowder. A cell phone was clipped to her belt, and Johnson wondered if she'd ever bothered to change the battery. He decided he wouldn't ask. She was having difficulty with his friendship with Sharon Wrightham, he knew, and even though he would never do anything to corrupt his relationship with Lora, he was not about to tell her. If she couldn't figure that out for herself, well then, maybe their relationship wasn't meant to be. He remembered a conversation he'd had years before with his grandfather. "Sometimes," he'd said, "though it is hard, you will have to leave behind things and sometimes people that you thought you knew to be true." He added a dirty breakfast dish to an already mountainous collection and walked the few steps to the door. He opened it just as Whitney approached.

"Good morning," he began. "Mind if we sit out here?" Whitney shrugged, and both sat on a gray and weathered board. It rested on two cinder blocks and passed for the top step.

"Let me guess? The house is a mess."

"A disaster would be closer to the truth. Can't seem to find a good maid service."

"Don't look at me," Whitney replied.

"I wouldn't think of it."

"Good. Maybe Sharon."

"Look," Johnson said, as he stood back up. "Maybe we should pick this up at another time when you can think straight."

"Fine. No problem. This was probably a bad idea anyway." She did not, however, stand up.

"So what are you waiting for?"

Whitney swallowed hard, and she knew it was her pride. "For you to sit back down," she said quietly, and the stubborn edge fell from her voice. Johnson sat down next to her, and noted a bit of moisture on her cheek.

"Are you all right?"

"Yes. Just a bit of dust in my eye. It'll clear up in a minute."

"Sometimes," Johnson began and chose his words carefully, "you can make things difficult." He put his hand on her shoulder, but she shrugged it off.

"Let's just stick to business, shall we?"

"Of course. Just the facts, ma'am."

"You're…I…we…"

"Need some help talking?"

"No! Maybe. It comes down to this case. I admit it's driving me nuts. I wake up in the middle of the night with all kinds of crazy scenarios running through my mind. Funny thing is many of them make perfect sense until the next morning."

Johnson listened intently, but then steered the conversation onto a new heading.

"I probably should warn you about something."

"Now what?"

"I gave out your cell phone number to a few folks."

"Let me guess."

"Yes Sharon. Also Bill Backus. Father Malley. I think Bodeman already has it."

"Why not just post the damn thing on the Internet?"

"I could, I suppose."

Whitney sat quietly, and again Johnson had to restart the conversation.

"I am going to tell you some things now that I swore I wouldn't tell to anyone. I want you to listen with an open mind until I'm through."

"So you're breaking your word to someone?"

"Yes. I'm telling you because I trust you, and despite our differences of late I respect your instincts."

"I guess I should be flattered."

"Don't let it go to your head. I'm sure you won't like what I'm going to say."

"Go ahead."

"Your theory about Sharon is simply not true, and I'm saying that not just because I consider her a friend. Her husband, Jonathan Wrightham, and Maclin set up the plane crash."

"She told you this?"

"Yes."

"What was their motive?"

"Revenge mostly. And to set an example for some kind of initiation."

"Initiation?"

"I don't know what it's all about. However, I can tell you with ninety-nine percent certainty that what I've just told you is true."

"So why doesn't she come forward with her story?"

"Fear. Not only for herself, but also for her sister, Lynn. Lynn could also substantiate her story but will not come forward for the same reason."

"So how does the bog lady fit into all this?"

"I don't know, but if she is Morgan Wrightham then there is certainly a connection somehow."

"OK. I'm going to play your game for a while. Let's suppose Wrightham is involved in both the plane crash and the death of his mother. We need motive and opportunity. Opportunity is not a problem, but I simply can't determine his motive in all this. I don't buy the revenge thing. And why would he eliminate his mother when he controlled everything anyway. Only a fool would risk a billion dollars on a stunt like that."

"I agree there has to be some missing pieces."

"On the other hand, Sharon would have had everything to gain from the elimination of the Wrightham heirs." Johnson rolled his eyes. "I listened to your confession," Whitney stressed, "now how about listening to mine." The statement was an order, not a question.

"Yes sir."

"Sharon had both motive and opportunity."

"I don't see how."

"And she's not quite as helpless as she lets on. I dug a little deeper through the information we received from VanHorst last night. Seems she was a computer programmer before Wrightham snapped her up."

"She told me she had no other skills."

"Maybe she wasn't quite as forthcoming as she could have been."

"I still don't see…"

"With her computer knowledge, she could very well have played a part in the plane crash."

"I can't believe she would deliberately hurt anyone."

"Nearly a billion dollars would have been a very powerful incentive to eliminate Maclin Ethek—assuming he still has a claim on the estate. Then her husband, when the time is right. The rest of you…" Whitney's voice trailed off without finishing the thought. Both sat silently staring out through the trunks of the pine trees, each believing the other was totally off the mark. Somewhere in the depths of Lora Whitney's consciousness was the seed of an idea. There was something, something obvious, that they were overlooking entirely. It was something Bodeman had said, but the thought lurked just beyond her ability to bring it into focus. She surprised herself by what she said next.

"If what you say is true, however, then we have to assume Sharon and probably Lynn are still in grave danger."

"I know. But, I couldn't convince her to leave, and at this point, it's doubtful Wrightham would let her out of his sight."

Both fell silent again. Johnson picked at a piece of rotting wood on the step, and Whitney stared out towards the highway.

"There is something else we should discuss," Whitney said finally.

"Yes?"

"It concerns the three of us."

"Sharon is a friend. I'm sure you have other men friends. It doesn't upset me."

"That's not…it's just…you're blinded by your emotions, and that's something I didn't think I'd ever see. Where is the logical minded man I met a year ago?"

"And you're not blinded by your emotions?"

"Maybe, but at least I can admit it."

"May I suggest something?"

Whitney shrugged.

"Let's pick up this discussion again after this case is behind you. Maybe we need some time."

"No problem here. However, this is one case that may never be solved."

Again silence separated the two, and then Johnson began again.

"Backus called me late last night. Actually very early this morning. Seems he has a very frightened houseguest. Lynn Bergen. She seems convinced Wrightham is up to something sinister. He also shared another interesting bit of information. Father Malley is not who he claims to be. His name is really James Edward Bell, and apparently he's connected to Rolland Woodlove, alias Mr. Parish, somehow."

"That's hard to believe, but does explain why VanHorst couldn't find out anything about him. I'll get his real name to Thomson and see where it leads. So how does he fit into all this?"

"Backus said it was all pretty mysterious, and that both Parish and Bell were part of some multinational group of observers."

"Observers?"

"He didn't elaborate, except to say the Bell/Malley personas are total opposites. While the Malley personality was the understanding priest, Bell turned out to be something of a hardnosed character who could have easily passed for an assassin. A hard look, bald head, he said, with a piece of one ear missing. He indicated to Backus there was still some unfinished business that needed to be taken care of and then he was going back to growing roses."

"Growing roses?"

"That's what Backus said. But it's the unfinished business part that has me worried. I can't help but believe he could very well be connected to Wrightham."

"And if your concern about Sharon is justified…where is she now?"

"I don't know. Possibly at their summer lodge on Leech Lake, or back at the Wrightham mansion in California."

"We could drive over to the Wrightham place. It's only about twenty-five minutes away," Whitney suggested. "Although I doubt I'd get past the gate without a search warrant."

"We could always say we were the neighborhood Welcome Wagon."

"I don't think they'd buy that."

The musical tone on Whitney's cell phone sounded and she unclipped it from her belt. She said hello, and then listened. Johnson was only inches away from the receiver, and could hear the frantic voice on the other end. A loud crack sounded, the voice suddenly stopped, and Whitney immediately stood up.

"What was that all about?" Johnson asked.

"That was your friend Sharon Wrightham. I didn't get it all, but from her voice I'd say she was terrified. Something about a helicopter ride."

His face twisted in fury, Jonathan Wrightham jerked the cell phone from Sharon's right hand and flung it against the rough logs of the wall where it shattered into several pieces. Mr. Bell stood behind him with his familiar hard blank expression of unemotional detachment. He had just returned from a bathroom break and found the door to the guest room open and Wrightham engaged in a confrontation with Sharon.

"I told you not to leave her alone," Wrightham snapped, and then to Sharon, "Where did you get the phone?"

"More importantly," Bell interjected, "Who did you call?"

"No one…the line was busy…"

"Liar!" Wrightham shouted.

"I was just trying to call my sister. You know I wouldn't do anything to put her life in danger."

"I sincerely hope not, because you both have a fragile lease on life." He turned to Bell. "I'm moving the schedule up today just to be safe. Tell Alfred to get everything ready on the chopper. We leave in fifteen minutes, and we're going to get this over with."

"What about your brother?"

"Maclin? He's upstairs sleeping like the baby he is. At this point he'd only get in the way."

Bell nodded, cast a quick glance at Sharon, and exited the room. Again she detected the hint of a smile, and wondered how anyone could get enjoyment out of the suffering of others. Wrightham stared with intense dissatisfaction at his wife. "Perhaps I need to teach you another lesson, my dear. One more for old times sake," he said and closed the door behind him. Bell was only a few steps down the hall when he heard Sharon Wrightham cry out in pain. He returned just as Wrightham was about to strike his wife for a second time. Bell said nothing, just stood silent in the doorway, watching.

"What the hell you looking at?" Wrightham asked.

Bell remained silent.

"This doesn't concern you."

Bell's cold stare cut through Wrightham, and he suddenly released Sharon from his grasp and walked out of the room without another word. Bell nodded to Mrs. Wrightham, smiled slightly, and left her alone with her thoughts.

"Call Sheriff Bodeman," Whitney directed as she tossed the cell phone to Johnson. Both raced for Whitney's SUV immediately after the phone connection went dead. Whitney had the vehicle rolling even before Johnson had the door closed. The tires shrieked and smoked and rubber burned as they turned onto Hwy200 and headed west. Driving at normal highway speeds, they would reach the Wrightham summer home on Leech Lake in twenty-five minutes, but this was not going to be a normal run. Within seconds, the SUV had accelerated to ninety miles per hour, and was still gaining speed. Johnson immediately called Bodeman's private number at the Emergency Services Building. He let it ring several times, before trying his home number. Bodeman's familiar deep voice sounded on the other end.

"Bodeman."

"Something's going down at the Wrightham estate. Sharon Wrightham may be in extreme danger. Whitney and I are on our way."

"Shit!"

"What?"

"The turbo went out on the Eagle."

"Thomson?"

"She'll be here momentarily with the state car. We'll get there as soon as we can."

"We have no firepower. Whitney is not in uniform."

"Understood. I'll see if any deputy is on duty close by. So what's going on?"

"I have a sick feeling Sharon Wrightham is going to take a dive out of a helicopter without the benefit of a parachute."

Johnson terminated the connection and turned to Whitney, whose face registered intense concentration, as she wove around the highway traffic. The SUV was her personal vehicle with no lights or siren. "I think we're going to be too late," Whitney stated.

"Once they get that chopper in the air…"

"There is absolutely nothing we will be able to do to prevent whatever happens next."

The rotor blade on the black helicopter sliced through the air but not with sufficient velocity to produce the necessary lift to get it off the ground. Alfred, who sat in the pilot's position, looked through the windshield at the approaching passengers. He had been the Wrightham family manservant for many years, and would do whatever he must do, no matter how unpleasant, to help maintain the Wrightham fortune. Mr. Bell, who held one arm of Sharon Wrightham, walked directly ahead of Jonathan.

Apprehension filled Sharon Wrightham as she approached the helicopter, and instinctively she tried to step back. Bell, however, held her firmly by the arm, and kept her moving forward.

"What's the matter, dear? Afraid of flying?" Wrightham laughed from behind. "Strap her in back with you," he directed Bell. "I'll sit up front with Alfred."

Bell nodded, squeezed her arm firmly, and felt her go limp in his arms. "She fainted," he advised Wrightham.

"Just as well. It'll make things easier."

Fifteen minutes after leaving his home, Johnson and Whitney turned off Hwy200 onto the Wrightham estate road, only to be confronted by a locked wrought iron gate. Going around it with the SUV was out of the question, as large boulders filled the space between the gate and the pine forest. Whitney briefly considered attempting to drive through the barrier, but realized it was doubtful the heavy gate would yield to the force of the SUV without killing the occupants. They left the vehicle, climbed over the boulders, and ran down the paved and weaving asphalt driveway. Ahead they could hear the increasing sound of a helicopter preparing to take off. As they rounded the final bend, a black helicopter ascended into the clear blue Minnesota sky.

"Take us straight up and hold at the three hundred foot level. Then head straight west out over the lake," Wrightham ordered through his headset. Alfred acknowledged with a nod, but after reaching the designated altitude, maintained a stationary position.

Wrightham turned to face Sharon. She was starting to come to. He felt just a prick of compassion. It would have been easier for her if she would have remained unconscious.

"We have a warning light," Alfred advised. "A loose seat belt."

"Bell can check it out." Wrightham grinned. He looked directly at his wife. "It's time." Soon this task would be over.

Sharon looked from her husband to Bell. He looked completely calm, with the same hint of humor in his otherwise cold eyes. She could only guess what was coming next, and all she could do was latch her fingers firmly onto the edge of the seat.

Bell checked his own seat belt, and then reached for the woman's, and hesitated. Every time he looked at her he couldn't help but see someone else. She was slowly regaining consciousness, and he was thankful his responsibility in this most unpleasant matter was coming to an end. Very soon he would be able to go back to the one thing that mattered in his life, his rose bed.

"Everything's ready to go back here," Bell said.

Wrightham looked directly into the conscious eyes of Sharon Wrightham.

"Good-by my dear," he said, and nodded to Bell.

Johnson and Whitney waved their arms wildly in the air attempting to get the attention of the pilot of the helicopter, but knew it was doubtful he had seen them, and knew it wouldn't have made much of a difference if he had. It hovered now, almost directly over head, and like a hawk that can remain nearly motionless in the face of a brisk wind, seemed poised, ready to strike at its pray on the ground. Instead, however, it listed slightly to one side, a door opened and a human being exited the aircraft. It appeared at first that the unfortunate individual would land in the water. However, they could only watch in horror as it quickly spiraled downward, arms and legs flailing frantically in the air, and landed face down with a sickening thud on the lawn less than fifty feet away. Johnson's chest ached with frustration and despair, and he could only hope that Sharon had somehow survived the fall. The helicopter immediately tilted forward, and moved away rapidly to the southwest, out over the rolling waves of the lake. Johnson and Whitney ran over to the body, and even though it was a wasted gesture, Johnson gently rolled it over on its back. From within the shattered face, two sightless eyes stared out into oblivion, frozen in an expression of total surprise.

"I just don't get it," Johnson said as he looked down upon the lifeless face of Jonathan Wrightham.

Whitney couldn't resist. "Now do you believe me?" she asked.

Chapter 19

Maclin Ethek had started out for the bathroom in his bathrobe but the sound of the helicopter rotor blades chopping the morning air prompted him to return without completing the necessary task. From the window of the bedroom on the top floor of the Wrightham summer home, he watched as Johnson and the policewoman inspected the remains of his half-brother. He felt no grief, only relief and moderate surprise at the turn of events. It occurred to him that there were now only one or two people standing between himself and a great deal of money. It would, however, be wise to remain absent from the extensive investigative presence that was now sure to occupy the property. The authorities would probably conduct a mere cursory search of the house, and he decided to wait out the investigation in the attic space just below the peak of the roof. He could then watch the proceedings on the ground through the louvered vent, and, when the opportunity presented itself, deal with at least one of the remaining obstacles.

Quickly Ethek completed his bathroom chore, and followed the upstairs hallway all the way to the south end, looking for the trapdoor. He turned a knob on the wall all the way to the left and immediately part of the ceiling began to hinge downward. A two by four section of the white ceiling tile opened revealing a short ladder, which Ethek ascended into the narrow attic space. He flipped a switch on a rafter directly overhead and the camouflaged door closed behind him. Except for a bit of light that entered the space through the louvered vents, the long narrow room was dark, and after some searching, Ethek found the string that turned on the one cheap porcelain light fixture. White motes danced in the meager light, which cast long shadows. The dust-covered bulb provided just enough light to make out half log rafters, and rough planking on the floor. The musty smell of the attic was combined with another sharp odor he couldn't identify. An animal squeaked and he dismissed it as merely a mouse. He hurried back to the north end, peered through the vent, and noted with satisfaction that he had a bird's eye view of the entire production below.

Bolt cutters made quick work of the padlock that secured the main gate to the Wrightham summer home, and several police and emergency vehicles with lights flashing followed Sheriff Bodeman and Sara Thomson in the state car along the winding driveway. As they approached the log home, Bodeman saw two people standing along the shoreline and a body lying on the green manicured lawn. He knew the deceased was not Sharon Wrightham as Whitney had called in to report the bizarre death of the multimillionaire. She had indicated the body had fallen from a sleek black helicopter, and he had immediately issued an APB on the aircraft.

Thomson exited the state car and walked over to the body. Bodeman hung back, and instead joined Johnson and Whitney on the sandy shore of the lake.

"What happened?"

"We were about two minutes too late," Whitney said.

A noise in the distance prompted the three to turn to the southwest. A black helicopter grew steadily larger. They watched as it came in low over the water and descended onto the green lawn several yards from where a cluster of people now surrounded the body. As soon as the rotor stopped spinning, a woman emerged from a rear door, and moments later the pilot stepped to the ground. Both walked directly over to Bodeman's group by the shore. Sharon immediately threw her arms around Johnson.

"Oh Charlie. It was horrible."

Whitney turned away, suddenly finding the waves of the blue waters an interesting diversion. Johnson held Sharon briefly and then turned to the pilot, a man he had met a year before at the Wrightham mansion in California.

"Hello Alfred."

"Mr. Johnson. I'm so pleased to see you again. Unfortunately...oh this is such a shock."

"This is Sheriff Bodeman. I'm sure he would like to ask you some questions."

"Of course. I'll tell you what I know, but since I was flying the helicopter, I don't know how much help I can be."

"Just tell me what happened as best you can," Bodeman said. Whitney took out a note pad and pencil.

"Mr. Wrightham insisted we take a ride out over the lake."

"Who's we?"

"Myself, Mrs. Wrightham, Mr. Wrightham, and Mr. Bell."

"Where's this Bell now?"

"I'll get to that. Mr. Wrightham requested a flight level of three hundred feet AGL over the lake, but after reaching that altitude, I noticed a warning light, which indicated a loose seat belt, so I held a steady position. Immediately, Mr. Bell checked his and Mrs. Wrightham's. They were in the rear seats. It never occurred to me it was Mr. Wrightham's that might be loose. Then something very strange happened."

"Yes?"

"Mr. Wrightham took off the ear phones, opened his door, and simply stepped out into thin air."

"You can verify that, Mrs. Wrightham?"

"I really thought Jonathan was going to try to...to harm me. That's why I called Deputy Whitney. I was so scared...I fainted...and when I came to, Jonathan was looking back at me with this mean, cruel look. I knew I was going to die."

"But you didn't," Whitney interjected.

"No. Jonathan's expression suddenly changed into one of pleasure or maybe contentment. He said something and then turned back towards the front, and the rest is just like Alfred described."

Charlie turned to Bodeman. "I know this isn't going to make much sense but Backus told me that this Mr. Bell and Father Malley are one and the same person. He described Mr. Bell as someone who looked like a hired hit man. Hard featured, not a hair on his head, with a piece of one ear missing."

"That's him," Sharon confirmed.

"Doesn't sound much like the Father Malley we know."

"Mr. Parish and he were apparently working together with Wrightham on something."

"Getting back to this incident, if I understand what Alfred and Mrs. Wrightham have said, no one laid so much as a hand on Wrightham."

"That's true, Sheriff," Sharon said. "I'd swear to it."

"Where's Mr. Bell now?" Whitney pressed.

"He ordered me to drop him off on the beach southwest of here," Albert said.

"Ordered?"

"He asked in a very persuasive way. I wasn't going to argue with him."

"You mentioned Wrightham said something just before he bailed out," Bodeman said to Sharon. "Do you recall what it was?"

"Something like…some people walk on water…or something like that."

Whitney hesitated, and then continued. "I couldn't help but notice the bruise under your eye."

"It was Jonathan…he…"

"With Jonathan dead," Whitney continued bluntly, "who inherits the Wrightham fortune?"

"I really don't know," Sharon shrugged. "Alfred would know."

"As things stand right now, you do my dear," Alfred offered. "Even this summer home."

"Would you mind if we looked around your house?" Bodeman asked.

Alfred noticeably straightened. "It is my sworn duty to protect the Wrightham estate. I must ask. Is Sharon considered a suspect in this tragedy?"

"She's merely a witness at this point."

"Perhaps it would be best if we secure the services of a lawyer."

"As you wish."

"I have nothing to hide," Sharon interjected. "You're welcome to look where ever you like."

"It's your home now, ma'am," Alfred said. "And I am now at your service, so the decision must be yours."

"Very well, Sheriff. Alfred can show you around."

"We should have things cleared up here in a few hours. But I'd appreciate it if you didn't leave the area until we can make some sense of this."

"Of course. I understand. But if you'll excuse me, I think I need to rest for a while."

Sharon cast one last glance at Johnson and then headed towards the door of the lakefront home. Bodeman and Alfred immediately followed, leaving Charlie Johnson and Deputy Whitney alone on the beach.

"This is truly confusing," Johnson began.

"Try to see past your friendship with Sharon for just a moment. Is it even conceivable to you that she may have hired this Mr. Bell to rid herself of her husband?"

"We've been over your theory."

"Listen. I'm not defending Jonathan Wrightham. He was undoubtedly a real asshole. Wife beater, and probably worse. But that simply adds another entry to the list of possible motives for Sharon to bump him off."

"But no one touched him."

"So Alfred and Sharon say. If my theory is correct, then they're not exactly credible witnesses. And if what Backus told you is true, then Mr. Bell could very well have been the instrument of Wrightham's death."

"I agree," Johnson said reluctantly, "that what you say could be true."

"Thanks for that," Whitney said sincerely. "The unfortunate thing is, short of a confession, I have absolutely no way to prove it."

The tiny African American woman left the group that milled about the body, and walked over to join Johnson and Whitney. Her diminutive form seemed small even in comparison to Whitney's less than average height.

"Seems we have another point for Whitney's theory," Thomson began and then motioned towards the body. "Not a pretty sight."

"Not the way I'd want to leave this world," Johnson stated.

"Anything that might indicate why he would want to take a walk out into thin air?" Whitney inquired.

"Nothing. We'll do a blood workup to see if there were drugs involved. You saw it happen. Did it look like someone threw him out?"

"I can't be positive but it really looked like he simply intended to go for a stroll. That's also the way the occupants of the helicopter described it."

"Then drug induced hallucination is probably the best hypothesis at this time. Certainly suicide seems unlikely." She faced Whitney directly. "VanHorst has managed to get a complete copy of Franklin Wrightham's original will. Also Jonathan and Sharon's pre-nuptial agreement. He said there wasn't much in any of it other that what we already suspected. Franklin's overriding desire seems to have been to maintain the family fortune. VanHorst is going to fax a copy of each to Sheriff Bodeman, immediately. He's sending the information to Forrest's house, so if you want to review it, stop over when you get the chance."

Thomson headed back towards Wrightham's body and Johnson began walking toward the Wrightham summer home. "Now where are you going?" Whitney asked.

"To see if Sharon needs anything."

"She just became a billionaire and you're going to see if she needs anything?"

"Something like that," Johnson smiled. "Don't worry. Forrest will be there to chaperone."

Inside the log home, Johnson found Sharon Wrightham sitting on the sofa in the sunroom staring out over the blue water of the lake, but Bodeman and Alfred were absent. From somewhere deep within the summer home he could hear Bodeman's gravelly voice, and knew he was searching for anything out of the ordinary that might explain Wrightham's recent violent end. Wrightham's arrogant personality certainly made anything but some form of execution highly unlikely. Much as he hated to admit it, he knew Sharon had the most to gain from her husband's death. Whitney was correct. The list of motives was long. Sharon heard him approaching from behind and turned to face him, just as Whitney entered the house behind him. The deputy leaned up against the wall, arms folded across her chest, and seemed content to listen. She had all she could do to keep from reading Sharon her rights.

"I had nothing to do with this," Sharon began anticipating Johnson's question.

"I believe you. However, it's not me you have to convince." He looked back over his shoulder, nodded to Whitney, and then refocused his attention on Sharon. "You told me before you signed an agreement with Jonathan before you became part of the Wrightham household."

"Yes. Jonathan called it a 'companion contract.'"

"What did it say?"

"I was guaranteed a great deal of money, and he received all he wanted from me."

"Is there anything in it to indicate what happens should either or both of you die?"

"I think it refers everything back to Franklin Wrightham's original will. Alfred would know."

"And Alfred says you get everything. What about Maclin?"

"What about him?"

"Does he stand to gain from Jonathan's death?"

"He and Jonathan had something of a love-hate relationship, and Jonathan sometimes threw him some scraps. Other than that, I can't think of any benefit to him."

Whitney listened intently to the conversation, and the nebulous bit of an idea she had before grew a fraction. "Is there anyone else you can think of who would benefit if your husband was out of the way?" she asked, and moved to stand next to Johnson.

Sharon struggled with a thought. "Maybe," she said finally.

"Who?"

"Mr. Parish might have."

"How well did Jonathan and Mr. Parish know each other?"

"They had some sort of business arrangement."

"What sort?"

"I don't know the details, but I know it didn't work out. Mr. Parish seemed very disturbed."

"How well did you know Bell and Parish?" Whitney persisted.

"Only through Jonathan. Bell watched me like a hawk, but…"

"But?'

"Mr. Parish called me on the phone at the Retreat right after the plane accident. He asked me a lot of questions."

"About?'

"My past mostly. Family history. How I became involved with Jonathan. I told him all I knew, which wasn't much. He also wanted to know about my sister, Lynn. It was all very friendly, but also weird."

"In what way?"

"I don't know. It was almost as if he were merely confirming what he already knew."

Johnson turned to Whitney. "According to Backus, Parish and Bell are working together in some way. He said the two had a disagreement on how best to proceed with whatever they were up to." He turned back to face Sharon. "Anything else you can tell us?"

"I really don't know except I thought Mr. Bell was going to hurt me, but now that I think back over everything, I wonder if in some strange way he was on my side from the beginning."

"What do you mean?" Whitney asked.

"Beneath the hardness of his face there was always something else, a hint of kindness or maybe humor. I always thought he just enjoyed scaring the hell out of people but now I wonder. Several times he managed to show up just when things didn't look good for me."

"That's understandable," Johnson added, "considering he also did a pretty good impression of a priest."

Despite the fact that VanHorst had indicated there was no new earth shattering news in Franklin Wrightham's will or the marriage contract, it was just after ten o'clock when Charlie Johnson headed for Sheriff Bodeman's home on Leech Lake to review the documents himself. Crime scene tape had been placed around the area where Wrightham had fallen from the sky, and the body, in the company of Sara Thomson, had been removed. A half-dozen law enforcement personnel still lingered on the grounds. Gradually, they would be breaking up and heading back to town. Bodeman told Thomson he would be the last man out, and Thomson had protested, indicating it would not be a good idea to leave the scene unsupervised by at least some law enforcement people. The sheriff assured her he was not planning to vacate the scene entirely, and was following up on an idea Whitney had proposed.

Johnson exited the Wrightham driveway in Whitney's new silver Chevy SUV, turned west on Hwy 200, and fifteen minutes later turned onto the short gravel driveway to Bodeman's lakefront home. Absently, he scanned the interior of Whitney's vehicle, and smiled inwardly to himself. Several empty white Styrofoam coffee cups and an empty donut box littered the floor. He glanced in the back and noted her winter survival kit which including a heavy woolen blanket, winter packs, extra jacket, a bag of candy bars, and several loose candles. Since it was late summer, it was probable the preparations were a carry over from the previous winter. The items were scattered about in a haphazard fashion, and he wished he'd had that information when she had commented on the condition of his house.

Johnson's thoughts turned to Sheriff Bodeman. Not everyone would let someone enter their home alone and without a second thought. Although he had served on occasion as a county deputy in an emergency capacity, he was not connected to law enforcement, and yet here he was participating in a homicide investigation. His normal income came from occasional lectures to students and various other groups on forest ecology—that was his expertise—and monthly payments he received for a house in town that he'd sold to the county. The very modest amount of money he made was barely sufficient to keep one person going, let alone two. He pondered his relationship with Lora Whitney. If it was to become a lasting relationship, he realized he'd probably have to get a real job. Certainly, he wouldn't consider living off Lora's deputy income. The way their relationship was headed, however, it might not even be a consideration. Still, he had to admit he enjoyed the challenge of investigative work. Maybe it would be an occupation to consider.

The key to Bodeman's door was where any self-respecting thief would look first, under the welcome mat. Johnson entered and immediately saw several sheets of printer paper on the floor near the far end of the kitchen counter, fall-out from the fax machine that rested on the counter directly above them. He spread out the information on the kitchen table, pulled up a chair, and vowed to read and understand every last word. Somewhere in the printed words there had to be something VanHorst had overlooked.

Two hours later with his stomach reminding him it was lunchtime, Johnson was more confused than ever. After getting past all the 'whereas' and 'therefores,' the marriage agreement seemed to be nothing more than a standard employment contract. Both parties outlined what each intended to provide to the relationship. What it boiled down to Sharon was to receive a hundred twenty five thousand dollars per year for 'services rendered.' The length of the contract was for five years, and there was no clause for early termination. There was also nothing in it to indicate what would happen if either party died. It was clear, however, that as Jonathan's lawful wife, she would almost certainly gain financially from her husband's death.

Johnson's efforts turned to Franklin Wrightham's original will. He read through it four times, and had to concede VanHorst was correct. Other than insisting the Wrightham fortune remain intact, there seemed to be no connection whatsoever to any future wife Jonathan might have. Even if there had been, it was doubtful that such a clause would hold up in court. The contest for the Wrightham fortune that Morgan, Jonathan, and Maclin had entered into was clearly stated, and an attachment provided by Alfred indicated that Morgan had won, but only after collaborating with Jonathan. Except for the family yacht, Maclin had ended up with nothing.

Johnson couldn't help but believe he, too, was overlooking something. He lay his head down on top of the papers, and attempted to clear his mind. There was another trail in this, he knew, that everyone had overlooked. But where was it, and to whom did it lead? A thought occurred to him and he shuffled through the papers again. There was, indeed, something missing. He read through the contract again, and there it was, conspicuous by its absence. Maybe it was just an oversight, but if it wasn't? Suddenly, all the pieces fell neatly into place. Quickly, he scanned Wrightham's will for the pertinent line. "My god!" he said aloud, and raced for Bodeman's phone.

Maclin Ethek watched through the louvered vent as the last of the police vehicles exited on the black asphalt driveway. He knew the Wrightham manservant, Alfred, and Sharon were still below him in the house. However, he'd heard other muffled voices, and so they were most likely not alone. Sharon would be weak and confused, or on the other hand, overconfident. Either way it was the perfect time to make his demands. He was about to turn his attention to other matters when another vehicle arrived in the driveway, a new lavender Cadillac.

Ethek moved toward the exit and the single light in the musty attic went out. After some groping, he managed to find and then flip the switch for the trap door, but it did not open. "What the hell?" he mumbled to himself, flipping the switch up and down several times. Slowly, the louvers on the vents on either end of the long narrow attic space began to close, and inside the meager sunlight dimmed to nothing. In the total silence and darkness, he stood confused and bewildered, and a flash of panic swept through him, as something soft brushed past his face. Instinctively he swung at the phantom, but succeeded only in striking a log rafter with his fist. Suddenly, the squeaking noise began again, but not from one, but several hundred startled voices. With the louvers closed, they, like him, were trapped and the colony of bats swarmed about the attic, deftly dodging the flailing arms of the hysterical human.

The first phone number that entered Johnson's mind was Whitney's cell phone number, and he let it ring several times before he realized the unit was lying outside the back door of the Bodeman's lakefront home on the front seat of her Chevy SUV where he had placed it. He thought of calling Emergency Services but any help from law enforcement was at least thirty minutes away in the wrong direction. He could have Emergency Services contact Bodeman on his car radio, portable, or even cell phone, but decided to call him directly from Whitney's cell phone. He could call and drive at the same time, not the safest policy, but time was now the critical factor. He threw the receiver back on the cradle and ran from the Sheriff's house. He was reasonably sure Bodeman and Whitney were no longer at the scene of the crime. If they were not and were unavailable, then attempting to call them would simply waste more valuable time.

Upon entering the SUV, Johnson picked up the cell phone, but instead of contacting Bodeman directly, decided instead to call the one number that might just prevent another tragedy. It took two valuable minutes to get the number through information, and he was thankful it wasn't unlisted. Hurriedly, he punched it in and then listened intently as it rang several times. The speedometer registered seventy when someone finally answered.

"Wrightham residence." The unidentifiable voice was muffled and echoed, as if the person was speaking through a culvert, and Johnson was uncertain even of the sex of the speaker.

"May I please speak with Sheriff Bodeman?"

"The Sheriff and Deputy are no longer present. Who's calling?"

"This is Charlie Johnson. May I speak with Sharon, then."

"Mrs. Wrightham is not available at the moment. Would you like to leave a message?"

"Just tell her I know what's going on."

"Do you?"

"Yes, and you won't get away with it."

"Of course I will. The flow of events has, unfortunately, necessitated certain actions. I hoped it wouldn't come to this. Please don't think badly of me."

"You don't have to do this. They're not a threat to you. For god's sake read the pre-nuptial agreement."

"It will all be over very soon."

"What are you going to do?"

"We're going to take a little ride. I so hope the water lilies are in bloom. Good-by, Charlie Johnson."

"Wait!"

Johnson flung the phone aside as soon as the connection terminated. If he could have, he would have rammed his foot through the floorboards.

In the warm afternoon sun, Lora Whitney stood with a pair of binoculars behind the smooth trunk of a red oak wondering if she was simply wasting her time. She had convinced Sheriff Bodeman to drop her off along the highway so she could return unseen to the Wrightham lodge. All investigators and emergency people were now absent. He'd given her his cell phone on the off chance something might develop. As an afterthought he also gave her his spare revolver, a .38 caliber Remington. It took her twenty minutes to return on foot under the cover of the forest.

Now, the thought that had been lurking just beyond the reaches of her consciousness crystallized in a remembered conversation with Bodeman.

"Approach this investigation with an open mind," he'd said. "Let the chips fall where they may. The answer to this is probably something no one has thought of." Partly out of jealousy, she realized she had been obsessed with proving Sharon guilty, but Johnson had also been equally blinded by his devotion to his friend. While she still felt Sharon Wrightham was no innocent babe, when one stood back and took a good look there were other potential suspects. Maclin Ethek certainly would have had good reason, if revenge were a good reason, to eliminate both his mother and his half-brother. His present whereabouts were unknown. The fact that he had been a passenger on the doomed airplane and not in the helicopter with his brother, however, indicated that there might be yet other players, possibly the mysterious pair of Mr. Parish, alias Rolland Woodlove, and Mr. Bell, alias Father Malley. According to the Feds, they were people who did not exist in any database, and that certainly was suspicious by itself. There was also the outside chance the Reverend Luke James, and Sharon's sister,

Lynn, were somehow involved, but there was nothing concrete to connect them to anything.

Somehow the string of events had begun with the death of the bog lady, who was probably Morgan Wrightham, then the intentional crash of the Tripacer, and finally the unexpected death of Jonathan Wrightham. It was even conceivable the kidnapping of Jennifer McGraig from the campground was somehow connected. What was disturbing was that the deaths might not yet be over. Somewhere, through it all, there had to be, as Charlie Johnson would say, a common trail.

Through an opening in the otherwise dense green foliage, she could clearly see the back door of the Wrightham summer home. A lavender Cadillac suddenly came into view, and parked adjacent to the split stone walkway to the back door of the summer home. She wondered if the answers followed the man, the Reverend Luke James, inside.

But something else was wrong. And like a bad itch one just can't reach, it kept scratching at her consciousness until finally the light bulb went on. The neatly manicured lawn, now partially enclosed with crime scene tape, was missing the lawn ornament, the shiny black corporation helicopter.

Chapter 20

▼

The sound of the rotating rotor blade above was barely audible though the headphones that fit snuggly over the ears of Sharon Wrightham. Soon after everyone had left the lodge, Alfred came from the upstairs panic-stricken. He'd indicated that someone unknown was somewhere in lodge, possibly dangerous and certainly uninvited, and that an expeditious departure was in her best interests. The quickest way off the premises was the helicopter, and so they left immediately. Looking at him, it occurred to her how much she now depended on Alfred. He had been about the only person in the family who had shown the least bit of compassion for her, and when this unpleasant business was completely in the past she'd have to arrange for an appropriate reward. It also occurred to her she didn't have the vaguest notion where they were headed, but at this point in time and with her financial future secure, it simply didn't matter. After all the abuse, insults, and suffering, it appeared her one wish had come true at last—to be free of Jonathan Wrightham, forever.

"I hope you don't think it bold of me, ma'am," Alfred began from his pilot's position, "but I've made arrangements to pick up your sister."

"That's very thoughtful of you, Alfred. It seems Lynn and I are going to have to count on you for a great many things for a while."

"She said she's very anxious to see you, and that she had much to discuss. You've both been through such a terrible experience. Just sit back and relax. I've taken care of everything."

* * * *

Lora Whitney was uncertain what to do next. She'd missed the take-off of the black helicopter, and so had no idea who was in it. Maybe everyone, and, except for Reverend James who had not reemerged from the doorway, the house might now be empty. She had turned Bodeman's phone off to maintain silence, but now reactivated it. The unit rang before she could get it back into her shirt pocket.

"Hello. This is Whitney."

"Where've you been? I've been trying to get through. This is Charlie. Where's the Sheriff?"

"The phone was off and he's heading back to town."

"Where are you?"

"Hiding out in the woods by the Wrightham lodge, just getting ready to pack up and leave."

"I'll be coming by the Wrightham driveway in a few minutes. Be there, and don't be late because if you aren't there I'm not waiting."

"What's the rush?"

"I found the missing trail."

"You did! And?"

"And I know where it leads."

"Where?"

"Right back to Buck Lake and the bones of Morgan Wrightham."

Seven minutes later, Johnson came to a sliding slow and go at the entrance to the Wrightham driveway, picked up Whitney, and immediately floored the SUV.

"Are you sure you don't want me to drive," Whitney asked as a motorist laid on the horn, and raised his middle finger as Johnson raced past.

"Did you learn anything new at the Wrightham estate?"

"Nothing other than the fact that the helicopter is now absent from the property, and for some reason the preacher, Luke James, is now making himself at home."

"Get on the phone and call Backus."

"Perhaps if you'll just tell me…"

"Dammit, Lora. For once in your life don't argue. Just do it! Every second counts."

"I don't know his number. I'll have to call information. What am I supposed to say to him?"

"Get him on the line, and then give me the phone."

Whitney secured the number from information, and had the system automatically dial it through. It rang several times, and she was about to terminate the call when the familiar voice of Bill Backus answered. She immediately handed the phone to Johnson. One-handed and on the shoulder of the road, he swerved past a semi truck that was already ten miles over the speed limit. Lora placed one hand firmly on the dash and the other on the door handle and tried desperately to remember the words to the Lord's Prayer.

"Bill," Johnson shouted into the phone. "Is Lynn with you?"

"Not at the moment. She received a call earlier, said it was time to take care of something having to do with her sister, and left."

"Did she say where she was going or when she'd be back?"

"It couldn't have been far, unless she's not worried about money. She had a cab pick her up. Now that I think about it, it was an airport cab, so she must have been going to the airport. As to getting back, I assume later today since all her stuff is still here. What's the problem?"

"We've been overlooking the most obvious answer. If Lynn should happen to come back, don't let her leave. Literally, tie her to a chair if you have to. Call Sheriff Bodeman and tell him Lora and I are headed to Buck Lake and to get there ASAP with back up. I have a good idea, but I'm not entirely sure what I'm up against."

"Will do. Is Lynn in some kind of trouble?"

"Big trouble, I'm afraid."

The black helicopter sat quietly on a fifty-yard circle of concrete reserved for the occasional rotor winged aircraft at the Bemidji airport. Cut out of a jack pine forest, the runways and buildings were surrounded by evergreens sixty feet tall. The spartan terminal building rose up out of the flat open space a half-mile away. Long rows of nearly identical tin aircraft hangers stretched for a considerable distance parallel to the main runway, and several private aircraft were tied down along the taxiway. At the moment, no aircraft were in the air, and no one was outside, except for one young woman. She stood next to the helicopter on the tarmac watching the arrival of an airport taxi. A light westerly breeze swept her long blonde hair with streaks of brown away from her face and past her shoulders. She wore her favorite clothes, a blue denim jumpsuit with embroidered yellow butterflies, and it seemed to flow over the graceful curves of her athletic body. In the warmth of the afternoon, she briefly regretted not wearing something cooler. Except that the woman who exited the taxi wore light green shorts and a matching short-sleeved blouse, she looked remarkably the same. A little shorter and fuller faced, she nonetheless had the same blonde hair. From a distance they could easily be mistaken for twins, although Lynn Bergen was several years older than her sister. They met in an arm-hugging embrace.

"I heard about Jonathan," Bergen began. "All in all, I can't say I'm sorry. How are you holding up?"

"Shocked, but otherwise OK. Probably even a little relieved."

"Any word yet on why he'd want to do a belly flop from several hundred feet?"

"None yet. Sara Thomson, the state investigator, said it would take a while to get the results of the blood workup."

"Blood workup?"

"They think he may have been drugged. There's no other explanation."

"What now?"

"Alfred was worried there might have been an intruder in the house, and so we decided to leave. He said he had contacted you so we could get together."

"It seemed like a good idea," Lynn agreed. "Would you mind very much if I stayed with you for a while? Until I...we can get this behind us? I feel like I'm imposing on Professor Backus."

Something about the sequence of events caused Sharon a moment of concern, but it's exact nature eluded her. Given the recent past, she was probably just being a bit paranoid. Everything had worked out as well as she could have hoped. Alfred joined them carrying a small brown wine case.

"Ladies," he said politely. "May I offer you a glass of white before we get started? Compliments of the Wrightham family stock." Sharon declined but Lynn took two offered glasses from Alfred, and handed one to her sister.

"Somehow, this seems inappropriate," Sharon protested.

"Nonsense," Lynn scolded, as Alfred poured a generous amount in each glass. "Here's to a new beginning."

Sharon's lips curled up in a weak smile. "It certainly is that." She sipped at the wine, and then noticed another vehicle approaching along the paved access road. As it drew closer, she could see the driver looking directly at her. It must be the wine, she thought, that was corrupting her eyesight. The man was someone she remembered clearly. Jonathan always had trouble remembering his name. He stopped the red convertible sports car several feet away, removed his sunglasses, and looked up over the windshield. A pencil thin mustache adorned his upper lip. Smith, his name was Smith. Confused she turned to Lynn. A silly grin spread across her sister's face, and then she felt herself relaxing into a peaceful slumber.

"Will you explain this to me before you get us both killed," Whitney pleaded as Johnson swerved to miss an oncoming red pickup truck. "Watch out! Jesus! At least stay in your own lane."

"Forty five minutes."

"What about forty five minutes?"

"Give or take that's how long it's going to take us to get to Buck Lake, assuming I can drive in on the ATV trail. If not, then add another fifteen minutes to a half hour."

"Why don't you run your theory past me on the off chance one of us survives your driving."

"Who has been the common denominator through all this?"

"Sharon? Ethek? I don't know."

"You said it yourself near the shore of Buck Lake."

"I did? I don't' recall…"

"It was supposed to be a joke, remember."

"Oh that. The butler."

Johnson glanced at his friend briefly and nodded.

"You mean Alfred? How could you come up with that crazy notion? He acts like a man who would faint at the first hint of violence."

"'Act' is the correct description. He's the common denominator through all this. He was present for all three events. The bog lady, he probably helped with the crash, and also the death of Jonathan Wrightham."

"He had opportunity, surely, but I fail to see the motive. He gets two hundred grand a year for the rest of his life."

"I agree that part is a little weak, but there isn't a better candidate."

"What about Sharon?" she asked with some hesitation.

"She had neither motive nor opportunity for all three events."

"I'd say about a billion dollars is a pretty strong motive, not to mention the physical abuse."

"She gets nothing. In fact she's out of a job."

"What?"

"I spent two hours this morning digesting every word of the pre-nuptial agreement, and also old man Wrightham's will. The pre-nup is nothing more than a standard contract which has, in this case, one very important piece missing."

"And that would be?"

"Nowhere is there any mention or documentation to indicate they were ever married."

"If they aren't husband and wife…"

"She is entitled to nothing, and a huge part of her motive goes out the window."

"Explain to me what all of that has to do with going back to Buck Lake."

"Flowers, specifically water lilies. When I called the Wrightham lodge looking for you or Bodeman, the person who answered—I'm assuming it was Alfred, but I have to admit it might not have been—said it was just about over, and he hoped the water lilies would be in bloom."

"Assuming?"

"The voice was distorted somehow, and not recognizable as either a man or woman."

"You think that Alfred is going back to Buck Lake to…"

"Eliminate the two people who he thinks stand in his way, just as he disposed of Morgan Wrightham. I tried to tell him on the phone they weren't a threat to him, but he wouldn't listen."

"I have to admit, it all sounds…like the craziest damn thing I've ever heard! What if you're wrong?"

"Then I have alternate scenario B. As much as I hate to admit it, Sharon and/or her sister, Lynn, are next in line."

"Sharon I understand, but why Lynn? How could she be involved?"

"Alfred told Sharon she was entitled to the estate, and at this point, I think she believes that. If something were to happen to Sharon…"

"Lynn might try to stake a claim? That's pretty hard to swallow. She's directly responsible for saving the victims of the plane crash, including you. And from what you've said, Sharon has no claim anyway."

"True, which leads me back to scenario A. Why would Alfred deliberately lie to Sharon, unless he had some ulterior motive?"

"What about scenario C? The mysterious pair, Parish and Bell?"

"I didn't want to make things complicated."

"Too late."

"In total truth, I have no clue where they fit in."

The black helicopter streaked through the air at a hundred fifty knots and reminded Alfred of a shark slicing through the ocean waters. As a slight man with limited strength, he always derived great satisfaction out of controlling such a complicated piece of machinery. With hydraulic aided controls and on-board computer navigation, flying really became as simple as riding a bicycle. Once you learned, you never forgot.

There was still a faint and distasteful odor inside the helicopter. Despite his best efforts, the disinfectants and deodorizers had not completely erased Luke James' earlier excretory accident. The man who sat across from him at that time was also present now. Mr. Smith was part of the team, his team, and was generally more reliable than Mr. Bell had been, who often came and went as he pleased. Smith sat, now, still as a stone watching the green tree-covered earth pass rapidly under them. The only indication of deeper thought was an occasional twitch of his thin mustache.

Alfred glanced quickly over his shoulder at the two women in the rear seat, one his temporary boss and the other a nuisance, one asleep and the other completely conscious. There was unpleasant work ahead, and, yet, as always, his overriding goal continued to be making sure the Wrightham fortune remained secure. Long ago he'd learned to turn emotional considerations aside, and make the goals of the estate his primary focus. Sometimes, however, one had to anticipate what was best for all concerned and take the initiative. He nodded toward

Smith, who seemed to awaken. He looked down at the moving map display.

"Fifteen minutes," he replied to the unspoken question. "Time to say good-by."

To Charlie Johnson it suddenly felt like they were crawling along while his companion hung on for dear life. Behind him was the highway and then the gravel road, and ahead was the last torturous two miles of the ATV trail. The meandering path was not meant for anything over four feet wide. Two ruts three feet apart and worn into the forest floor wound around mature oak and aspen, up hardwood ridges and through grassy swales, through mud holes and over boulders.

The white trunks of two large aspen, one on each side, framed the road ahead.

"They're too close together," Whitney said calmly. "We better walk," and was about to unbuckle her seat belt. Instead of stopping, Johnson pushed the accelerator to the floor, and the SUV surged ahead. "You're not…oh shit!" Whitney moaned, as the solid trees neatly trimmed the rearview mirrors from the vehicle.

Brush and limbs scraped against the pristine paint job of the new silver SUV and the thought occurred to Whitney she was two weeks late on the last payment. Her stomach and chest hurt from the seat belt and shoulder strap that dug into her flesh as she bounced around like a marble in a tin can. At least, she reasoned, the straps kept her head from going up through the roof. She glanced at Johnson. He remained white knuckled, both hands clutching the steering wheel with his focus straight ahead. He'd put his entire being behind the assumption that something dreadful was going to happen directly ahead, and he was the only one who could stop it. She wondered what would happen if everything he believed to be true turned out to be false; that when they finally arrived, only a lily pad covered and bog encircled lake and a couple trumpeter swans would greet them. What if none of his assumptions turned out to be true, and they were risking life and limb for nothing? Her SUV could be replaced, as it almost certainly was going to have to be, but what about his pride? Seeing the intense look on his face almost made her wish something bad was about to occur.

As if in answer to her thoughts, Johnson grumbled something barely audible.

"God, I hope this is all for nothing. Sorry about your Chevy. I'll buy you a new one."

"How much farther?" A loud grinding drowned her words, as the undercarriage slid over a huge rock. The smell of antifreeze began to seep in through the heater vents.

"We're practically there."

"Maybe we should stop and walk. Good for us. Good for my Chevy."

"No time."

"Where are they going to be?"

"There's only one place open enough to land that helicopter. Right where the ATV trail hits the floating bog. Right where you were standing when you watched us gather up the remains. Just beyond that ridge directly ahead."

"I must have fainted," Sharon Wrightham said. She recognized the back seat of the Wrightham helicopter and her sister who gently shook her shoulders.

"I thought so at first. You colasped before I could even taste the wine. But you've been out for a long time. We left the airport, and just set down in the woods by a lake. Alfred said we have some kind of problem, but I'm beginning to wonder. Something's not right here. Alfred and his friend are out somewhere, inspecting something."

"Just before I fainted...I can't remember clearly. Was there someone else?"

"Only Alfred's friend."

"I thought for sure...maybe it was just a dream. I've fainted before, but only for a few minutes. What friend?"

Alfred appeared in the open door. "Why don't you two ladies get out for some fresh air," he advised. "This may take some time."

"What's wrong?"

"Navigation went out."

"Navigation? Surely you can fly in broad daylight without the navigation computer."

"Of course. Just wanted to be safe. But you're going to absolutely love this place. We just happened to set down by a beautiful lake of white and yellow water lilies. Unfortunately it looks like they're past their prime, but the the view is gorgeous."

With her sister's help, Sharon moved unsteadily around the chopper and looked out over the lake. The scenic view was truly remarkable, like a post card, as Alfred had said. He came to stand next to the women.

"How long are the repairs going to take?" Lynn asked.

"Not long."

"Would I have time to take Sharon down to the shore and pick a flower?"

"Of course. In fact, you took the words right out of my mouth."

A loud bang, almost like a gun shot, sounded behind them, then an increasing roar, and finally a battered and muddy SUV sailed over the ridge leaving two feet of daylight under the wheels, and skidded to rest within six feet of them and the black helicopter. Steam erupted from under the hood as soon as the engine died. A man and woman, somewhat unsteady on their feet, exited from either side, and stood together facing the startled trio. Alfred and Lynn seemed to retreat slightly, but Sharon took a step forward.

"I'm…I'm overwhelmed. What's…why are you…what's going on?"

Charlie Johnson had been so determined to get to Buck Lake, he hadn't given serious thought to what he was going to say when he arrived. Now, standing face to face with Alfred, Lynn, and Sharon he realized he still didn't know for certain who to confront. Whitney, however, took the initiative, and a chance. It was time, she decided, to trust Charlie's instincts.

"We have reason to believe you are in grave danger," she stated and then turned to face Alfred, "from you." Whitney thought his reaction would be either shock or denial, but instead the slight fragile-looking man with the round face merely smiled.

"Even if what you say is true, my dear, as you can clearly see, these ladies are in fine physical health, and in no danger of imminent collapse. Just what do you intend to do? Arrest me for something that hasn't happened yet?"

Whitney studied the meek man before her. Her instincts and training told her to have her weapon at ready, but he posed no visible threat that she could determine. He was clearly unarmed, and appeared to be no match for her, let alone Charlie, in a physical confrontation. Still, she rested her hand on the grip of Bodeman's revolver just to be safe.

"Then you won't have any problem with Sharon and Lynn returning with us to the station for questioning and protective custody."

"Of course not. However, how do you intend to get there? Your transportation seems to be out of commission. It would be so much easier if you all just rode with me."

"No need to be concerned," Johnson interjected. "We'll find our way."

Lynn, who had been at first stunned and then confused, suddenly pointed behind the deputy. Both she and Johnson whirled at the same time, and Whitney instinctively drew the .38 as she turned. A single shot rang through the air and Whitney cried out in sudden pain, dropping the revolver to the ground. Blood seeped from a gash along the back of her right hand from the path of a 9mm bullet. She covered it with her left hand to stop the flow. Johnson took a step toward the intruder who held the weapon. Sharon immediately came to Whitney's side, produced a white handkerchief, which she began wrapping around the flesh wound.

"You can call me Mr. Smith, and it seems I have to remind you yet again to refrain from doing anything stupid, Mr. Johnson. I'd advise you to take a close look at this firearm. It's not like the little pea shooter I had the last time we met." Charlie immediately recognized the man with the pencil thin mustache who had escorted Jerry Koler and him into the green Tripacer at the Retreat. Johnson's only weapon, he knew, was going to have to be reason. Alfred moved to stand next to Smith, and Charlie addressed him directly.

"As I told you on the phone, Sharon is not a threat to you. She is not entitled to any of the Wrightham fortune. Surely you must have known she and Jonathan were never legally married."

"A very clever lie. I was present at the ceremony. In fact, I arranged the ceremony."

"Then where is the paperwork, the documentation? A ceremony, even if there are a lot of toasts and speeches means nothing unless the paperwork gets duly filed with the court. There is none of that." He turned to Sharon. "Do you recall signing anything other than the pre-nuptial agreement?"

"Nothing. Jonathan said that's all we'd need."

Alfred shrugged. "I'm so sorry, but at this point I can't afford to take your word for it."

While intent on the conversation, Charlie Johnson was also doing some mental arithmetic. If Backus had called Bodeman immediately after their conversation, the sheriff should only be twenty or thirty minutes behind him. Saving lives might just depend on his ability to keep everyone talking until the cavalry arrived.

Smith's lips parted in a thin wide smile, and Johnson realized he was daring him to reach for the gun that lay on the ground by his feet. The time might come, but not at the moment.

"You have to trust me," he said to Alfred.

"Trust? I don't believe in trust. First I trusted Franklin Wrightham. We started out partners, you know. I was just a young naïve kid, and Wrightham, a wolf. Everyone thinks he was this great economic wizard. Who do you think advised him on when to buy and when to sell? He could add and subtract but he couldn't read people. You see, that's my gift. I can see a person and know exactly what they're thinking. Right now you're thinking that if you can buy a little time help might arrive, or Mr. Smith will lower his defenses just a bit. I assure you. It won't happen."

"So if you're so smart, how come Franklin Wrightham ended up rich and you ended up the butler?"

"That's beside the point. The important thing for you to realize is he ended up dead."

"And what about Morgan?"

"She spent money like it rained from the sky. Running all over Europe with her male whores. It was my money. I had a right to protect it."

"Ethek?"

"There was a chance he might be able to claim a portion of the estate in the future. I couldn't allow that. I had Mr. Smith put him on the doomed Tripacer with the rest of you. Ironically, he was the one who planned his own accident."

"But he survived."

"Right about now he's wishing he would have died quickly. Starvation and dehydration, I've heard, are the worst ways to go."

"And finally Jonathan."

"He was the one person I thought I could deal with. He was very smart, but also very reckless. Then he had this wild idea of joining some make believe all powerful family of multinationals."

"Parish and Bell?"

"A couple shysters. Real con men. Sharon met them. She can tell you. Jonathan actually gave them a million dollars in cash. The old man, Parish, had him hypnotized. I was able to use that to my advantage when the time came. You see, everything has been neatly tied up except for these two lovely ladies."

"So you kill off all the heirs. What could you possibly gain from that?"

"Please, Mr. Johnson. Don't patronize me. You know and I know that Franklin's original will calls for the entire estate to be split between UCLA cancer research center and yours truly, Alfred Ginnus, should there be no heirs. Half of nearly a billion dollars is preferable to a modest two hundred thousand a year, wouldn't you say?"

"You won't get away with this. Backus knows. Bodeman knows."

"Look out over this deceptively beautiful lake. It is surrounded by nearly eighty acres of floating bog. I can merely pick a place at random, make a hole in the surface vegetation, and the four of you will disappear into history. Even if the sheriff suspects where to look, he'll never find the faintest trace. Miss Whitney will tell you. Without a body it is very difficult to prove anything."

"You're going to have to get us there first."

"If you made the slightest threatening move, I'm afraid your good friend will be the first to leave us." He directed his attention to Smith who had not once shifted this focus from the brown skinned man with the long black hair. "Did you get the cameras in place?"

"Everything is set."

"Cameras?" Johnson asked.

"I like to watch. My own version of home movies, you might say,"

"You're sick."

"And you've done an effective job of stalling for time. I really am very sorry about this. However, it is time to get this unpleasant, yet necessary, task behind us and move on. We can make this as painless or difficult as you like."

During the conversation, Johnson had gradually inched his way towards Smith and Alfred, with the three women grouped behind him. He knew he'd take at least one, and probably more, hits before he could reach Smith. Mentally, he determined his chances at less than ten percent. Still, it was better than going quietly into the night. His own death was irrelevant, but the death of his friend was much more disturbing. Perhaps if he could somehow make the first lunge and Lora could get the .38 on the ground, she and the sisters would stand a chance. It was their only hope. Alfred was looking at him curiously, and then smiled his polite smile. Slowly, he walked toward Johnson and retrieved the weapon from the ground.

"It wouldn't have worked anyway, Mr. Johnson. Please don't make things difficult."

Yet there was still something else, maybe someone else, as twice Johnson had noticed movement from within Whitney's broken Chevy. Directly behind Smith, steam continued to rise from the engine compartment. It was only in his peripheral vision he had detected movement, and that had been several minutes before. Then the familiar whistled tune of *This Old Man*, filled the silence of the moment, and a head appeared just beyond the ridge. The head grew into a body and all present turned with undisguised fascination at the man who now stood thirty feet away at the edge of the forest.

"Hi yawl. Nice day for a stroll in the woods wouldn't you say." Sharon and Lynn couldn't help but involuntarily gasp at the strange figure. Whitney and Alfred stared in wonder, but Smith nodded knowingly. Johnson breathed a sigh of relief, which was more of hope than certainty. The man's head and face were almost completely covered with curly brown and disheveled hair. He wore army combat fatigues, and held a high-powered rifle across his chest, which he stroked like it was the family pet. His white teeth flashed through his beard when he spoke, revealing one silver colored tooth. But his most obvious feature, and the one that was impossible to ignore, were his eyes. They seemed to glow red, like two hot coals, and looked piercingly and unblinking at the man who held the 9mm.

"What's your interest in this?" Smith asked immediately.

"I's just passin' through. I don't like to butt into other folk's affairs, but it looks like you boys is havin' a bit o' trouble."

"You know this man?" Alfred asked. Smith had not once let his aim shift from Johnson.

"I know of him. He's in the business. For obvious reasons, they call him Bullet."

"Bullet. That's a very strange name."

"They say he's terminated over a hundred people. Even bit one man to death."

"Well, Mr. Bullet, if that's what you like to be called, you've interrupted a bit of personal business here. What can I do for you?" Alfred asked.

"Like I said. I's just passin' through."

"Then pass through," Smith ordered.

"Afraid I just can't do that." He briefly shifted his gaze to Sharon. "That woman. If she dies, you die."

"I don't think you're seeing the complete picture. Two guns to one. I think you'd lose."

The red eyes narrowed to thin slits, and when he spoke, the folksy southern accent was absent.

"Did you ever see what a two hundred twenty grain bullet traveling twice the speed of sound can do to a human body?" He continued to stoke the rifle fondly with his right hand, and then slowly placed his finger through the trigger guard.

"You'd die trying," Smith stated.

"We all are going to die sometime. It might as well be now, but I assure you I will have company today in hell."

For the first time, Smith hesitated. The man's calm exterior was deceiving. The man known as Bullet was well known, even legendary in certain circles. How he happened to be here at this precise moment only added to the mystical accounts of his exploits. Smith struggled in indecision and was thankful when Alfred arrived at a decision.

"I can see you are a determined man, fully expecting to lay down your life for these people. Therefore, I suggest a compromise."

The folksy accent returned to Bullet's voice. "Well, now. Why didn't I think of that? Just what did yawl have in mind."

"We all go our separate ways."

"I can live with that. What do you folks think?" The question was directed at the man with the long black hair and the woman deputy, but his eyes never left Smith.

"Sounds fair," Johnson happily agreed.

"OK. You folks move over by me, and Alfred and Mr. Smith can mosey on over to the helicopter."

Three women and two men stood well away from the rotating blade as the black helicopter slowly rose into the late afternoon sky. The blast of air sent leaves and bits of twigs outward in a hundred foot circle. There was a momentary glitch in the sound of the engine, but did nothing to slow its rise to just over treetop level. The nose pitched forward, the aircraft rapidly gained airspeed, and quickly disappeared from view. Sharon and Lynn accompanied Whitney back to the Chevy to get the first aid kit to better treat the flesh wound. Johnson extended his hand to the man who he had met before.

"Seems I need to thank you once again."

"Like I said. I's just passin' through."

"You were in the back of Lora's Chevy under the wool blanket on the floor."

"True, and you nearly killed me on the way in. Where did you learn to drive like that?"

"I don't drive much. I guess some things are born of desperation."

"Very true."

"It took me a while, but I know who you are."

"Really? There are times even I don't know who I am."

"And you slipped a moment ago."

"Did I?"

"You mentioned Alfred by name. Therefore, you've met him before."

Bullet smiled through the hair. "I must say. You've really lived up to your profile."

"I have to ask. Other than the obvious, why the interest in Sharon?"

For just a moment, a flash of despair filled the man's eyes. "She reminds me of someone I once knew."

"And what about the million dollars?"

"Other than a necessary tool, we really don't have much use for money. I'll probably give most of it away."

Somewhere off in the distance a booming explosion sent sound waves cascading through the forest. Johnson looked questioningly at Bullet.

"Bad fuel," he said, and disappeared into the undergrowth.

Chapter 21

The dreaded time had come. The fifty six year old man with a warm pleasant smile and thinning light brown hair placed his right hand on the door handle and hesitated. Awaiting him inside the red brick building was the college board of trusties and several of his own peers who literally held his professional life in their hands. He had considered not going at all. There would be a multitude of questions, most of which he could not answer. He'd listen politely to their concerns about scientific ethics, the reputation of the institution, and then they'd lay the Unrequested Leave of Absence before him. It was at that point they would fully expect him to exchange it for an official resignation. That was the way these things worked. No one would outwardly accuse him of anything. He'd not admit any wrongdoing. It was one of those arrangements designed to give something to everyone. Except he had no intention of resigning. If they wanted him to leave, they'd have to fire him, and even with the Greenland episode on his record that would not be an easy job. With his tenure, he could drag out the process for years. It would end up costing the university thousands to try to remove him permanently.

Two students, a young man and woman, approached and he absently opened the door for them. They stopped half way through the opening and turned to face him.

"Are you Professor Backus?" the shy brunette asked.

"Call me Bill," he said automatically. "And yes, I am."

"My name is Mary Carter, and this is my friend Marty. We're in your freshman geology class winter semester. My sister, Lois, had you for a teacher a couple years ago."

"Lois Carter. Sure, I remember her. How's she doing?"

"Very well. I just want you to know I'm in your class because of her. She said you were the best teacher she ever had."

Backus nodded a thank you and the two young people continued on their way. The chance meeting was a wake up call. He knew now he couldn't drag the university through a prolonged battle. He might eventually win, but it would inevitably be the students who would suffer. The money the university would have to spend on the legal process could be much better spent in the classrooms and laboratories of the institution he loved so much. No, when the time came he'd agree to whatever the board demanded and get on with his life. Maybe flipping burgers wouldn't be so bad. At least he'd be close to the food.

Resigned to his fate, he walked down the long corridor to the meeting room. The familiar and unique odor of people and classrooms and the business and art of learning and instruction was something he knew he'd never forget. A dark haired woman in a gray suit appeared out of a side door, and he recognized the executive secretary to the president of the college. Her eyes caught his before he could find a place to hide. Her reaction to his presence was not at all what he expected.

"Professor Backus? Why are you here?"

"The meeting on my current status. The Unrequested Leave of Absence hearing?"

"Oh no. I'm so sorry. Didn't anyone call you? That's been cancelled."

"And when is the rescheduled date?"

"It hasn't been rescheduled that I know of."

"I'm a little confused."

"Why don't you drop in to President Freeman's office while you're here? I'm sure he'd like to thank you personally, and also talk a little about the announcement ceremony."

"I guess. What ceremony?"

"Come now. Don't be modest. Just go right in. I'm sure he can set aside what ever he's doing."

A genuine and warm smile flooded her face, and she nodded towards the door to the president's office. A couple thoughts filled Backus' head. First, in all his years at the university he'd never been in the president's office before, and second he was either dreaming or this woman had lost her mind. Tentatively, he knocked on the office door, and a voice from within called out, "Come in." Backus opened the door about a foot and peeked around the edge. The heavy set man with thin gray hair looked up from his desk and a broad welcoming grin spread across his face.

"Professor Backus. Come in. Come in. So good of you to stop by." Freeman hurried around his desk to greet him, and shook his hand like a pump handle. "I just want to take this moment to thank you so very much. With the budget shortfalls, the gift to the university will be a tremendous help. Don't worry. We don't intend to spend it all at once."

"Gift?"

"I have to admit. We all thought it was some kind of prank at first. No one really thought the check was genuine. I almost threw it away."

"Check?"

"Well, what did you expect? It was signed only, The Family. But one doesn't throw away a cashier's check for ten million dollars without at least giving it the benefit of a doubt."

"Well, certainly not."

"I don't know who these people are, but I just want to thank you for convincing them to invest in our institution. And don't worry. The half million dollars reserved for your Greenland research is sitting in a separate account ready whenever you are."

"It is?"

"I have to ask. With all that capital at your disposal, what do you intend to do now."

"Well, I've given it a lot of thought, and this year at least…"

"Yes."

"I'm going to teach."

The brown-skinned man with the long black hair wasn't sure he was in the right place. Papers, reports, and brown manila folders no longer sat in bunches, but had been neatly filed away in the wall file cabinets. Wads of paper had magically moved from the floor to the wastebasket. A computer monitor and keyboard rested on the desk with only a phone for company. Rummaging through a desk drawer, a huge man, in width if not height, looked at Johnson, threw up his hands, and frowned.

"I can't find a damn thing in here. I never should have given in to Calway. It's going to take a month just to locate everything."

"I have to admit walking in here was a little bone chilling. For a minute I thought we had a new sheriff."

"Don't start."

"Bumped into Audrey Bechworth on the way in."

"I hope that wasn't literally. She'd probably sue you. I keep telling her the case against Saulo and Cook is out of my hands, but she's been in here every other day like clockwork."

"The answer is obvious. She has a huge crush on you. Can't resist your animal magnetism."

"I'll tell you what you can do with your 'animal magnetism.' You…"

The diminutive form of Sara Thomson appeared and she knocked lightly on the door jam.

"Hope I'm not interrupting anything."

"No, not really. You just saved Johnson's life is all."

"Really?"

"A joke," Bodeman stressed. "It was a joke. We're still waiting for Sharon Wrightham and her sister."

"What about Officer Whitney? I really wanted to talk to her. If she ever gets tired of the North Country, I have a place for her in St. Paul."

"She's been fighting a bug off and on for a couple weeks now," Johnson offered. Bodeman gave Johnson a quizzical look but made no comment.

"Nothing serious I hope."

"Could be one of those long-term illnesses, right Charlie?" Bodeman offered, a comment that struck Johnson as downright confusing. He was about to have Bodeman explain, when Sharon Wrightham and Lynn Bergen entered. Bodeman found chairs for everyone and then sat behind his desk.

"We were able to identify the remains in the burned out chopper and they are those of Alfred Ginnus, house servant and one time partner of Franklin Wrightham, and the other was Arthur Kampfey, alias, Mr. Smith. Sharon had requested that we do a search for anything on James Edward Bell, and, I think, under the circumstances, we owe her the courtesy of providing that information." Bodeman nodded to Thomson and she picked up where Bodeman left off.

"We had assumed that Bell was an alias, just as were Malley, and his Bullet persona, but strange as it may seem we have located an address for a James Edward Bell in west central Minnesota. He does seem to generally match the age and description of our Bell."

"I feel I owe him my life," Sharon began. "I'd like to get in touch with him to thank him somehow."

"From what we've been able to piece together he is a very dangerous man. Probably capable of murder."

"Yet he saved my life on several occasions."

"There have been volumes written about the criminal mind, and yet no one knows for sure how it works. I can give you his last known address. Just so you know, we've already checked it out and found nothing."

"Thanks. It's a place to start." She turned to face Charlie. "I own you a great deal."

"You owe me nothing. What are you going to do now?"

"I've had some computer training, but I think I want to do something for people. I don't know what yet. Jonathan essentially confiscated everything I was supposed to make so Lynn and I are going to help each other out for now. It's weird. I've been going by the name Wrightham for so long it feels like my real name."

"So your real name is Sharon Bergen?"

"Yes."

"I don't know. Bergen and Bergen has a nice ring to it."

"It does, doesn't it."

"Otherwise, I could use a maid," Johnson joked, but quickly added. "I don't think that's for you."

Thomson wrote an address on the back of a business card and handed it to Sharon.

"This is the best I can do on Bell. Good luck."

All rose as the sisters stood up to leave. Sharon hesitated a moment and then threw her arms forcefully around Johnson. "Thanks for everything. You really are special."

Bodeman just couldn't resist a comment after they had left.

"Ah shucks, it weren't nothing ma'am."

"You're just jealous because on a scale of one to fifty Sharon is a fifty and Audrey, your new love interest, is in the single digits."

"What do you expect? She's a lawyer for crying out loud." He turned his attention back to Thomson. "Other than Cook and Saulo, do we have anyone left in this mess to press charges against?"

"Just so you know, Sheriff Forrest Bodeman, I became a bona fide lawyer before I went into forensics."

"Oops."

"And the only one left is the one we started out with, Maclin Ethek."

"Who seems to have eluded us once again."

"Do you really want to hear the kicker? Maclin Ethek is the sole surviving heir to the Wrightham estate."

Johnson pondered for a moment. "I wonder if he realizes he's now a millionaire."

Fifteen minutes later, Thomson left the office, leaving Bodeman and Johnson alone once again.

"What do you hear from Jerry?"

"Jerry?"

"Jerry Koler. Remember him. Your good friend. The one who saved your ass and managed to get the Tripacer down in almost one piece."

"He's back in LaCrescent. Last I heard the headaches had quit and he was back to work at the SciOgen Corporation." Johnson started to leave but turned to face Bodeman when he'd reached the doorway. "I just wanted to let you know Lora and I are on speaking terms again."

"Good to hear. Anything else you want to tell me?"

"Not that I can think of. Oh. It's none of my business but…"

"But you're going to ask anyway?"

"And you said I was the one who completed other people's thoughts."

"Two can play that game. Fire away."

"I was wondering what you decided about the civic club's request for you to become a 'front man,' I believe you said, for law and order in the county. You know. Speaking to the Ladies Aid, the kiddies and such."

Bodeman mumbled something unintelligible under his breath.

"I didn't catch that."

"I said *yes*," he growled. "Now get out of here before I arrest you for loitering."

Bergen and Bergen emerged from the Emergency Services and Law Enforcement building into the gray mist of a September morning. Lynn noticed a familiar man sitting on a park bench on the front lawn.

She nodded to her sister who continued on towards their car, but Lynn walked in a direct line towards Bill Backus. He stood to greet her, and they sat down together on the damp bench. Both were silent for some time, until Backus began.

"Well, I have my old job back."

"That's good. Real good."

"Let's see. What else. My third wife informed me she's in love with our neighbor and wants a divorce."

"I'm sorry."

"I'm not."

"I…"

"I've also been trying to convince wife number two to rejoin AA. I've pulled together her doctor, some family and friends, and we're going to do an intervention."

"Intervention?"

"Sort of a tough-love confrontation with the facts."

"And what about you?"

"What about me?"

"When are you going to quit worrying about everyone else and start living your own life?"

"I don't know. I don't know any other way to be."

"I better go. Sharon is waiting. I don't know how to say this so I'll just say it. I'm thirty seven years old and not getting any younger so don't wait too long."

"For what?"

"Good-by Bill. Good luck."

She was several paces away when the fog lifted.

"I'm getting a group of students together for an October fossil hunt in eastern Montana."

Lynn stopped and turned to face him.

"So?"

"So I'm going to need a female chaperone. It'd be rough. Sleeping on the ground. Cooking over campfires. Stuff like that. You know of a mature lady who would be interested in the job?"

"I might."

At first the bats had been terrifying, calling out in their shrill squeaking voices, and flitting around his head. He'd heard they carry rabies, and other diseases, and for some reason he couldn't get past the thought of one biting into his exposed neck. He'd expected his eyes to eventually become accustomed to the darkness, but that required at least an infinitesimal amount of light, and the attic was as dark as a cave, and he continued to flounder in total blackness.

Gradually, as hunger pains began to rake his side, the bats took on a new significance. He'd managed to kill one, he'd stuffed it into a shirt pocket, but he hadn't yet reached the point where he could sink his teeth into the furry flesh. Then there was the problem of water. He could survive many days without food. Dehydration would kill him in a matter of hours. It occurred to him blood might substitute for water, and there was always the bats.

His mouth was already parched, his throat raw. He'd remained silent at first, fearing arrest by the hoard of police officers and investigators that he knew must be investigating his brother's death. When it finally occurred to him that they were the only ones who could save him, it was too late. No one answered his calls, then screams. Finally, when his vocal cords failed, he could make no sound at all. Occasionally, he thought he heard someone in the house directly below him, but he realized it must be wishful thinking. He could only guess how much time had passed, but it seemed like days.

He'd kicked at first one and then the other louvered vent until his feet ached, but they were made of steel, not the usually flimsy aluminum. He sat now in the dark empty space with the dead bat in his hand. Was it worth it? Was he simply delaying the inevitable? When there were no more bats, then what? He closed his eyes against the darkness, opened his mouth, and bit down on his first meal in his new home.

Maclin Ethek rested his head against a rafter in a corner of the attic and a restless sleep temporarily saved him from madness. Somewhere in the murky world of dreams, he was a child hiding in a culvert from his father. It was a game, and he laughed. Suddenly, the culvert seemed to close around him, preventing movement forward or back, and yet he continued to hear his father's laughter.

The man with the long, hook like nose and ears that seemed glued to the side of his head relaxed on the brown sofa in the sun room that overlooked the blue waters of the lake. He'd spent the better part of two days struggling over his next course of action. The frantic calls, then screams, had diminished to whimpering and then subsided altogether. He'd realized almost immediately the person in the attic space was his son, yet how he'd managed to get trapped there was beyond him. Still, it was a bit of good fortune. He could simply walk away from the log mansion and never have to worry about the little rodent ever again.

Yet, he hadn't been able to. Maybe some of the message he preached had penetrated his otherwise self-serving personality. Compassion was something alien and it had turned a simple decision into an agonizing act of mental contemplation. Twice he'd left the house and stood with his hand on the door handle of the lavender Cadillac, only to retreat back inside. He knew if he waited much longer, starvation and dehydration would settle the question for him. The time to act was now, or never.

"Well, God. If you're really up there, I'm going to leave Maclin's fate in your hands."

The Reverend Luke James drew a quarter from his pocket, and flipped it into the air. He caught it on the downward spiral, and cupped it in his hands.

"Heads for life. Otherwise, I walk away and never look back." He flipped the coin on the back of his wrist, and peeked through spreading fingers. "Crap," he said, and looked up toward the ethereal. "Would you go best two out of three?"

The light mist gathered slowly on the windshield of the white rental car, and the wipers at the slowest intermittent setting was all that was required to keep it clear. The two women sat quietly in the front, an unusual occurrence for the sisters who often found they could chat endlessly about just about anything. Both were now free of a yoke of terror, but the expected exuberance and joy was tempered by reflection and anticipation. Before she could get on with her life, Sharon Bergen needed to find the man, Bell. She wasn't even sure what she would say or do when she found him, but she knew it was something she had to do. Her sister, the only family she had anywhere in the world, had volunteered to ride along for company and moral support. When she thought about it, that was the glue that held all of womanhood together.

The address Thomson had given her took her down Hwy 371 through Brainerd to Little Falls, and then west on Hwy 27. Just before Long Prairie, a winding road turned north. The rolling land was mostly farm with random patches of woods and cornfields, pasture and ponds. She glanced again at the address and began searching for the name, Bell.

They almost went past the driveway but at the last moment Lynn saw the mailbox with the correct name lying next to the road in the ditch. Grass grew up in the center of the infrequently used driveway, and two narrow tracks led to an abandoned farmhouse. A vast field of drying corn eight feet tall nearly encircled the building. Sharon parked the car in the tiny unmowed lawn.

"Looks like a dead end," Lynn said. "Just like Thomson said."

"I really hoped…"

"We can check with the neighbors. Someone may know something."

Sharon stared at the old two-story farmhouse. The siding that had once been white as snow had now peeled back to gray weathered wood. Windows were broken. The roof sagged. Shingles missing. Dreams shattered.

"They call them 'temporaries,'" Sharon said at last.

"What?'

"The Europeans call our homes temporaries. We make ours out of wood to last a generation. They make theirs out of stone to last for centuries."

"We're a relatively young nation. Still growing. Still evolving."

Sharon seemed not to hear. "Someone builds his dream, and fifty years later it's bulldozed to the ground for the next dream. It just seems so sad."

"There's someone here." Lynn interrupted.

The front door opened and an old woman, bent and haggard, slowly shuffled toward the driver's side of the car. Her worn gray dress scraped along in the dirt and grass, and a stained yellow scarf framed a wrinkled face a century old. In sharp contrast to her drab appearance, the stem of a brilliant red rose was stuck though a buttonhole of her faded green sweater. Sharon rolled down her window, and was about to speak, but the senior began before she could offer a hello.

"This ain't no truck stop. What you want?" One eye looked directly at Sharon but the other seemed to be focused on the ground. "You lookin' at my bum eye?"

"No ma'am. We're looking for someone that used to live here."

"You know I was pretty like you once. Men followed me around like a herd of bulls after a cow in heat."

"Yes ma'am. The man we're…"

"You know I used to live right there in the Big Sky country."

"Colorado?"

"Not Colorado, silly. Montana. Great Falls, Montana. Now that's God's country. None of them damn mosquitoes out there neither. I'm going back, ya know."

"I'm sure you are."

"You think I'm just a senile old woman don't you? Can't even see straight. Well let me tell you something, deary. I still have control of my bowels. When you get to be as old as me, it's a blessing, ya know."

"I wish you the best, really, but we're looking…"

"Did I tell you I'm going to Montana? Leaving right away today. Soon's you leave. What is it you want again?"

"We're looking for a man by the name of James Edward Bell. He used to live here."

"Well don't no more. Did once I heard, though."

"Do you know where he went?"

"Gosh yes. Just up the road a mile or so. Right by the church."

"Do you think he's home?"

"Ol' Jimmy boy? Sure. He's a regular home body."

"Thanks ma'am."

"Say, what you gals want anyway. This ain't no truck stop, ya know."

Sharon backed out of the driveway, and turned north toward a tall white church steeple that seemed to grow up out of the rolling prairie. Within minutes she parked the car in the gravel parking area.

"This is strange," Lynn stated. "Where does he live? There isn't another house for a mile."

"Oh no," Sharon exclaimed, and ran from the car towards a stone covered field. Immediately, her sister understood, and followed more slowly. In amongst the headstones, a single engraving stood out on the most prominent. Covering the complete gravesite was a dense thicket of red roses. Lynn came up next to her sister, and read the names that were carved in the granite. Mother Marie Ann Bell, Baby Daughter Nora June Bell, Father James Edward Bell. Whether from extreme sadness or frustration, Sharon Bergen sank to her knees and wept. Lynn put her hand on her shoulder but could offer no comfort.

The grief stricken moment was interrupted by a young girl's voice.

"Pardon me. Are you Sharon Wrightham?"

Sharon looked up into the face of a young teenage girl. Her hands were dirty, as were the knees of her denim jeans.

"Should I know you?"

"Oh no. I was just out back with the flower garden."

"Then how do you know who I am?"

"Someone came by earlier and said if a lady was to come and visit that grave, I was to give that person the briefcase. Said her name would be Sharon Wrightham. Are you Sharon Wrightham?"

"Well, no. That is I used to be. I'm Sharon Bergen now."

"That's good enough for me." She turned and ran back to the church and returned with a black briefcase. Somehow it looked familiar, but then all briefcases looked the same.

"Thank you," she called out to the retreating girl.

"Well, open it," Lynn insisted.

Sharon stood it upright and pushed the two round buttons outward. The latches popped up and the front fell forward revealing neat bundles of green paper.

"My god!" Lynn gasped. "Is it real?"

Sharon picked up a bundle and thumbed the thousand dollar bills like a deck of cards. She set it aside in favor of a plain white envelope. The hand written note on the front said: *I know you'll put this to good use. JB*

Lynn made the connection before Sharon. "If we go back now, he might still be there."

"No matter," Sharon said thoughtfully. "I know were he's going."

EPILOG

The light drizzle that had fallen steadily for two days had served to dampen everyone's mood, but provided little in the way of moisture. In late afternoon of the second day, a sudden thundershower broke the spell, and the low-pressure system moved off to the east dragging the gloom along with it. The gray clouds began to pull apart, and warm sunlight shown through the ragged holes.

Charlie Johnson stared out from the kitchen window of his grandparent's home noting the change in weather. Thoughts of Grandmother standing in that exact place flooded his mind. Firmly etched in his thoughts was the image of her in her forest green dress, with long black hair with streaks of white. She looked out for Grandfather, "Trying to keep him out of trouble," she always said.

He remembered his conversation with Parish. Such a strange man. Probably nothing more than a con artist, yet very insightful. He knew now that he'd meant for him to realize that Grandfather would always be alive in his heart. Somehow, that made accepting his death easier.

He'd put the last of two weeks worth of dirty dishes in the sink drainer to drip dry, when a battered silver Chevy SUV pulled to a stop under the pine trees. Lora Whitney stepped out and stretched her five foot two height to its fullest extent. He wondered if she had any other clothes besides her deputy uniform and the faded blue jeans, red plaid shirt, and the hat advertising gunpowder. This time he waited until she knocked lightly on the front door.

"Come in," he called out.

She stepped inside cautiously and looked around the corner into the kitchen. "Hi."

"Just had to prove to you I really do do the dishes now and then. Care to take a walk?"

"Where to?"

"I thought we'd walk back to Grandfather's favorite place. By the lake under the white pine."

Ten minutes later they stood on the pine ridge that overlooked the blue water. The wind had rotated around to the northwest, and the brisk breeze carried the familiar scent of a fresh water lake though the pine boughs.

"Grandfather is buried there," Johnson said. There was no grief in his voice, it was simply a statement of fact. After a long silence, he turned to face Lora directly. "I see you managed to get the Chevy out of the woods. Much damage?"

"Let's put it this way. When the insurance adjuster came out, he just laughed."

"I'll figure out a way to replace it."

"No need. You were right all along."

"I was just lucky."

"I don't think luck had much to do with it."

An awkward silence separated the two for nearly a minute.

"So," Johnson began again. "I hope you're feeling better."

"Feeling better?"

"The flu bug."

"Oh that. It wasn't the flu."

"What was it then?"

"Can we sit down? There's something…"

"You're accepting Thomson's offer to work in St. Paul."

"No."

"Sharon went back out west."

"This doesn't concern Sharon."

"I'm losing my touch. What then?"

"I have something to tell you," Whitney said seriously. "Been trying to tell you for some time. Something that you have a right to know. Something I've suspected but it took Pam Calway's insight for it to really hit home."

"Don't worry. I already know about the freckle on your…"

"Quit kidding for once. This is important."

"I'm listening."

"I've missed two," Lora said bluntly, "and it's the first time in my entire adult life."

"Missed two what?"

Whitney threw up her hands in frustration. "For an intelligent man, you're pretty dense. What do you think?"

"You've lost me."

"There's a baby on the way and you're the father," Whitney stated matter-of-factly.

"A what? How did that happen?"

"What do you mean, how did that happen? The usual way, you thick-headed…"

"You know what I mean. I thought women took, you know, stuff to prevent this kind of thing."

"Before I met you I had no need to, and then after I met you…" Whitney had begun strong, but now her resolve was slipping away. "I've never had relations…sex…with a man before."

"Neither have I," Charlie quipped, but quickly realized this was not the time to try to be funny.

Lora looked down and did not throw anything back. Lately her emotions had been unpredictable, happy one moment and on the verge of tears the next. Charlie's reaction to the news was not what she had expected. He seemed to be pulling away from her, physically and emotionally, as if she had some contagious disease. Maybe she had read more into their relationship than was really there. He had always been very good at evading talking about his true feelings, a characteristic, she knew, that she shared. "We don't have to get married," she said finally. "We don't even have to live together. I can raise…"

"What are you babbling on about? We're already married."

"What? How?"

"At least in my mind. From the first night we spent together, I've considered you my partner for life. A marriage isn't a piece of paper, and a couple 'I dos.' It's a state of mind. I will never leave you unless you want me to. I guess I just assumed you felt the same. But if you don't want to…"

"Now I am upset!"

"Now what did I do?"

"Do you think I'm the kind of woman who would sleep with a man if I didn't love him?"

The fog began to clear in Johnson's head, and Lora's meaning rang clear. He couldn't admit it to her just yet, however. "So who's the poor soul who has to put up with you?"

"Do I have to spell it out for you," Whitney began, but then noticed Johnson's ear-to-ear grin.

Whitney, however, wasn't laughing. "So where do we go from here?" she asked directly. "I need to know. I don't like uncertainty. And don't give me that 'we're already married' line. You just can't drag me off into the bushes and consider that a wedding."

"I don't remember doing much dragging."

"I'm being serious."

"How about I cut out my heart and hand it to you on a platter?"

"No thanks," Whitney smiled, "but a ring would be nice."

The September night grew still and cold. A long and peaceful silence joined the two, as they lay together side by side on the bed of evergreen boughs facing the warmth and light of the campfire. The heavy woolen blanket from Whitney's SUV covered them nearly completely, with only their faces visible to reflect the firelight. Whitney lay closest to the fire, with Johnson behind. He put his arms around her breast, and pulled her tightly to him.

"My heart sings," he said quietly, "and it is because of you, and the baby."

"I love you, too. Does that scare you?"

"Not at all…well, maybe a little. My Universe just grew a little bigger, and Grandfather would say that's a good thing."

The sky remained clear during the night, and the temperature dropped steadily, reaching forty-two degrees by six AM. Slowly, Johnson eased his body away from Whitney and faced the rising sun. Things often were different in the morning. Great ideas and plans of the night before seemed foolish with the morning light. But not this morning. He folded his half of the blanket over the woman, and touched her red cheek lightly with his hand. She responded by grumbling something unintelligible in her sleep. He made his way down the steep slope of the pine ridge to the water's edge, and was engulfed in the morning fog. It had been Grandfather's way to begin each day with a thanksgiving prayer to the Great Mystery. He thought of the woman who slept by the burned out coals of the campfire. He wanted to say so much, but the words that came to mind were inadequate, nearly blasphemous. In the end he could only think of two that came close.

"Thank you," he said aloud.

He turned away from the still water to return up the ridge, but something in the morning mist along the shore made him hesitate. At first he thought it might be a deer coming for a morning drink. It seemed to glide ever closer, until the outline of a man with long, pure white hair in brown buckskin clothing broke through the fog. Charlie's heart raced and a tear streamed down his cheek as a voice from the forest spoke to him.

"Hello *Amikons*. I have been watching you."

For more information contact:
Terry Oliver Mejdrich
mejdrich@means.net
mejdrichto@yahoo.com

0-595-30806-6

Printed in the United States
31401LVS00002B/43-60